THE GREAT MATRIX

Hilary began, dimly through the darkness of the caves, to sense, if not quite to see, the glowing nexus of a great matrix. Above it, shadowed—not perhaps a physical figure at all, Hilary could see, sketched dimly on the darkness, the figure of a woman, kneeling, golden chains enshrouding her, all faintly glowing flame-color. Sharra; the goddess of the forge-people, here imaged, not on their altar, exactly, but so near as made no matter.

Now she could see it. In the Ages of Chaos, when this thing had first been shaped, it had been traditional to house these things in the shape of weapons: and this one was fashioned to be set in the hilt of a great two-handed sword. Hilary moved swiftly to take up the sword in both hands. It was suprisingly heavy. In the overworld she was accustomed to moving without weight, but an object like this—a matrix, she knew, had form and body through all the various levels of consciousness—had weight and substance even in the overworld. *Now,* she thought, *I have it in my hands, and I shall return to Arilinn as swiftly as I can.* She turned to retrace her steps, but as the matrix moved away from the altar, she heard a great cry.

Sharra! Protect us, golden-chained one!

Beneath her feet, the very ground was beginning to burn. She went on, stepping carefully through the spreading patches of fire, reminding herself that the fire was illusion, intended to frighten her; it was not real. *It cannot hurt me.*

Now the very soles of her slippers were beginning to smolder; she felt sharp pain in the soles of her feet.

Anguish seized her, and faintness; she stumbled, dropping the matrix. Before she could seize it again she was spiraling, choking, through layers of smoke, into a well-known room and Ronal and Callista were looking down at her in fright.

Hilary burst into tears. "I nearly had it," she said, weeping.

"We must let the big matrix go, at least for now," Leonie said. But she looked somehow troubled, as if touched by a premonition of the future.

A Reader's Guide to DARKOVER

THE FOUNDING:
A "lost ship" of Terran origin, in the pre-empire colonizing days, lands on a planet with a dim red star, later to be called Darkover.
    DARKOVER LANDFALL

THE AGES OF CHAOS:
1,000 years after the original landfall settlement, society has returned to the feudal level. The Darkovans, their Terran technology renounced or forgotten, have turned instead to freewheeling, out-of-control matrix technology, psi powers and terrible psi weapons. The populace lives under the domination of the Towers and a tyrannical breeding program to staff the Towers with unnaturally powerful, inbred gifts of *laran.*
    STORMQUEEN!
    HAWKMISTRESS!

THE HUNDRED KINGDOMS:
An age of war and strife retaining many of the decimating and disastrous effects of the Ages of Chaos. The lands which are later to become the Seven Domains are divided by continuous border conflicts into a multitude of small, belligerent kingdoms, named for convenience "The Hundred Kingdoms." The close of this era is heralded by the adoption of the Compact, instituted by Varzil the Good. A landmark and turning point in the history of Darkover, the Compact bans all distance weapons, making it a matter of honor that one who seeks to kill must himself face equal risk of death.
    TWO TO CONQUER
    THE HEIRS OF HAMMERFELL

THE RENUNCIATES:

During the Ages of Chaos and the time of the Hundred Kingdoms, there were two orders of women who set themselves apart from the patriarchal nature of Darkovan feudal society: the priestesses of Avarra, and the warriors of the Sisterhood of the Sword. Eventually these two independent groups merged to form the powerful and legally chartered Order of Renunciates or Free Amazons, a guild of women bound only by oath as a sisterhood of mutual responsibility. Their primary allegiance is to each other rather than to family, clan, caste or any man save a temporary employer. Alone among Darkovan women, they are exempt from the usual legal restrictions and protections. Their reason for existence is to provide the women of Darkover an alternative to their socially restrictive lives.

THE SHATTERED CHAIN
THENDARA HOUSE
CITY OF SORCERY

AGAINST THE TERRANS
—THE FIRST AGE (Recontact):

After the Hastur Wars, the Hundred Kingdoms are consolidated into the Seven Domains, and ruled by a hereditary aristocracy of seven families, called the Comyn, allegedly descended from the legendary Hastur, Lord of Light. It is during this era that the Terran Empire, really a form of confederacy, rediscovers Darkover, which they know as the fourth planet of the Cottman star system. The fact that Darkover is a lost colony of the Empire is not easily or readily acknowledged by Darkovans and their Comyn overlords.

REDISCOVERY (with Mercedes Lackey)
THE SPELL SWORD
THE FORBIDDEN TOWER
*STAR OF DANGER
*THE WINDS OF DARKOVER

AGAINST THE TERRANS
—THE SECOND AGE (After the Comyn):

With the initial shock of recontact beginning to wear off, and the Terran spaceport a permanent establishment on the outskirts of the city of Thendara, the younger and less traditional elements of Darkovan society begin the first real exchange of knowledge with the Terrans—learning Terran science and technology and teaching Darkovan matrix technology in turn. Eventually Regis Hastur, the young Comyn lord most active in these exchanges, becomes Regent in a provisional government allied to the Terrans. Darkover is once again reunited with its founding Empire.

*THE BLOODY SUN
 HERITAGE OF HASTUR
*THE PLANET SAVERS
*SHARRA'S EXILE
*THE WORLD WRECKERS
*RETURN TO DARKOVER

THE DARKOVER ANTHOLOGIES:

These volumes of stories edited by Marion Zimmer Bradley strive to "fill in the blanks" of Darkovan history, and elaborate on the eras, tales and characters which have captured readers' imaginations.

 THE KEEPER'S PRICE
 SWORD OF CHAOS
 FREE AMAZONS OF DARKOVER
 THE OTHER SIDE OF THE MIRROR
 RED SUN OF DARKOVER
 FOUR MOONS OF DARKOVER
 DOMAINS OF DARKOVER
 RENUNCIATES OF DARKOVER
 LERONI OF DARKOVER
 TOWERS OF DARKOVER
 MARION ZIMMER BRADLEY'S DARKOVER
 *SNOWS OF DARKOVER

(*forthcoming in DAW Books editions in 1994)

Marion Zimmer Bradley's

Darkover

DAW BOOKS, INC.

DONALD A. WOLLHEIM, FOUNDER

375 Hudson Street, New York, NY 10014

ELIZABETH R. WOLLHEIM
SHEILA E. GILBERT
PUBLISHERS

Contents

Introduction

One of the strangest things in my life as a writer has been the success of the Darkover Books—not simply as books, but the way in which the self-contained universe of Darkover has become not only self-sustaining, but has encouraged other writers to write their own stories, first about Darkover, and then, increasingly, in their own self-created universes. I was the very first, although since then, many writers, especially women—I need only name Mercedes Lackey and Jacqueline Lichtenberg—have encouraged others to write in their own universes. I think there are many reasons for this; some more feminist than others.

Women are not and were not encouraged to create universes of their own; especially in the days when I entered fandom. In other writings I have spoken of those days in the forties and fifties when women were not only not encouraged to write, but were not encouraged even to read very much—and then nothing but Nancy Drew, Sue Barton, and various saccharine romances, meant to convey the idea that a woman's only duty and pleasure was to secure a man—by fair means or foul didn't much matter; she'd be accused of the foul ones anyhow. No one born in these post-Star Trek days can imagine quite how segregated all writing and, indeed, all mental activity was. And by and large, girls cooperated in this segregation, insisting that educators were right; the only degree worth having was Mrs., and a girl who wanted to work should obviously be prepared to neglect her God-given responsibilities to home and children—and to accept all kinds of abuse for so doing.

Yet there have obviously been women in science fiction and fantasy from the beginning. The very field of science fiction was created by a woman, Mary Shelley, author of FRANKENSTEIN. The "Gothic novels" which preceded today's fantasy were created by one "Mrs. Radcliffe" and her imitators. The difference was simple; a woman had to be, as I was, and as most of my better known predecessors from Charlotte Bronte on were, obsessed, prepared to ignore the brainwashing given in schools to all females. One woman at a mid-seventies' woman's meeting I attended said that no woman could possibly escape her brainwashing. I stood up and called her a liar to her face; I was living proof, and so was everybody else in the room, that some of us had managed to escape it—or none of us would have been there.

But, in a sense, she was right. The vast majority of girls in my school seemed brainwashed to me—and I have heard similar stories from everybody else, from Leigh Brackett and Catherine L. Moore to Joanna Russ and Diana L. Paxson. The many woman who wrote, from Ms. Bronte to me, from Leigh Brackett to C.L. Moore, were obsessed. They were prepared to ignore anything and everything, from their stern Victorian fathers to their brainwashed mothers, in order to write.

Everyone familiar with women writers knows the famous answer of William Wordsworth to Charlotte Bronte when that lady sought his support for her writing; but anyone who, like so many of today's teenagers, thinks the past "Irrelevant" should remember that Wordsworth told Charlotte to finish the dishes first. This, unfortunately, is an answer which we have heard *ad nauseam*, all of us, starting with Andre Norton and ending with the little girls who write for my anthologies, one of whom is about thirteen.

I was the very first writer to encourage other writers to write in my universe. Not everybody approved; Lester Del Rey told me that he, for one, would never consent to read one single word of Darkover fiction written by anyone else. All I can say to that is that it is a free country and he is entitled to his opinion. It's his loss. Most of the Darkover stories were about as good as any slush anywhere, which means not very good, at least at first; but after reading a lot of it, I came to the conclusion that a lot of it—being written by women who were obsessed with writing—was readable. If there were the kind of conspiracy in science fiction that the louder and more obnoxious feminists kept insisting, Don Wollheim—about whose masculinity no one ever had any question—would never have agreed to let me publish an anthology of fan writings.

But he did; and here we are. For the anniversary of the tenth of these anthologies I have decided—for the benefit of Mr. Del Rey and his ilk—to publish my own shorter Darkover stories all in one place.

Here they are.

—*Marion Zimmer Bradley*

FREE AMAZONS

Nothing in a fairly long and eventful career as a writer has ever surprised me as much—except perhaps the success of MISTS OF AVALON, which I never liked that much, thinking THE INHERITOR a much better book—as the success of the Free Amazons; both as a concept and as individual books. I suppose I must have created an archetype or something.

It all started while I was writing the first published—not the first written but the first published—of the commercial Darkover books; which I called PROJECT JASON, and which the original editor called THE PLANET SAVERS, a title I did not and do not like. While writing this book I cannibalized a file drawer full of my early and unsuccessful Darkover stories; and while I was plotting the story, with the aid of an ancient textbook on writing by, I think, the late John D. McDonald—I had a dream.

This was one of the few dreams I can remember clearly from an entire lifetime of fairly lucid dreams. In it, a group of adolescents—not unlike the ones I went to school with—were engaged, as so many of the young people were then, in 1956 or thereabouts—in playing complex war games; in the dream I was a member of a girls' band of soldiers. I was captured by a gang of boys and I was asked who we were. I made the answer that many girls liked to be a boy with the boys, but that most of us—and I have no idea where this came from; it didn't describe me, at any rate—preferred to be a girl with the boys. Half asleep, chewing over the dream, I came up with the phrase "I'm not neutered, though some of us are," a phrase I was later to apply in the words of Kyla, the first Free Amazon, who wasn't; and later to apply to Camilla n'ha Kyria, one of my later free Amazons, who WAS.

Here is my own favorite of the early Free Amazon stories; "To Keep the Oath." "Amazon Fragment," which follows, was the first appearance of Camilla, a fragment intended to be part of the first Free Amazon novel, which was meant to center on Camilla and for which Kindra was invented. The next story, "House Rules," arises from a controversy arising from a somewhat stupid and not very well thought-out idea I had based on a local household of feminists which had the policy—which I stupidly adopted for my Amazon households—that no male over five could live in an Amazon household. And lastly one of my best short stories—I am not a very good short story writer—"Knives," which I think was the first to embody the idea that something which seems at the time to destroy one's own life can be a blessing in disguise. I often say that I never know what my stories are about till years after I write them; "Knives" was the first of my stories for which I figured out the underlying "message" within 20 years.

To Keep The Oath

by Marion Zimmer Bradley

The red light lingered on the hills; two of the four small moons were in the sky, green Idriel near to setting, and the tiny crescent of Mormallor, ivory-pale, near the zenith. The night would be dark. Kindra n'ha Mhari did not, at first, see anything strange about the little town. She was too grateful to have reached it before sunset—shelter against the rainswept chill of a Darkovan night, a bed to sleep in after four days of traveling, a cup of wine before she slept.

But slowly she began to realize that there was something wrong. Normally, at this hour, the women would be going back and forth in the streets, gossiping with neighbors, marketing for the evening meal, while their children played and squabbled in the street. But tonight there was not a single woman in the street, nor a single child.

What was wrong? Frowning, she rode along the main street toward the inn. She was hungry and weary.

She had left Dalereuth many days before with a companion, bound for Neskaya Guild House. But unknown to either of them, her companion had been pregnant; she had fallen sick of a fever, and in Thendara Guild House she had miscarried and still lay there, very ill. Kindra had gone alone to Neskaya; but she had turned aside three days' ride to carry a message to the sick woman's oath-mother. She had found her in a village in the hills, working to help a group of women set up a small dairy.

Kindra was not afraid of traveling alone; she had journeyed in these hills at all seasons and in all weathers. But her provisions were beginning to run low. Fortunately, the innkeeper was an old acquaintance; she had little money with her, because her journey had been so unexpectedly prolonged, but old Jorik would feed her and her horse, give her a bed for the night, and trust her to send money to pay for it—knowing that if she did not, or could not, her Guild House would pay, for the honor of the Guild.

The man who took her horse in the stable had known her for many years, too. He scowled as she alighted. "I don't know where we shall stable your horse, and that's certain, *mestra*, with all these strange horses here . . . will she share a box stall without kicking, do you suppose? Or shall I tie her loose at the end?" Kindra noticed that the stable was crammed with horses, two dozen of them and more. Instead of a lonely village inn, it looked like Neskaya on market-day!

"Did you meet with any riders on the road, *mestra*?"

"No, none," Kindra said, frowning a little. "All the horses in the Kilghard Hills seem to be here in your stable—what is it, a royal visit? What is the matter with you? You keep looking over your shoulder as if you expect to find your master there with a stick to beat you—where is old Jorik, why is he not here to greet his guests?"

"Why, *mestra*, old Jorik's dead," the old man said, "and Dame Janella trying to manage the inn alone with young Annelys and Marga."

"Dead? Gods preserve us," Kindra said. "What happened?"

"It was those bandits, *mestra*, Scarface's gang; they came here and cut Jorik down with his apron still on," said the old groom. "Made havoc in the town, broke all the ale-pots, and when the menfolk drove 'em off with pitchforks, they swore they'd be back and fire the town! So Dame Janella and the elders put the cap round and raised copper to hire Brydar of Fen Hills and all his men to come and defend us when they come back; and here Brydar's men have been ever since, *mestra*, quarreling and drinking and casting eyes on the women until the townfolk are ready to say the remedy's worse than the sickness! But go in, go in, *mestra*, Janella's ready to welcome you."

Plump Janella looked paler and thinner than Kindra

had ever seen her. She greeted Kindra with unaccustomed warmth. Under ordinary conditions, she was cold to Kindra, as befitted a respectable wife in the presence of a member of the Amazon Guild; now, Kindra supposed, she was learning that an innkeeper could not afford to alienate a customer. Jorik, Kindra knew, had not approved of the Free Amazons either; but he had learned from experience that they were quiet guests who kept to themselves, caused no trouble, did not get drunk and break bar stools and ale-pots, and paid their reckoning promptly. *A guest's reputation,* Kindra thought wryly, *does not tarnish the color of his money.*

"You have heard, good *mestra*? Those wicked men, Scarface's fellows, they cut my good man down, and for nothing—just because he flung an ale-pot at one of them who laid rough hands on my little girl, and Annelys not fifteen yet! Monsters!"

"And they killed him? Shocking!" Kindra murmured, but her pity was for the girl. All her life, young Annelys must remember that her father had been killed in defending her, because she could not defend herself. Like all the women of the Guild, Kindra was sworn to defend herself, to turn to no man for protection. She had been a member of the Guild for half her lifetime; it seemed shocking to her that a man should die defending a girl from advances she should have known how to ward off herself.

"Ah, you don't know what it's like, *mestra,* being alone without the goodman. Living alone as you do, you can't imagine!"

"Well, you have daughters to help you," Kindra said, and Janella shook her head and mourned. "But they can't come out among all those rough men, they are only little girls!"

"It will do them good to learn something of the world and its ways," Kindra said, but the woman sighed. "I wouldn't like them to learn too much of that."

"Then, I suppose, you must get you another husband," Kindra said, knowing that there was simply no way she and Janella could communicate. "But indeed I am sorry for your grief. Jorik was a good man."

"You can't imagine how good, *mestra,*" Janella said

plaintively. "You women of the Guild, you call your-selves free women, only it seems to me I have always been free, until now, when I must watch myself night and day, lest someone get the wrong idea about a woman alone. Only the other day, one of Brydar's men said to me—and that's another thing, these men of Brydar's. Eating us out of house and home, and just look, *mestra,* no room in the stable for the horses of our paying customers, with half the village keeping their horses here against bandits, and those hired swords drinking up my good old man's beer day after day—" Abruptly she recalled her duties as landlord. "But come into the common room, *mestra,* warm yourself, and I'll bring you some supper; we have a roast haunch of *chervine.* Or would you fancy something lighter, rabbit-horn stewed with mushrooms, perhaps? We're crowded, yes, but there's the little room at the head of the stairs, you can have that to yourself, a room fit for a fine lady, indeed Lady Hastur slept here in that very bed, a few years gone. Lilla! Lilla! Where's that simpleminded wench gone? When I took her in, her mother told me she was lack-witted, but she has wits enough to hang about talking to that young hired sword, Zandru scratch them all! Lilla! Hurry now, show the good woman her room, fetch her wash-water, see to her saddlebags!"

Later, Kindra went down to the common room. Like all Guild-women, she had learned to be discreet when traveling alone; a solitary woman was prey to questions, at least, so they usually journeyed in pairs. This subjected them to raised eyebrows and occasional dirty speculations, but warded off the less palatable approaches to which a lone woman traveling on Darkover was subject. Of course, any woman of the Guild could protect herself if it went past rude words, but that could cause trouble for all the Guild. It was better to conduct oneself in a way that minimized the possibility of trouble. So Kindra sat alone in a tiny corner near the fire-place, kept her hood drawn around her face—she was neither young nor particularly pretty—sipped her wine and warmed her feet, and did nothing to attract anyone's attention. It occurred to her that at this moment she, who called herself a Free Amazon, was considerably less

constrained than Janella's young daughters, going back
and forth, protected by their family's roof and their
mother's presence.

She finished her meal—she had chosen the stewed
rabbit-horn—and called for a second glass of wine, too
weary to climb the stairs to her chamber and too tired
to sleep if she did.

Some of Brydar's hired swords were sitting around a
long table at the other end of the room, drinking and
playing dice. They were a mixed crew; Kindra knew
none of them, but she had met Brydar himself a few
times, and had even hired out with him, once, to guard
a merchant caravan across the desert to the Dry Towns.
She nodded courteously to him, and he saluted her, but
paid her no further attention; he knew her well enough
to know that she would not welcome even polite conversation when she was in a roomful of strangers.

One of the younger mercenaries, a young man, tall,
beardless and weedy, ginger hair cut close to his head,
rose and came toward her. Kindra braced herself for the
inevitable. If she had been with two or three other
Guild-women, she would have welcomed harmless companionship, a drink together and talk about the chances
of the road, but a lone Amazon simply did NOT drink
with men in public taverns, and, damn it, Brydar knew
it as well as she did.

One of the older mercenaries must have been having
some fun with the green boy, needling him to prove his
manhood by approaching the Amazon, amusing themselves by enjoying the rebuff he'd inevitably get.

One of the men looked up and made a remark Kindra
didn't hear. The boy snarled something, a hand to his
dagger. "Watch yourself, you—!" He spoke a foulness.
Then he came to Kindra's table and said, in a soft, husky
voice, "A good evening to you, honorable mistress."

Startled at the courteous phrase, but still wary, Kindra
said, "And to you, young sir."

"May I offer you a tankard of wine?"

"I have had enough to drink," Kindra said, "but I
thank you for the kind offer." Something faintly out of
key, almost effeminate, in the youth's bearing, alerted
her; his proposition, then, would not be the usual thing.

Most people knew that Free Amazons took lovers if and when they chose, and all too many men interpreted that to mean that any Amazon could be had, at any time. Kindra was an expert at turning covert advances aside without ever letting it come to question or refusal; with ruder approaches, she managed with scant courtesy. But that wasn't what this youngster wanted; she knew when a man was looking at her with desire, whether he put it into words or not, and although there was certainly interest in this young man's face, it wasn't sexual interest! What did he want with her, then?

"May I—may I sit here and talk to you for a moment, honorable dame?"

Rudeness she could have managed. This excessive courtesy was a puzzle. Were they simply making game of a woman-hater, wagering he would not have the courage to talk to her? She said neutrally, "This is a public room; the chairs are not mine. Sit where you like."

Ill at ease, the boy took a seat. He was young indeed. He was still beardless, but his hands were callused and hard, and there was a long-healed scar on one cheek; he was not as young as she thought.

"You are a Free Amazon, *mestra*?" He used the common, and rather offensive, term; but she did not hold it against him. Many men knew no other name.

"I am," she said, "but we would rather say: I am of the oath-bound—" The word she used was *Comhi-Letzis*— "A Renunciate of the Sisterhood of Freed Women."

"May I ask—without giving offense—why the name Renunciate, *mestra*?"

Actually, Kindra welcomed a chance to explain. "Because sir, in return for our freedom as women of the Guild, we swear an oath renouncing those privileges that we might have by choosing to belong to some man. If we renounce the disabilities of being property and chattel, we must renounce, also, whatever benefits there may be; so that no man can accuse us of trying to have the best of both choices."

He said gravely, "That seems to me an honorable choice. I have never yet met a—a—a Renunciate. Tell me, *mestra*—" His voice suddenly cracked high. "I suppose you know the slanders that are spoken of you—tell me, how does any woman have the courage to join the Guild, knowing what will be said of her?"

"I suppose," Kindra said quietly, "for some women, a time comes when they think that there are worse things than being the subject of public slanders. It was so with me."

He thought that over for a moment, frowning. "I have never seen a Free—er—a Renunciate traveling alone before. Do you not usually travel in pairs, honorable dame?"

"True. But need knows no mistress," Kindra said, and explained that her companion had fallen sick in Thendara.

"And you came so far to bear a message? Is she your *bredhis*?" the boy asked, using the polite word for a woman's freemate or female lover; and because it was the polite word he used, not the gutter one, Kindra did not take offense. "No, only a comrade."

"I—I would not have dared speak if there had been two of you—"

Kindra laughed. "Why not? Even in twos or threes, we are not dogs to bite strangers."

The boy stared at his boots. "I have cause to fear—women—" he said, almost inaudibly. "But you seemed kind. And I suppose, *mestra,* that whenever you come into these hills, where life is so hard for women, you are always seeking out wives and daughters who are discontented at home, to recruit them for your Guild?"

Would that we might! Kindra thought, with all the old bitterness; but she shook her head. "Our charter forbids it," she said. "It is the law that a women must seek us out herself, and formally petition to be allowed to join us. I am not even allowed to tell women of the advantages of the Guild, when they ask. I may only tell them of the things they must renounce, by oath." She tightened her lips and added, "If we were to do as you say, to seek out discontented wives and daughters and lure them away to the Guild, the men would not let any Guild House stand in the Domains, but would burn our houses about our ears." It was the old injustice; the women of Darkover had won this concession, the charter of the Guild, but so hedged about with restrictions that many women never saw or spoke with a Guild-sister.

"I suppose," she said, "that they have found out that we are not whores, so they insist that we are all lovers of women, intent on stealing out their wives and daughters. We must be, it seems, one evil thing or the other."

"Are there no lovers of women among you, then?"

Kindra shrugged. "Certainly," she said. "You must know that there are some women who would rather die than marry; and even with all the restrictions and renunciations of the oath, it seems a preferable alternative. But I assure you we are not all so. We are free women— free to be thus or otherwise, at our own will." After a moment's thought she added carefully, "And if you have a sister you may tell her so from me."

The young man started, and Kindra bit her lip; again she had let her guard down, picking up hunches so clearly formed that sometimes her companions accused her of having a little of the telepathic gift of the higher castes; *laran.* Kindra, who was, as far as she knew, all commoner and without either noble blood or telepathic gift, usually kept herself barricaded; but she had picked up a random thought, a bitter thought from somewhere, *My sister would not believe* ... a thought quickly vanished, so quickly that Kindra wondered if she had imagined the whole thing.

The young face across the table twisted into bitter lines. "There is none, now, I may call my sister."

"I am sorry," Kindra said, puzzled. "To be alone, that is a sorrowful thing. May I ask your name?"

The boy hesitated again, and Kindra knew, with that odd intuition, that the real name had almost escaped the taut lips; but he bit it back.

"Brydar's men call me Marco. Don't ask my lineage; there is none who will claim kin to me now—thanks to those foul bandits under Scarface." He twisted his mouth and spat. "Why do you think I am in this company? For the few coppers these village folk can pay? No, *mestra.* I too am oath-bound. To revenge."

Kindra left the common room early, but she could not sleep for a long time. Something in the young man's voice, his words, had plucked a resonating string in her own mind and memory. Why had he questioned her so insistently? Had he a sister or kinswoman, perhaps, who had spoken of becoming a Renunciate? Or was he, an obvious effeminate, jealous of her because she could escape the role ordained by society for her sex and he could not? Did he fantasy, perhaps, some such escape from the demands made upon men? Surely not; there were simpler lives for men than that of a hired sword! And men had a choice of what lives they would live— more choice, anyhow, than most women. Kindra had chosen to become a Renunciate, making herself an outcaste among most people in the Domains. Even the innkeeper only tolerated her, because she was a regular customer and paid well, but he would have equally tolerated a prostitute or a traveling juggler, and would have had fewer prejudices against either.

Was the youth, she wondered, one of the rumored spies sent out by *cortes*, the governing body in Thendara, to trap Renunciates who broke the terms of their charter by proselytizing and attempting to recruit women into the Guild? If so, at least she had resisted the temptation. She had not even said, though tempted, that if Janella were a Renunciate she would have felt competent to run the inn by herself, with the help of her daughters.

A few times, in the history of the Guild, men had even tried to infiltrate them in disguise. Unmasked, they had met with summary justice, but it had happened and might happen again. At that, she thought, he might be convincing enough in women's clothes; but not with the scar on his face, or those callused hands. Then she laughed in the dark, feeling the calluses on her own fingers. Well, if he was fool enough to try it, so much the worse for him. Laughing, she fell asleep.

Hours later she woke to the sound of hoofbeats, the clash of steel, yells and cries outside. Somewhere women were shrieking. Kindra flung on her outer clothes and ran downstairs. Brydar was standing in the courtyard, bellowing orders. Over the wall of the courtyard she could see a sky reddened with flames. Scarface and his bandit crew were loose in the town, it seemed.

"Go, Renwal," Brydar ordered. "Slip behind their rear-guard and set their horses loose, stampede them, so they must stand to fight, not strike and flee again! And since all the good horses are stabled here, one of you must stay and guard them lest they strike here for ours ... the rest of you come with me, and have your swords at the ready—"

Janella was huddled beneath the overhanging roof of an outbuilding, her daughters and serving women like roosting hens around her. "Will you leave us all here unguarded, when we have housed you all for seven days and never a penny in pay? Scarface and his men are sure to strike here for the horses, and we are unprotected, at their mercy—"

Brydar gestured to the boy Marco. "You. Stay and guard horses and women—"

The boy snarled, "No! I joined your crew on the pledge that I should face Scarface, steel in hand! It is an affair of honor—do you think I need your dirty coppers?"

Beyond the wall all was shrieking confusion. "I have no time to bandy words," Brydar said quickly. "Kindra—this is no quarrel of yours, but you know me a man of my word; stay here and guard the horses and these women, and I will make it worth your while!"

"At the mercy of a woman? A woman to guard us? Why not set a mouse to guard a lion!" Janella's shrewish cry cut him off. The boy Marco urged, eyes blazing, "Whatever I have been promised for this foray is yours, *mestra,* if you free me to meet my sworn foe!"

"Go; I'll look after them," Kindra said. It was unlikely Scarface would get this far, but it was really no affair of hers; normally she fought beside the men, and would have been angry at being left in a post of safety. But Janella's cry had put her on her mettle. Marco caught up his sword and hurried to the gate, Brydar following him. Kindra watched them go, her mind on her own early battles. Some turn of gesture, of phrase, had alerted her. *The boy Marco is noble,* she thought. *Perhaps even Comyn, some bastard of a great lord, perhaps even a Hastur. I don't know what he's doing with Brydar's men, but he's no ordinary hired sword!*

Janella's wailing brought her back to her duty. "Oh! Oh! Horrible," she howled. "Left here with only a woman to look after us ..."

Kindra said tersely, "Come on!" She gestured. "Help me close that gate!"

"I don't take orders from one of you shameless women in breeches—"

"Let the damned gate stay open, then," Kindra said, right out of patience. "Let Scarface walk in without any trouble. Do you want me to go and invite him, or shall we send one of your daughters?"

"Mother!" remonstrated a girl of fifteen, breaking away from Janella's hand. "That is no way to speak— Lilla, Marga, help the good *mestra* shove this gate shut!" She came and joined Kindra, helping to thrust the heavy wooden gate tightly into place, pull down the heavy crossbeam. The women were wailing in dismay; Kindra singled out one of them, a young girl about six or seven moons along in pregnancy, who was huddled in a blanket over her nightgear.

"You," she said, "take all the babies and the little children upstairs into the strongest chamber, bolt the doors, and don't open them unless you hear my voice or Janella's." The woman did not move, still sobbing, and Kindra said sharply, "Hurry! Don't stand there like a rabbit-horn frozen in the snow! Damn you, *move*, or I'll slap you senseless!" She made a menacing gesture and the woman started, then began to hurry the children up the stairs; she picked up one of the littlest ones, hurried the others along with frightened, clucking noises.

Kindra surveyed the rest of the frightened women. Janella was hopeless. She was fat and short of breath, and she was staring resentfully at Kindra, furious that she had been left in charge of their defense. Furthermore, she was trembling on the edge of a panic that would infect everyone; but if she had something to do, she might calm down. "Janella, go into the kitchen and make up some hot wine punch," she said. "The men will want it when they come back, and they'll deserve it, too. Then start hunting out some linen for bandages, in case anyone's hurt. Don't worry," she added, "they won't get to you while we're here. And take that one with you," she added, pointing to the terrified simpleton Lilla, who was clinging to Janella's skirt, round-eyed with terror, whimpering. "She'll only be in our way."

When Janella had gone, grumbling, the lackwit at her heels, Kindra looked around at the sturdy young women who remained.

"Come, all of you, into the stables, and pile heavy bales of hay around the horses, so they can't drive the horses over them or stampede them out. No, leave the lantern there; if Scarface and his men break through, we'll set a couple of bales afire; that will frighten the horses and they might well kick a bandit or two to death. Even so, the women can escape while they round up the horses; contrary to what you may have heard, most bandits look first for horses and rich plunder, and women are not the first item on their list. And none of you have jewels or rich garments they would seek to strip from you." Kindra herself knew that any man who laid his hand on her, intending rape, would quickly regret it; and if she was overpowered by numbers, she had been taught ways in which she could survive the experience undestroyed; but these women had had no such teaching. It was not right to blame them for their fears.

I could teach them this. But the laws of our charter prevent me and I am bound by oath to obey those laws; laws made, not by our own Guild-mothers, but by men who fear what we might have to say to their women!

Well, perhaps at least they will find it a matter for pride that they can defend their home against invaders! Kindra went to lend her own wiry strength to the task of piling up the heavy bales around the horses; the women worked, forgetting their fears in hard effort. But one grumbled, just loud enough for Kindra to hear, "It's all very well for *her*! She was trained as a warrior and she's used to this kind of work! I'm not!"

It was no time to debate Guild House ethics; Kindra only asked mildly, "Are you proud of the fact that you have not been taught to defend yourself, child?" But the girl did not answer, sullenly hauling at her heavy haybale.

It was not difficult for Kindra to follow her thought; if it had not been for Brydar, each man of the town

could have protected each one his own women! Kindra
thought, in utter disgust, that this was the sort of thinking that laid villages in flames, year after year, because
no man owed loyalty to another or would protect any
household but his own! It had taken a threat like
Scarface to get these village men organized enough to
buy the services of a few hired swords, and now their
women were grumbling because their men could not
stand, each at his own door, protecting his own woman
and hearth!

Once the horses had been barricaded, the women clustered together nervously in the courtyard. Even Janella
came to the kitchen door to watch. Kindra went to the
barred gate, her knife loose in its scabbard. The other
girls and women stood under the roof of the kitchen,
but one young girl, the same who had helped Kindra to
shut the gate, bent and tucked her skirt resolutely up to
her knees, then went and brought back a big wood-
chopping hatchet and stood with it in her hand, taking
up a place at the gate beside Kindra.

"Annelys!" Janella called. "Come back here! By me!"

The girl cast a look of contempt at her mother and
said, "If any bandit climbs these walls, he will not get
his hands on me, or on my little sister, without facing
cold steel. It's not a sword, but I think even in a girl's
hands, this blade would change his mind in a hurry!"
She glanced defiantly at Kindra and said, "I am ashamed
for all of you, that you would let one lone woman protect us! Even a rabbit-horn doe protects her kits!"

Kindra gave the girl a companionable grin. "If you
have half as much skill with that thing as you have guts,
little sister, I would rather have you at my back than
any man. Hold the axe with your hands close together,
if the time comes to use it, and don't try anything fancy,
just take a good hard chop at his legs, just like you were
cutting down a tree. The thing is, he won't be expecting
it, see?"

The night dragged on. The women huddled on hay-
bales and boxes, listening with apprehension and occasional sobs and tears as they heard the clash of swords,
cries and shouts. Only Annelys stood grimly beside Kindra, clutching her axe. After an hour or so, Kindra said,

settling herself down on a hay-bale, "You needn't clutch it like that, you'll only weary yourself for an attack. Lean it against the bale, so you can snatch it up when the need comes."

Annelys asked in an undertone, "How did you know so well what to do? Are all the Free Amazons—you call them something else, don't you?—how do the Guild-women learn? Are they all fighting women and hired swords?"

"No, no, not even many of us," Kindra said. "It is only that I have not many other talents; I cannot weave or embroider very well, and my skill at gardening is only good in the summertime. My own oath-mother is a mid-wife, that is our most respected trade; even those who despise the Renunciates confess that we can often save babes alive when the village healer-women fail. She would have taught me her profession; but I had no talent for that, either, and I am squeamish about the sight of blood—" She looked down suddenly at her long knife, remembering her many battles, and laughed; and An-nelys laughed with her, a strange sound against the frightened moaning of the other women.

"*You* are afraid of the sight of blood?"

"It's different," Kindra said. "I can't stand suffering when I can't do anything about it, and if a babe is born easily they seldom send for the midwife; we come only when matters are desperate. I would rather fight with men, or beasts, than for the life of a helpless woman or baby . . ."

"I think I would too," said Annelys, and Kindra thought: *Now, if I were not bound by the laws of the Guild, I could tell her what we are. And this one would be a credit to the Sisterhood . . .*

But her oath held her silent. She sighed and looked at Annelys, frustrated.

She was beginning to think the precautions had been useless, that Scarface's men would never come here at all, when there was a shriek from one of the women, and Kindra saw the tassel of a coarse knitted cap come up over the wall; then two men appeared on top of the wall, knives gripped in their teeth to free their hands for climbing.

"So here's where they've hidden it all, women, horses, all of it—" growled one. "You go for the horses, I'll take care of—oh, you would," he shouted as Kindra ran at him with her knife drawn. He was taller than Kindra; as they fought, she could only defend herself, backing step by step toward the stables. Where were the men? Why had the bandits been able to get this far? Were they the last defense of the town? Behind her, out of the corner of her eye she saw the other bandit coming up with his sword; she circled, backing carefully so she could face them both.

Then there was a shriek from Annelys, the axe flashed once, and the second bandit fell, howling, his leg spouting blood. Kindra's opponent faltered at the sound; Kindra brought up her knife and ran him through the shoulder, snatching up his knife as it fell from his limp hand. He fell backward, and she leaped on top of him.

"Annelys!" she shouted. "You women! Bring thongs rope, anything to tie him up—there may be others—"

Janella came with a clothesline and stood by as Kindra tied the man, then, stepping back, looked at the bandit, lying in a pool of his own blood. His leg was nearly severed at the knee. He was still breathing, but he was too far gone even to moan, and while the women stood and looked at him, he died. Janella stared at Annelys in horror, as if her young daughter had suddenly sprouted another head.

"You killed him," she breathed. "You chopped his leg off!"

"Would you rather he had chopped off mine, mother?" Annelys asked, and bent to look at the other bandit. "He is only stabbed through the shoulder, he'll live to be hanged!"

Breathing hard, Kindra straightened, giving the clothesline a final tug. She looked at Annelys and said, "You saved my life, little sister."

The girl smiled up at her, excited, her hair coming down and tumbling into her eyes. There was a cold sleet beginning to fall in the court; their faces were wet. Annelys suddenly flung her arms around Kindra, and the older woman hugged her, disregarding the mother's troubled face.

"One of our own could not have done better. My thanks, little one!" Damn it, the girl had *earned* her thanks and approval, and if Janella stared at them as if Kindra were a wicked seducer of young women, then so much the worse for Janella! She let the girl's arm stay around her shoulders as she said, "Listen; I think that is the men coming back."

And in a minute they heard Brydar's hail, and they struggled to raise the great crossbeam of the gate. His men drove before them more than a dozen good horses, and Brydar laughed, saying, "Scarface's men will have no more use for them; so we're well paid! I see you women got the last of them?" He looked down at the bandit lying in his gore, at the other, tied with Janella's clothesline. "Good work, *mestra,* I'll see you have a share in the booty!"

"The girl helped," Kindra said. "I'd have been dead without her."

"One of them killed my father," the girl said fiercely, "so I have paid my just debt, that is all!" She turned to Janella and ordered, "Mother, bring our defenders some of that wine punch, at once!"

Brydar's men sat all over the common room, drinking the hot wine gratefully. Brydar set down the tankard and rubbed his hands over his eyes with a tired "Whoosh!" He said, "Some of my men are hurt, dame Janella; have any of your women skill with leech-craft? We will need bandages, and perhaps some salves and herbs. I—" He broke off as one of the men beckoned him urgently from the door, and he went at a run.

Annelys brought Kindra a tankard and put it shyly into her hand. Kindra sipped; it was not the wine punch Janella had made, but a clear, fine, golden wine from the mountains. Kindra sipped it slowly, knowing the girl had been telling her something. She sat across from Kindra, taking a sip now and then of the hot wine in her own tankard. They were both reluctant to part.

Damn that fool law that says I cannot tell her of the Sisterhood! She is too good for this place and for that fool mother of hers; the idiot Lilla is more what her mother needs to help run the inn, and I suppose Janella will marry her off to some yokel at once, just to have help in running this place! Honor demanded she keep silent. Yet, watching Annelys, thinking of the life the girl would lead here, she wondered, troubled, what kind of honor it was, to require that she leave a girl like this in a place like this.

Yet she supposed it was a wise law; anyway, it had been made by wiser heads than hers. She supposed, otherwise, young girls, glamored for the moment with the thought of a life of excitement and adventure, might follow the Sisterhood without being fully aware of the hardships and the renunciations that awaited them. The name Renunciate was not lightly given; it was not an easy life. And considering the way Annelys was looking at her, Annelys might follow her simply out of hero-worship. That wouldn't do. She sighed, and said, "Well, the excitement is over for tonight, I suppose. I must be away to my bed; I have a long way to ride tomorrow. Listen to that racket! I didn't know any of Brydar's men were seriously hurt—"

"It sounds more like a quarrel than men in pain," Annelys said, listening to the shouts and protests. "Are they quarreling over the spoils?"

Abruptly the door thrust open and Brydar of Fen Hills came into the room. "*Mestra,* forgive me, you are wearied—"

"Enough," she said, "but after all this hullabaloo I am not like to sleep much; what can I do for you?"

"I beg you—will you come? It is the boy—young Marco; he is hurt, badly hurt, but he will not let us tend his wounds until he has spoken with you. He says he has an urgent message, very urgent, which he must give before he dies . . ."

"Avarra's mercy," Kindra said, shocked. "Is he dying, then?"

"I cannot tell, he will not let us near enough to dress his wound. If he would be reasonable and let us care for him—but he is bleeding like a slaughtered *chervine,* and he has threatened to slit the throat of any man who touches him. We tried to hold him down and tend him willy-nilly, but it made his wounds bleed so sore as he struggled that we dared not wait—will you come, *mestra*?"

Kindra looked at him with question—she had not thought he would humor any man of his band so. Brydar said defensively, "The lad is nothing to me; not foster-brother, kinsman, nor even friend. But he fought at my side, and he is brave; it was he who killed Scarface in single combat. And may have had his death from it."

"Why should he want to speak to me?"

"He says, *mestra*, that it is a matter concerning his sister. And he begs you in the name of Avarra the pitiful that you will come. And he is young enough, almost, to be your son."

"So," Kindra said at last. She had not seen her own son since he was eight days old; and he would, she thought, be too young to bear a sword. "I cannot refuse anyone who begs me in the name of the Goddess," she said, and rose, frowning; young Marco had said he had no sister. No; he had said that there was none, now, that he could call sister. Which might be a different thing.

On the stairs she heard the voice of one of Brydar's men, expostulating, "Lad, we won't hurt ye, but if we don't get to that wound and tend to it, you could die, do ye' hear?"

"Get away from me!" The young voice cracked. "I swear by Zandu's hells, and, by the spilt tripes of Scarface out there dead, I'll shove this knife into the throat of the first man who touches me!"

Inside, by torchlight, Kindra saw Marco half-sitting, half-lying on a straw pallet; he had a dagger in his hand, holding them away with it; but he was pale as death, and there was icy sweat on his forehead. The straw pallet was slowly reddening with a pool of blood. Kindra knew enough of wounds to know that the human body could lose more blood than most people thought possible without serious danger; but to any ordinary person it looked most alarming.

Marco saw Kindra and gasped, "*Mestra*, I beg you—I must speak with you alone—"

"That's no way to speak to a comrade, lad," said one of the mercenaries, kneeling behind him, as Kindra knelt beside the pallet. The wound was high on the leg, near the groin; the leather breeches had broken the blow somewhat, or the boy would have met the same fate as the man Annelys had struck with the axe.

"You little fool," Kindra said. "I can't do half as much for you as your friend can."

Marco's eyes closed for a moment, from pain or weakness. Kindra thought he had lost consciousness, and gestured to the man behind him. "Quick, now, while he is unconscious—" she said swiftly, but the tortured eyes flicked open.

"Would you betray me, too?" He gestured with the dagger, but so feebly that Kindra was shocked. There was certainly no time to be lost. The best thing was to humor him.

"Go," she said, "I'll reason with him, and if he won't listen, well, he is old enough to take the consequences of his folly." Her mouth twisted as the men went away. "I hope what you have to tell me is worth risking your life for, you lackwitted simpleton!"

But a great and terrifying suspicion was born in her as she knelt on the bloody pallet. "You fool do you know this is likely to be your deathwound? I have small skill at leechcraft; your comrades could do better for you."

"It is sure to be my death unless you help me," said the hoarse, weakening voice. "None of these men is comrade enough that I could trust him . . . *mestra,* help me, I beg you, in the name of the merciful Avarra—I am a woman."

Kindra drew a sharp breath. She had begun to suspect—and it was true, then. "And none of Brydar's men knows—"

"None. I have dwelt among them for half a year, and I do not think any man of them suspects—and I fear women even more. But you, you I felt I might trust—"

"I swear it," Kindra said hastily. "I am oath-bound never to refuse aid to any woman who asks me in the name of the Goddess. But let me help you now, my poor girl, and pray Avarra you have not delayed too long!"

"Even if it was so—" the strange girl whispered—"I would rather die as a woman, than—disgraced and exposed. I have known so much disgrace—"

"Hush! Hush, child!" But she fell back against the

pallet; she had really fainted, this time, at last; and Kindra cut away the leather breeches, looking at the serious cut that sliced through the top of the thigh and into the pubic mound. It had bled heavily, but was not, Kindra thought, fatal. She picked up one of the clean towels the men had left, pressed heavily against the wound; when it slowed to an ooze, she frowned, thinking it should be stitched. She hesitated to do it—she had little skill at such things, and she was sure the man from Brydar's band could do it more tidily and sure-handed; but she knew that was exactly what the young woman had feared, to be handled and exposed by men. Kindra thought: *If it could be done before she recovers consciousness, she need not know* ... But she had promised the girl, and she would keep her promise. The girl did not stir as she stepped out into the hall.

Brydar came halfway up the stairs. "How goes it?"

"Send young Annelys to me," Kindra said. "Tell her to bring linen thread and a needle; and linen for bandages, and hot water and soap." Annelys had courage and strength; what was more, she was sure that if Kindra asked her to keep a secret, Annelys would do so, instead of gossiping about it.

Brydar said, in a undertone that did not carry a yard past Kindra's ear, "It's a woman—isn't it?"

Kindra demanded, with a frown. "Were you listening?"

"Listening, hell! I've got the brains I was born with, and I was remembering a couple of other little things. Can you think of any other reason a member of my band wouldn't let us get his britches off? Whoever she is, she's got guts enough for two!"

Kindra shook her head in dismay. Then all the girl's suffering was useless, scandal and disgrace there would be in any case. "Brydar, you pledged this would be worth my while. Do you owe me, or not?"

"I owe you," Brydar said.

"Then swear by your sword that you will never open your mouth about this, and I am paid. Fair enough?"

Brydar grinned. "I won't cheat you out of your pay for that," he said. "You think I want it to get round these hills that Brydar of Fen Hills can't tell the men from the ladies? Young Marco rode with my band for half a year and proved himself the man. If his foster-sister or kinswoman or cousin or what you will chooses to nurse him herself, and take him home with her afterward, what's it to any of my men? Damned if I want my crew thinking some girl killed Scarface right under my nose!" He put his hand to sword-hilt. "Zandru take this hand with the palsy if I say any word about this. I'll send Annelys to you," he promised, and went.

Kindra returned to the girl's side. She was still unconscious; when Annelys came in, Kindra said curtly, "Hold the lamp there; I want to get this stitched before she recovers consciousness. And try not to get squeamish or faint; I want to get it done quick enough so we don't have to hold her down while we do it."

Annelys gulped at the sight of the girl and the gaping wound, which had begun to bleed again. "A woman! Blessed Evanda! Kindra, is she one of your Sisterhood? Did you know?"

"No, to both questions. Here, hold the light—"

"No," said Annelys. "I have done this many times; I have steady hands for this. Once when my brother cut his thigh chopping wood, I sewed it up, and I have helped the midwife, too. You hold the light."

Relieved, Kindra surrendered the needle. Annelys began her work as skillfully as if she were embroidering a cushion; halfway through the business, the girl regained consciousness; she gave a faint cry of fright, but Kindra spoke to her, and she quieted and lay still, her teeth clamped in her lip, clinging to Kindra's hand. Halfway through, she moistened her lip and whispered, "Is she one of you, *mestra*?"

"No. No more than yourself, child. But she is a friend. And she will not gossip about you, I know it," Kindra said confidently.

When Annelys had finished, she fetched a glass of wine for the woman, and held her head while she drank it. Some color came back into the pale cheeks, and she was breathing more easily. Annelys brought one of her own nightgowns and said, "You will be more comfortable in this, I think. I wish we could carry you to my bed, but I don't think you should be moved yet. Kindra, help me to lift her." With a pillow and a couple of clean sheets she set about making the woman comfortable on the straw pallet.

The stranger made a faint sound of protest as they began to undress her, but was too weak to protest effectively. Kindra stared in shock as the undertunic came off. She would never have believed that any woman over fourteen could successfully pose as a man among men; yet this woman had done it, and now she saw how. The revealed form was flat, spare, breastless; the shoulders had the hardened musculature of any swordsman. There was more hair on the arms than most women would have tolerated without removing it somehow, with bleach or wax. Annelys stared in amazement, and the woman, seeing that shocked look, hid her face in the pillow. Kindra said sharply, "There is no need to stare. She is *emmasca*, that is all; haven't you ever seen one before?" The neutering operation was illegal all over Darkover, and dangerous; and in this woman it must have been done before, or shortly after puberty. She was filled with questions, but courtesy forbade any of them.

"But—but—" Annelys whispered. "Was she born so or made so? It is unlawful—who would dare—"

"Made so," the girl said, her face still hidden in the pillow. "Had I been born so, I would have had nothing to fear ... and I chose this so that I might have nothing more to fear!"

She tightened her mouth as they lifted and turned her; Annelys gasped aloud at the shocking scars, like the marks of whips, across the woman's back; but she said nothing, only pulled the merciful concealment of her own nightgown over the frightful revelation of those scars. Gently, she washed the woman's face and hands with soapy water. The ginger-pale hair was dark with sweat, but at the roots Kindra saw something else; the hair was beginning to grow in fire-red there.

Comyn. The telepath caste, red-haired ... this woman was a noblewoman, born to rule in the Domains of Darkover!

In the name of all the Gods, Kindra wondered, who can she be, what has come to her? How came she here in this disguise, even her hair bleached so none can guess at her lineage? And who has mishandled her so? She must have been beaten like an animal . . .

And then, shocked, she heard the words forming in her mind, not knowing how.

Scarface, said the voice in her mind. *But now I am avenged. Even if it means my death* . . .

She was frightened; never had she so clearly perceived; her rudimentary telepath gift had always, before, been a matter of quick intuition, hunch, lucky guess. She whispered aloud, in horror and dismay, "By the Goddess! Child, who are you?"

The pale face contorted in a grimace which Kindra recognized, in dismay, was intended for a smile. "I am— no one," she said. "I had thought myself the daughter of Alaric Lindir. Have you heard the tale?"

Alaric Lindir. The Lindir family were a proud and wealthy family, distantly akin to the Aillard family of the Comyn. Too highly born, in fact, for Kindra to claim acquaintance with any of that kin; they were of the ancient blood of the Hastur-kin.

"Yes, they are a proud people," whispered the woman. "My mother's name was Kyria, and she was a younger sister to *Dom* Lewis Ardais—not the Ardais Lord, but his younger brother. But still, she was highborn enough that when she proved to be with child by one of the Hastur lords of Thendara, she was hurried away and married in haste to Alaric Lindir. And my father—he that I had always believed my father—he was proud of his red-haired daughter; all during my childhood I heard how proud he was of me, for I would marry into Comyn, or go to one of the Towers and become a great and powerful sorceress or Keeper. And then—then came Scarface and his crew, and they sacked the castle, and carried away some of the women, just as an afterthought, and by the time Scarface discovered who he had as his latest captive—well, the damage was done, but still he sent to my father for ransom. And my father, that selfsame *Dom* Alaric who had not enough proud words for his red-haired beauty who should further his ambition by a proud marriage into the Comyn, my father—" She choked, then spat the words out. "He sent word that if Scarface could guarantee me—

untouched—then he would ransom me at a great price; but if not, then he would pay nothing. For if I was—was spoilt, ravaged—then I was no use to him, and Scarface might hang me or give me to one of his men, as he saw fit."

"Holy Bearer of Burdens!" Annelys whispered. "And this man had reared you as his own child?"

"Yes—and I had thought he loved me," Camilla said, her face twisting. Kindra closed her eyes in horror, seeing all too clearly the man who had welcomed his wife's bastard—but only while she could further his ambition!

Annelys' eyes were filled with tears. "How dreadful! Oh, how could any man—"

"I have come to believe any man would do so," Camilla said, "for Scarface was so angry at my father's refusal that he gave me to one of his men to be a plaything, and you can see how he used me. *That* one I killed while he lay sleeping one night, when at last he had come to believe me beaten into submission—and so made my escape, and back to my mother, and she welcomed me with tears and with pity, but I could see in her mind that her greatest fear, now, was that I should shame her by bearing the child of Scarface's bastard; she feared that my father would say to her, *like mother, like daughter,* and my disgrace would revive the old story of her own. And I could not forgive my mother—that she should continue to love and to live with that man who had rejected me and given me over to such a fate. And so I made my way to a *leronis,* who took pity on me—or perhaps she, too, wanted only to be certain I would not disgrace my Comyn blood by becoming a whore or a bandit's drab—and she made me *emmasca,* as you see. And I took service with Brydar's men, and so I won my revenge—"

Annelys was weeping; but the girl lay with a face like stone. Her very calm was more terrible than hysteria; she had gone beyond tears, into a place where grief and satisfaction were all one, and that one wore the face of death.

Kindra said softly, "You are safe now; none will harm you. But you must not talk any more; you are weary, and weakened with loss of blood. Come, drink the rest of this wine and sleep, my girl." She supported the girl's head while she finished the wine, filled with horror. And yet, through the horror, was admiration. Broken, beaten, ravaged, and then rejected, this girl had won free of her captors by killing one of them; and then she had survived the further rejection of her family, to plot her revenge, and to carry it out, as a noble might do.

And the proud Comyn rejected this woman? She has the courage of any two of their menfolk! It is this kind of pride and folly that will one day bring the reign of the Comyn crashing down into ruin! And she shuddered with a strange premonitory fear, seeing with her wakening telepathic gift a flashing picture of flames over the Hellers, strange sky-ships, alien men walking the streets of Thendara clad in black leather . . .

The woman's eyes closed, her hands tightening on Kindra's. "Well, I have had my revenge," she whispered again, "and so I can die. And with my last breath I will bless you, that I die as a woman, and not in this hated disguise, among men . . ."

"But you are not going to die," Kindra said. "You will live, child."

"No." Her face was set stubbornly in lines of refusal, closed and barriered. "What does life hold for a woman friendless and without kin? I could endure to live alone and secret, among men, disguised, while I nursed the thought of my revenge to strengthen me for the—the daily pretense. But I hate men, I loathe the way they speak of women among themselves, I would rather die than go back to Brydar's band, or live further among men."

Annelys said softly, "But now you are revenged, now you can live as a woman again."

Again the nameless woman shook her head. "Live as a woman, subject to men like my father? Go back and beg shelter from my mother, who might give me bread in secret so I would not disgrace them further by dying across her doorstep, and keep me hidden away, to drudge among them hidden, sew or spin, when I have ridden free with a mercenary band? Or shall I live as a lone woman, at the mercy of men? I would rather face the mercy of the blizzard and the banshee!" Her hand closed on Kindra's. "No," she said, "I would rather die."

Kindra drew the girl into her arms, holding her against her breast. "Hush, my poor girl, hush, you are overwrought, you must not talk like that. When you have slept you will not feel this way," she soothed, but she felt the depth of despair in the woman in her arms, and her rage overflowed.

The laws of her Guild forbade her to speak of the Sisterhood, to tell this girl that she could live free, protected by the Guild Charter, never again to be at the mercy of any man. The laws of the Guild, which she might not break, the oath she must keep. And yet on a deeper level, was it not breaking the oath to withhold from this woman, who had risked so much and who had appealed to her in the name of her Goddess, the knowledge that might give her the will to live?

Whatever I do, I am forsworn; either I break my oath by refusing this girl my help, or I break it by speaking when I am forbidden by the law to speak.

The law! The law made by men, which still hemmed her in on every side, though she had cast off the ordinary laws by which men forced women to live! And she was doubly damned if she spoke of the Guild before Annelys, though Annelys had fought at her side. The just law of the Hellers would protect Annelys from this knowledge; it would make trouble for the Sisterhood if Kindra should lure away a daughter of a respectable innkeeper, whose mother needed her, and needed the help her husband would bring to the running of her inn!

Against her breast, the nameless girl had closed her eyes. Kindra caught the faint thread of her thoughts; she knew that the telepath caste could will themselves to die ... as this girl had willed herself to live, despite everything that had happened, until she had had her cherished revenge.

Let me sleep so ... and I can believe myself back in my mother's arms, in the days when I was still her child and this horror had not touched me.... Let me sleep so and never wake ...

Already she was drifting away, and for a moment, in despair, Kindra was tempted to let her die. *The Law forbids me to speak.* And if she should speak, then Annelys, already struck with hero-worship of Kindra, already rebelling against a woman's lot, having tasted the pride of defending herself, Annelys would follow her, too. Kindra knew it, with a strange, premonitory shiver.

She let the rage in her have its way and overflow. She shook the nameless woman awake, knowing that already she was willing herself to death.

"Listen to me! Listen! You must not die," she said angrily. "Not when you have suffered so much! That is a coward's way, and you have proven again and again that you are no coward!"

"Oh, but I am a coward," the woman said. "I am too much a coward to live in the only way a woman like me can live—through the charity of women such as my mother—or the mercy of men like my father, or like Scarface! I dreamed that when I had my revenge, I could find some other way. But there is no other way."

And Kindra's rage and resolution overflowed. She looked despairing over the nameless woman's head, into Annelys's frightened eyes. She swallowed, knowing the seriousness of the step she was about to take.

"There—there might be another way," she said, still temporizing. "You—I do not even know your name, what is your name?"

"I am nameless," the woman said, her face like stone. "I swore I would never again speak the name given me by the father and the mother who rejected me. If I had lived, I would have taken another name. Call me what pleases you."

And with a great surge of wrath, Kindra made up her mind. She drew the girl against her.

"I will call you Camilla," she said, "for from this day forth, I swear it, I shall be mother and sister to you, as was the blessed Cassilda to Camilla; this I swear. Camilla, you shall not die," she said, pulling the girl upright. Then, with a deep resolute breath, clasping

Camilla's hand in one of hers, and stretching the other to Annelys, she began.

"My little sisters, let me tell you of the Sisterhood of Free Women, which men call Free Amazons. Let me tell you of the ways of the Renunciates, the Oath-bound, the *Comhi-Letzii* ..."

Amazon Fragment

by Marion Zimmer Bradley

Years afterward, neither Camilla nor Rafaella could ever remember exactly what had triggered their original quarrel. Somewhere there must have been some initial remark, some small individual episode, which set off a series of silly, pointless squabbles, of rude remarks and covert insults, of endless bickering; but neither of them could ever trace it back and find the spark which had set all this tinder ablaze.

But it seemed to Rafaella, this winter, that Camilla had for no known reason taken a bitter dislike to her, and went out of her way to pick quarrels over everything. She remembered one bitter dispute over a barnbroom which they were both using in the stable one day, as a result of which Camilla had—accidentally, she insisted—shoved her into the manure pile. And another, in the kitchen, where she had stumbled and scattered a pile of trash which Camilla had laboriously swept up, and because Camilla had loudly accused her of doing it on purpose, she did not, (as normally, she insisted, she would have been glad to do) help the other woman sweep it up again.

But Camilla—it seemed to Rafaella—was forever making remarks about women who flaunted their lovers, and when Rafaella, one night in the music room, had laughingly admitted to one or two of the younger women that she had reason to believe she might be pregnant, Camilla had muttered "Harlot!" and gotten up to leave the room. Rafaella had flared, "None of *your* lovers would ever give you so much," and Camilla had slapped her face.

That episode had gotten them both called up in House meeting before the Guild-mothers, who, without listening to the remarks they had exchanged—Mother Lauria said sharply that she had heard all the insults young women could put on one another and was not interested—admonished them to try and live at peace. Afterward the Guild-mothers, aware of their hostility, tried to assign them separate tasks; Camilla was working in the city, and Rafaella living in the house and working in the Guild House garden, so that they really did not come in contact very often. Not nearly often enough to quarrel as often as they did. It soon seemed that they could not be in the same room without quarreling, and they made a point of seating themselves at opposite ends of the room in dining room and House meeting.

The final episode was triggered one night when they happened to be at the same time in the third-floor bath, and (by accident, Rafaella always insisted) Rafaella ran without looking into Camilla, knocking her off balance and splashing her with dirty water. Camilla turned on her furiously.

"Now see what you have done, you fat bitch!" Her thick nightgown was clinging wetly to her knees, sopping.

"Bitch yourself," Rafaella retorted, angry because for once it had really been an accident and she had actually opened her mouth to apologize, to hand Camilla the towel in her own hand, when Camilla turned on her.

Camilla did not answer. She picked up a basin at hand, and doused the gallon or so of cold, soapy bathwater over Rafaella's head.

Shocked, spluttering, furious, frantically pushing ice-cold, soapy hair out of her face, blinded, Rafaella picked up a pitcher and flung it at her.

"I'll break your head, you *emmasca* cat-hag!"

The pitcher, which was made of stoneware and heavy, struck Camilla on the shoulder, knocking her almost to the floor. She stumbled and went down; a woman behind her caught her and helped her to her feet. Camilla whirled; her clothes were spread out on a stool, and she caught up her dagger from her belt.

"You filthy whore, how dare you!" She rushed at Rafaella, and Rafaella gripped at the knife in her boots, in sheer reflex—self-defense, she justified herself later. And then they were fighting in deadly earnest, slipping on the wet stone floor of the bath, Camilla hampered by her long nightgown. It took four women to drag them apart, and both were bleeding from long, painful cuts; Kindra, roused from sleep to deal with the matter, looked grave.

"You two have been keeping the house in an uproar for half a season," she accused. "This cannot go on. While it was only harsh words, we held our peace, but this—" she looked, shocked, at the slash along Rafaella's bare arm, the two cuts on Camilla's face, "this is serious, this is oath-breaking. You are sworn, like all of us, to live at peace, as kin and sisters."

Camilla hung her head. In the slashed, dripping nightgown, she looked ludicrous. Rafaella saw Kindra's eyes on hers and wanted to cry.

Kindra said quietly, "Daughters, I ask you now to kiss one another, beg each other's pardon, and swear to live at peace as sisters should. Will you now obey me, and we need carry this no further."

Rafaella looked at Camilla with cold, fastidious distaste—as if, Camilla said later, I was something with a hundred legs that you had found in your porridge. "I'd rather kiss a *cralmac*!"

"Rafaella, my child, this is not worthy of you," Kindra said.

Camilla said, in shaking rage, "Let her keep away from me, and I will promise to keep my hands off her dirty throat. I will promise no more!"

Kindra stared from one to the other of them, angry and appalled. "We cannot have this here! You know that!"

"Then send me away," Camilla flared, "where I need not listen night and day to her taunting! There are other Guild Houses in the Domains!"

Rafaella's eyes rested on Camilla; she felt her lip curl as she said, "Perhaps that would settle it best. I am trying to stay as far away from her as I can, but it seems the House is not big enough for us both. If she chooses to leave here, that would solve everyone's problem."

Kindra shook her head. "You are my oath-daughters, both of you; that would be no solution. Children," she pleaded, "will you not, for my sake, sit down together and talk this through?" She held out a hand to each of them; Camilla lowered her eyes and pretended not to see, and Kindra said in despair, "Will you leave me no choice but to bring this before the judges?"

"Oh, Kindra," Rafaella said, and her eyes filled with tears, "I have tried, truly I have, but I can't live with her! One of us must go, even if—" she heard her voice catch in a sob, "even if it must be me!"

Would Kindra actually send her away? She thought, wretchedly, *Does she care more for that* emmasca *than for me?* A year ago she would have flung herself into Kindra's arms and cried, promising to do everything Kindra asked. She moved toward Kindra, on the verge of breaking down, longing for Kindra to take her into her arms, but Kindra frowned and drew back. She said, and her voice was hard, "It is not to me, Rafaella, but to Camilla, that you must make your apology."

"To *her?*" Rafaella was cold and incredulous. "Never!" She wanted to cry out, *Kindra, don't you love me anymore at all?* But she swallowed the words back, knowing she had no right to speak them.

Kindra took Camilla's long fingers in hers. She said "Kima, my child, you are the elder, and you have been one of us longer. She is a child. Will you yield? I should not ask it. Yet I do."

Camilla's voice was husky; but her eyes were tearless and her face like stone. "It is unfair for you to ask it, Kindra. You know I would do anything for you save this, but I have done nothing to merit her persecution—"

"Nothing?" Rafaella cried, "You—"

"Rafi!" Kindra's voice was not loud; but it cut Rafaella off in mid-syllable.

Camilla went on, steadily, "If she will apologize, I will accept her apology, and carry this no further, but I will not crawl to her and beg forgiveness for allowing her to ill-use me!"

Kindra sighed. She said, "You have left me no choice," and summoned the women who had disarmed them. "Keep them in separate rooms while I send for the judges."

Left alone, frightened as the night crawled on, Rafaella heard the words of her oath echoing in her mind.

And if I prove false to my oath, I shall submit myself to the Guild-mothers for such discipline as they see fit, and if I fail, let them slay me like an animal and consign my body unburied to corruption and my soul to the mercy of the Goddess....

Oath-breaking. She had once heard her father say that the most vicious crime was to turn drawn steel against kinfolk; she had been brought up on the ballad of the outlaw berserker who had slain his brethren and been exiled by his last remaining sister ... and she had drawn her dagger on Camilla. True, Camilla had first come at her with a dagger. But perhaps the woman had only been trying to frighten her ... it need not have come to a fight. The slash on her arm smarted and throbbed; no one had troubled to bandage it. *By oath, Camilla is my sister ... mother and sister and daughter to every other woman oath bound to the Guild. And I drew my dagger on a kinswoman, the more so because she, too, is Kindra's oath-daughter.*

But Kindra could not help her now.

She does not love me at all! She would not pledge herself to me ... she loves Camilla better than me!

At last one of the women came and summoned them, and Rafaella saw the pale angry face of her fellow culprit. They stood side by side before the four Guild-mothers, their slashed garments and small wounds telling the tale, and Kindra added that they had refused, before witnesses, to compromise or amend their quarrel. Mother Callista, the oldest of the Guild-mothers, and one of the judges of the Guild, said at last. "This is oath-breaking," and Rafaella trembled.

What will they do to me? she wondered.

Mother Lauria said, "You, Camilla n'ha Kyria, Rafaella n'ha Doria, stand before me. This is no game; I ask you two for the last time if you are willing to join hands, exchange a kiss as sisters, and pledge to amend your quarrel before it is too late. You will have no other chance."

Camilla said, her hands clenched into hard fists, "I would rather you killed me, than apologize without fault and grovel before her!"

Callista said, "Rafaella, will you apologize?"

Rafaella had the craven thought, *If I do, then perhaps they will only punish her ... if I break down now and apologize, they will think I do so because I am afraid of punishment, and they will know I am more cowardly, that she is braver and more defiant than I am! Show myself cowardly before her? Never!*

She said, spitting the words out, "Beat me, then, or kill me if you will! Is this Amazon justice?"

"Kill you?" Mother Callista laughed, not amused. "We are not Guardsmen, to challenge your defiance, and reward you for your stubbornness because you are able to disguise it as heroism. You stand here, then, ready to submit yourselves to punishment? Or will you apologize and pledge to live at peace?"

Rafaella felt her stomach lurch, her knees almost too weak to hold her upright. *What are they going to do to us?* She wanted to cry out, beg for mercy, but before Camilla's cold, defiant face she thought she would rather die there and then, than show herself afraid. Neither of them spoke, and at last Mother Lauria shrugged.

"On your own heads, then, you silly, stupid girls! You have left us no choice. Go and fetch the chains."

Chains! Rafaella thought in horror. *This is worse than I feared....*

Camilla was deathly white; Rafaella wondered for a moment if she would faint. Mother Lauria said, "Make sure neither of them has any weapons."

They stood side by side, each trying to ignore the other's presence as they were searched to the skin. Rafaella was shaking, but before Camilla's iron control she resolved she would not betray any sign of her terror.

Mother Callista stretched her hand out and one of the women handed her a pair of handcuffs, joined by a short length of chain, not more than three inches. She said, "You two have refused to keep your oath of your free will, and will not pledge to live together at peace. Now you will be chained together wrist to wrist; you will eat together, sleep together, work together and live together until you have learned to live in company as sisters must do. When you discover that neither of you can take so much as a single step without her sister's cooperation, then you will learn a lesson that whatever we do of necessity involves another. Most of us learn this lesson less painfully. Camilla, are you left-handed?"

"Yes," said Camilla reluctantly.

"Give me your right hand, then. Rafaella, are you left-handed?"

"Right."

"That is good; otherwise you would have had to flip a coin, and abide by the lot." Her mouth tight with angry distaste, she buckled the handcuffs on their wrists.

Some of the women watching giggled a little, nervously. One of them intoned, "May you be forever one," mocking the phrase of *catenas* marriage, and frowned at the Guild-mother's angry look.

"Leave them now," Mother Callista said, "and go up to bed, all of you. This shameful episode is finished."

Camilla said nervously, "What do we do now?"

Mother Callista said indifferently, "That is for you to decide. Together." She rose without a backward glance and went out of the room. Kindra looked at them for a moment and seemed about to speak, then she, too, turned and went up to bed.

One of the women who had witnessed the quarrel said, "Maybe now you silly brats will stop keeping us in an uproar night and day—and if you want to fight, you'll have all the time you want to do it where it won't bother anyone else!"

Rafaella sat with tears rolling down her face. *Unfair, cruel, humiliating! How could Kindra have let them do this to me? Why didn't Kindra warn me what would happen? Doesn't she love me at all? They all hate me, they're all taking Camilla's part. . . .*

She moved automatically to wipe away her tears and felt the metal cuff jerk hard on her hand, pulling Camilla's wrist up toward her eyes. Camilla yanked hard on it and said, "Stop that, damn it!"

Rafaella began to cry, sobbing helplessly, her free hand up to her face. Camilla said coldly, "Now you may weep, when it is too late to mend matters."

"And what did you do to mend them?" Rafaella demanded, snuffling.

Camilla's voice was icy. "Nothing. You need not remind me what a fool I am."

For a long time neither of them moved. The fire burned low and the room was very dark. Rafaella saw out of the corner of her eyes that Camilla raised her hand to her face as if she was wiping away tears, but thought, *Her crying? That* emmasca? *I don't think she's human enough to know how to cry!* And indeed, Camilla made no sound or movement.

Rafaella felt weary, incapable of coherent thought. She had never been so tired in her life. How would she stand this? How long would it last? Since the Guildmother said they would eat together and work together and sleep together, she wondered if it would be many days. How could she possibly endure it, to have her enemy always at her elbow? She shuddered, and saw Camilla turn to stare angrily at her.

She wished she was safely in her own room, her own bed. But how could she go to bed with Camilla chained to her wrist? This was worse than a beating! She would not make the first move, nor ask that they go upstairs.

Although, soon or late, I must go up to the bathroom— sooner, rather than later, since I have been pregnant ... well, I will not ask her.

And she felt that she had won a kind of victory when it was Camilla who finally muttered, "I suppose we cannot sit here all night. Shall we go upstairs, then?"

"I don't mind," Rafaella said ungraciously, but it was hard to keep pace with Camilla's long steps, and Rafaella stumbled and fell on the stairs, dragging Camilla down; Camilla swore.

"Will you break my shins, too, damn you?"

"Do you think I break my own leg to spite *you*, bitch?"

"How do I know what you are likely to do?"

Rafaella lapsed into furious silence. Even years later she remembered the angry humiliation of having to relieve herself with the other woman at her elbow, and the struggle she had not to cry. *I won't give her the satisfaction!* Camilla herself behaved with complete, calm aloofness, as if she were completely alone. Rafaella wondered how she could accept it so calmly.

(Years later Camilla said to her, "I wanted to scream, to cry for hours, to slap you. But you were so arrogant, so aloof, as if you didn't know I was there. I felt I couldn't behave worse than you did, I had to pretend to be calm ... then, too, I had had more practice than you in enduring humiliations. You did not know, then, how much I had endured in the way of torment, that I could endure this, too. ...")

Rafaella said coldly, "Well, are we to sleep on the floor in the hallway here?"

"Where they can all jeer at us in the morning? Not likely!"

Rafaella said reluctantly, "There is room in my bed."

"You would like to wake all your friends, then, to jeer at me?"

Rafaella realized that the three other women who slept in her room knew nothing of what had happened. "Would you rather wake *your* friends?"

"*What* friends?" Camilla asked, "I sleep alone—which I am sure you have never done in your life—and at least in my bed we will not be seen!"

Discouraged, Rafaella muttered assent. In Camilla's room she had to struggle one-handed to get off her boots. Camilla was already undressed, in the slashed, still-damp nightgown she had been wearing. Rafaella decided not to take off anything else.

Rafaella slept badly, in her clothes, and on an unaccustomed side. Every time she stirred, the handcuffs jerked her awake again. When she woke, she felt abruptly the surging, uneasy nausea which she had felt only a few times before, but which the Guild-mothers had told her some women suffered in early pregnancy; she sat up, sick and retching, and Camilla grumbled, waking abruptly, "Lie down! What in the devil—"

"I'm sick," Rafaella mumbled miserably, and hurried off down the hall, Camilla angrily stumbling behind. She knelt over the basin, retching, sunk in hopeless misery. Devra, there early for kitchen-duty, came to wipe her face with a cold cloth.

"Poor Rafi, I hoped you would escape this—" she broke off, staring in angry shock at Camilla.

"What—"

Rafaella was too sick and wretched to explain. Camilla said briefly, "We fought. This is how they punished us."

Devra stared in dismay. "But Rafi, this is terrible, when you are sick—does Kindra know? Can she do this to you *now*?"

Rafaella could not answer; she could only think, *I brought it on myself.* Camilla was standing there, her face turned away in angry disgust. Stumbling to the room for her boots, Rafaella found that she was crying helplessly.

"Oh, shut up," Camilla shouted. "Is that all you can think to do, cry all the time?"

"I—I can't help it—"

"It's bad enough to be kept awake all night with you jerking around, and wake up with you throwing up all over everything, do I have to listen to you bawling all day, too? Shut up or I'll slap you soft-headed!"

"Just you try it!"

Camilla raised her hand for a blow, but discovered that the force of the slap threw her off balance. They fell together in a tangle on the bed. Camilla, swearing, hauled herself upright.

"Where are you going now?" Rafaella demanded.

"To wash myself, dirty pig, and dress, or don't you wash? And am I to go to breakfast in my dirty nightgear?"

Rafaella said shakily, "I'm not hungry." She felt she could not face the room full of women.

But Camilla said coldly, "I am. I'm not pregnant," and Rafaella had no choice but to trail along awkwardly to the bath where Camilla awkwardly washed herself with one hand. She turned her face stubbornly away while Camilla dressed. The room was full of women who stared or giggled or whispered to one another. Rafaella supposed every woman in the Guild House knew the story by now. In the dining room they had to argue again about where they would sit; finally they balanced awkwardly on the end of the bench. Rafaella could not eat, though she drank a little hot milk. Kindra, at a nearby table, turned and looked at them, but, though it seemed to Rafaella that her glance was sympathetic, she did not speak.

"Ah," someone jeered, "so you have wedded *di catenas,* you two?"

"Camilla is a Dry Towner, to put her woman in chains!"

Rafaella began to realize what she had never recognized before; Camilla was not particularly well liked. Most of the taunts were aimed at her; what few expressions of sympathy were spoken, came to Rafaella. But most of the women seemed to avoid them, embarrassed.

It was a miserable day, punctuated with insults and occasional slaps, jerking at the cuffs that bound them, hobbling awkwardly around the house to their assigned tasks. After a time they began to be able to walk without pulling one another off balance, but they still argued angrily over almost every step and when, toward evening, Rafaella began to cry with exhaustion, Camilla slapped her again, and Rafaella turned and grabbed at her throat. They went down together, fighting, clawing, gripping at any part of each other they could reach, sobbing with rage and humiliation ... they could not, with their hands chained together, even get a good grip on one another's hair!

Abruptly, Rafaella began to laugh. She lay back, released Camilla, and lay laughing helplessly on the rug.

"What's so damned funny?"

"You are," Rafaella gurgled, "and I am. We are. Can't you see how idiotic we are? Here we are fighting this way and we can't even get *at* each other—any more than we can get *away* from each other!"

Camilla began slowly to chuckle. She said, "And I can't even run away without taking you along." They laughed together till the tears ran down their faces, Rafaella holding her sides with pain.

"My shoulder," Camilla groaned. "I think it's broken—"

"Did I do that? I'm sorry, I didn't mean—oh, this is ridiculous—"

"It isn't hurt, I guess. Just pulled. Did I hurt you?" Camilla asked, "I didn't want—" she helped the other girl to her feet. Rafaella stumbled on the stairs and Camilla reached out and steadied her. Surprised, Rafaella thanked her.

"Don't thank me," Camilla grumbled. "If you fall, I am sure to break my knee!"

In the bathroom, Rafaella looked wistfully at one of the tubs.

"I wish I could have a bath. But I don't see how—"

Camilla began to laugh. "I don't think there is a tub big enough to hold us both."

For some reason that struck them both as funny, too. Camilla said, roughly, "If you will wash my face, I will wash yours."

Weakly, tears of laughter dripping down their faces, they washed one another. As they went down to dinner, Rafaella said shyly, "Before we go in—let us agree where to sit so we don't have to haul on one another before the rest of them—"

Camilla shrugged. "As you will. Where we sat this morning, then?"

When they had found a seat, Camilla said harshly to the serving-woman, "Here, you, we can't chew our meat like dogs. They have not given us back our knives; we must have something to cut our meat with!"

Kindra heard them. She said, "Here," and handed her own knife to Camilla, watching while they cut up the meat into bites. When Camilla had finished, she sheathed it again without comment and walked to her own seat. Rafaella watched her walk away, wondering, *Is she gloating over us?*

After dinner some of the women gathered in the music room to hear Kindra and Devra sing ballads; Rafaella and Camilla sat on a cushion to listen, but the novelty of the sight was wearing off and no one paid any attention to them. When they separated to go upstairs, Rezi stopped beside Rafaella and nudged her.

"I thought you boasted of never sharing your bed with a woman, Rafi!"

Rafaella felt hot crimson suffusing her face. She knew Kindra was watching them. Camilla snapped "Let her alone!"

"Why, Camilla, gallantry? And after only one night in her bed? Tell me, what is this magic which a woman of her kind can cast on you, so that already you guard her like a lover—"

"Shut up, damn you," Camilla said, her voice dangerously quiet. "I will not always be chained."

"So now the sworn foes are *bredhin'y*?" someone else jeered. "Like bride and groom, strangers before, and afterward—"

Camilla said in an undertone "Let's get out of here. We don't have to stay here and listen to that."

They got out of the room hurriedly, to a chorus of jeers, catcalls, and ribald jokes. On the stairs, looking at the tears in Rafaella's eyes, Camilla said quietly, "I am sorry about that, Rafaella. I would not willingly have exposed you to that kind of joke. I know they do not like me, but I had thought they were your friends—"

Rafaella swallowed hard. She said, "I thought so, too."

"But they take it out on me because I have brought this on you," Camilla said bitterly, and was silent. "I am older than you, and I first drew my dagger. You should have told Kindra that. Why did you not?"

Rafaella bent her head. She mumbled, "I don't know."

She had thought of it. And then she thought, *If they send me away, even in disgrace, I have kinsmen and kinswomen, I will not be wholly alone. But Camilla is* emmasca *and I once heard Kindra say that her kin had cast her off. She has nowhere else to go.*

She said instead, "I must have clean clothes for tomorrow. Will you come to my room while I fetch them?"

"Of course. Though I hope your roommates are not there . . ." Camilla said, stifled. "I am afraid of them . . . they all dislike me, and you are so popular—"

Rafaella said, really shocked, "Why, everyone in the house likes you!"

"No," said Camilla, bitterly, "they are carefully polite to me because I am *emmasca, mutilata* . . . no one truly likes me save Kindra, and now she will hate me, too, because I have brought trouble and disgrace upon you, her pet and darling. . . ."

"Kindra does not love me at all," Rafaella said, and began to cry. Camilla looked at her in dismay. "She took your part against me, Camilla . . . and I thought she loved me . . ." and all the old hurt surged over her again. Trying to keep back her sobs, she went to her chest and took out a fresh tunic and under-tunic, clean breeches and stockings. She said "I do not want to sleep in my clothes again...."

"You need not," Camilla said, and then, bitterness breaking through, "unless you are afraid to undress in my presence, knowing I am a lover of women...."

"Don't be silly," Rafaella said. "That never occurred to me; do you think I even listened to their rude jokes?" Then she realized, suddenly, that Camilla was not joking. "But you are serious! Truly, I never thought it!"

"If you did not, it is sure you are the only one who did not," Camilla said. Rafaella stopped and stood very still, looking at the taut face, the thin mouth. It seemed that she was seeing Camilla for the first time, and something that had been no more than a word, an insult, suddenly became real to her. She thought; perhaps she was even Kindra's lover, perhaps it was for her sake that Kindra would not pledge to me ... but she was afraid and ashamed to say the words. Finally she said, feeling the words awkward on her lips, "That was not—not necessary, Camilla. I do not care what they say."

What can I say to her? I loved Kindra and I never really understood, and now I do not know what to say to her. I feel like a fool.

And Kindra loved me, too. But if she loved me as she said, why did she drive me into the arms of a man? Shaking, suddenly aware of a thousand things beyond her knowledge, feeling suddenly very young and childlike, she turned her eyes away from Camilla. She said "Will you unfasten my cuffs, please? I cannot reach the buttons on that wrist."

They helped each other undress; but although Camilla did not remove her under-tunic, as she turned to get out of her trousers, Rafaella saw what she had not seen that morning when the other woman dressed, the terrible scars all along Camilla's shoulders and back. She drew a long breath of consternation.

This must be why she never bathes in the common room, why she always sleeps alone. How came she by those dreadful scars?

Camilla said, very low, "Now you have seen. Now you can spread the tale of my—my degradation, of how I am doubly mutilated...."

Rafaella turned away. She said, "Hell, no. I have troubles enough of my own to worry about."

Camilla drew a long breath. "I had thought ... Kindra would have spoken to you of this. It is told from here to Dalereuth, I suppose, in the Guild Houses; how I had to be stripped naked at my oath-taking because I had nothing like to a woman's form, and—and they would not believe me a woman...."

Rafaella said "You wrong Kindra if you think she would spread such a tale. Nor has any woman who saw you stripped spoken of it to me. But how came you so scarred, Camilla?"

"I—I would rather not speak of it," Camilla said. "I was very young, but I do not like to remember it ... perhaps some day I will tell you. But I—I cannot talk about it."

"As you like," Rafaella was quiet as they climbed into bed and shifted about for a comfortable place. Rafaella woke suddenly, hearing her companion scream aloud, moan, start upright, wildly flailing her hands.

"Don't. It's all right, Camilla—it is only me, there is no one to harm you...."

Camilla started and shivered, staring at her in the darkness.

"Oh—Rafi—I am sorry I woke you—"

"I am only sorry you cannot sleep without nightmares."

Camilla said after a long minute, "I was afraid. I—there was a time when I was tied—like an animal—and beaten like an animal, too. Mercifully, I have forgotten much, but sometimes I still have nightmares...."

"Why, this must be worse for you than for me, then," Rafaella said, compassionately. *Tied like an animal ... beaten like an animal ... what can have come to her?*

"Camilla," she said at last, "I am sorry. Our quarrel was my fault; I splashed you with dirty water and I should have apologized and never let it come to this. Tomorrow I will go to Kindra and tell her, and ask that I alone should be punished. You can be freed, then, and need not have nightmares of being tied up."

Camilla bent her head. She said, "You make me ashamed. I knew you would apologize and I didn't want

that, because that would mean you were better than I.
I think if you had apologized I would have pretended
not to hear, so I need not acknowledge it."

"Then we are both to blame," Rafaella said, hesitating, "Will you—will you exchange forgiveness with me,
Camilla?"

"Willingly—oath-sister." Camilla used the ritual
phrase, *com'hi-letzis*.

Rafaella leaned over and lightly kissed her on the lips;
wondering, touched Camilla's face with her fingertips.
No one in the Guild House had ever seen Camilla cry.
Even when she had been brought in from the battle in
the hills with a great wound in her leg and it had to be
cleansed and cauterized with acid, she did not cry out
or weep!

Camilla said, "I always wanted to be your friend.
You were Kindra's kinswoman, and for that alone I
would have loved you. And yet I could not refrain
from making a quarrel with you and bringing this upon
you. . . ." her voice broke. "And because you are
beautiful and everyone loves you, and because you are
pregnant."

"But you are the best fighter in the house, everyone
admires your courage and your strength."

"I am a freak," Camilla said, her voice shaking, "An
emmasca, not a woman at all."

"But Camilla, Camilla—" Rafaella protested, dismayed, putting her arms around the older woman; it had
never occurred to her that Camilla, who had, after all,
chosen to undergo the neutering operation, could possibly feel like this. She was not to know for many years
why Camilla had had this choice forced upon her, but
she sensed tragedy and it made her gentle.

"I thought you despised my womanhood; you taunted
me for being pregnant—"

"Taunted you? If I did, it was only out of envy—"
Camilla said, choking.

Rafaella said incredulously, "Envy? Of this insane—
insane trouble I have gotten myself into? And I have
been hating myself for being such a fool, vulnerable. . . ."

"Envy because you are to have a child," Camilla said,
"and I never shall, now . . . nor, I suppose, really want

to, though sometimes it seems to me hard ... nor could I ever, I suppose, make myself vulnerable in such a way. Is it worth it, Rafaella? Is it really such a delight to you, what you do with men, enough to make up for all the risks?"

"I suppose you would not think it so," Rafaella said, trying not to remember that her reasons had been quite otherwise, "you who are so defiant about being a lover of women."

"Defiant?" Camilla shrugged. "Perhaps. If you had had my experience, you would not think so much, perhaps, of what men desire of women." She turned her eyes away, but Rafaella, thinking of the terrible scars Camilla bore, guessed at something too dreadful to be spoken. She put her arms around the older woman in silent sympathy, but Camilla was rigid, unmoving. She said, "I did not die. That is what I cannot forgive myself. To live with the memory. That is what none of my kins-women could forgive me; that I lived when a decent woman would have died." She pulled herself free of Rafaella's arms. "Don't touch me, Rafaella, I'm not fit to live."

"Don't say that, Camilla, don't—" Rafaella said, holding her.

After a moment the older woman shuddered and said "I'm sorry. I get like that sometimes. And when I heard you were pregnant, it seemed I could not bear my hate— that you were young, lovely, cherished ... but it was myself I hated ... for all the things I would never have or enjoy...." She smiled, bleakly, in the dark. "It is all born of nightmares. Forgive me, Rafaella."

"I think," Rafaella said, subdued, turning her hand within the chain so that her hand lay within Camilla's, "that I should ask you to forgive me instead, *breda*."

"We will forgive one another, then," Camilla said, squeezing the soft hands. "Come, you must sleep, it is not good for a woman with child to lose sleep this way. Here, will you sleep better like this?" She eased the pillow under Rafaella's side and neck. "Lie quite still, and when you wake up tomorrow, maybe you will not be sick and I can sleep a little longer."

They were chained together for another three days;

but now they had learned to help one another, and it cemented a friendship which was to endure lifelong, and to go so deep that in years after, neither could ever remember why they had quarreled.

House Rules

by Marion Zimmer Bradley

"Here is my book, Mama," Loren said. "Will you hear me read?"

"Certainly." Lora felt the skinny little boy leaning against her knee and felt the tears welling up again inside her. Two more months and then Loren must be sent to his father. *To be made into the kind of man I despise, the kind of man who fills Amazon Guild Houses.* Because of the rules of the Guild House that a boy child may not live among women, and Loren was no longer a baby.

Janna came bursting in, her hair long and messy around her shoulders. "Mama, what's for dinner?"

"I haven't thought about it yet, Janni," Lora said. "Why don't you go out in the kitchen and see if there are any potatoes left; I'll fry them in goose fat."

"I'm tired of potatoes," Janna said, "When will we have meat again?"

"When we can afford it." Lora said. "Janna, why are you wearing your holiday smock?"

"Because it's the only decent dress I have," Janna whined. "Am I supposed to go around in breeches all the time like you and Marji?"

"Why not? What is wrong with them? You can work properly in them," Lora said, but she might as well have spoken to the wind.

It is Cara's doing. We should never have taken her into the House; she was very bad for Janni, Lora thought. She hardly knew her nice obedient child in this sullen brat who seemed to spend all her day arranging her hair and painting her nails, who would not work in the barn or the fowl house because she hated to get her hands dirty, and last week she had caught Janni, hardly ten years old, lingering at the gate, twisting her curls and simpering as she talked to young Raul of King's Head Farm. Ten, and already making eyes at the lads. What did we do wrong, Marji and I? Janna was one of the reasons I fled from Darren, a few days after Loren was born ... so Janna would not be pushed into being a stick in a pretty frock, good for nothing but to dress up, simper at boys, and giggle and talk about boys.

Marji called from the back door, "Lora? Are you home?" and Lora pushed her unwilling daughter into the kitchen.

"Take the skins from the potatoes and slice them," she ordered, and Janna sulked.

"I spend all my time in kitchen work. If I lived with Papa at least there would be kitchen-women to do the work for me. I am a kitchen slave, that's all. And I have to be one because you and Marji—"

"That's enough," Lora commanded. "There are no kitchen slaves in the Guild; but you know no other work as yet. Marji and I do our share of the kitchen work, but I have other work to do. I have to bathe the baby before supper and you are not yet big enough to do that. And Marji is working this week getting in Farmer Coll's hay."

"The women said she could have married Farmer Coll," Janna grumbled, "and she wouldn't have to slave in the fields all the time."

And that, Lora thought, would have been a good trade? Coll was forty-nine, and had buried three wives already.

"I'll run away, like Cara," Janna grumbled. "I saw her today; she said when she and Ruyval are married I can come and live with her. At least she's a woman, a natural woman."

"That's *enough*, Janna," Lora commanded and went through to the front hall, where Marja n'ha Carisse was taking off her boots. They hugged each other, and Marji asked, "Nice day?"

"No, Janna's at it again. Spent the whole day playing about with her hair and down at the gate simpering to talk with that wretched Raul from the farm. Cara's simply ruined her. All she thinks of is clothes and boys."

"We should have sent Cara away a year ago," Marji agreed. "I did not realize how much harm she was doing Janna. I was like that at her age, thinking of nothing but clothes and boys; she'll get over it. We did."

"But not in time," Lora wailed. "Now she wants to go and live with her father, and keeps threatening it. It's bad enough that I have to send Loren—how can I bear to give up my baby girl, too!"

"There, there," Marji said comfortingly. "You are protected by the Oath, and the magistrate said Janna could live with you. But if she wants to go, it will do her no good to stay here. Next time she threatens to go to her father, don't just let her go, *make* her go. She'll learn. How is my baby?"

"I haven't bathed her yet," Lora said submissively, and Marji held her. "It won't hurt her to go without a bath for a night. You look so tired, Lori. It's too hard on you, being saddled with all the children while I get out among human beings all day. When haying is over I will stay home for a while and you can find work; it's not fair you should have Callie as well as your two all day, all year."

"Callie is giving me no trouble, at least. At that size, as long as I keep her dry and fed, she makes no other demands." Lori said. "And speaking of Callie, I hear her. . . ."

She ran into the next room, returning after a moment with a tousled, sleepy two-year-old. Marji kissed her daughter, and, carrying her over her arm, went through into the kitchen where Janna was sullenly peeling cold boiled potatoes. "Here, Janni, give those to me, I'll make a cream sauce for them, and the farm wife gave me some bacon; I'll cook it for supper." She set about preparing the meal. "No, sit down, Lori, you're worn out. Where is Lynifred?"

"A messenger came from Arilinn; a man there has a sick horse and she went to doctor it; she will not be back till tomorrow," said Lora.

"Did you remind her that we need leather for boots for the children?"

"Yes; she said she would bring some, and then I can make boots for Janna and Callie as well as the ones

Loren will need," said Lora, and began to cry again. Marji patted her shoulder, dished up the potatoes and fried bacon, then sat down with Callie on her knee and began to feed her daughter.

When the smaller children were in bed, and Marji and Lora were tidying the kitchen, Marji said "I saw Cara in the market. She and that boy were married. . . ."

"Goddess protect her," Lora said, "Cara is not sixteen!"

"Not before time, though," said Marji. "She is beginning to show."

"Well, she had nowhere else to go, after we threw her out," said Lora, "I feel it's my fault. We should have been more patient with her."

"But, my dear," Marji said, "we could not keep her, not when she was stealing from us. We forgave her a dozen times, but she was never a true Renunciate in spirit. Going about with her tunic unlaced down to *here*—" she gestured, "and spending all her time gawking and giggling about with the boys instead of staying properly in the house and helping you with the children! We should have sent her to Neskaya or Thendara for proper training—we had no Guild-mistress here to teach her proper behavior. And then we went into her chest and found all your best holiday skirts retrimmed—and she had sworn she had not seen them—"

"Oh, I know; but still, I feel I failed her, I tried to treat her like my own child—"

"And so did I, and so did Lynifred," said Marji, "but done is done, and she seems happy. I only hope Janna does not follow in her footsteps."

"That's what worries me," said Lora. "But perhaps if she lives with her father for a year or two, she will appreciate the Guild House. Come, my dear, let's lock up for the night."

Lying sleepless at Marji's side, while her freemate slept, Lora thought of how they had established the first small Guild House this side of the river, with three women; herself—and her daughter Janna, then five, and the infant Loren, still at the breast—fleeing from her husband who had beaten her and abused her.

Worst of all, he had forbidden her to read, or to read to Janna . . . books, he said, only kept a woman from what was proper for her. When he had wanted to betroth Janna, at five, to the thirty-year-old lord of the nearby estate, she had rebelled and fled to the Neskaya Guild House to take the Oath.

Then she had met Marji, newly come to the Guild, pregnant at that time with Callie. When her husband kept on pestering the Neskaya Guild House, the Guildmother had sent them both to establish a Guild House here in this little village, with Lynifred, a veteran Renunciate almost fifty years old. For more than a year the village had treated them like outcasts, especially when they took in the runaway Cara at fourteen, until Lynifred managed to save a dozen horses who had been poisoned by witchgrass, and Lora went down to the village and offered to teach women the special skills of midwifery that she had learned in the Arilinn Guild House. Now they had been, to some degree, accepted; women in need of a midwife were as likely to summon her as the dirty, slatternly old woman who had been the village midwife since anyone could remember. Lynifred was now the local horse-doctor, all the better liked because she was not above removing a bone from a cat's throat, or splinting the leg of a dog caught in a trap. "They are the Goddess' creatures, too," she said, "even if they are not riches like horses or cattle."

The trouble had started, she thought, when Cara discovered boys and in no Amazon spirit had decided she wanted to experiment with them. This Janna had heartily followed, too, against Lora's prohibition.

Cara had seemed interested only in catching a husband. Well, now she had one, and Lora honestly hoped the girl was happy.

Marji hired herself out to work in the fields, which was awkward, because Farmer Coll wanted to marry her, and had accused her of trying to snare him with spells; fortunately there was not too much superstition in the village. Still it was an awkward situation, since Coll was regarded as a good catch, and the local women, many of whom would have liked to be Farmer Coll's wife, felt angry because Marji scorned what they thought so valuable, while Marji only wished Coll would marry one of them, and be done with it.

Lora knew she must sleep; there were only three more days before Loren must go to his father, and she supposed Janna would choose to go, too. Deeply as Lora loved her daughter, she knew Janna was not happy; but she did not think Janna would be happy in her father's house either; and she shrank from the thought of losing both children.

She felt she had not slept at all when she heard sounds in the kitchen, and roused up to go and make up a fire; Lynifred had ridden in at dawn and with her was another woman, muffled in cloak and boots against the early chill.

"This is Ferrika, midwife at Armida," Lynifred said. The strange woman wore an Amazon earring but wore ordinary skirts, not the usual breeches and leather boots.

"I must work among ordinary people," Ferrika said. "There is no sense in antagonizing them before they know me."

Lora put on a kettle for tea, and cooked a big pot of oatmeal porridge, and with it fried a little of the bacon Marji had brought home. The women sat with their feet to the fire, drying their snow-stiffened cloaks, and Ferrika asked for the news.

"Only that a fosterling whom we had to ask to leave has married, and is running about already showing her pregnancy less than a tenday past the marriage," said Lora despondently. "It says little for our care of her."

"I am sure the villagers know her ways as well as we do," Lynifred said. "It is not a reflection on your quality as a mother, Lora."

"I am not so sure of that," Lora answered. "Janna is beginning to imitate her—nothing in her head but boys, and fussing with her clothes."

"Almost all teenage girls are like that," Ferrika said, "unless they have had an early and dreadful lesson in what conformity can bring on girls in this world. When Janna sees Cara a drudge to her husband she will be glad to know how she can escape that fate."

"I wasn't," Lynifred said, and Ferrika laughed.

"Nor I," said Lora. "Nevertheless I married when the

time came, thinking it better to have my own house and kitchen than work in my mother's. And even so, if I had married a decent man—though I thought my husband good when we were married."

"And so he might have been," said Ferrika. "It is not his fault that he did as his father and grandfather had done before him. Be sure you raise your son better than that, to know what women need, and that women are human, too, and not slaves."

"But how can I raise my son to be anything at all?" Lora asked, finally bursting into tears, "when I must send him to be reared by Aric and turned into the very kind of man I most despise?"

"When does he go?" asked Ferrika.

"Day after tomorrow," said Lora.

"Why are you sending him? Why not keep him here?"

"It is required by the rules," Lora said.

"Whose rules? Tell me which provision of the Oath requires it?"

"I have been told since Loren was born that I must prepare myself to give him up to his father when he is five years old—"

"Yes," said Ferrika, "so they told you at Neskaya. In the larger Amazon houses it is a solid rule, yes—many boys of fifteen or more living under the same roof with many women, would indeed be disruptive. But tell me, are your two housemates pressuring you to send him away? Some Renunciates wish to be free of all male creatures, including little boys."

Lynifred turned from the fire and said, "No; I told Lora to defy the bastard and keep the boy herself. Marji feels the same."

"What I truly wish," said Marji, coming into the kitchen with Callie in her arms, "is that we could keep Loren, whom we all love, and send away Janna, who is turning this house upside down. I'm sorry, love; you know I love your daughter, but she's driving us all mad, and if she goes Cara's way, that's no credit to a House of Renunciates."

"She's right," said Lora, sobbing. "Why do we have to send a harmless baby away just because he's male, and keep that one because she had the luck to be born a girl?"

Ferrika said, "Under most conditions, boys—especially tough street-reared boys—cannot be housed with women without trouble; I could tell you some stories—there was a time in Thendara House when we kept boys till they were ten, and the experiment did not work. Even their mothers were glad to see them go. It was not safe even for the younger girls in the house; and when we let the boys stay past puberty it was disaster. So in general conference it was decided that they should be sent away before five, and *certainly* before puberty. But in this, every house may make its own rules." And she quoted the Renunciate Oath.

"*'I alone shall determine rearing and fosterage of any child I shall bear.'* If it goes against your conscience to send him to his father, then, Lora, it is your duty to find a foster father or guardian for him who will not—as you said—turn him into the very kind of man you most despise."

"I thought it was part of the Renunciate law that my son could not live with me after he was five."

Ferrika smiled. "No," she said, "you are confusing the law for all Renunciates, and the house rules of each group. In the larger houses it is established that no woman may be forced to live with men or boys; but here you may make such rules for your house as you all agree on. You might even make it known, so that some women who are considering leaving the larger houses because they cannot bear to part with young sons, could come to you here—"

"It's a thought," said Lynifred. "If young men were to be raised by Renunciates, some awareness of what women really are and what men can be might some day go into the world outside the Guild Houses." She drew on her boots. "I'll take Loren out with me and teach him horse-doctoring, now he's big enough to spend a day away from his mother."

Lora thought, *Lynifred could raise a man better than most men could; certainly better than his father could. She'll raise him to be strong, honorable, hardworking, and to understand that a woman can be so as well.*

"What will my husband say?" she asked.

Ferrika replied gently, "If you care what he says, Lora, you are in the wrong place."

"I don't really care what he says," Lora answered, "but I dread having to face him while he says it."

"I think we all do," Marji said, "but we'll back you up. I don't think any magistrate would rule that he is more fit to be a parent than you."

"Send Janna to him," Lynifred suggested, "and if a year of being a kitchen drudge, wash-woman, and baby-tender for her stepmother—and worse, treated as if she had no brains—does not send her fleeing back to us here, then perhaps she deserves to stay in that world."

"But I couldn't bear to see Janna go back to that—" Lora began.

"If it's what she wishes, you cannot keep her from it," said Marji. "Because we want this life, we cannot demand it must be for her."

Lora bent her head, knowing that Marji was right; Janna must be free to choose as she had chosen.

"So," said Lynifred, "we are all here; shall we call this a House meeting, and pass a rule that boys may live here, if the women in the house all consent, till puberty, and that girls reared here must live a year outside the house before they take the Oath? It makes good sense to me."

"And to me," said Marji. Lora wiped her eyes and said, "I am not yet able to determine what makes sense to me. I am only so grateful that I am not to lose my son."

"And your daughter," Marji said. "A year treated as girls are treated in, say, Neskaya village would no doubt, have brought Cara back to us. Janna will be back."

"I hope so," Lora murmured, but she was not so sure. Nevertheless if Janna wanted that kind of life she could not be denied it. And if other women came here with their sons, it could be a beginning for a nucleus of men raised not to despise women. That was worth doing whatever became of them.

"I agree," she said smiling, and began to cut leather for a set of boots for Loren. He would soon need a scabbard for his first sword, too.

Knives

by Marion Zimmer Bradley

Marna shivered on the cold steps as she heard the bell
jangle somewhere inside the house—this strange house
which she had never expected to approach. The sign, she
knew, said that this was the Guild House of the *Comhi-
Letzii;* but Marna could spell out only a few letters. Her
stepfather had told her mother that there was no point
in teaching a woman to read more than enough to spell
out a public placard, or sign her name to a marriage
contract. Her own father had had a governess for her,
insisting that she should share her brother's lessons. She
swallowed hard, the pain like a knife at her throat, remembering her father. He would have protected her,
when even her mother would not. No, she told herself,
she would not cry, she must not cry.

She wondered which one of them would open the
door; maybe the tall one she had seen at Heathvine,
riding astride like a man, her little bag of midwife's supplies on the saddle behind her. *I could have spoken to
her at Heathvine,* Marna thought. But then she had been
too frightened, too intimidated. Her stepfather would
surely have killed her if he had suspected. . . . She
winced, as if she could feel his hard hands on her, the
knife again, sharp at her throat. He had forbidden her
to speak to the Amazon midwife, and emphasized the
threat with heavy pinches which had left her upper arm
bruised and blue.

She looked around apprehensively, as if Ruyvil of
Heathvine might come around the corner at any moment. Oh, why didn't they open the door? If he found
her here, he would surely kill her this time!

The door opened, and a woman stood in the doorway,
scowling. She was tall and wore some sort of loose dark

garments and for a moment Marna did not recognize the midwife who had come to Heathvine. But the woman on the threshold recognized the girl.

"Is your mother ill again, *Domna* Marna?"

"Mother is well." Marna felt her throat close again in a sob. *Oh, yes, she's well, so well that she can't risk losing that handsome young stranger she calls husband. She'd rather think her eldest daughter a liar and a slut.* "And the baby, too."

"Then how may I serve you, mistress?"

Marna blurted out, "I want to come in. I want to—to join you. To stay here as one of you."

The woman lifted her eyebrows. "I think you are too young for that." Then she noticed the way Marna was looking around her, glancing back at the open plaza, the main street running up toward it, as if an assassin's knife sought her. What was the girl afraid of? "We need not stand and talk on the doorstep. Come in," she said.

Marna heard the great bronze hasp close with a shiver of relief that ran all down through her. Now she remembered the midwife's name. "*Mestra* Reva—"

"We do not accept young women here; you should go to Neskaya or Arilinn for that."

Neskaya was four days' ride away; Arilinn was away on the other side of the Kilghard Hills. She had never been to either place; the Amazon might as well have told her to go to the Wall Around the World! She swallowed hard and said hopelessly, "I do not know the way."

And she had no horse, and any traveler she might ask to take her there would be as bad as *Dom* Ruyvil, or worse. . . .

"How old are you?" the woman asked.

"I shall be fourteen at Midwinter."

Reva n'ha Melora sighed, taking in the girl's twisting hands; fine hands which were not worn with work; the good stuff of her gown and shawl and shoes. "We are not allowed to accept the oath of any woman before she is full fifteen years old. You must go home, my dear, and come back when you are grown up. It is not an easy life here, believe me; you will work very much harder than in your mother's kitchen or weaving-rooms, and you have obviously been brought up to luxury; you would not have that here. No, dear, you had better go home, even if your mother is harsh with you."

Marna's voice stuck in her throat. She whispered, "I—I *cannot* go home. Please, please don't make me go."

"We do not harbor runaways." Marna saw Reva's eyes flash like blue lightning. "Why can't you go home? No, look at me, child. What are you afraid of? Why did you come here?"

Marna knew she must tell, even if this harsh old woman did not believe her. Well, she could be no worse off; her mother had not believed her, either. "My stepfather—he—" She could not make herself say the words. "My mother did not believe me. She said I was trying to make trouble for her marriage—" She swallowed again; she would *not* cry before the woman, she would not!

"So," said Reva at last, frowning again at the girl. Yes, she had seen, at Heathvine, how Dorilys of Heathvine doted on her handsome young husband; *Dom* Ruyvil had feathered his nest well, marrying the rich widow of Heathvine. But Reva had seen, too, that the swaggering young man cared little for his wife.

Marna blinked fiercely, trying to hold back tears. "It began while my mother was carrying little Rafi—Mother wouldn't believe me when I told her!" she sobbed. "I *didn't* want to," she said, through the sobs. "I didn't, I really didn't. I was so afraid—he—he threatened me with a knife, then said he would tell Mother I had tried to entice him—but I never played the harlot, I didn't—" She looked down at the tiled floor, trying not to cry. She thought she felt a gentle touch on her hair, but when she looked up, *Mestra* Reva was striding around the room angrily.

"If what you tell me is true, Marna—"

"I swear it, by the blessed Cassilda!"

"Listen to me, Marna," the woman said. "This is the only circumstance under which we may shelter a girl not yet fifteen: when her natural parent or guardian has abused her trust. But we must be very sure, for the laws forbid us to take in ordinary runaways. Has he made you pregnant?"

Marna felt crimson flooding her face; she had never been so ashamed in her life. "He said—he said he had not, he had done—done something to prevent it, but I don't know—I wouldn't know how to tell—"

Mestra Reva said something obscene, stamping her foot; Marna flinched.

"Not you, child. I cursed the laws which say that a man is so wholly master in his own house that his wife and womenfolk are no more protected than his horses and dogs. Such a man should be hung at the crossroads with his *cuyones* stuffed in his mouth! Well, stay, then," she said with a sigh. "It may make trouble, but that is why we are here. You walked all the way from Heathvine?"

"N–no," she stammered. "He came to market—he is drinking in the tavern, and I slipped away, telling him I wanted to buy some ribbons—he even gave me a few coppers—and I ran. Mother had made me come, she wanted me to choose some laces for her, and when I begged her not to send me with Ruyvil, she slapped me and said she was sick of my lies—" Marna looked down again at the floor. Ruyvil had boasted, on the ride in, that on the way back they could find the shelter of a travel-hut, and this time, he promised, she would like it and she would not need to be threatened with a knife . . . That was why she had taken this desperate step, she could not bear it, not again.

Reva saw her trembling hands, the shame in her face, and did not question any further. It was obvious that the girl was telling the truth and that she was frightened. "Well, you may as well stay and have some supper. Hang your cloak in the hall." She led her along into a big stone-floored kitchen where four women were sitting at a round wooden table.

"Go and sit there, beside Gwennis, Marna," said Reva, pointing. "She is the youngest of us here, Ysabet's daughter." Gwennis was a girl of twelve or thirteen; Ysabet a dumpy, muscular-looking woman in her forties. Beside her was a tall, scrawny woman, scarred like a soldier; she was introduced as Camilla n'ha Mhari. The last was a small gray-haired woman they called Mother Dio.

"This is Marna n'ha Dorilys," said Reva. "She is too young to take the oath here, but she will be here as foster-daughter, since her natural guardians have abused their trust; she may cut her hair and promise to live by our rules and take oath when she is fifteen." She dipped Marna a ladleful of soup from the kettle over the fire. Mother Dio, at the head of the table, cut Marna a chunk of the coarse bread and asked if she would have butter or honey. The soup was good, but Marna was too tired to eat, and too shy to answer any of the questions the girl Gwennis asked her. After supper they called her to the head of the table, and the old woman cut off her hair to the nape of the neck.

"Marna n'ha Dorilys," she said, "you are one of us, though not yet oath-bound. From this day forth, our laws forbid you to appeal to any man for house or heritage; and you must learn to appeal to none for protection, and to defend yourself. You must work as we do, and claim no privilege for noble birth; and you must promise to be a sister to every other Renunciate of the Guild, from whatever house she may come, and shelter her and care for her in good times or bad. Do you promise to live by our laws, Marna?"

"I do."

"Will you learn to defend yourself and call on no other for protection?"

"I will."

Mother Dio kissed her on the cheek. "Then you are welcome among us, and when you are old enough, you may take the Renunciate's oath."

Marna's neck felt cold and exposed, immodest; she looked at her long russet hair on the floor and wanted to cry. Ruyvil had played with her hair and fondled the nape of her neck; now no man would ever say again that she had lured him with her beauty! She looked at their coarse mannish garments, the long knives in their belts, and shivered. They all looked so strong. How could she ever learn to protect herself with a knife like that?

"Come, Marna," said Gwennis, taking her hand. "I am so glad you have come, there is no one here that I can talk to—I am so glad to have a sister my own age! The girls in the village are not allowed to talk with me, because they say my breeches and short hair are immodest. They call me mannish, a she-male, as if I would teach them some wickedness—you'll be my friend, won't you? I mean, you *have* to be my sister, it's the law of the Guild House, but will you be my friend, too?"

Marna smiled stiffly. Gwennis was not like any other girl she had ever known, and Marna's mother would not have approved of her either, but she had always obeyed her mother's rules, and much good it had done her! "Yes, I'll be your friend."

"Take her upstairs, Gwennis, and show her the house," said Reva. "Tomorrow we can find her some clothes—your old tunic and breeches will fit her, Ysabet. And tomorrow, Camilla, you can show her something of knife-play and self-protection before you are on your way back to Thendara."

"You must go to the magistrate for a report, Reva," Camilla said, "for you have been at Heathvine and you know her family. You can tell them how likely it is that Ruyvil had abused this girl as she said. I met with that fellow Ruyvil when he was still a homeless nobody; I can well imagine he might use his own step-daughter foully."

Later that night, before she was tucked into a trundle bed in Gwennis' room, Reva came in and asked Marna a number of questions. When Reva made her take off her shift, she remembered nasty things she had heard of the Guild House, but the woman only examined her briefly and said, "I think you were lucky; you are probably not pregnant. Dio will brew you a drink tomorrow and if your courses are only delayed by shock and fear, we shall know it soon. But I can testify you have been badly treated; a man who takes a willing girl does not leave *that* kind of mark. This is so I can swear to the magistrate that you have been raped, and were not, as your mother said, just playing the harlot. Then we may lawfully shelter you. Go to sleep, child, and don't worry." And Marna fell asleep like a baby.

The Guild House of Aderes was not a large one; only four women lived regularly in the house, although sometimes traveling Amazons like Camilla stayed there for a few days or a season. Reva, the midwife, provided most of their cash income; otherwise they lived by selling the fine kerchiefs they wove from the wool of their animals. Marna, who had been taught to do fine embroidery, encouraged them to decorate the kerchiefs with pretty patterns. They also had an herb garden and sold medicines, and when their cows were fresh they took butter to market. It was a hard life, as Reva had said: they spent most of their days in weaving or working in their garden. For days, Marna trembled at every knock on the door, fearing *Dom* Ruyvil had come to drag her away, but soon she grew calm. She enjoyed her new life. Some of the things she learned were a delight; she was taught to read, and soon could write a good hand. She did not like cooking and scrubbing floors, but every woman in the house had to take turns at the heavy work, as they did with the shearing, spinning, and weaving of the wool. The old emmasca, Camilla, who had been a mercenary soldier and lived in Thendara Guild House, gave Marna a few lessons in knife-play and unarmed combat, but Marna was not very skilled at it; she was timid and clumsy, and the more Camilla yelled at her, the more helpless she felt.

When she was older, they told her, they would send her to Thendara Guild House for the regular half-year of re-training. Meanwhile she must learn their ways. Mostly they kept her in the house and garden, but one day Gwennis was sick, and they sent her to the market with butter. She had been there several times with Mother Dio or Ysabet, and knew the basic rules of Amazon behavior in public: to speak to no man except on business, not to talk to the village girls, who might be punished for associating with her. Marna thought this was foolish. The girls should know that there was a better life than slaving as drudges for their parents until some man bought them like animals! But the law was the law, and in order to exist at all, the Amazons had been forced to make compromises. One was that they might not recruit any woman who did not seek them out of her free will. Marna suspected that a little discreet recruiting was done anyway, but while she was still too young for the oath, she must obey their rules meticulously.

So she walked along, her eyes bent strictly on business; she went to the dairy-woman's market stall and gave the woman her butter. Mother Dio had told her they needed honey; she had packets of herb dyes in her pocket, and she should try to barter for it. Marna spent a pleasant hour in the market, and finally started back to the Guild House, the crock of honey wrapped in a burlap sack; she had traded it for some madder dye.

It was beginning to grow dark. As she passed the tavern, a young man unhitching his horse from the rail, so drunk that even at this distance Marna could smell the stale reck of wine, called to her, "What about it, girl, want to spend the night with me? Hey—don't be so damned unfriendly!" He turned and staggered toward her. "Aaah—one of those bitches trying to wear a sword like a man!" He caught heavily at her arm. "What you want to spend your life with those women for? Why don't you want to be a real woman, huh?" He fumbled at her.

Marna, shaking, pulled herself free and fled, clutching at the crock of honey. The man yelled drunkenly, "Aaah, go on, who the hell wants one of you bitches anyhow!"

Her heart beating, racing, her mouth dry, Marna tried to compose herself. Was there something about her, that she looked like that kind of girl? *Dom* Ruyvil had accused her of leading him on, too, even when she cried and tried to stop him. What did she do that made men act that way? She put her hand on her knife hilt. If the man had really tried to hold her, could she have drawn her knife, tried to frighten him away with it? Could she have found the courage to strike?

Half blinded by tears, she did not see where she was going until she ran into a tall, heavy man on the cobbled street. She murmured a well-bred apology, then felt her arm seized in a heavy grip, and heard a hated voice.

"So, little Marna! You lying slut, you've made a fine mess of my life—Dori came near to sending me away! Running and whining to those filthy bitches, and now you're one of them!"

She struggled to free herself of the heavy grip.

"You! Ruyvil!"

"You will say stepfather, or *dom*, when you speak to me," he snarled.

"I won't!" she cried. "You're not my father and I owe you nothing—not respect, not obedience, nothing!"

He slapped her, hard. "No more of that! You're coming home where you belong. Look at you—brazen as you please in boots and breeches, your hair cut off, showing your—" He used a filthy word. "Come on, you—I've got a horse, and I'm going to take you home to your mother, and by Zandru's toenails, if you tell her any more tales, I'll break every bone in your body!"

She faced him, shaking, but braced by what the women had told her; she must learn to defend herself and appeal to none for protection. "Everything I said to mother and the magistrate was true—"

"Ah, you wanted it, you dirty little slut, you can't tell me you weren't making eyes at every stable-boy and armsman—"

"I *do* tell you that!" she retorted. "You can lie all you want to my mother, but you know perfectly well what the truth is—"

"You can't speak to me like that!" His heavy hand knocked her sprawling to the ground; she lay there in terror, watching his knife come out of its sheath. . . . With some last resource of strength she scrambled to her feet, grabbed up the miraculously unbroken honey-crock, and ran like a *chervine,* dodging into an alley; no skirts to hamper her this time! She pounded in panic on the door of the Guild House; but by the time Gwennis opened the door, her breathing had quieted. No, she must not tell. They had made it so clear she must learn to defend herself.

And I couldn't defend myself, she thought in despair. *I couldn't get my knife out of its sheath at all, I never thought of it, I ran like a rabbit-horn! I should have killed Ruyvil, thrust my knife into his guts! But I was afraid. . . .*

Did he really think I led him on? Is there something about me that makes men think that? That other man, the drunken one at the tavern, he thought so, too. . . .

"You're out of breath," Gwennis said. "What's the matter, Marna, have you been running?"

"Yes—it was late, and dark, and cold, I ran to warm myself," Marna said, and was angry at herself for lying. But Gwennis, she knew, had been trained to defend herself. How she would despise Marna if she knew what a weakling she was!

Marna stayed in the house after that, as much as she could, and every time she went out of doors, it seemed to her that *Dom* Ruyvil must be lurking around every corner. But as time went by, she grew less afraid and at last she was willing to go to the market again. In three months, she would be fifteen and could take the oath lawfully; and then she would be safe. At this season there was a good harvest of herbs, and the women of the Guild House shared a stall with the dairy-woman who sometimes sold their butter. Marna spread out the little packets of herbs meticulously, proud of the delicate lettering she had done on the front of each packet—she wrote the clearest hand in the house, now, and designed all their embroideries. As she finished, she looked up to hear a familiar voice.

"Is your golden-flower well dried? If it is, I will have two packets—Marna!" the woman said with a gasp, and Marna stared into her mother's face.

"Marna! So this is where you went! Oh, Marna, how could you? Oh, my little girl—where is your pretty hair? What have they done to you, those awful women! Marna, won't you even kiss your mother in greeting?"

Marna wanted to cry. She wanted to shout, *Yes, it was* Dom *Ruyvil who abused me, but it was you who let him do it, you who wouldn't believe your own daughter* ... but before her mother's weeping face she could not stand and refuse her. She hugged her mother, thinking, *Now I am taller than she is, I am bigger than she is—she could never learn to defend herself.*

"Oh, you look so grown up and so—so stern and awful!" Dorilys of Heathvine said, "Have they made you swear to all kinds of evil things, my poor baby? Oh, blessed Cassilda, I will never forgive myself—"

Marna kept her voice hard. "So you believe me at last?"

"Oh, Marna—" Her mother spread out her hands. "What could I do? He said he would take his son and leave me—and I was alone in the world, your brother is in Thendara now as a cadet, I am alone with the babies—and if Ruyvil is angry with me, what shall I do? A woman has no choice but to live with her husband— and if I had made complaint to a magistrate, he would have beaten me or worse—"

"It's all right, Mother, I understand," said Marna, with a choking pain in her throat. She did *not* understand. She would never understand. If she had a daughter, if a man had treated her daughter that way, she certainly would not have continued to love the man, to share his bed! She would have called the magistrates, had Ruyvil thrown into the middle of the street! But her mother had not even had the strength or the good sense to run away.

"Marna—oh, my little girl, won't you come home? I promise you—you can have one of the maids to sleep in your chamber—he will never bother you again, I promise you! I miss you so, there is no one I can talk to, no one I care about—"

"No, mother," said Marna gently, but without pity. "I will never live under your roof again. I will come and see you sometimes when *Dom* Ruyvil is away from home, if you will send me word; or you can come and visit me at the Guild House."

"The Guild House? What could I possibly—Ruyvil would be very angry with me if I spoke to such women!"

"Oh, Mother," Marna said impatiently, "they are women just like you, except that they do not let men beat and abuse them! They are honest women who live by weaving and selling herbs!"

"Hmmph! What evil things have they taught you? What man will marry you now?"

"None, I hope!" Marna said crossly. "Believe what you like, Mother, I would not change my life for yours! And if you think I live an evil life in the Guild House, why, get up the courage of a goose and come and visit us and see for yourself how I spend my days!"

When her mother had gone weeping away, Marna ran after her—she had forgotten the packets of golden-flower; yes, she must take it, she looked pale. No, forget the money, she had picked and dried it herself, it was a gift ... and as she began packing up the wares in the booth, for the sun was going down, she felt better. Yes, in spite of her anger, she loved her mother, was glad to see that she was alive and well.

Unless that bastard Dom *Ruyvil kills her some day, beating her, or keeping her bearing children until she dies of it!*

Well, there was nothing she could do. She said, "Where is Ysabet with the pack animal, Gwennis? We should load it, to be home before dark. There is not much to load, we have sold all the embroideries and all the kerchiefs but three."

"The embroidered ones sell better," Gwennis said. "You were right, Marna. Who was that woman you were talking to?"

"My mother," said Marna, and said no more.

Gwennis, full of questions, stopped at the look on Marna's face; she said only, "Here, help me untie this bridle-rope, we will have everything ready for Ysabet when she comes—Zandru spit fire!" she swore, as the rope twisted on the edge of the booth, something caught, and the packets of herbs and the kerchiefs came cascading down, with crocks of butter. The girls scrambled to pick them up, but one crock of butter had split and slimed the kerchiefs and the cobbles in front of the stall.

"Well, I will go and borrow a mop, and clean it," said Gwennis heavily, looking around the half-deserted market; most of the stalls were empty now and the shadows were falling, red and thick, across the marketplace. "Rinda at the tavern will lend me a mop, I bandaged her ankle when she sprained it."

"Don't leave me alone," Marna begged, "it's so dark, wait till Ysabet comes with the horse!"

"But someone could slip and fall and break their neck!" said Gwennis, shocked. "Don't be such a coward, Marna! You must learn to be alone."

Gwennis went, and Marna, shivering, packed up the herbs. Then a rough hand seized her, and a voice she feared and hated growled, "So here's where you've been hiding, eh? Filthy slut, I'll teach you to talk like that to your mother. She told me she'd seen you here. You're coming home with me now, and no nonsense about it! Feel this?" Marna felt a knife-edge at her throat. Ruyvil pressed hard; she felt the skin break, and blood trickle down.

"Now will you behave?"

In deadly fear, Marna nodded and the knife moved away from her throat. Ruyvil's hands were rough on her. He said, "Now you come on, without any more fuss. Make a laughing-stock of me, will you, telling tales so your mother can't get decent maids to stay, and complaining to a magistrate about me? I tell you, Marna, I'll teach you a lesson if it's the last thing I do! You're coming home where you belong, and people are going to see that I can rule my family and my womenfolk and no damned magistrates butting in! Fine thing, when a man can't handle his own affairs without the government on his back! It's not as if you were any real kin to me, as if I'd done you any harm!" He gave her wrist a vicious twist. "Give me your hands!" She saw a length of rope in them: he would tie her, drag her home—

She wrenched away, screaming. He jerked at her, flung her down. "Marna, I'll kill you for that!" he rasped. She grabbed at her knife, clumsily, in deadly terror. Oh, he would kill her, with that knife—but better that than be dragged home knowing he could do his worst—but suddenly he had her knife, too, and she cursed her clumsiness.

"You let her alone!" came a scream behind them, and Gwennis swung the heavy mop-handle; Ruyvil's mouth burst open with blood. Swearing, he ran at Gwennis with his sword, and Marna, grabbing up her blade, hardly knowing what she did, thrust herself between them; her Amazon knife, not quite a sword, was braced right against Ruyvil's belly.

"Make one move," she said, astonished at how loud and firm her voice sounded in the deserted market, "and I'll run this right through you, *step*father!"

He howled in rage. "Put that thing down! What the hell—?"

Gwennis had scrambled to her feet, recovered her own knife. She came and took Ruyvil's sword, saying, "I ought to cut his throat. But we have trouble enough here. I'll tie his hands and he can get loose later—who's to say if the magistrate would believe us? Here, Marna, you tie him, you can make a better knot than I can. He won't get *that* loose before we're safe in the Guild House. And if he wants to tell how two girls under fifteen bested him, well, let him talk and be a laughingstock!"

Ysabet came with the pack-animal and looked at the furious, cursing Ruyvil, his hands tied behind him. She said, "Listen to me, *Dom* Ruyvil, your stepdaughter, whom you have abused, is being sent to Neskaya Guild House; do you want a public examination by *leronis* so that everyone in the countryside knows she told the truth?"

He calmed at last and said sheepishly, "No. I will swear—"

"Your oath is not worth a piece of fresh horse dung," said Ysabet, "but if you do not molest us further we will leave you alone, though I would willingly make you incapable of molesting any woman again." She gestured with the knife and Ruyvil flinched and howled, begging, pleading, weeping. Marna wondered why she had ever been afraid of him.

As they went homeward in the dusk, Gwennis said—Ysabet had walked a little ahead with the horse—"If your stepfather was following you, lying in wait for you, why didn't you tell us?"

"I was ashamed," Marna muttered. "So much was said about learning to defend myself, not asking any other for protection—"

"Yet you must protect your sisters, and they must protect you," Gwennis chided gently, an arm around Marna's waist. "That is what the oath is all about, that we swear to care for one another—would you not have protected your mother? You found courage to draw your knife when he menaced *me*—"

Marna began to weep. She could not protect her mother from Ruyvil; her mother did not want protection, would not appeal even to her sisters. Worse, her mother had thought so much of Ruyvil that she would not protect her own daughter. For the first time since she had come to the Amazon house she wept and wept, sobbing even after they were inside the Guild House. Gwennis was alarmed at her crying and sent for Reva, who gave her wine, and finally slapped her.

"I can live with what Ruyvil did to me," Marna said, hiccoughing, tears still streaming from her eyes, "and I can defend myself against any man now. But what I cannot bear, is that my mother would not protect me, that she would even let her daughter be misused, rather than lose the man she loved ... that she did not love *me* enough to quarrel with him. ..." She cried and cried, clinging to Reva, while the older woman, kinder now, held and comforted her.

"But that is what the Amazon oath is all about," Gwennis repeated. "Any of us will protect you, as your mother should have done; as women must always protect each other. I can't make your mother care for you as she should have done—what's done is done and there's no mending it. But you have an oath-mother now, and many sisters. And you were strong to defend *me*, if not yourself!"

"You didn't deserve it," Marna sniffed. "I mean, *you* hadn't done *anything*. I couldn't let him hurt you!"

Gwennis' arms were around her. "But *you* hadn't done anything either, and *you* didn't deserve it, either," she said fiercely, "and if that old wicked man made you think you did, then that's worse than what he did to you in the first place!" She kissed Marna on the cheek. "I'll miss you, sister, if they send you to Thendara for training," she said, "but you'll come back, when you've learned how to defend yourself and how to live with everything you have to live with, *breda*." Shyly, she took her knife from its sheath. She said, "You defended me when you wouldn't defend yourself. Will you exchange knives with me, Marna?"

After a wide-eyed moment, Marna drew her own knife, and solemnly, they put their knives, each into the other's sheath, then embraced. Marna said, almost crying again, "I do not want to go away! I love you all, and you have been so good to me—"

"But you have sisters everywhere," Reva said gently. "Soon you will take the oath; and then you will be one with us."

Marna put her hand on Gwennis' knife in her sheath. Yes, her sister's knife had been drawn in her defense; now she could draw it in her own. One woman had failed her, but, looking around at her sisters, she knew that no one of them would ever fail her. With amazement, she realized that *Dom* Ruyvil had not destroyed her; he had driven her into a new life, a real life. What she thought was the end of the world had brought her here.

He had set her free.

HILARY

The Hilary stories were all originally written as sketches for a proposed Darkover novel which should have been the first Darkover collaboration, a book about Hilary Castamir. I first mentioned Hilary, and her many problems, in THE FORBIDDEN TOWER. Elisabeth Waters, who later became my secretary cum children's governess and Lord High Everything else, had started on her own first book before I got around to starting the Hilary novel I had envisioned, for which I wrote "The Lesson of the Inn." By then Elisabeth had won the very first Gryphon Award, given by Andre Norton for an unpublished novel by a new woman writer, so she had a contract for her own novel and no time to work on a collaboration.

So, as I had done with the story "Blood Will Tell," years before, which became sketches for the novel SHARRA'S EXILE, I wrote several stories on my own about Hilary. "The Keeper's Price" and "Firetrap" are the only stories in this book which are not entirely my own work; but I had so much input on each of them, that I still think of them as partly mine. Another story in the "Hilary cycle," "Playfellow," is Elisabeth's, rather than mine, so I am omitting it from this volume. It appears in RED SUN OF DARKOVER. (DAW 1987)

"Hilary's Homecoming" and "Hilary's Wedding" are the only new, totally original stories in this volume. Both were written especially for this anthology and have never appeared in print anywhere—not even in a fanzine—before.

Firetrap

by Elisabeth Waters and
Marion Zimmer Bradley

". . . and while the season is slack, and there is so little to do," commented Leonie, "it will be good practice for all of you to look everywhere you can think of for abandoned matrixes. Some of them have been forgotten from the Ages of Chaos. I have also heard rumor that Kermiac of Aldaran is trying to train matrix workers in his own way. That sort of thing should not be allowed, but the Council says that if I intervene, I will be recognizing that Domain; and so for the time being I can do nothing. In time to come—well, enough of speechmaking," she concluded. "It should be enough to know that in this you serve our people."

She went away, and the little group of younger workers in training gathered to look after her, each one secretly hoping that he or she would be the one to reclaim one of the lost matrixes from the Ages of Chaos; perhaps one of the old, forbidden matrix weapons from that Age.

"There is rumored to be an ancient one in our family since the early days," said Ronal Delleray. "I did not realize how important it could be. I do not think it is a dangerous one; I could lay my hands upon it at any moment."

"Then you should do so. Leonie will be pleased," said young Hilary, the under-Keeper. Hilary Castamir was about fifteen; slender to the point of emaciation, her dark-copper curls lusterless, her spare-boned face bearing the insignia of longstanding poor health. She would have been pretty if she had not been so sickly-looking; even so, she had grace and fine features, the mark of the Comyn strong in them. "And if Leonie is pleased enough—"

She broke off, but Ronal knew what she did not say, though like all Keepers Hilary had learned early to barricade her thoughts even from her fellow workers in the Tower. *If Leonie is pleased enough with me, she will not speak again of sending me away.* They all knew that HIlary was a telepath of surpassing skill, but that her health was not robust enough for the demanding work of the Tower, especially that of a Keeper.

The new young apprentice, Callista Lanart-Alton, looked even more frail, but she managed somehow to avoid the devastating attacks of pain and even convulsions which again and again confined Hilary to bed, or kept her out of the relay screens for ten days or so of every moon. And as Callista grew older, nearer to the time when she could take on in full all of a Keeper's responsibilities, the day grew nearer when Hilary, for her very life, must be released and sent away.

Ronal was fond of Hilary, with a little more than the bond which bound Tower worker to Tower worker. Though he was not at all the kind of man who would ever have pressed his attentions upon this sick girl, who was also a Keeper; the discipline of concealing this fondness from her, even in thought, would be, he sometimes thought, the destruction of him. But he told himself grimly that it was good discipline—for if Leonie had caught so much as a hint of it he would at once have been sent away. Leonie loved Hilary and no worker would have been allowed to trouble her peace for a moment. So he quietly hung on.

"Are you willing to search for your family's matrix?" Hilary pressed on. "Whatever we may discover, or not, Leonie is right; it would be good practice."

Ronal demurred. "I do not think my father will want to give it up." But he already knew that he would do whatever Hilary wanted.

"I am sure Leonie will be able to persuade him," Hilary said. "When shall we start?"

"Tonight, then?" they agreed, and separated, arranging when to meet again.

*   *   *

Later that night, Hilary and Ronal met in the deserted Tower room—they had decided they need not disturb the others, although they were accompanied by Callista, who had agreed to monitor for them. She was about thirteen, no more, a tall, slender child without as yet the slightest sign of oncoming womanhood.

"Shall I search for it?" asked Ronal. "I know exactly where it has been kept all these years."

"If you wish," Hilary agreed, "and Callista shall monitor for you, then."

"See you later," he said, and was off into the overworld. Ten minutes later he was back, a matrix clenched in his hands. "Found it lying about on a high shelf in the library," he said. "Nobody but my father even knew what it was. I heard of another one, too; one is lying on an altar of the forge-folk. Father spent some time in a Tower; that is how he knew what it was. He visited the forge-folk to have them make a sword, and saw it there. It is supposed to be a talisman of their fire-goddess; but it is at least ninth-level. I do not know if I can get it—"

"No, that is work for a Keeper," Hilary said. "Leonie would want to do it herself, I suppose; although I am perfectly capable of it. Except that I should know where to look; there is, after all, more than one village of forge-folk. Meanwhile, let us see what you have here," she said, taking the matrix from him. It was coated with dust, dull blue. She brushed away the dust. "I can well believe that it has been lying about in a library all these years, forgotten. It must have been overlooked when we called in all the matrixes, a couple of generations ago. One like this would be easy to overlook. Let me see if it was ever a monitored matrix."

She laid it carefully in a cradle and activated a small screen. For a long time she was silent, light from the screen coming and going, and reflecting on her narrow face. The other two leaned close. At last, Hilary switched off the screen, the lights fading, and said, "I still do not know all its history, and it is not important enough to do timesearch to find it out; but it is very old. It may have been made before the Towers—oh, yes," she said in reply to Ronal's startled glance. "It is an artificial one, perhaps one of the first ones made. I wish

I knew who made it. Oh, well—" She wrapped it carefully in insulating silks and said, "Your father did not mind giving it up?"

"No," said Ronal, "I don't suppose he knew he was; when I appeared to him, he thought he was dreaming of me. When he finds out that I have really been home, even in spirit, he will be so busy saying I should have first shown myself to my mother that he will not get around to scolding me for the loss of the matrix for years—if ever. It means nothing to him, and so it belongs here; Leonie may discover a use for it—or if not, destroy it."

"Which will be safer for all concerned," Hilary agreed. "Do you want to go after the one the forge-folk hold tonight?"

"No," said Ronal, a little reluctantly; Hilary looked tired and ill, and he knew if she overstrained herself Leonie would be angry. Much as he enjoyed working together like this, elementary caution could not be neglected. And another thing: "Leonie might wish to seek for this one herself. It is a large and an important one, perhaps not to be left to a couple of apprentices."

When Leonie heard of the ninth-level matrix, she was eager to seek it for herself. Therefore they gathered in one of the Tower rooms the next night.

"Which village of forge-folk holds it? I think I have heard of it—this great lost matrix. It will not be altogether welcome to them—that such a matrix should go behind Tower walls and be lost to them, but I think I can persuade them."

Ronal did not doubt it; it would take a braver man than he knew to stand against the wishes of Leonie Hastur.

He supposed she had once been remarkably beautiful, this Keeper; certainly she had been behind Tower walls all of his life, and during most—if not all—of the lives of his parents—and for all he knew, of his grandparents. He found himself wondering how old she was; with some women, especially of Hastur blood, after they reached a certain age, it was impossible to tell their age because although they were not actually withered, or emaciated, there was something about them; they might have been any age or none. It was still possible to see that Leonie had been beautiful, just possible; it was perhaps the only remnant of her humanity. She looked almost unreal in the stiff, formal Keeper's veils of deep crimson.

"I will go," she said. "Keep watch for me."

Thus saying, she slipped out of her body. To the young people watching, there was no apparent difference, except for an almost imperceptible slumping and a somewhat vacant look in the eyes that were still as blue as copper filings in flame, but they all knew she was not there. She had gone heaven knows where into that strange unknown realm of the overworld, where time and space were not tangible, and only thought existed. Things were not what they seemed in the overworld, but could under certain conditions be manipulated—by thought alone.

The night wore away; after a long time, Leonie—who had, to all appearances, remained motionless in her chair—began to stir and struggle. Callista, instantly alert, murmured, "She's not breathing," but before she could intervene, Leonie pitched out of her chair, falling forward, in a flutter of crimson, breathing heavily in normal unconsciousness.

Ronal cried out, bending over to lift the Keeper. She half-roused at the touch, murmured, "Too strong for me—" and slipped back again into unconsciousness. Ronal lifted the apparently lifeless body and carried her into her shielded room. He waited there until Leonie's attendants had applied various restoratives and determined that she was suffering only from shock and exhaustion.

When he returned to the others, Hilary had already slipped into Leonie's vacated chair.

"No, Hilary," Ronal demurred. "If it was too strong for Leonie, what do you think you can do alone?"

"Do you know how much Leonie has been overworking lately?" Hilary shot back. "That is what led to her collapse; any task she might have undertaken could have done the same. And I will finish what she started. There is no question now that there is something to find, and it must be found before they have time to transfer it to a better hiding place." As Ronal still hesitated, she added persuasively, "I might as well; I will be good for nothing tomorrow, and probably not for another tenday."

"Perhaps if you rest now—" Ronal began.

"No." Hilary shook her head definitely. "It doesn't work that way. Right now I'm riding on the wave of energy I always get a day in advance. We might as well take advantage of it."

Ronal shrugged helplessly; stronger men than he had failed to deter a Keeper when her mind was set on something.

"Besides, if I go now, at once, I can follow her traces," Hilary said.

And Ronal could say only, "You know best."

Hilary took her place in the chair, wrapping herself in a long woolly robe over her regular working robe, shrugged a bit to make herself comfortable, and slipped out of her body.

Hilary found herself at first on what appeared to be a gray featureless plain, without visible landmarks except, behind her, the rising Tower of Arilinn—not the real Tower as it appeared in the outer world, but what she knew to be the idealized form of that structure. It had been a landmark in the overworld for many generations, and before it, Hilary saw shining footprints, tracks with a faint silver luster. *Leonie's? Did she leave these marks for me?*

Since her main thought had been to follow in Leonie's footprints, she set out quickly along the trail, knowing that it would fade to invisibility all too soon. She moved without conscious thought, unaware of the motions of walking; her only aim to follow that almost imperceptible trail before her where Leonie had gone. She was so intent on following in Leonie's footsteps that it seemed to her to be no time at all—though to the watchers in the outer world it was a considerable time—before she found herself at the entrance to a great dark cave, one of—she was not sure how she knew this, perhaps some intangible trace of Leonie's thought—a great labyrinth of caves which made networks all through the foothills of the mountains. This was the home, she knew, of the strange people known as the forge-folk.

She had no personal knowledge of them, but she had been told by Leonie that they were the first group on Darkover to discover mastery over metals. Darkover was a metal-poor world; from the very earliest days, metal had assumed an almost sacred significance. The small amounts of metal necessary to shoe a horse, to edge a weapon, and other uses, dictated by necessity—in the beginning it had been necessary to make certain that the allocation of metals was made by real need, and not by greed. Still, human nature was always at work, and economic forces had also dictated some accommodation to human status desires which had nothing to do with actual need. Therefore, various political expediencies had made it desirable for powerful persons—and above all the Hasturs and the Comyn—to keep in favor with the forge-folk. Therefore they had been given certain privileges, especially relating to the use of matrixes, traditional from the days before the Ages of Chaos. *But even with these privileges,* Hilary thought, *they should not be keeping a ninth-level matrix, even if it has become a sacred object to them.* She should reclaim it for the Comyn, and for the Towers, where it could not be abused by anyone who might have a fancy to do so. Such a matrix represented a very real danger to the Comyn and to the people of the Domains. And if Hilary could recapture it, the danger was lessened.

The movement, at the speed of thought, had brought her past several glowing forges, and she began, dimly through the darkness of the caves, to sense, if not quite to see, the glowing nexus of a great matrix. Above it, shadowed—not perhaps a physical figure at all, Hilary could see, sketched dimly on the darkness, the figure of a woman, kneeling, golden chains enshrouding her, all faintly glowing flame-color. Sharra; the goddess of the forge-people, here imaged, not on their altar, exactly, but so near as made no matter

Now she could see it. In the Ages of Chaos, when this thing had first been shaped, it had been traditional to house these things in the shape of weapons; and this one was fashioned to be set in the hilt of a great two-handed sword. Hilary moved swiftly to take up the sword in both hands. It was surprisingly heavy. In the overworld she was accustomed to moving without weight, but an object like this—a matrix, she knew, had form and body through all the various levels of consciousness—had weight and substance even in the overworld. *Now,* she thought, *I have it in my hands, and I shall return to Arilinn as swiftly as I can.* She turned to retrace her steps, but as the matrix moved away from the altar, she heard a great cry.

Sharra! Protect us, golden-chained one!

Heaven help us, she thought. The forge-folk, even the guardian of the altar, were aware that the matrix had been touched by an intruder! Now what to do? In her astral form she could not physically struggle for it; her only hope lay in getting back to Arilinn so swiftly that they could not overtake her.

But which way was Arilinn? In the labyrinth of caves, she had become confused. Somehow she must find her way out. The traces, faintly shining, of her own footsteps on the way in were still there. She began to move along them, fighting for breath—it was smoky and hard to breathe. Well, that did not matter; Callista, monitoring her bodily functions would see to it that she kept breathing. She told herself firmly that the heat and smoke were illusions, and struggled on.

As she went on, retracing her earlier steps, she became aware of a glow. Neither ahead or behind her; it seemed to be actually beneath her feet. Down below, on a level somewhere below these astral caves, there was fire. *They have set it here to frighten me,* she thought, and tried to quicken her step as much as she could without losing sight of the faint trace of her own footsteps she needed to find her way back—back to Arilinn.

Beneath her feet, the very ground was beginning to burn. She went on, stepping carefully through the spreading patches of fire, reminding herself that the fire was illusion, intended to frighten her; it was not real. *It cannot hurt me.*

Now the very soles of her slippers were beginning to smolder; she felt sharp pain in the soles of her feet. *It is only illusion,* she told herself, clinging tightly to the matrix, stepping gingerly over the floor of the cave and across the glowing flames. *It is all an illusion—*

Anguish seized her, and faintness; she stumbled, dropping the matrix. Before she could seize it again she was spiraling, choking, through layers of smoke, into a well-known room. She was in Arilinn, abruptly back in her body, conscious of burning pain through the soles of her feet, and Ronal and Callista were looking down at her in fright.

When she could speak she gasped, "Why did you pull me out? I had it—"

Callista murmured, "I'm sorry, but I had to. I dared not leave you longer. Your feet were burning!"

"But that is all illusion, isn't it?" Hilary asked.

"I don't know," said Callista, bending to pull off Hilary's slippers with deft hands. They all gasped at the scorched and blackened shoes, and looked in dismay at the mass of blisters on the reddened flesh.

"You won't be doing much walking for a few days," Ronal said harshly.

Hilary sighed, feeling the familiar preliminary stabs of pain through her abdomen.

"Oh, well," she said, "I wasn't planning on doing much walking for about a tenday anyhow. Callista, will you help me to my room? And I'd better have some golden-flower tea, too."

Later that day, Leonie came to visit her. At the tender solicitousness in the older Keeper's face, Hilary burst into tears. "I nearly had it, but Callista and Ronal pulled me back," she said, weeping.

"No, no, child; they did it to save your feet—if not your life. I heard you were badly hurt."

Hilary wriggled her bandaged toes. "Not as badly as all that," she said.

"All the same, I think they did right. We must let the big matrix go, at least for now. At least, if it is so well guarded by the forge-folk, no outsider can use it to do us harm," Leonie said, "and the forge-folk do not have the type of *laran* to use it as a weapon." But she looked somehow troubled, as if touched by a premonition of the future.

The Keeper's Price

by Marion Zimmer Bradley
with Lisa Waters

The pain had started.

Hilary was aware of it even in her sleep, but, knowing that her body needed at least another two hours' rest, she tried to ignore it. But the gnawing discomfort deep in her body would not be ignored; after an hour she gave up the futile attempt and threw on a robe, slipping silently down the stairs to the stillroom to make herself a cup of golden-flower tea. She knew from experience that it would numb the cramping pain, at least a little.

It might also, she thought, settling back into her bed, make her sleepy. At least that was what the other women said. Somehow it never seemed to work that way with Hilary. It only made her arms numb and her head feel fuzzy, and the room seemed unbearably warm as things swam in and out of focus. The effects of the tea wore off all too quickly, and the heavy cramping pains, contractions, Leonie called them, became worse and worse, moving up from her abdomen to her stomach to her heart, so that she felt constricted and aching, struggling for breath.

She had only to call, she knew, and someone would come. But in a Tower filled with telepaths, help would be there when she absolutely needed it. And she didn't want to disturb anyone unless she had to.

After all, she thought wryly, *this happens every forty days. They should be used to it by now. Just Hilary again, going through her usual crisis, disturbing everybody as usual.*

The circle had been mining metal the night before, and everyone had gone to bed late and exhausted, especially Leonie. Leonie of Arilinn had been Keeper since she was a young girl; now she was an old woman – Hilary did not know how old—training Hilary and the new child, Callista Lanart, to be Keepers in her place. For the last half-year Hilary had been able to work at Leonie's side, during the heavy stresses of the work, taking some of the burden from the older woman. She wasn't going to drag Leonie out of bed to hold her hand. They wouldn't let her die. Maybe this month it would be only the cramping pain, the weakness; after all, there wasn't a woman in Arilinn who didn't have some trouble when her cycle started. It was simply one of the hazards of the work. Maybe this time it would subside, as it did in the other women, before she went into crisis, without the agonizing clearing of the channels. . . .

But they couldn't wait too long, hoping it would clear spontaneously. Last time, wanting to spare her the excruciating ordeal, Leonie had waited too long; and Hilary had gone into convulsions. But that wouldn't happen for hours, maybe for days. Let Leonie sleep as long as she could. She could bear the pain till then.

Hilary adored Leonie; the older woman had been like a mother to her ever since she had come to Arilinn, five years before, a lonely, frightened child of eleven, enduring the first testing of a girl with Comyn blood, the loneliness, the waiting until, when her woman's cycles began, she could begin serious training as Keeper. She had been proud to be chosen for this. Most of the young people who came here were selected as monitor, mechanic, even technician—but very few had the talent or potential to be a Keeper, or could endure the long and difficult training. And now Hilary was near to that goal. Had all but achieved it; except for one thing. Every time, when her cycles started, there was the pain, the cramping contractions quickly escalating to agony, and sometimes to crisis and convulsions.

She knew why, of course. Like all matrix workers, she had begun her training as a monitor, learning the anatomy of the nerve channels which carried *laran*—and, unfortunately, also carried the sexual energies. Hilary had known, from the time she agreed to take training as a Keeper, that she must pay the Keeper's price; ordinary sexuality was not for her, and she had solemnly sworn, at thirteen, a vow of perpetual chastity. She had been taught, in all kinds of difficult and somewhat frightening ways, to avoid in herself even the slightest sexual arousal, so that the lower nerve centers which would carry these energies were wholly clear and uncontaminated, the channels between the centers nonfunctional.

Only, somehow, the channels were *not* clear at this time, and it puzzled all of them. Hilary, who lived under Leonie's immediate supervision, and rarely drew a breath Leonie did not know about, knew that her chastity was not suspect; so it had to be something else, perhaps some unsuspected weakness in the nerve centers.

The only thing that pulled Hilary through each moon, and sent her back to work again in the screens, was her desire not to fail Leonie. She could not leave Leonie to shoulder the burden alone, not when she was so close to her goal. Leonie had been letting her, now, take a part of the burden as Keeper, at the center of the circle, and Hilary knew, without conceit, that she was capable and strong, that she could handle the linked energies of a circle up to the fourth level without too much drain on her energies. Soon, now, Leonie would be free of at least a part of the burden.

Little Callista showed promise and talent; but she was only a child. It would be a year before she could begin serious training, though she was already living with the carefully supervised life of a pledged Keeper and had been allowed to make provisional vows; it would be years before she would be old enough to take on any part of the serious work. There was so much work to do, and so few to do it! Arilinn was not alone in this; every Tower in the Domains was short-handed.

The last effects of the tea were gone. Outside the window it was sunrise, but no one was stirring. Now the pains seemed to double her into a tight ball; she rolled herself up and moaned to herself.

· *Don't be silly,* she told herself. *You're acting like a baby. When this is over you'll hardly remember how much it hurt.*

Yes, but how much longer can I stand this?

*As long as you have to. You know that. What good is
your training, if you can't stand a little pain?*

Another wave of pain washed over her, effectively si-
lencing the inner dialogue. Hilary concentrated on her
breathing, trying to still herself, to let the breath flow in
and out quietly, one by one monitoring channel after
channel, trying to ease the flow of the currents. But the
pains were so violent that she could not concentrate.

It's never been this bad before! Never!

"Hilary?" It was the gentlest of whispers. Callista was
bending over her, a slight long-legged girl, her red hair
loosely tied back, a heavy robe flung over her nightgown.
She was barefoot. "Hilary, what is it?"

Hilary gasped, breathing hard.

"Just—the usual thing."

"I'd better get Leonie."

"Not yet," Hilary whispered, "I can manage a little
longer. Stay with me though. Please. . . ."

"Of course," Callista said. "Hilary, your nightgown is
soaking wet; you'd better get out of it. You'll feel better
when you're dried off."

Hilary managed to pull herself upright, to slide out of
the gown, drenched with her own sweat. Callista brought
her a dry one from her chest, held it while Hilary slipped
it over her head; maneuvering deftly, so carefully that
she did not touch Hilary even with a fingertip.

She is learning, Hilary thought, and looked with wry
detachment at the small scarred-over burns on her own
hands; remnants of the first year of her training. In that
year she had been so conditioned to avoid a touch, that
the slightest touch of living flesh would create a deep
blistered burn exactly as if the other flesh were a live
coal. Callista's scars were still red and raw; even now
she would punish herself with a deep burn if she touched
anyone even accidentally. Later, when the conditioning
was complete, the command would be removed—Hilary
was no longer forbidden to touch anyone, the prohibition was no longer needed; she *could* touch or be touched, with great caution, if it was unavoidable—but no
one touched a Keeper; even in the matrix chamber, a
Keeper was robed in crimson so that no one would touch
her when she was carrying the load of the energons. And

among themselves, even when the conditioning was no more than a memory, they used the lightest of fingertip-touches, more symbolic than real. Hilary, settling back on the clean dry pillow—Callista had changed the pillow-cover, too—wished rather wistfully that she could hold someone's hand. But such a touch would torment Callista and probably wouldn't make her feel any better.

"It's really bad this time, isn't it, Hilary?"

Hilary nodded, thinking, *She is still young enough to feel compassion. She hasn't yet been dehumanized....*

"You're lucky," Hilary said with effort. "Still too young to go through this. Maybe it won't be so bad for you...."

"I don't know how you bear it—"

"Neither do I," Hilary murmured, doubling up again under the fresh wave of violent pain, and Callista stood helpless, wondering why Hilary's struggles hadn't yet waked Leonie.

"I made her promise to sleep in one of the insulated rooms last night," Hilary said, picking the unspoken question out of the child's mind.

"Did you get all the copper mined?"

"No; Romilla broke the circle early; Damon had to carry Leonie to her room, she couldn't walk ..."

"She's been working too hard," Callista said, "but Lord Serrais will be upset; he's been badgering us for that copper since midsummer."

"He won't get it at all if we kill Leonie with overwork," Hilary said, "and I'm no good one tenday out of every four."

"Maybe overworking is why you get so sick, Hilary."

"I'd get sick anyway. But overworking does seem to make it worse," Hilary muttered, "I don't have the strength to fight off the pain anymore."

"I wish I'd hurry and grow up so I could be trained, and help you both," Callista said, but suddenly she was frightened. Would this happen to her too?

"Take your time, Callista, you're only eleven.... I'm glad your training is going so well," Hilary murmured, "Leonie says you are going to be really great, better than I am, so much better ... we need Keepers so badly, so badly...."

"Hilary, hush, don't try to talk. Just try to even out your breathing."

"I'll live. I always do. But I'm glad you're doing so well. I'm so afraid. . . ."

"That you won't be able to work as a Keeper anymore?"

"Yes, but I have to, Callista, I have to—"

"No you don't," said the younger girl, perching on the end of Hilary's bed, "Leonie will release you, if it's really too much for you. I heard her tell Damon so."

"Of course she will," Hilary whispered, "but I don't want her to be alone with all the weight of the work again. I love her, Callista. . . ."

"Of course you do, Hilary. We all do. I do, too."

"She's worked so hard, all her life—we can't let her down now! We can't!" Hilary struggled upright, gasping. "The others—there were six others who tried and failed, and there were so many times she tried to train a Keeper only to have her leave and marry—and Callista, she's not young, not strong enough anymore, we may be her last chance, she may not be strong enough to train Keepers after us, we *have* to succeed—it could be the end of Arilinn, Callista—"

"Lie down, Hilary. Don't upset yourself like this. Just relax, try to get control of your breathing, now." Hilary lay back on the bed, while Callista came and bent over her. Light was beginning to filter through the window of her room. She did not speak as Callista bent over her, but her thoughts were as tormented as her body. There must be Keepers, otherwise darkness and ignorance closed over the Domains. And she could not fail, could not let Leonie down.

Callista ran her small hands over Hilary's body, not touching her; about an inch from the surface of the nightgown. Her face was intent, remote. After a little she said, troubled, "I'm not very good at this yet. But it looks as if the lower centers were involved, and the solar plexus too, already—Hilary, I'd better waken Leonie."

Wordless, Hilary shook her head. "Not yet." The cramping pain had moved all through her body now, so that she found it hard to breathe, and Callista looked down, deeply troubled. She said, "Why does it happen, Hilary? It doesn't happen with the other women—I've monitored them during their cycles—and they—" She stopped, turning her eyes away; there were some things from which a Keeper turned her mind and her words away as she would have turned her physical eyes from an obscenity, but they both knew what the quick equivocal glance meant: *and they are not even virgins.* . . .

"I don't know, Callista. I swear I don't," Hilary said, feeling again the terrifying sting of guilt. *What forbidden thing can I have done, not knowing, that the channels are not clear? How can I have become contaminated . . . what is wrong with me? I have kept my vows, I have touched no one, I have not even thought any forbidden thought, and yet . . . and yet . . .* another wave of pain struck her, so that she turned over, biting her lip hard, feeling it break and blood run down her chin; she did not want Callista to see, but the child was still in rapport with her from the monitoring, and she gasped with the physical assault of it.

"Callista, I have tried so hard, I don't know what I have done, and I can't let her down, I can't . . ." Hilary gasped, but the words were so blurred and incoherent that the young girl heard them only in her mind; Hilary was struggling for breath.

"Hilary, never mind, just lie quiet, try to rest."

"I can't—I can't—I've got to know what I have done wrong."

Callista was only eleven; but she had spent almost a year in the Tower, a year of intense and specialized training; she recognized that Hilary was fast slipping into the delirium of first-stage crisis. She ran out of the room, hurrying up the narrow stairs to the insulated room where Leonie slept. She pounded on the door, knowing that this summons would rouse Leonie at once; no one in Arilinn would venture to disturb Leonie now except for a major emergency.

After a moment the door opened, and Leonie, very pale, her graying hair in two long braids over her shoulders, came to the door. "What is it? Callista, child!" She caught the message before Callista could speak a word.

"Hilary again? Ah, merciful Avarra, I had hoped that this time she would escape it—"

Then her stern gaze flickered down Callista; the robe buttoned askew, the nightgown dragging beneath it, the bare feet.

This is no way for a Keeper to appear before anyone! The harsh reproof of the thought was like a mental slap, though aloud she only said, and her voice was mild, "Suppose one of the others had seen you like this, child? A Keeper must always present a picture of perfect decorum. Go and make yourself tidy, at once!"

"But Hilary—" Callista opened her mouth to protest, caught Leonie's eyes, dropped her own gray eyes and murmured, "Yes, my mother."

"You need not dress if your robe is properly fastened. When you are perfectly tidy, go and send Damon to Hilary; this is too serious for Romilla alone. And I will come when I can."

Callista wanted to protest—*Waste time in dressing myself when Hilary is so sick? She could be dying!*—but she knew this was all a part of the discipline which would make her, over the years, into a schooled, inhumanly perfect machine, like Leonie herself. Quickly she brushed her red hair and braided it tightly along her neck, slipped into a fresh robe and low indoor boots of velvet which concealed her bare ankles; then she knocked at the door of the young technician, Damon Ridenow, and gave her message.

"Come with me," Damon said, and Callista followed him down the stairs, into Hilary's room.

A Keeper must always present a picture of perfect decorum—even so, Callista was shocked at the effort Hilary made to compose her limbs, her voice, her face. She went and stood beside Hilary, looking compassionately down at her, wishing she could help somehow.

Damon sighed and shook his head as he looked down at Hilary's racked body, her bitten lips. He was a slight, dark man with a sensitive, ascetic face, the compassion in it carefully schooled to impassivity in a Keeper's presence. Yet it came through, a touch of faint humanity behind the calm mask.

"Again, *chiya*? I had hoped the new medicines would help this time. How heavy is the bleeding?"

"I don't know—" Hilary was trying hard to control her voice; Damon frowned a little, and shook his head. He said to Callista, "I don't suppose—no, you cannot touch anyone yet, can you, child? Leonie will be here soon, she will know—"

Leonie, when she came, was as calm, as carefully put

together as if she were facing the Council. "I am here, child," she said, laying the lightest of touches on Hilary's wrist, and the very touch seemed to quiet Hilary somewhat, as if it stablized her ragged breathing. But she whispered, "I'm so sorry, Leonie—I didn't want to—I can't let you down—I can't, I can't—"

"Hush, hush, child. Don't waste your strength," Leonie commanded, and behind the harshness of the words there was tenderness, too. "Callista, did you monitor her?"

Callista, biting her lip, composed herself to make a formal report on what she had discovered. The older telepaths listened, and Damon went over the monitoring process for himself, sinking his mental awareness into the girl's tormented body, pointing out to Callista what she had missed.

"The knots in the arms; that is only tension, but painful. The bleeding is heavy, yes, but not dangerously. Did you check the lower channels?"

Callista shook her head and Damon said, "Do it now. And test for contamination."

Callista hesitated, her hands a considerable distance from Hilary, and Damon's voice was harsh.

"You know how to test her. Do it."

Callista drew a deep breath, schooling her face to the absolute impassivity she knew she must maintain or be punished. She dared not even form clearly the thought, *I'm sorry, Hilary, I don't want to hurt you*—she focused on her matrix, then lowered her awareness into the electrical potential of the channels. Hilary screamed. Callista flinched and recoiled, but Leonie had seen, and forced swift rapport so that Callista, immobilized, felt the wave of sharp pain flood through her as well. She knew the lesson intended—*you must maintain absolute detachment*—and forced her face and her voice to quiet, concealing the resentment she felt.

"Both channels are contaminated, the left somewhat more than the right; the right only in the nerve nodes, the left all the way from the center complex. There are three focuses of resistance on the left—"

Damon sighed. "Well, Hilary," he said gently, "you

know as well as I what must be done. If we wait much longer, you will go into convulsions again."

Hilary flinched inwardly with dread, but her face showed nothing, and somewhere, in a remote corner of her being, she was proud of her control.

"Go and fetch some *kirian,* Callista, there is no sense waking anyone else for this," Leonie said, and when the child returned with it, she was about to run away. But Leonie said, "This time, you must stay, Callista. There may be times when you must do this unaided, and it is not too early to learn every step of the process."

Callista met Hilary's eyes, and there was a flash of rebellion in them. She thought, *I could never hurt anyone like that* ... but despite her terrible fear, she forced herself to stand quiet.

Will they make me go through it this time in rapport with her ... ?

Damon held Hilary's hand, giving her the telepathic drug which would, a little, ease the resistances to what contact they must make with her mind and body, clearing the channels. Hilary was incoherent now, slipping rapidly into delirium; her thoughts blurred, and Callista could hardly make them out.

Once again to lie still and let myself be cut into pieces and then stitched back together again, that is what it feels like ... *and they are training even little Callista to be a torturer's assistant* ... *to stand by without a flicker of pity.* ...

"Gently, gently, my darling," Leonie said, and the compassion and dread would communicate itself to Hilary and added, "when it is over, it will be better."

She is so cruel, and so kind, how do I know which is real? Callista could not tell whether it was her own thought or Hilary's. She knew she was tense, numb with fear, and forced herself to breathe deeply and relax, fearing that her own tension and dread would communicate itself to Hilary and add to the other girl's ordeal; and she watched with amazement and dread as Hilary's taut face relaxed, wondered at the discipline which let Hilary go limp; Callista forced herself to calm, to detachment, watching every step of the long and agonizing process of clearing the blocked nerve channels.

When they were sure she wasn't going to die, not this time anyway, they left her sleeping—Callista, feeling Hilary slip down into the heaviness of sleep under the sedative they had given her, felt almost light-headed with relief; at least she was free of pain! Damon went to find himself a delayed breakfast, and Leonie, in the hallway outside Hilary's door, said softly, "I am sorry you had to endure that, little one, but it was time for you to learn; and you needed the practice in detachment. Come, she will sleep all day and perhaps most of the night, and when she wakes, she will be well. And next month we must make sure she does not overwork herself this way at this time."

When they were in Leonie's rooms, facing one another over the small table set in the window, and Leonie was pouring for them from the heavy silver pot, Callista felt tears flooding the back of her throat. Leonie said quietly, "You can cry now, if you must, Callista. But it would be better if you could learn to master your tears, too."

Callista bent her head with a silent struggle; finally she said, "Leonie, it was worse this time, wasn't it? She's been getting worse, hasn't she?"

"I'm afraid so; ever since she began work with the energons. Last time it took her three days to build up enough energy leakage to go into crisis."

"Does she know?"

"No. She doesn't remember much of what happens when she's in pain."

"But Leonie—she wants, so terribly, not to disappoint you—" *and so do I,* thought Callista, struggling again with her tears.

"I know, Callista, but she'll die if she keeps this up. She is simply too frail to endure the stress. There may be some kind of inborn weakness in the channels—I am to blame, that I accepted her without being certain there was no such physical weakness. Yet she has such talent and skill—" Leonie shook her head sorrowfully. "You may not believe it, Callista, but I would gladly take all her pain upon myself if it would cure her. I feel I cannot bear to hurt her again like that!"

Before the vehemence in the older woman's voice Callista was shocked and amazed.

Can she still feel? I thought she had taught herself to be wholly indifferent to the sufferings of others, and she would have me.

"No," Leonie said, with a remote sadness, "I am not indifferent to suffering, Callista."

But you hurt me so, this morning.

"And I will hurt you again, as often as I must," Leonie said, "but, believe me, child, I would so much rather . . ." She could not finish, but, in shock, Callista realized that she meant what she said; Leonie would willingly suffer for *her*, too . . . suddenly, Callista knew that instead of indifference, Leonie's level voice held agonized restraint.

"My mother," Callista burst out, through the restraint, "will I suffer so, when I am become a woman?"

Could I endure it? Time and again, to be torn by that kind of pain . . . and then to be torn apart by the clearing process . . .

"I do not know, dear child. I truly hope not."

Did you? But Callista knew she would never dare to put her unspoken question into words. Leonie's restraint had gone so deep that even to herself she had probably barricaded even the memory of pain.

"Isn't there anything we can do?"

"For Hilary? Probably not. Except to care for her while we can, and when it is truly too much for her to endure, release her." It seemed now to Callista that Leonie's calm was sadder than tears or hysterical weeping. "But for you—I do not know. Perhaps. You might not wish it. If I had my way," Leonie said, "every girl coming to work here as Keeper would be neutered before she comes to womanhood!"

Callista flinched as if the Keeper had spoken an obscenity; indeed, by Comyn standards she had. But she said obediently, "If that is your will, my mother—"

Leonie shook her head. "The laws forbid it. I wonder if the Council know what they are doing to you with their concern? But there is another way. You know that we cannot begin your training until your cycles of womanhood are established—"

"The monitors have said it will be more than a year."

"That is late; which means there is still time."

Callista had eagerly awaited the first show of blood, which would mean that she was a woman grown, ready to begin her serious training as Keeper; now she had begun to think of it with dread. Leonie said, "If we were to begin your training now, it would make certain physical alterations in your body; and the cycles probably would not begin at all. This is why we are not supposed to begin this training until the Keeper-novice is come to womanhood, the training changes a body still immature. And then you would never have the problem Hilary has had ... but I cannot do this without your consent, even to save you suffering."

To be spared what Hilary suffered? Callista wondered why Leonie should hesitate a moment.

"Because it might mean much to you, when you are older," Leonie said. "You might wish to leave, to marry."

Callista made a gesture of repugnance. She had been taught to turn her thoughts away from such things; in her innocence she felt only the most enormous contempt for the relationship between men and women. Secure in her chastity, she wondered why Leonie believed she could ever be false to the pledge she had sworn to perpetual virginity.

"I will never wish to marry. Such things are not for me," she said, and Leonie shook her head, with a little sigh.

"It would mean that you would remain much as you are now, for the cycles would not begin. . . ."

"Do you mean I wouldn't grow up?" Callista did not think she wished to remain always a child.

"Oh, yes," Leonie said, "You would grow up, but without that token of womanhood."

"But since I am sworn to be Keeper," said Callista, who had been taught a considerable amount of anatomy and knew, at least technically, what that maturity meant, "I do not see why I should need it."

Leonie smiled faintly. "You are right, of course. I would that I had been spared it, all those many years."

Callista looked at her in surprise and wonder; never

had Leonie spoken to her like this, or loosened even a little the cold barricade she kept against any kind of personal revelation.

So she is not . . . not superhuman. She is only a woman, like Hilary or Romilla or . . . or me . . . she can weep and suffer . . . I thought, when I was grown, when I had learned my lessons well and had come to be Keeper, that I would learn not to feel such things or to suffer with them. . . . It was a terrifying thought, a new terror among the terrors she had known here, that she would not safely outgrow those feelings. She had believed that her own sufferings were only because she was a child, not yet perfected in learning. *I had believed that to be a Keeper one must outgrow these feelings, that one reason I was not yet ready was that I still had not learned to stop feeling so. . . .*

Leonie watched her, without speaking, her face remote and sad.

She is such a child, she is only now beginning to guess at the price of being Keeper. . . .

But all she said aloud was, "You are right, of course, my dearest; since you are sworn to be Keeper, you do not need that, and you will be better without it, and if we should begin your training now, you will be spared."

Again she hesitated and warned, "You know it is against custom. You will be asked if I have fully explained it to you, what it will mean, and if you are truly willing; because I could not, under the laws made by those who have never stepped inside a Tower and would not be accepted if they did, do this to you without your free consent. Do you completely understand this, Callista?"

And Callista thought, *She speaks as if it were a great price I must pay, that I might be unwilling. As if it were deprivation, something taken from me. Instead it means only that I can be Keeper, and that I need not pay the terrible price Hilary has had to pay.*

"I understand, Leonie," she said, steadily, "and I am willing. When can I begin?"

"As soon as you like, then, Callista."

But why, Callista wondered, *does Leonie look so sad?*

The Lesson of the Inn

by Marion Zimmer Bradley

Hilary Castamir rode head down, her gray cloak wrapped tightly about her, the cowl of her cloak concealing her face. She did not turn to look her last on Arilinn.

She had failed....

She would never, now, be known as Hilary of Arilinn, or grow old in the service of the most ancient and prestigious of the Towers of the Seven Domains; revered, almost worshiped. Keeper of Arilinn. Never, now. She had failed, failed....

It would be Callista, then, who would take Leonie's place when the old sorceress finally laid down her burden. *I do not envy her,* Hilary thought. And yet, paradoxically, Hilary knew that she did envy Callista.

Callista Lanart. Thirteen years old, now. Red hair and gray eyes like all the Altons—like Hilary herself, for Hilary, too, had Comyn blood. Why should Callista succeed where she had failed?

Leonie had tried to soften the blow.

"My dearest child, you are neither the first nor the last to find a Keeper's work beyond your strength. We all know what you have endured, but it is enough. We can ask no more of you." Then she had spoken the formal words which formally released Hilary from the vows she had sworn at eleven years old. And half of Hilary was shaking with craven relief. Not to have to endure it anymore, never again to await, in helpless terror, the attacks of pain which swept over her at the time of her women's cycles, never again to endure the excruciating clearing of the nerve channels....

Or worse than that, again and again, the desperate hope that this time it would be only the cramping, spasmodic pain, the weakness that drove her to bed, sick and exhausted and drained. *That* she could endure, she had endured; she had patiently swallowed all the medicines which were supposed to help it and somehow never did; she never lost the hope that this month the pain would simply subside as it did in the other women. But every month there was the terror, too, and the guilt. What is it I have done that I ought not to have done?

What have I done? Why do I suffer so? I have faithfully observed all the laws of the Keepers, I have touched no man or woman, I have not even allowed myself to think forbidden thoughts. . . . Merciful Avarra, what am I doing wrong that I cannot keep the channels pure and untainted as befits a virgin and a Keeper?

All the training she had endured, all the suffering, all the terror and the guilt, the guilt . . . all gone for nothing. And there was always the suspicion. Always when a Keeper could not keep her channels clear there was suspicion, never spoken aloud, but always there.

The channels of a virgin, untainted, are clear. What is wrong with Hilary, that these nerve channels, these same channels which in an adult woman carry sexuality, cannot remain clear for unmixed use of laran? Even Leonie had looked at her in sharp question, a time or two, the unspoken doubt so clear to the telepath girl that Hilary had burst into hysterical crying, and even Leonie could not doubt the utter sincerity of bewilderment.

I have not broken my vow, nor thought of breaking it. I have faithfully kept all the laws of a Keeper, I swear it, I swear it by Evanda and Avarra and by the Blessed Cassilda, mother of the Domains. . . .

And so, in the end, Leonie had had no choice but to send Hilary away. Hilary was almost hysterical with relief that her long and agonizing ordeal was at an end; but she was still sick with guilt and terror. Who would ever believe in her innocence, who would believe that she had not been sent away in disgrace, her vows broken? Sunk in misery, she did not even turn to look her last on Arilinn.

Seven years, then, gone for nothing. She would never again wear the crimson robes of a Keeper, nor work again in the relays . . as they crossed the pass, there was one narrow space where they had to dismount and walk carefully along the narrow trail while the horses were led along the very rim of the chasm; and as she looked down into the dreadful gulf dropping away to the plains a thousand feet below, it came into her mind that she could take a single careless step, no more, it would be so easy, an accident, and then she need never again face the thought of failure. No one could ever look at her, and whisper when she was not in the room that here was the Keeper who had been sent from Arilinn, no one knew why. . . .

One single false step. So easy. And yet she could not summon up enough resolution to do it. *You are a coward, Hilary Castamir,* she told herself. She remembered that Leonie herself, and the young technician Damon Ridenow, who had sometimes come to help Leonie with the clearing of her channels, had praised her courage. *They do not really know me; they do not know what a coward I am. Well, I will never see them again, it does not matter. Nothing really matters. Not now.*

Toward mid-afternoon, as they came down into a valley outside the ring of mountains which shut the Plains of Arilinn away from the outside world, they stopped at an inn to rest the horses. Her escort said that she would be conducted to a private parlor inside the inn, where she could warm herself and have some food if she wished. She was weary with riding, for she had risen very early this morning; she was glad of a chance to dismount, but when the escort, in automatic courtesy, offered her his help, she had scrambled down without touching him, so skillfully that she had not even brushed his outstretched hand.

And when a strange man in the doorway held out his hand, with a soft, polite, "Mind the steps, *damisela,* they are slippery with the snow," she had drawn back as if the touch of his hand would contaminate her beyond recall, and had opened her lips to flay him with harsh words. And then she remembered, with a dull sensation of weariness. She was not, now, wearing the crimson robes which would protect her against a careless touch, even a random look. Her gray hooded cloak was the ordinary traveling dress of any noblewoman; even though she shrouded her face deep within it, it would not wholly protect her. It seemed, as she went through the hallway to the inn, that she could feel eyes on her everywhere.

Do all men, always, watch women this way? she wondered. And yet no man's eyes had rested on her for more than a moment, as they might have rested on a horse or a pillar; it was only that they looked at her at all, that their eyes were not automatically withdrawn as they had been in Arilinn when she rode forth with the other women of the Tower, that everyone did not step aside, as she had been accustomed to their doing, waiting for her to pass.

In the room to which the servant conducted her, she unfastened her cloak and put back the hood, she went to the fire to warm herself; but she did not touch the jug of wine which had been sent to her.

After a long time she heard a soft sound at the door. A woman stood there, round and plump-bodied, enveloped in a capacious apron; she might have been the innkeeper's wife or daughter, or a servant. She said with soft courtesy, "I will make up the fire freshly for you, my lady," and came to put fresh logs on it. Then she blinked in astonishment. "But you are still wearing your cloak, *damisela*. Let me help you." She came, and Hilary started to recoil, automatically ... no human being had laid so much as a fingertip on her garment, not for years. Then she remembered that this prohibition no longer applied to her, and stood statue-still, suffering the impersonal touch of the woman's hands, removing her cape and the scarf around her neck.

"Will you have your shoes off as well, my lady, to warm your feet at the fire?"

"No, no," said Hilary, embarrassed. "No, I will do very well—" She stooped to unfasten her own traveling-boots.

"But indeed, you must not," said the woman, scandalized, kneeling to draw them off, "I am here to serve you, lady—ah, how cold your feet are, poor little lady, let me rub them for you with this towel...." She insisted, and Hilary, acutely embarrassed, let her do as she would.

I did not know how cold my feet were until she told

me. I have been taught to endure heat and cold, fire and ice, without complaint, even without awareness ... but now that she was aware of the cold, she shivered as if she would never stop.

The woman took a steaming kettle off the hob of the fireplace and poured something hot into a cup. "Now drink this, little lady," she said compassionately, "and let me wrap you in your cloak again. It will warm you now. Here, put your feet up to the fire like this," she said, drawing a footstool around so that Hilary found herself deep in a chair with the soles of her feet propped up to the blazing fire. "Have you dry stockings in your saddlebags? I think you must have them on, or you will take cold." And almost before Hilary knew it, her feet were toasty warm in dry stockings, and she was sipping at the hot spicy brew which, she suspected, had had something a good deal stronger than wine added to it. A sensation very like pleasure began to steal over her.

I have not been this comfortable in a long time, she thought, almost with a secret guilt, *a long long time.* Her head nodded and she drowsed in the heat. Some time later she awoke to discover that a pillow had been tucked behind her head in the armchair, and someone had covered her with a blanket. She had not slept so well for a long time, either.

The thought began to stir faintly in her consciousness. *I have been taught to be indifferent to all these things, indifferent to pain, cold, hunger, isolation. Such thoughts are not worthy of a Keeper. I learned to endure all these things,* she thought. *And still I failed....*

Outside in the hallway she heard soft voices; then there was a tentative knock on the door. Quickly Hilary turned her skirt down over her thin knees. *Even if I am no longer a Keeper,* she thought, *I must behave as circumspectly as one, lest my behavior give them cause to think I was sent away from Arilinn for something I have done.* She got to her feet and called, "Come in."

The leader of the escort sent by her father stood hesitantly in the door, saying diffidently, "My lady, the snow has begun to fall so thickly that we cannot go on. We have arranged to remain here for the night, if it please you."

If it please me, she thought. But the words were only formal courtesy. *What could they possibly do if it did not please me? Try to force their way through the storm, and perhaps lose the way or be frozen in a blizzard?* She did not look at the man; her face was turned away, as always in the presence of strangers, and she longed for the protection of her hooded cloak, hanging on the chair to dry. She said with aloof courtesy, "You must do as you think best," and the man withdrew.

Later she heard voices along the hall.

"Look, I don't care who the *vai domna* is, unless she is the Queen's own self or Lady Hastur. Once and for all, we are crowded and overworked down here, with the storm and all these travelers; no one has leisure to go back and forth along all these corridors with trays and special meals now. The worthy lady can just haul her honorable carcass down to the common room like everyone else, or she can stay in her precious private parlor and go hungry, for all I care."

Hilary's anger was purely automatic. How dared they speak like that? If a Keeper of Arilinn chose to honor their wretched little inn, how dared they refuse her the protection of her privacy? Then, dully, Hilary remembered. She was no longer Keeper, no longer even a *leronis* of Arilinn. She was nothing. She was Hilary-Cassilde Castamir, second daughter of Arnad Castamir, who was only a minor nobleman on a small-holding in the Kilghard Hills. She remembered, dimly, like something in a dream, something her father had said to her. It had been the year before she went to Arilinn, but already she had been tested and had begun to dream of being one of the great Keepers. She had been about nine years old.

"Daughter, the servants and vassals have tasks much harder than ours, much of the time. You must never needlessly make their lives harder; it is not worthy of a noblewoman to give orders only for the pleasure of seeing yourself obeyed."

Hilary thought; *I need nothing, I will tell them I am not hungry, then I can remain here in peace, untroubled. They need not spare anyone to wait on me.* But there was a good smell of cooking all along the hallways, and

Hilary reflected that in order to tell them this, she would need to go down to the common room anyhow. And she had breakfasted early, and scantily, and had had nothing since except the drink the woman had given her. She put her light veil about her head, and went along the passageway to the common room.

As she came in, the woman who had waited on her before came toward her; Hilary stopped in the doorway, overcome by shyness and the impact of the crowded room, more people than she had seen in one place in many years; men, women and children, strangers, all overtaken by the storm. The woman led her quickly to a small corner table, apart from the others, where she could sit in the shadow of the projecting fireplace and not be seen. The four men of her escort were eating and drinking heartily, laughing over their food and wine; the leader came and inquired courteously if she had everything she needed. She murmured a shy assent without raising her eyes.

The woman was still standing protectively beside her. "My name is Lys, my lady. Will you have wine, or hot milk? Food will be brought to you in a moment. The wine is from Dalereuth and quite good."

Hilary said shyly that she would rather have hot milk. The woman went away and after a while a great fat woman, swathed to the neck in a great white apron, came around, lugging a huge bowl the contents of which she ladled out onto every plate. She passed Hilary's isolated table and ladled out a great dollop of whatever it was onto her plate, then passed on to the next table. Hilary stared in consternation. It was some kind of stew, great lumps of boiled meat and some kind of thickly cut coarse vegetables, white and orange and yellow.

Hilary was rarely hungry. She had been ill so much that she almost never thought with any pleasure of food. When she had been doing heavy and strenuous work in the matrix screens, she was ravenous and ate whatever was put before her without tasting; not caring what it was, so long as it replaced the energy her starved body needed. At other times she cared so little for food that the others in her circle tried hard to think up special dainties which, delicately served, might tempt her fickle appetite just a little. This stew from the common dish looked appalling. But it smelled surprisingly good, hot and savory, and after all she could not sit there and seem to disdain the common fare. She took a bite, squeamishly, and then another; it tasted as good as it smelled, and she ate it all up, and when the woman Lys came around with her hot milk she stirred honey into it and drank all of that, too, surprised at herself.

While the adults in the room were busy at eating and drinking, two young children had come and knelt on the hearth, their tartan skirts spread around them. One of the little girls had opened a little bag she carried and spilled out some small cut and colored pebbles. Hilary knew the game; she had played it with Callista, to try to divert the homesick child in her first loneliness. As they cast the stones, one of them fell on the edge of Hilary's green skirt; they looked at her, too shy to come and fetch it, and Hilary bent down and held out the small carved stone to them.

"Here," she said, "come and take it." It did not occur to her to be shy with the children.

The taller of the little girls —they were about six and eight, with long tails of white-blonde hair down their backs—said, "What is your name?"

"Hilary."

"I'm Lilla, and my little sister is Janna. Would you like to play with us?"

Hilary hesitated, then realized that in the darkness of the room, they probably took her for a child like themselves. Rising early at Arilinn that morning, she had simply tied her hair at the back of her neck without bothering to do it up. The little girl urged, "Please. It isn't so much fun to play with only the two of us," and it reminded her of something Callista had said once. She smiled and sat down on the hearth beside them, carefully tucking in her skirts. Lilla said, "You can have first turn if you want to, since you are our guest," and at the child's careful politeness, she wanted to giggle. She thanked Lilla and shook the toys out on the floor.

After a time the woman Lys came back to clear away the plates and mugs, and looked startled to see Hilary on the floor with the children. Recalled, Hilary looked around for her escort; they were wrangling with the housekeeper, near the door. The children scrambled to their feet. Lilla said politely, "My mother will be looking for us. Thank you for playing with us. I must take my little sister to bed," but small Janna came up, held out her arms wide and gave Hilary a moist kiss and a hug.

Hilary, too shy to return the kiss, felt tears start to her eyes. No one had kissed her in so many years. *My mother kissed me, in farewell, when I went to the Tower. No one since, not even my mother when I visited her, not my sisters; they had been told of the taboo, that I was to touch no one, not with a fingertip. Callista did not kiss me when we parted. Callista, who will be Lady of Arilinn. Callista will make a good Keeper; she is cold, she finds it easy to keep to all the laws and rules of the Tower . . .* and again she felt the weight of her guilt and shame, the weight of failure. For a few minutes, playing with the little girls, she had forgotten.

The escort and the innkeeper were still arguing, and the woman Lys broke away from them and came toward Hilary. She said, "Lady, my master cannot displace any guest who has bespoken a room before you. But I have offered—it is mean and poor, lady, but the room I share with my sister and her baby has two beds; I will share my sister's bed and you may have mine, you are very welcome." And as Hilary hesitated, "I wish there were some place more worthy of you, lady, but there is nothing, we are so crowded, the only alternative is to spread your blankets in the common room with your soldiers, and that a lady cannot do. . . ."

"You are very kind." She felt dazed by many shocks. She had eaten in a room full of strangers, played with strange children, now she was to share a room with two strange women and to sleep in a servant's bed. But it was preferable, of course, to sleeping among her soldier escort. "You are very kind," she said, and went with Lys, only half conscious of her escort's look of relief at this solution.

The room was dark and cramped and not warm, but floor and walls were scrubbed clean, and the linen and quilts heaped on the beds were immaculate. Between the two beds was a cradle, painted white, and on the other bed, a woman sat, holding a chubby baby across her lap and dressing it in clean clothes. Lys said, "This is my sister Amalie. *Domna,* I must go and finish my kitchen work. Make yourself at home; you can sleep there, in my bed." Hilary's saddlebags had been brought and shoved into the cramped space at the foot of the beds, and Hilary began to rummage for her nightgear. The woman with the baby was looking at her curiously, and Hilary murmured a shy formula of greeting.

"It is most kind of you to share your room with a stranger, *mestra.*"

"I hope the baby will not keep you awake, lady. But she is a good baby and does not cry very much." As if to give her the lie direct, the baby began to wave its small fists and shriek lustily, and Amalie laughed.

"Little rogue, would you make a liar of me? But she is hungry now, my lady, she wants her supper; afterward she will sleep."

"I have heard that it is good for them to cry," Hilary said timidly. "It helps their lungs to grow strong. How old is the baby. What is her name?"

"She is only forty days old," Amalie said, "and since my husband is a hired sword to *Dom* Arnad Castamir, I named her for one of the lord's daughters; Hilary."

So the baby is my namesake. Couldn't the woman do better for her child than to give her the name of a failure, a disgraced Keeper? But she could not say that. She said, "My name is Hilary, too," and held out her hand to the chubby screaming child. The fist waved, encountered Hilary's finger and gripped it surprisingly hard. Amalie was unfastening her dress; she was thin, but Hilary was surprised to see her breasts, grotesquely swollen, it seemed to the point of deformity. The nipples already oozed white. Amalie lifted the baby, crooning.

"There, you greedy puppy," she said, and the small rosy mouth fastened hard on the swollen nipple, the crying choking off in mid-scream. The baby made small gasping noises as she sucked, waving her clenched fists rhythmically, in time to the sucking gulps. Hilary had never seen a woman nursing her child before—at least, not since she was old enough to remember.

"I heard them say in the inn that you were coming

from Arilinn," Amalie said. "Ah, you must be happy to
be coming home to your mother, and she will be happy
too. I think it would break my heart if some day my
daughter went so far from me." She stroked the baby's
forehead with a tender finger, brushing the colorless
curls away from the tiny face. "They live such sad and
lonely lives in the Tower, poor ladies. Were you very
unhappy there, very glad to come away?"

Not a word or whisper of disgrace. Nothing but, you
will be glad to be coming home to your mother. *My
mother,* Hilary thought. *My mother is a stranger; she has
become a stranger to me. And yet once we were close . . .
as close as that,* Hilary thought, looking at the woman
with the child at her breast. *My mother need not be a
stranger now. Perhaps, when she knows how hard I tried,
she will not blame me for my failure. . . .*

The baby's fists were still clenching and unclenching
rhythmically as she sucked, her toes curling up with eagerness. The woman's eyes were closed. She looked
happy and peaceful. Suddenly Hilary felt a pain in her
own breasts, a cramping down through her whole body,
not unlike what she felt at the time of her recurrent
ordeal, only now, for some reason, it was not particularly
painful or even unwelcome. It was so intense that for a
moment she thought she would faint, and clutched the
bedpost; then quickly she turned away and began to
rummage again in her saddlebags for her nightgown.

She got into bed, and lay watching the nursing, feeling
strangely drained. The pain had gone, but her breasts
felt strange, tense, as if she could feel the nipples rub-
bing hard against her thick nightgown. The woman finally drew the baby, sated and blissful, from her breast,
fastened up her nightgown, and carried her to Hilary
where she lay in the strange bed.

"Would you like to hold her for a minute, *Domna*?"

Hilary held out her arms, and Amalie put the baby
into them; she held her awkwardly against her own meager breasts. Full and sleeping, the baby squirmed, nuz-
zling her mouth against Hilary's nightgown, and the
woman laughed as the little flailing hands closed on Hilary's breast.

"You will find nothing there, greedy one, and you are

as full as a suckling pig already," she scolded, teasing, "but a year or two from now, well, she would have better luck looking there, perhaps, lady?"

Hilary blushed, looking down at the baby in her arms, drawing her finger over the soft little head. It felt like silk, feathers, nothing in the world had ever felt so soft to her. The soft sleeping weight against her body made her feel depleted, with a pleasant exhaustion. When Amalie picked up the baby to tuck her into the cradle, Hilary's arms felt suddenly cold and empty, and after the light was out she lay listening to the soft breathing of the women and the child, feeling the curious ache in her body. What must it feel like, to nurse a child that way, to feel that hungry tugging at her breasts? She felt her nipples throbbing again. She had never been conscious of them before, they had simply been there, part of herself, like her hair and her fingernails. She put her hands over them, awkwardly, trying helplessly to calm the aching; she felt cold, an empty shell, shivering, finally pulling the pillow toward her and hugging it tight, in an attempt to quiet the strangeness she could not calm. Suddenly, exhausted by strangeness and fatigue, she slept.

When she woke the room was filled with sunlight, and Amalie and the baby had gone, and Lys was saying apologetically, "I am sorry to waken you, my lady, but your escort sent to say you should be ready to ride within the hour."

Hilary sat up in bed and blinked; she had slept unusually long and late.

"You can wash yourself here, lady, I have brought you some hot water. I will bring your breakfast if you like."

"I can come to the common room for breakfast," Hilary said, "but I will be glad of your help in lacing my gown." She gave Lys a gift of money before she left. When the woman protested, saying it was unnecessary, she said, "Give it to your sister, then, and tell her to buy something pretty for the baby."

On the steps of the inn, crowded because the unexpected guests of the storm were readying themselves for departure, and the courtyard was thick with horses and men, she suddenly heard, around the corner, a man's voice.

"Who is the pretty young lady in the green gown and the gray cloak? I saw her last night in the common room, and again this morning, but I do not know her by name."

It was one of the escort who answered. "She is the lady Hilary Castamir; we are bringing her from Arilinn. I have heard she found the work there too hard and too taxing to her health, so she is going home to her family."

Now it will come, Hilary thought, braced for the indecent jests about a Keeper who found it too difficult to keep her virginity, the rude speculations, the talk of broken vows, disgrace . . . but the first speaker only said, "I have heard that the work there is difficult indeed. It would have been a great pity for such a young woman to live all her days shut inside a Tower, and grow at last as gray and gaunt as the old sorceress of Arilinn. She is only a pretty girl now; but if I am any judge, one day she will be one of the loveliest women I have ever seen. I hope the bride my father one day chooses for me will be even half so lovely."

Hilary listened, shocked—how dare they talk of her this way? Then, slowly, it dawned on her that they were actually complimenting her, that they meant her well. She wondered if she was really pretty. It had never occurred to her even to think about it. She knew, in a vague way, that most women cared a good deal about whether men thought them pretty; even those women in Arilinn itself who did not live under a Keeper's laws, the monitors and mechanics and technicians there, went to great pains to keep themselves prettily dressed and attractive when they were not working. But she, Hilary, had always known such things were not for her. She dressed for warmth and modesty, she wore the crimson robes from which all men turned away their eyes by instinct, she had been taught to give no time or thought to such matters.

The women in the Towers, those other women who need not live by Keeper's laws, they know what it is to think of men as the men think of them. . . .

Hilary had always known that the women and men in Arilinn lay together if they would, had been aware in the vaguest of ways that the women found pleasure in such things; but she, a Keeper, a pledged virgin, had been taught, in all kinds of ingenious and demanding ways, to turn her thoughts elsewhere, never to give such a thought even a moment's mental lease, never to know or understand what went on all around her, to numb all the reflexes of her ripening body.... Hilary stood paralyzed on the stairs, motionless under the impact of a thought which had just come to her; remembering the curious pain in her breasts last night as she watched the nursing child.

I have denied myself all this. Even the pleasures of warmth and food. I have taught my body to feel nothing, except pain ... that I could not barricade away, but except for the pain I could not deny, I had refused to know that I had a body at all, thinking of it only as a mechanical contrivance for working in the relays, not flesh and blood. I learned to feel nothing, not even hunger and thirst. And perhaps the pain was the revenge my body took for letting it feel nothing more than that ... for allowing it no comfort, no pleasure....

The leader of her escort came and bowed.

"Your horse is ready, lady. May I assist you to mount?"

She started to mount without assistance; in the old way. Then she thought, in surprise, *Why, yes, you may.* She said, with a smile that surprised him, and herself, "I thank you, sir." Momentarily, and from habit, she tensed as he lifted her, then relaxed, and let him lift her into the saddle.

"Are you comfortable, my lady?"

She was still too timid to look at him, but she said softly, "Yes, I thank you. Very comfortable."

As they rode out of the courtyard, she put back her hood, luxuriating in the warmth of the sun on her face.

I am pretty, she thought defiantly. *I am pretty, and I am glad.* She looked back at the inn, with a warmth akin to love, and for a moment it seemed she had learned more in the single night there than in all the years that had gone before.

I can kiss a child. I can hold a baby in my arms, and think about what it would be like to hold a baby of my own, to have my own baby at my breasts. I need not feel guilty if men look at me and think I am pretty. And tomorrow I shall see my mother, and I shall throw myself in her arms, and kiss her as I used to do when I was a very little girl.

I can do anything.

Poor Callista. She will be Lady of Arilinn, but she will never have any of this.

I am free!

By the time she rode up out of the valley, she was singing.

Hilary's Homecoming

by Marion Zimmer Bradley

i

At Syrtis they turned off the Great North Road and took the road which curved away eastward into the foothills of the Kilghard Hills. Hilary Castamir had never believed she could be so weary of riding. At the very best of times she was not much more than an indifferent horsewoman, and this was hardly the best of times. She had been in the saddle for almost three days now; the road from Arilinn was long and rough to her horse's feet.

She was eager to reach home and to see her mother and father, not to mention her brother and the little sisters, one of whom had been born since she left home for the Tower, where she had gone when she was only ten years old. She was now seventeen, though she looked younger—a slender sickly-looking girl, painfully thin. She might have been pretty had she looked a bit more healthy.

But now everything, even the anticipated sight of her parents, had slipped away in her weariness. She dearly wished to be out of the saddle and to rest somewhere; but in this company, of course, it would be unseemly to show signs of weariness or fatigue. A Keeper, she reminded herself, must always be the perfect model of the decorum of the Arilinn Tower. Then, painfully, she reminded herself: *but I am a Keeper no more.* She had been sent away like a parcel of unwanted goods, disgraced—

No, she told herself firmly; *not in disgrace. Leonie had written to her parents last month and made it very clear.*

Hilary had dwelt in the Arilinn Tower for nearly seven

127

years and Leonie, who had chosen her for Keeper, had no fault to find with her. It was only that her health had failed and she had had to be dismissed, at last, to avoid a complete breakdown. For this reason Leonie had not arranged a marriage for her, as was usually done on the infrequent occasions when a maiden was dismissed from the Tower. Her parents might choose to do so when she had recovered her health.

As they turned off the Great North Road on to the smaller branch road which led more deeply into the Kilghard Hills, a rider on a fine black horse, a green cadet cloak about his shoulders, broke loose from where he was posted at the crossroads and came riding toward them. As he came near, Hilary realized it was her older brother Despard.

He must be quite nineteen now. She had not set eyes on him for many years. He looked very much as Hilary would have looked if she were older and in robust health; his cheeks were round and as red as the dwarf crab-apples on the trees in the fence-rows, glowing with cold and excitement.

He bowed in his saddle and said with unexpected formality,

"My lady—?"

"Just Hilary, Des," she said. "You don't have to be formal with me any more; didn't Mother tell you? That's all over now; I'm home for good."

His eyes clouded.

"They didn't tell me anything," he said. "What happened, sister? Or shouldn't I ask?"

"You can ask me anything you like," she said, "and I'll tell you everything. But Leonie wrote to tell Mother and Father; I thought for sure they would have told you."

"No; as I said, they told me only that you were coming home. I thought at first it must be for a visit; but the way Mama looked, I didn't dare ask for details. What happened?"

Hilary smiled. Knowing her mother, she should have been prepared for this.

"Nothing's really wrong," she said. "It's just that I was sick so often I disrupted the life of the Tower. So they felt I shouldn't stay there any longer." She felt a strange disquiet; had Leonie's letter gone astray? But she put that thought away.

"Have you been very long on the road?" Despard asked.

She smiled wearily; it made her look older and desperately emaciated; she could read that in her brother's dismayed reaction.

"You really don't look well, Hilary; we should hurry and get you home."

"Thanks. I'd really be glad to be inside—and rest."

"Well, let's be off, then," Despard said, and spurred his horse to ride alongside the guards who escorted her. Hilary pulled herself upright, thinking, *Just a little farther now.*

A wooden rail fence lined the road here, and after a little way she saw plots of kitchen gardens and a few fruit trees and berry bushes. Finally she saw the familiar tidy yard, at the end of which was the stairway to the imposing front door of paneled dark wood. At the top of the stairs stood a young girl Hilary did not know. She saw the Guards and Hilary and yelled, "Mama, she's come!"

A tall woman came from inside the door; for a moment, Hilary did not recognize her mother. *Domna* Yllana Castamir was tall and slender. In adolescence she must have looked very much the way Hilary did now; but unlike Hilary, she had never been pale and gaunt.

Hilary reined in her horse thankfully. For the moment, all she could think of was the cessation of motion. She said, a little faintly, "Mother—"

"Well, Hilary girl, how are you? You're thinner, but I can't say it's becoming to you. Well, I suppose you must be tired from riding. Come in; our guests are here, and you'll be expected at dinner."

"Come, come, Mother, let the girl get her riding-cloak off before you start ordering her about," interrupted the small, slight, withered man who appeared at her side. Hilary recognized her father, *Dom* Arnad Castamir. In her childhood he had seemed enormous, imposing and powerful; now she could see he was an old man, quite overshadowed by his more aggressive wife. He came down the stairs to Hilary, held out his arms, and helped her from the saddle, leaning forward to embrace her. He had the familiar smell she remembered from her childhood—horse, sweat, and the brew of medicinal herbs and cinnamon that he took for his cough. He hugged her hard and said, "You're too thin, my girl; haven't they been feeding you in that Tower?"

"Oh, yes, they were all very good to me," Hilary said. "But that's why I'm here, of course; my health was breaking down. Didn't Leonie write to you?"

"Oh, yes, the Lady Leonie wrote," her mother said. "But so vaguely that we were worried." She led Hilary into the hall and took off her gray cloak.

"Make haste, my love; you will soon be expected at dinner in the hall; we invited our neighbors, so that they can see for themselves that you have nothing to hide. As you surely know, when a Keeper is dismissed so suddenly, there is certain to be gossip."

"Of course I have nothing to hide," said Hilary in exasperation. "I thought Leonie had told you; I have almost lived in her pocket for seven years, and anyone who could commit the slightest indiscretion under Leonie's eyes—"

"Oh, but she would have to say that for her own protection," said her mother. "After all, you have been in her care for all these years, and you know as well as I that no Keeper is ever dismissed at such short notice if she has behaved herself properly. Is there nothing you want to tell me, Hilary?"

Now it dawned on Hilary just what her mother must be thinking. In shock and horror, she said, "Mother! I heard it said once that there was nothing so evil as the mind of a virtuous woman! Can you dare to think I have misbehaved myself? It would take a stronger will than mine to—misbehave, or worse, under the Lady Leonie's eye. Nor have I ever been tempted to—to misbehave in that way." She spoke firmly and with conviction; her mother looked skeptical.

"Oh, come, daughter, you forget I was a girl myself."

"Well, I can only think you must have been a different kind of girl!" Hilary snapped.

Lady Yllana said angrily, "How dare you speak to me that way?"

Hilary was instantly contrite, her voice thickening with unexpected tears. "Oh, Mother, I did not mean to be rude, but truly, Leonie told no more than the truth. And—" she flared, suddenly angry, "if you do not believe me, send for the midwife at Castamir and let her testify for herself."

"Hmph! The lady's no more than human," began Lady Yllana. But *Dom* Arnad interrupted, "Come, now, Yllana, you mustn't speak that way about the Lady Leonie. Let the girl sit down and rest. She looks frightfully tired."

"I am. Thank you, Papa," Hilary murmured and sank down on one of the old blackened-oak settles in the hall.

"Yes, rest a bit, my dear; you'll want to comb your hair and arrange it before dinner in the Hall," said her mother. "Oh, don't get that ridiculous look, child; you can't hide yourself away behind Tower walls as you've been doing for these last years. You're a part of this family now; and, like it or not, you might as well get used to the fact that you have duties to it. Oh, it's just the family of your brother's wife. You don't know Cassilda that well? Soon after we sent you to the Tower—" Hilary knew that in return for sending a daughter to the Tower, her brother's marriage to a lesser Hastur family's daughter had been arranged.

"I know Cassilda Di Asturien, yes," she said wearily. "I met her on one of my visits here a few years ago; she was pregnant then. I did not hear if her child was a girl or a boy." It must now, she thought, be three or nearer four years old.

The expected diversion was successful. In thinking of her grandchild, her mother forgot her younger daughter.

"The child is a boy," she said fondly. "I think I had written to you of that. He's about the same age as my own youngest; but I forgot. You have not yet seen your youngest sister."

"You did write me about that," Hilary said, grateful for the new turn the conversation had taken. "Maellen, is it not? It is not a family name; I am not familiar with it."

"Maellen," her mother replied. "There was a Hastur princess by that name, or so I am told; your father wished to name her Cassilda, but there is a Cassilda behind every tree in this Domain."

"And Maellen is now what—five?"

"You will see her at dinner," her mother answered. "Yes, five—a little older than my grandson, who is another Rafael, as if there were not enough Rafaels in the Domains." Her tone made it obvious that this was not her choice of name. "The boy should have been named for Despard's father—or for *her* father. Well, come along to dinner, my dear; you are really much too thin; you are not really ill, are you?"

Hilary wondered frantically what her mother *thought* they had been talking about. But her early training was strong; in compliance she rose, fumbling in the purse at her waist and taking out a little bone comb, with which she made a few hasty passes through her hair. Although earlier she had been hungry, having eaten nothing since they set forth that morning, she now felt the very smell of food would sicken her. She only wanted to lie down; but she knew her mother would not be dissuaded, and so she thought that the second best would be to sit quietly in a corner of the dining room.

"You're making rather a mess of that," her mother remarked, taking the comb from Hilary's shaking hands and tugging it briskly through the wind-tangled curls. "There; now you look a bit more civilized. Well, come along, my dear." She took Hilary's arm firmly in hers and, followed by Despard and her father, went into the hall.

"It looks just the same," she remarked. Her mother seized on the comment, and said in an aggrieved voice, "There, Arnad, I told you we should have the carpets or at least the curtains replaced; it's just as it was when Hilary and Despard were little children." Hilary wanted to say she had meant the phrase for compliment, but she knew her mother would not hear. She so seldom did.

At the end of the table, the place for honored guests, a woman was seated—a woman Hilary hardly recognized. This was the mother of Despard's wife Ginevra.

"Lady Cassilda," she said, "I wish to present my daughter Hilary; she is on leave from Arilinn Tower where she is in training to become a Keeper."

Hilary wondered why her mother had spoken in the present tense. Perhaps it was natural that her parents—her mother, anyway—would not wish to confess to having a failed Keeper in the family.

Well, sooner or later the woman would have to know; but perhaps she would not be here long enough. Lady Cassilda inquired politely about the health of Lady Leonie, to which Hilary replied that Leonie was well, but suffering from overwork at the moment. She felt the surge of Ginevra's unspoken criticism: *Why, then, are you here instead of being at her side?* Ginevra, of course, was too polite to speak it aloud. Hilary sat, unspeaking, letting Cassilda Hastur's disapproval flood over her. Someone passed her a platter of roast rabbit-horn and boiled whiteroot and she took some on her plate without bothering to see what it was. For all she knew, it could have been roast heart of banshee. She had grown unaccustomed to eating meat in Arilinn, where most of the Keepers were vegetarian by custom. She struggled to chew a bite but felt it would not go down. Her mother was talking quietly with Cassilda about some clever doings of their grandson. Hilary struggled to chew and swallow, knowing she dared not be sick here—nor would her mother be likely to excuse her so soon. With a fierce effort she managed to swallow. Her meals at Arilinn were usually taken alone, in peace. Crowded family affairs like this were rare, almost nonexistent. It was hard for her to eat at all, let alone remember proper table manners and protocol.

She tried to concentrate on what Despard was saying to her, and on the little girl who had come into the room. This, she guessed, was the little sister she had never met. Maellen had fine feathery red curls, and Hilary found herself wondering if the younger girl was enough of a telepath that she would be chosen for the Tower in some unknown future. It was, of course, far too early even to make an intelligent guess.

The little girl paused at her knee and asked "Are you my big sister Hilary? Mama told me about you."

"Yes, I am."

"Why aren't you in the Tower now?"

Hilary smiled. "Because I got ill, and they had to send me away."

"If you're ill," the child asked reasonably, "why aren't you in bed?"

That, Hilary thought, was an excellent question; it was a pity she did not have an equally excellent answer. At last she said, "Mama wanted me to be at dinner tonight."

"Oh." The child asked no more, and Hilary thought that, small as she was, the child already knew her mother was not to be questioned. "Can I sit in your lap?"

"If you like," Hilary said, and lifted the little girl to her knee. Maellen snuggled against her.

Cassilda Hastur, hearing them, asked, "Yes, Hilary; if you have come here from the Tower, how is it that you join us tonight?"

"I did as my parents willed," replied Hilary.

Despard interrupted, "Cassilda, I should like you to know my sister Hilary. . . ."

Lady Castamir interrupted, "But, Hilary, you are eating nothing. Do let me give you some of this excellent roast rabbit-horn," and placed a well-carved portion on Hilary's plate. Hilary distinguished herself by being very thoroughly sick all over the table and her neighbors.

ii

A little while later, when Hilary had been taken to bed, and the guests had departed, Lady Castamir stood angrily glaring at her.

"How could you behave so? Now the gods alone know what they'll be thinking."

"Nothing worse than what *you* seem to be thinking," Hilary interrupted.

Her mother glared at her. "Don't you be impertinent, Miss. Now that you have shown yourself in such shape before noble neighbors, how do you think we are to get you married?"

"Mother," said Hilary evenly, "I am not in any state to be married. This was one reason why they sent me home; if I was not well enough to remain at Arilinn, how could you think me well enough to marry?"

"Don't be foolish; if you are not to be Keeper, of course you must marry, and as soon as possible." Yllana Castamir snapped. "What other kind of life is there for a respectable young woman? And you are already seventeen."

"Hardly senile," Hilary commented. "And I could always cut my hair and become a Renunciate, as a daughter of Aillard recently did."

"Do be serious," her mother said crossly. "Women of our rank cannot do as we wish; there is a duty laid upon us. Of course, spending so many years in the Tower, doing as you please—"

Hilary thought that this was the last way she would have chosen to describe her years at Arilinn, constantly subject to Leonie's will.

"At least you have not been bound to carry out your duty to clan and family," her mother said harshly. "But now that you have been sent away, you *are* so bound. You will be well enough by the end of this tenday, I should hope, that we can arrange a small function. Once it is known that we have a marriageable daughter, all of our kinfolk will come, I imagine."

"I cannot keep you from imagining whatever you like," Hilary said wearily, feeling as if one of the Terrans' earth-moving machines had rolled over her. It did not matter what she said; her mother would not listen to her anyway.

iii

For the next three or four days, Hilary was carried along by her mother's brisk commands. A seamstress was summoned, and a number of beautiful dresses ordered. At any other time, Hilary would have been delighted; but it was so obvious that these were intended only to show her off in the marriage market, that she felt very cynical about them.

At the end of that tenday, her mother and father gave a small dance. Everyone from Syrtis and the nearby village came. Hilary, who did not feel much like dancing, spent much of the evening alone, listening to the musicians. Then her brother Despard led two young men to her.

"Rafael Hastur—the son of the Regent—and his paxman Rafael Syrtis," he said.

Young Rafael Hastur bowed; he was a handsome young man about thirty.

"I believe we may have met when we were children at just such an affair as this, *damisela;* it was the year before you were taken to the Tower."

"I remember," Despard said. "Hilary was too young to dance even with kinsmen, and so she and I watched the musicians from the top of the stairs. You two came upstairs with your sister Cassilda and we danced a set with the governess and the fencing-master."

Hilary smiled. "I remember, too," she said. "But I have spent so much time isolated in Arilinn that I have never danced at a public dance."

Rafael Hastur said, "Then I must just claim you as kin, *damisela*—or should I say, cousin—and take this dance. If you will honor me—" He held out his hands to her. She did not feel much like dancing, but she felt it would please her mother to see her dancing with the only son of the Hastur. Afterward, Rafael Syrtis said that if she was his lord's kin, she must accept him as kin, too; and she danced with him, and with Despard. Then she had to sit down with a glass of cider, to recover her strength. Her mother chose this time to ask if she had danced much. Hilary told her about the two Rafaels, and her mother snorted.

"A waste of time, my dear; Rafael Hastur is betrothed to his cousin Alata Elhalyn. As for the Syrtis boy, he's only the son of Lord Danvan's hawkmaster. He's reputed to be a lover of men *and* a *cristoforo*," she said. "And he wouldn't be any good to you; I heard he was pledged to one of the Hastur foster-children, but the girl's to be married to Kennard Alton. If Lord Hastur wouldn't have him for his own foster-kin, he wouldn't allow him to marry *you*."

"Mother," Hilary protested, "Don't you ever think about anything else?"

"Not until you're properly married off!" said Lady

Yllana and went off again, returning quickly with a burly red-haired man.

"*Dom* Edric Ridenow," she said, "allow me to present my daughter Hilary, who until a few days ago was pledged to the Arilinn Tower."

He bowed. "I believe you know my brother, Damon Ridenow," he remarked. "He has mentioned your name; he came from the Tower, and is now hospital-officer in the Guards."

"I know Damon quite well," Hilary said. "We were friends for many years and I think he was a close friend to Leonie, too."

As much, she thought, *as any man can be friend to a pledged Keeper.* Hilary had come to believe that, whatever reason Leonie had given for dismissing Damon, the older woman had begun to think of him in a way she must not lawfully think of any man. And so, of course, Damon had had to go. Hilary was happy to know he was in the Guards now. She hoped, sooner or later, that she would see him. *Now,* she thought, *if mother would scheme to marry me to him*—but she was sure no such idea would ever cross her mother's mind. No such luck.

"I suppose, since you are from Arilinn, you are fond of hunting, *damisela*?" Hilary was about to explain that the state of her health had not allowed her to do much riding or hawking, but Lady Yllana broke in.

"Certainly Hilary is fond of hawking," she said, her hands gripping Hilary's arm in a way that defied her to say a single word of denial. Edric smiled, his eyes taking in Hilary's *decolletage* in a way she did not like at all. She remembered Damon speaking of this brother scathingly as "the red fox."

But she could not help thinking that if he was Damon's brother, it was not altogether unlikely he should have some of Damon's virtues. And if it would make her mother happy, she might as well hunt with him; she did know a little of it. So it was arranged for the following day.

Before she went to bed that night, her mother burbled, "Aren't you excited, you silly girl? A Comyn lord, and it's all too obvious that the man's looking for a wife.

And he's heir to the head of the Domain! How would you like to be Lady Ridenow?"

Hilary felt somewhat shaky—it had been a long evening—but she said she could probably do worse, and her mother left her to sleep.

iv

The next morning Hilary woke, not feeling like hunting, or to tell the truth, doing anything whatever except staying where she was and sleeping. However, she knew what her mother would have said to that; so she got up and dressed, drank a little milk, and went down to her horse.

She found *Dom* Edric already there, aboard a great gray mare. She thought that even this substantial beast must bear his weight with some difficulty. *Dom* Edric was nothing at all like Damon: he was huge—gross, even—where Damon was slight and slender; he was rough-spoken where Damon was impeccably polite. And he looked at her—well, she thought, she must learn to expect that. She was no longer a Keeper, protected by her crimson robe. She wondered if all men in the world looked upon women like that—as if she were a sweet-shop window before a hungry small boy. If so, the task of readjustment would be harder than she had ever thought.

But perhaps he had never been taught otherwise. She could not expect him to behave with the courtesy of a Tower technician, but perhaps he did not know she found his look offensive. "I knew your brother Damon very well at Arilinn," she said. "Have you never spent time within Tower walls, *Dom* Edric?"

His laugh was as gross and mountainous as everything else about him. "Me? In a Tower? All Gods forbid, Lady Hilary. Damon's not my kind at all. Gods only know how the same dam whelped us both! I never thought too well of Damon. When he left the Tower, I hoped he'd become more the image of a man, but he hasn't. Men in the Tower are a sickly lot—no guts to any of 'em that I ever saw. O'course, one expects that in a lady," he simpered—there was really no other word for it—and Hilary's heart sank.

She said, "Damon told me once that most Comyn men are lacking in either brains or guts; it's rare to find them with both—"

"Aye," Edric answered, "Damon got the brains and I got the guts."

And you're proud of it, Hilary thought. A man of Edric's type could brag of having no brains, and was unwilling to credit his brother with courage. It was not so much that Damon lacked courage, as that Edric lacked imagination. She said so, and Edric remarked, "Aye, and I thank the Gods for it. As I see it, imagination's all very well for the ladies; but who wants a man with so much imagination that he can't act when he must?"

I, for one, Hilary thought. Already she knew Edric had too little *laran* to read her thoughts. *Well,* she thought doggedly, *he may have other virtues.* She put all of her energies to the task of staying in the saddle; she was at the best of times only an indifferent rider.

After being Keeper at Arilinn, the thought of being married off to someone completely lacking in *laran* seemed to Hilary all too much like being coupled with a dumb animal. But her mother, who had precious little *laran* of her own, was unlikely to think of that as a reason for stopping any such marriage. Hilary braced herself for the proposal she knew was coming, and steeled herself to do what her family required. *No one,* she thought, *escapes a marriage of this kind. I have known that since I was younger than Maellen. . . .*

The cool air had put some color in her cheeks and Hilary did not realize how pretty she looked in her riding habit. She knew that she was nice-looking; men had looked at her since she was thirteen years old, but her status as Keeper had protected her from any but the subtlest and most genteel approaches. She knew that *Dom* Edric could—and should—look upon her with desire. This did not precisely revolt her. She had known some women who had been given in marriage to men indifferent to women, and knew how unfortunate they were. Hard as it was to be given in marriage to a desire she had carefully been trained not to feel, there were many women who suffered at finding themselves married to a man who kept his desires for a handsome guardsman, or worse, some horrid little pageboy.

The intensity of Edric's stare disquieted her; she did not much like him, and almost for the first time Hilary thought what it would be like to be bound to a man who could never share her innermost self. She had known so few men except the telepaths of Arilinn, and now she was being offered openly to this crude person who boasted of his lack of imagination and sensitivity as if they were virtues. It was not a good life to which to look forward; but if this was her duty, she thought, trying to quell her rebellious spirit, she would marry Edric. And after all, what alternative did she have? She had hoped she would be given a few months to readjust; she should have known better.

Edric had drawn his horse up close to hers. He smiled and said, "I'm a plain man, Hilary; I won't beat around the bush. You must know that my family and yours are both looking forward to marrying us off. Does that suit you?"

Hilary thought, *at least he has the virtue of honesty.* She looked up at him with a little more liking because of it, and said, "It's true. My mother told me that you had come here looking for a wife."

Edric asked, "And shall I ask you formally to marry me, then?"

She said demurely, "If that is what you wish to do." *Why,* she thought, *perhaps the poor fellow is only inarticulate, then,* and smiled.

He said, "We will consider it done, then," and added, "I am hungry; perhaps we should tell your mother when we stop for lunch."

"If you like. I think it will make her very happy," said Hilary. She did not really feel much like eating, and did not see how he could be hungry after his enormous breakfast; but perhaps the poor fellow only gobbled because he was shy and could not think of anything else to do. She knew that some of the younger men in the Towers gobbled greedily to conceal nervousness; and it occurred to her that she might like Edric all the better for a few faults.

"Well, we've had no hunting yet," he said, deftly unhooding his falcon and letting it fly. Hilary had done little hunting at Arilinn, although a few of the women were avid falconers, some even training their own birds. So she watched with interest as the falcon soared aloft. Damon, she knew, had been a most competent falconer; and little Callista was already adept enough with her own—a great hawk like Edric's.

Edric's falcon was not unlike Damon's favorite bird; she said so, and Edric replied without much interest, "It probably is Damon's. I've always felt falconry was a sport mostly for women; certainly no man I know, except for Damon, cares to handle birds that much. Well, better him than me, I reckon. If he wants to train falcons for all the ladies, it saves me the trouble of worrying about a strange falconer on the place. But, when you're married to me, and Damon trains your falcons, make sure that's *all* he does for you."

Hilary blushed. His meaning was unmistakable even without the aid of telepathy, and the remark came just short of being improper. Her father, or Despard, or Damon, would never have spoken so in her presence— and certainly would not have grinned and chuckled so suggestively. Still, she clung to the thought that a man speaking to his promised wife need not observe so many courtesies.

Edric's eyes were on the falcon; Hilary could not see so far, but Edric put spurs to his horse and raced toward where she could just see it descending on some small wild thing in the grass. By the time she reached it he was standing in his saddle, crossly calling off one of the dogs. The quarry was probably a squirrel; it was being torn to pieces by falcon and dogs, and there was nothing left of it except a few scraps of blood-stained fur.

Edric scowled. "Hardly worth the trouble; still, it makes a man hungry." Hungry, Hilary thought, was the last thing it made her feel. In fact, she felt as if she would not want to eat again for a long, long time. Still, she controlled herself, knowing her mother would be very vexed if she showed any sign of distaste.

The hunting party returned home, and it was not long before the entire family was gathered. Edric said to her father, "Hilary and I have something to tell you, and I hope you will be pleased, sir."

Her mother asked, "Does this mean, *Dom* Edric, that there's a wedding in the offing?" Edric nodded gruffly, and her mother smiled at Hilary; it had been a long time since her mother had looked so approvingly at her.

Her father glanced doubtfully at Edric, and then said, "Whatever Hilary wants is fine with me," and gave Edric a hearty handclasp, following it with a warm hug.

Despard grinned and said "Whatever Hilary wants—if this is your choice, sister—"

Her father was opening a bottle of homemade apple wine. "I laid this wine down before Despard was born," he said. "We drank the first of it at his wedding and now we shall celebrate Hilary's upcoming marriage."

Hilary accepted a goblet and drank in her turn. Then weariness and exhaustion overcame her, and she collapsed into her father's arms.

She came to herself a little when she was carried up the stairs. "It was only—the smell of blood—" she tried to explain, and lost consciousness. When she woke, Edric was gone. Her mother, at the bedside, looked cross.

"I hope you realize, you foolish girl, what you've done," she said angrily. "*Dom* Edric was most apologetic, but he said that he must have a wife who is neither sickly nor frail. He fears you cannot give him a healthy son, Hilary; the Ridenows have been free of the infertility which has plagued so many of the Domains, and he dares not pledge himself to an unhealthy woman."

"Good enough for him," said Despard wrathfully. "Why doesn't he go marry the swineherd's daughter, if that's all he wants in a woman?"

Domna Yllana was beyond speech as she looked at Hilary. When she found her voice, she snarled, "Well, I've done my best; I wash my hands of you!"

No such luck, Hilary thought. But she might, at least, get a couple of months to recover her strength.

"Yes, Mother," she said weakly. Her eyes caught Despard's behind *Domna* Yllana's back and he smiled.

Hilary's Wedding

by Marion Zimmer Bradley

"I don't understand you at all, Hilary," *Domna* Yllana said with a look of frustration. "Your own wedding gown, and it might as well be a new pinafore for your sister. I never had anything so fine till after Despard was born; if I had, I would have been wild with excitement. One would think it was someone else's wedding, not yours at all."

It isn't mine, thought Hilary, *it's yours and Papa's—the one you would have liked to have.* However, she had learned by now not to say so. She turned around, asking, "What is it, Maellen?" as her youngest sister came into the room.

"Mama, there are messengers from Armida, and Lord Damon himself is with them; he has a message for you." Maellen was now a coltish eleven, all knees and elbows, protruding gawkily from her torn pinafore, her red curls tangled and half uncurled.

"Oh, dear, I hope you did not greet him looking like *that,* Maellen," her mother said, but broke off as Damon Ridenow himself came into the room and bent over Hilary's hand.

"Don't scold her, I beg of you, *vai domna,*" he said to *Domna* Yllana; "I have come to bid you to a naming-feast at Armida, and of course Callista bade me come to you first of all."

"Oh, has Ellemir borne her child? She will be so happy!" Hilary exclaimed.

"No," Damon said, "Next tenday, perhaps; she is still dragging about, as big as the side of the barn, or so it seems. No, Callista bore Andrew a daughter ten days gone, and she wishes to call her daughter 'Hilary'; so I

143

came to you to be certain you were not of those who thinks it ill luck to name a child after a living person."

"No, of course I am not," said Hilary, delighted. "I shall have a naming-gift for the little one. Is Callista well, then? And Ellemir?"

Damon grinned—as happily, Hilary thought, as if the child were his own. "I am happy to say that both are well, and barring something unforeseen," he made a superstitious gesture, "this time, all Gods be thanked, nothing will go wrong."

"I am so happy for Ellemir," Hilary said, "I have not seen either of them since the wedding." It had been quite a scandal in the country round. The twins of Armida had been married, Ellemir to Damon and Callista to a stranger, a Terran, named Anndra Carr—and that not by the *catenas* but in a simple freemate declaration before witnesses. But both marriages, as far as she knew, had gone well, and the folk at Armida were no less popular than ever. Of course, whatever an Alton of Armida chose to do was assumed to be well done.

Damon touched Hilary's hand; his eyes fell on the wedding gown on the rack. "Yours? May I ask when the wedding is to be held?"

"We were making ready to send out messages bidding you to the wedding," Hilary said, "I could not possibly be married without my oldest friend in attendance." She recalled, on the day she left Arilinn, Damon had met with her in the courtyard and had kissed her in farewell—the first human touch she had borne in seven years.

He said, with a trace of the old familiarity, "So you are to have a wedding. I hope it may be as lucky as mine; a marriage should be a happy thing. Do I know the fortunate man?"

Hilary thought, *Probably better than I do,* but aloud she only said, "I believe you knew him when you were cadet-master in the Guard. His name is Farrill Lindir; he has four children by his first wife, so he need not care if I do not give him a son."

"Oh, Hilary," *Domna* Yllana interrupted in despair. "Isn't she dreadful, Damon? Why, her health is so much improved. I beg of you, Lord Damon, don't listen to her! No doubt, at this time next year, he'll be sending out a bidding to a naming-feast at Miron Lake."

"I certainly hope he does not count upon that," Hilary interrupted. "If it is a child he wants, no doubt he'll return me like a sack of grain from the mill; but he wishes for a noble wife, one of unquestioned birth and position. But no doubt he has heard of why my betrothal to Edric Ridenow went amiss; and everyone for miles around knows my health is not that much improved. Nor do I care much for babes—I would rather it was me he wanted, not a brood mare."

Domna Yllana interrupted, "Surely this is no seemly speech for a maid almost on the eve of her marriage!" but Damon laughed.

"So Callista has said many times; but now that her own child is more than a vague idea, she is not only reconciled to having her but has become fond enough of her daughter. And if she were not, there are more than enough women in the Domain for that." He smiled at Hilary, ignoring her mother, and said, "It was a gift of Arilinn which kept this child for me; you know after Ellemir's first child was born so much too soon, it was a woman from the college of midwives at Arilinn Village who told Ellemir what she should do to keep her from such misfortune this time. And so I will soon invite you to the naming feast of my own first son."

Hilary said with an attempt at formality, "I am happy for you, Damon; I know how much Ellemir has wanted a child." She thought *If it had been you came courting me instead of Edric*— She quickly dropped that thought, knowing Damon would pick it up. *But when we both dwelt in the Tower, I was but a little girl—and Callista even more so—and he could never see any woman but Leonie.* Knowing Damon would pick that up, too, she looked away from him with a new shyness.

Damon bent and kissed the tips of her fingers, "May you be as happy as I am with Ellemir, *breda*," he said. Hilary stood on tiptoe and brushed his cheek with her lips, then withdrew, coloring a little, as she saw her mother's eyes upon them.

When Damon had left them, *Domna* Yllana scowled. "You wretched girl! Why, if you wanted to be married, did you not make sure of *Dom* Damon before ever you left the Tower?"

"Mother," Hilary protested, "when Damon left the Tower, I was young and had never thought of any future but to be Keeper at Arilinn. I thought no more of Damon that way than of one of my father's grooms!" And she thought, *I am afraid to ask how she thinks I should have made sure of him, or how that would have availed me anything but for both of us being sent away for misconduct.*

Domna Yllana's cheeks reddened with a dull color, and—not for the first time—Hilary suspected her mother had some *laran*, though flawed and incomplete. But *Domna* Yllana only said aloud, "We have on our estate somewhere, too, a midwife trained at Arilinn. If she helped Lady Ellemir, we should have her look at you."

"Perhaps," Hilary said, and hoped her mother would forget it again.

But nothing much happened that day on the estate but for a long colloquy with the cooks about the cakes and wine to be served at the wedding. Personally, Hilary thought this was a lot of fuss for nothing; they had vetoed her first choice of an apple nut cake.

"I can't imagine why, since I am to be the bride in question, and it is *my* favorite cake," Hilary protested.

But *Domna* Yllana only laughed and said, "Don't be silly, it isn't at all a suitable cake for a wedding. *Dom* Farrill would think I didn't know what was proper!"

When Hilary stubbornly requested further explanation, her father pinched her cheek and said, "I don't understand either, my love; but your mother knows about these things and I don't. Better listen to her." Hilary, realizing he was probably right, had said no more.

The wedding gown was finished and hung in Hilary's clothespress. She had tried it on, but when she wanted to show it to her father and Despard, her mother had said harshly that it was ill-luck for anyone but the bride and her attendants to see her dressed before the wedding. Hilary wondered why, then, it would not be bad luck for her mother to see it; and since *Domna* Yllana had fashioned it for her, how her mother could have made it without seeing it. Again, she knew better than to ask.

It was only a day later when the horsemen rode into the courtyard. The foremost among them said they were from Lake Miron and asked, "Is it you, *damisela* Hilary, who was to marry *Dom* Farrill?"

"It is I," Hilary returned with poise and self-possession; but she already knew, from the man's taut face, what news he would give her. She heard him say it, like an echo. *Dom* Farrill had been thrown by a half-broken horse, and his head had split open. That last detail they thought to spare her, only calling it a riding accident; but she knew it anyway.

She felt no great personal grief, for she had barely known the man; but it was a dreadful thing for a young life to be so suddenly snuffed out. "I cannot tell you how greatly I regret this," she said, shaking her head sadly; inwardly, she felt nothing but a relief she was too worldly-wise to show. She offered the riders refreshment, already knowing her mother's grief would be greater than her own.

Indeed, when *Domna* Yllana heard the news, she was as shaken as if she had lost a son. It was she who felt it necessary to tell the riders that Hilary was truly heartbroken, but too dignified and self-possessed to show her grief publicly.

When Hilary expressed her true feelings to her father, he looked troubled. "Don't say such things before your mother; she was really looking forward to your wedding."

"I know," said Hilary, making a face. "Between ourselves, rather more than I was."

He looked at her guiltily. "I know; also between ourselves, I'm not sorry to keep my little girl a few more years. How old are you now, my darling?"

"Nearly twenty-three," Hilary said, grimacing. "A confirmed old maid for certain."

He looked abashed. "Oh, surely there is time enough," he said, and hugged her.

Domna Yllana seemed resigned. She said crossly to Hilary, "I suppose even Maellen will be married before you will! I knew when you wanted to show Arnad your wedding gown that some evil would come of it," she added with a grim look as if she had foreseen all this. Trying to comfort her, Hilary agreed to consult the Free Amazon midwife on the estate; she had never been willing to speak with the woman before. But now she thought it might be a good thing to be completely well again.

A couple of days later *Domna* Yllana brought the midwife to her. To Hilary's surprise, the Renunciate did not wear the riding garb she had always associated with Renunciates, but an ordinary skirt and overdress. Her hair was fastened in a net. Hilary, looking closely, saw that the skirt was cut somewhat shorter than most dresses—for riding, probably.

"I am astonished you do not appear like the Guild House Renunciates, with short hair and breeches."

"Oh, I wear breeches when I must, but when I am in the villages, I dress so as not to alienate the women I must serve—or their husbands," the woman said, her eyes twinkling.

"What is your name, *mestra*?"

"Allier n'ha Ferrika, my lady."

"And—how old are you?" Hilary asked with real curiosity. "You look no older than I."

"I probably am not," the woman said. "I was twenty-two a few days before Midsummer. I learned this work at my mother's knee; I have been doing it since I was fifteen. Women of my kind, my lady, work from the time they are big enough to gather eggs."

"I am twenty-two also," Hilary said, "and I worked long and hard when I was in Arilinn." And as she spoke, she thought, *But now I am doing nothing! A working woman like this must despise me for my idleness.*

"I dwelt for a couple of years in Arilinn, to learn the midwife's art," the woman said. "I saw you, from time to time, riding out with the old sorceress; I doubt not at all that your life in the Tower was harder than mine in the Guild House."

Hilary flushed; had the woman been reading her thoughts? After a moment she put the question.

"No, my lady; I am not of those gifted with *laran*, but in Arilinn everyone knows how hard the sons and daughters of the Comyn must work, and what a toll it may take of them. And my mother's favorite apprentice works at Armida. She came there to care for Lady El-lemir, and she saw how hard it was for Lady Callista to cast off those same shackles. Everyone in Arilinn knew you were not as healthy and strong as the Lady Callista." She colored a little. "I fear in Arilinn—as everywhere else in the Domains, my lady—we have not much better to do than speak of the comings and goings of our bet-ters," she said defensively. "Surely you know how women gossip. Perhaps they should not, but they do, and that's all there is to it."

"Oh, I'm familiar enough with that," Hilary said. "Even here on my father's estate I am gossiped about enough. And I know that in Arilinn, a mouse can hardly stir in the walls before half the people in the countryside are offering us kittens to catch it. I grew used to that my first year there." It was not particularly pleasant to think that her health had been discussed throughout the midwives college there; but it was simply part of living in Arilinn, which, after all, carried enough privileges that she must accept its few disadvantages as well. She grinned almost mischievously at the woman.

"Fair enough; I suppose you heard also when my mar-riage with Lord Edric Ridenow came to nothing."

Allier said quickly, "Only that there had been talk of some such alliance, but it ended because of your ill-health. Did you want very much to marry him, my lady?"

Hilary could not keep from laughing. "I think I could have borne the loss without weeping," she said, "but my mother was wonderfully cross. That is why she has sent for you, that my health may not lose us another valuable alliance. My mother feels that it will be a disgrace if I am not properly married off before my younger sister Maellen is old enough to wed."

Allier looked straight at her. "And you are willing to be married off that way, my lady?"

Hilary shrugged a little. She said equivocally, "It will please my mother if I am not ill; and what is more, I cannot abide the thought of continuing to spend ten days of every forty in bed. I have already made enough embroidered pieces for a dozen or more hope chests for myself and Maellen, and I am weary of it."

Allier smiled. "Well, we shall see what can be done."

Hilary felt that Allier had really been asking her something else, but she was not sure quite what.

"Tell me, what remedies have they given you?"

"I have drunk enough golden-flower tea to drown the very Tower itself, both here and in Arilinn. And there have been many other things as well—I cannot remember them all—black hawberries, bitter herbs, in fact everything they could think of."

"Ah, some herb-wives would treat the black rot with a dose of golden-flower. Have you—" she hesitated, then asked, "Forgive me, my lady. Have you miscarried a child? Or did anyone give you a potion to rid you of an unwanted child?"

Hilary chuckled.

"No," she said. "I do not think the Goddess Avarra herself could manage to conceive a child under Leonie's sharp eyes. I dared not even think of such things in her presence! I have had no opportunity, and I am not an oathbreaker."

"True; even *laran* has its drawbacks." The young Renunciate agreed.

"Nor, I must say, has the man been born who would or could tempt me from my vows. No, not even Damon," Hilary said. "You may believe that or not—my mother does not—but it is true."

"I have no *laran*," the woman said, "but I know when I am being told the truth. I believe you, my lady."

Hilary sighed and relaxed. "What do you think you can do for me?"

"I can promise you nothing; but we know more about these things than women before us knew. In Leonie's time it was fashionable to say the sickness was in the mind; and while a sickness in the mind can be harder to cure than one of the body, there were those who thought if the illness was all in the mind, it was just a matter of making up your mind to be free of it."

Hilary sighed "I know; I have lost count of those who thought my illness all in the mind. Even Leonie, I think, kind as she always was, never ceased to believe that I was making myself ill in some way that she, and certainly I, did not understand."

"We know better now," Allier told her. "Whether or not we can make you entirely well is not within my knowledge; but we will try."

"Thank you, Allier," Hilary said. "And you know, now that I think on it, I truly do not wish to be married off for my family name nor for the children I might have, even though it is the fate of almost every woman in the Domains."

"I would be the last to think ill of you for that," Allier said. "Of course, that is the one fate a Renunciate need never fear."

Hilary sighed. "Alas, I have neither talent nor will to defy my family and live as a Renunciate, even were such a path open to me. I fear I could not face my family and wage war for that right, although such as you will think me cowardly for believing so."

Allier smiled. "Courage is of all kinds," she remarked. "I have often said that you strove with more courage in Arilinn than I would ever have had. I would have given in and come home within three months. You were there, I think, for almost seven years. No, my lady, *coward* is not a word I would ever use for you."

After this, they returned to the subject of what the woman thought could be done for Hilary. They soon agreed that she should ride with Allier to her home in the village, since Hilary was experiencing one of her episodes of reasonable health. It would be convenient to have the Renunciate's supply of herbs and medicines close at hand.

"We will try one of the simpler remedies first," Allier said. "Even if it does you no good, it will do no harm. With some of the stronger remedies, you must be watched carefully day and night, and I am not free this tenday to take leave of my other patients and stay near enough to you to make certain that you have no trouble."

"That is pleasing to me," Hilary said. "But the old woman on the estate has already dosed me with enough of her brews that I have little faith in any of them."

"Still, we will try them," Allier said. "And if I were

you, I would not undervalue the power of faith; but I believe you have already put the work of faith to the test. Here." She alighted from her saddle horse, and went into her small cabin; Hilary followed and found the woman rummaging among the flasks and vials on a long shelf. She asked Hilary, "Do you know anything of the healer's art, my lady?"

"Very little. Callista knows much more of herbs than I," Hilary said. "But I know enough to know that your equipment is of the best. I think we had hardly so much in the Tower itself."

"Perhaps not, for I know something of the Terran medical arts; their medical men and women make use of remedies more powerful than those at my command. Only at last resort would I make use of those with you. And before doing so, I must consult with my Terran colleagues."

Hilary shook her head; "I dare say my mother would be afraid of this kind of consultation."

"Well, perhaps it will not come to that."

Although Hilary did not share the exaggerated fear of the Terrans that some of the less educated men and woman in the Domains had, she hoped fervently it would not, indeed, come to that. Allier packed up some of her medicines in a bag that fitted to her saddle, and added a few candies flavored with sweetroot. "I promised your little sister some of these," she said.

As they came out into the courtyard, they found a young man waiting. Allier bowed to him.

"Vai dom?"

The young man made a deep bow to Hilary. She recognized him as one of the youngsters who had been at Arilinn for half a year while she was there. "Forgive me for disturbing you, Lady Hilary. I have brought *Mestra* Allier one of my mother's favorite dogs. I think she has a bone in her throat, and it is beyond my skill or that of the beast-leech on our estate. If I might trouble you, *mestra. . . .*"

"Let me see her," said Allier, getting down from her horse. "Ah, poor creature," she crooned. The little dog, small and silky, whined and whimpered and drooled in distress.

"Do what you can for her, and my mother will be suitably grateful."

"Master Colin, I would do as much for any stray mongrel; but you must must hold her head for me." She signaled and Colin climbed off his pony and took the little dog's head. "So. There. There, poor girl—" she patted the dog's head, and bent over her with her long, sharpened forceps. "Hold her, so—good dog, good girl—" A moment later, having extracted the bone, she patted the little dog's head and set her down; the dog licked her hands and whimpered with relief.

Young Colin smiled "I am very grateful to you, *mestra*. She is my mother's pet, and Mother would not have lost her for any amount of gold. How can I repay you?"

"Feed her no more bones of birds; dogs can chew many bones, but not those. For myself I need nothing, *vai dom;* only tell your mother that when anyone speaks ill of the Renunciates in her hearing, to speak no evil of us herself, even if she cannot in conscience come to our defense."

Colin sighed; "I fear that will not be easy to ask of my mother, for she does not know any of you personally; but I will bear her the word. And no one shall speak ill of your Order in *my* hearing; that I vow to you." He fumbled in a purse. Allier shook her head, but he said, "For anyone in the village who cannot pay for your aid, then," and the woman tucked the gold coin into her purse. "I thank you, *dom;* some of these old women cannot pay for bandages or linen even for a shroud."

Colin bowed and rode away, and Allier said to Hilary, "Do you then know *Dom* Colin of Syrtis?"

"I know him; he was for some months at Arilinn."

"Perhaps he did not speak to you because he was anxious for the little dog. Or perhaps, not expecting to see you here, he did not recognize you."

"Oh, but he called me by name," Hilary protested. It troubled her a little to think that Colin might not have wanted to speak with her. Or did he think her still sacrosanct, Keeper, not even to be spoken to as a friend? Or even—oathbreaker? Had he not heard that she had been sent away from the Tower? Did he, perhaps, despise her for that?

A few days later, Hilary and her family rode to Armida for the naming-feast of Callista's daughter. She did not at first see Ellemir, but as she bent over the cradle in which the younger Hilary lay, Damon came into the room. He admired the baby's gift from Hilary, a golden locket with a lovely green stone, not precious, but both tasteful and pretty, at its center. Then he turned to Hilary and said, "Ellemir is still abed. She bore me a son two days ago, and I would like to show him to you."

"I should like nothing better, Damon, though I do not know Lady Ellemir nearly so well as Callista. I am sorry I have nothing but goodwill to bring as a gift; I did not know the boy had been born. Yes, Damon, I would be happy to see your son."

Damon smiled and led her up the stairs to a room where Callista was attending Ellemir. As she approached, a familiar form straightened up from where she was bent over the cradle.

"Greetings *vai domna;* I am glad to see you so well," Allier said, cheerfully. "How do you like this fine boy?"

"He is beautiful, Damon; I am very happy for you." Now, whatever should happen to Ellemir, Damon might remain at Armida by right; and she had never seen him look so content.

"Do you like my son, *vai domna*?" asked Ellemir.

Hilary bent and kissed the tiny face; the baby wrinkled up his red features and began to scream. Allier put him into Ellemir's arms.

Hilary said, "He is beautiful, Ellemir, though he does not seem to like me as much as I like him! And not *vai domna,* but Hilary. Damon is my oldest friend from Arilinn."

Ellemir smiled, even though she did not look perfectly happy; Hilary knew that she was somewhat jealous of the hold his old friends from Arilinn had on Damon. Still, sooner or later Ellemir must know she was no threat where Damon was concerned—no more than Hilary's brother Despard or her own little sister. At that moment the door swung wide, and young Colin Syrtis came into the room.

"I have a gift for your son, Damon," he said, and then broke off, staring at Hilary.

"I am glad to see you looking so well, *vai domna*. So Damon has been showing you our new little Guardsman?"

"Oh—I knew not that this boy was destined for the Guards—is it so, Damon?"

Damon grinned and said, "That destiny no Comyn son can escape if he has two sound legs and his eyesight."

Hilary said, looking at the child's clear blue eyes, "That he has, at least, and I am glad of it. But it is possible he may, like his father, be destined for the Tower."

"He will not," said Damon, "Others have more of foresight than I; but he will not enter a Tower, that I know."

"I trust, then, that he may at least be a good Guardsman," said Hilary, and Colin grinned. "No question of that; not with Damon for his father! May I ride home with you, *damisela*? There is something I would say to your mother and father."

"I should welcome it," Hilary said demurely.

She was pleased with Colin's company, which made the long road less tiresome. As they neared Castamir, he said abruptly, "Are you not even curious about what I would say to your parents, Hilary?"

She sighed, forced to take note of it again.

She said slowly, "I wish it had not come up. I suppose you are going to ask my mother and father for permission to request my hand in marriage; but my mother will be so disappointed when your family makes it clear that you must have a healthy wife, capable of giving you children. I will, I confess, feel very sorry when that happens. I would rather have a friend than a suitor."

She went on doggedly, "We have been friends; and at this moment I would rather have you as a friend than marry any man the Gods ever made. I do not have so many friends as that."

Colin looked at her and sighed. He asked, "Why should you believe that it must inevitably come to nothing, Hilary? Or that we cannot remain friends, whether we marry or not?"

She sighed, too, then said warily, "Because you are akin to Comyn and must have a wife who can give you healthy sons. I am sure you have heard that I have been three times handfasted, and each time, the man or his parents have broken the contract; it is not likely that your parents would allow you to marry me."

"As for that," Colin said, "I am a third son; and I know what havoc arises in a family with too many sons. Like Damon's, my family had five sons, all but one of whom lived and thrived. I cannot offer you a Domain, but the best of it is that at least I may marry to please myself, and not the Head of my family. And so, Hilary, I do not intend to consult them."

"But your mother and father would wish you to marry someone of a more powerful family."

"If they do—and I do not think they do—they may wish for whatever they like, but I am not obliged to pay heed. Believe me, Hilary, I do not intend to marry at their or anyone else's bidding."

Hilary could not keep a tinge of bitterness out of her voice.

"Well, you may ask—for all the good I think it will do you."

Colin said gently, "I wish only to ask if such a request would displease you, Hilary."

Hilary laughed a little. "Oh, no," she said, "I thought I had made that clear; I only did not wish to face disappointment when the marriage plans come to nothing—as I am sure they will."

"That is all I ask," Colin said gently.

Later that day Hilary's father called her into the room. "An offer has been made for you, sweetheart; would it please you to be married into the Syrtis family?"

"It would please me greatly," said Hilary truthfully. "Colin spoke of this to me—no, do not be cross with him, Papa, he only asked me if such a request would be distasteful to me."

"And what answer did you give to him?"

"I told him I should like it very much," she answered.

"I confess, I hope these arrangements do not fall through." Had it really come to pass that she was being married for herself, and not for the sake of a dynastic alliance? The Syrtis folk had been Hastur allies for many years, and she still feared when they knew of Hilary's poor health, his family would not like it.

But as the months went by and she met *Domna* Camilla, she began to believe in her good fortune, to be married to a man she actually knew and thought well of; and she liked Colin's parents. Actually, she found herself wishing they had been her own parents. She felt a little guilty about that. The folk of Syrtis were richer than her own people, and she felt guilty about that, too. Maybe, she thought, that was why they cared less about the trappings of the wedding. Or perhaps, with so many sons, they were simply getting used to weddings by now.

Meanwhile, the Renunciate had been trying various of her medicines and potions on Hilary; so far, none of them had had much effect on her, although some seemed to make matters worse. One afternoon Hilary felt quite tired, and had stayed in bed. She was listlessly playing a game of castles with Maellen when *Domna* Yllana brought her up word that Colin's mother had called and wished to see her.

"Of course she must not see you like this!" *Domna* Yllana's voice was filled with distress. "What would she think?"

Hilary found it too much trouble to think. Whatever Allier had given her had made her much drowsier than golden-flower, but as far as she could tell, had had no other effect.

"Perhaps she will think I am really sick, and that I am not pretending illness to escape marrying her son?" she inquired.

"Hilary, what a dreadful thing to say!"

"Well, it's what *you* think, isn't it?"

"Of course not, darling; but couldn't you make just a little effort? To get up and come downstairs?"

Hilary said dizzily, "No, I couldn't. I thought you learned that from my first night here; do you really want me to throw up in the noble lady's lap?"

Hilary did not really care about much of anything. Allier's potion had made her feel drowsy; it was simply too much trouble to put her mind to anything at all. Of course, her mother could not let it go at that; she fussed over Hilary interminably, insisting that the girl comb her hair and put on a fresh and pretty bed jacket. When at last Lady Syrtis came into the room, Hilary was groggy and exhausted. Maellen had successfully resisted her mother's admonitions to go and get into a fresh pinafore. "It's not me the noble lady's coming to see," she had announced, and settled down where she was, on Hilary's bed.

Lady Syrtis greeted Maellen, then looked anxiously at Hilary's pale face. Hilary's mother left the room to prepare refreshments.

"I did not mean for you to put yourself to any trouble, my girl," she said. "I can see that you are not well. I beg of you," she added, "don't trouble yourself to sit up. I wished only to know if you had any preferences about the wedding."

"None whatever," Hilary said faintly. "If I had my preferences, it would be as small and private a ceremony as might be."

Lady Syrtis said almost regretfully, "I wish I had known that earlier; I have already invited many of our kin, and I cannot now ask them not to come, or they may feel that some of us have something to conceal. I am sorry; if I had known you felt that way, I would have asked only the family. But your mother gave me to understand you wanted full ceremony, and we were anxious to honor you."

Hilary sighed. There was no reason to create enmity between her mother and her new relatives, so she said, "I believe my mother must have misunderstood something I said when I was a child too young to understand how much trouble such a wedding could be. Believe me, I am not eager for ceremony. I had enough of that in Arilinn to last me a lifetime."

"I can well believe it, my dear," said Lady Syrtis. "I do wish I had known; but for now, rest well and try to grow strong." She bent and kissed Hilary, patted the cheek of the silent Maellen, and withdrew.

Hilary had almost fallen asleep again when her mother came into the room; one glance told Hilary she was angry.

"What is this you have been telling Lady Syrtis? That you do not want a big ceremony?"

"She did say that," Maellen, still at the foot of the bed, pointed out. "I heard her."

"Silence, Miss," commanded Lady Castamir. "Well, Hilary, have you made fools out of all of us here?"

No, Hilary thought, *you have done that admirably for yourself.* But she did not say so. "Mother, I said only that if it had been left to me, I would have been content with repeating my vows before our two families; but you and Papa would not have it so."

"Don't be foolish, my girl. If you sequester yourself on your wedding day, they will all think you have something to hide."

"I know, Mother," Hilary said placatingly. "I know it has gone too far for that; but I beg you, speak no more of ceremony for this wedding! It is already as if you were planning the marriage of King Stefan."

"It is only for our daughter and our close relatives," said her mother with a definite sense of injury. "And it is all for your sake, my love." She went out, and soon returned, saying that Colin was below, and would speak with his bride. "Now, don't for heaven's sake say anything of this to him," she demanded. Hilary, already feeling like a captive of some great Terran earth-moving machine, promised.

A few days later, Hilary, feeling much better, rode out with Colin to Allier's cottage. The woman was in her courtyard readying herself for a trip to the village as Colin rode into the yard.

"A word with you, *mestra.*"

"We must speak here; we have no Stranger's Room as we do in a proper Guild House If we allowed strange men to come within, what sort of house do you think the villagers would take it for?"

"I had never thought of that," Colin said. "There is a proverb, 'Surely there is nothing so evil as the mind of a virtuous woman.' "

"Unless," said Allier, "it is the mind of a virtuous man. Still, those minds and tongues do exist; and I must live with them."

"My promised wife is with me," Colin said, as Hilary rode into the yard. "I truly think she is chaperon enough against those evil tongues."

"Oh, to be sure," Allier said. "Come in, Lady Hilary, while *Dom* Colin puts up the horses."

"With pleasure," Hilary said. She entered the woman's little cottage, sat down, and told her everything.

"I feel so guilty because I have let things go this far," Hilary confessed. "I don't know how I can stop it now."

"Nothing is easier, but it does need some courage," Allier commented. "Just say to your mother that you do not want a grand festival."

"But that makes it sound—oh, dear—ungrateful for all the trouble she has taken," Hilary said. "I do not want to alienate her."

"Then I do not see that you have any choice," Allier said. "You are, in fact, ungrateful, but you do not want to anger her by saying so."

"How well you know me," Hilary answered, a little ruefully. "I don't have the courage of—of my father's wake-hounds. They, at least, will bark to wake up the night watchman."

"No, you are not very good at barking, Hilary," Allier said. "Could you speak of this to Colin?"

"Oh, yes," Hilary said. "I think I could speak of *anything* to Colin."

"Well, I am relieved at that," Allier said, "For if there was anything of which you could not speak to Colin, I would certainly say you should not marry him."

Hilary asked, "Is that Renunciate wisdom?" One of the first things she had learned from her mother as a small child was that, as a matter of course, there were many things which could not be said to Papa.

"No, it is only plain common sense," Allier replied. "I would not marry except as a freemate—my oath prevents it; but even if I were free, I would not marry a man from whom I felt I must conceal anything. You have already made a good start on this by insisting on telling Colin of your health problems. I dare say your mother felt it best to say nothing of that."

"Why, you're right," Hilary confessed.

"And she made it clear that one of a wife's duties was to say as little as possible about the state of her health, even after they were married." While it was true that Hilary knew such conversation could be boring, she had become accustomed at Arilinn to hearing the state of her health discussed at great length by everyone there.

"I suggest, then, that you tell Colin exactly how you feel," Allier said. "And if he feels you must carry it through in spite of everything, I suggest that you wind up your courage and do so. Otherwise, I bid you remember that a marriage in essence consists of only *a meal, a bed, and a fireside.*"

As they rode homeward, Hilary told Colin everything, as Allier had suggested. He looked so full of solicitude that Hilary felt like breaking down; but she only said, "Tell me the truth, Colin, how much of this ceremony do you really want?"

"No more than you do," he said, rather unhappily. "Surely you know that all this ceremony is to please the family of the bride; I was told by your parents that you must have a wedding worthy of the former Keeper of Arilinn. But I confess, I do not see what difference it makes."

"Then we are in total agreement," Hilary said with a breath of relief. "I was told that only a great ceremony would please you and your kin, and was made to feel ungrateful for not wanting it—as if it would dishonor you and your noble kinfolk."

Colin's face lit up. "Then let us have less ceremony, by all means," he said. "I have always thought a wedding should please bride and husband, and I was willing to go along with whatever you wished. But if it is not your true will—and if we are both agreed—?"

"Of one thing you should be sure," Hilary said, "My mother and father will be angry with us—or at least my mother will be. Papa will not mind, except that he will have to bear my mother's wrath."

Colin sighed. "Darling, if you will forgive me for saying so, I care not a raisin for your mother's wrath."

Hilary felt the most extraordinary sense of relief and lightness; she giggled helplessly and murmured, "To be perfectly truthful, neither do I, Colin; but I am not brave enough to say so!"

He turned in the saddle to look at her. "Then, my love, I think there is nothing left to do but to decide where and when we wish to go."

She could not think of what she wished to do, or where they could go to do it. She did not wish to bring down her parents' wrath upon any of the villagers who might lend them a roof. Finally she suggested in desperation that perhaps Allier would know, or be able to suggest something.

They met with Allier the following day and unfolded their dilemma to her; she listened a moment, then grinned.

"I was wondering when you would get around to asking me. I do not fear the wrath of your family. I do not depend on anyone in your village for my livelihood, but only on my Guild-mother. Rather, they dare not offend me—or who would serve the women in your village? And where would they be if my Guild refused to send them Healers or a midwife? You will borrow my cottage, of course."

Once it was determined, Hilary set herself to deciding what their first meal together, at their first fireside, should be. She herself knew almost nothing of kitchen arts. In the Tower, there had been servants to do everything. So she decided that she would take ready-to-eat food. By telling her mother that she and Colin planned a day's ride, she got one of the kitchen women to pack them a generous lunch, including many of her favorite dainties. With a little glimmer of mischief, she even had them pack an apple nut cake; everyone on the estate knew it was her favorite. And now this would be her wedding cake after all, she thought with a sly smile; there would be no one to say it was not suitable.

One of the kitchen women, who had been Hilary's

nurse when she was very small, saw the smile. "You are merry, Mistress," she said with a hint of question. Hilary merely said, "If I cannot be merry on the eve of my wedding, when should I be?" She hugged the woman exuberantly. When the house folk heard that she had cheated them of their festival, at least someone would know how happy she had been.

But she grew pensive as she and Colin rode out. For the last two or three years she had heard much from Damon of the struggle Callista had had to lay down the burden of the Tower; she had refused to join with Leonie when the folk of the Tower would have met to strip Damon of his powers. She was still frightened; because of Allier's ministrations, it might be easier for her. She could probably consummate her marriage without danger; but she might be among those failed Keepers who kill their prospective husbands without meaning to, and even the bare possibility frightened her. Colin, too, was of the Tower. She had been brought up on stories which made the point that a man who takes a Keeper—even with her own consent—risks his life and sanity. Did Colin fear her?

"Not much," he said, "but life is full of fears. If I was prone to be afraid, I would never ride a horse for fear he might slip the reins, nor hunt for fear a huntsman's arrow would strike me, nor ever leave my fireside and go out of doors for fear stray lighting might strike me from the sky. A man cannot live his life in fear, Hilary; there is risk every time I set foot out of my bed, when it comes to that."

"Ah, you are braver than I," Hilary said, "I am afraid of everything."

"But when you are married to me," Colin said, "you will not need to be afraid, for you will have nothing to be afraid of."

"I hope not," Hilary replied as they drew up their horses in front of Allier's cottage. She evidently was not within; but she had left the latchstring out for them. Hilary went in while Colin tied the horses and gave them hay. The cottage consisted only of one big room which served as kitchen, living room, and bedroom. A large four-poster bed took up a good deal of the space. Hilary had not found the bed remarkable when she was here before, but now she could not take her eyes from it. Colin came in and she went at once to build up the fire. He bent beside her and said, "Let's build it together— our first fireside. . . ."

In spite of the fire, Hilary felt cold. Perhaps, she thought, she would feel better with something warm to drink. She found a saucepan hanging over the hearth, and poured the cider into it. Within minutes it was steaming away merrily. She unpacked the nut cake and borrowed Colin's knife to cut two generous wedges.

"Our wedding feast is ready, Colin," she said. Colin turned around and placed the treats and cider on the big bed.

"Come here, Hilary," he said matter-of factly, and offered his hand to help her onto the patchwork quilt. Then he sat beside her, and put his arm around her.

"So," he said quietly, holding the mug to her lips, "it is done. We have shared a bed, a hearth, and a meal; you are my wife. There is time enough for everything else when we have leisure and we are ready. Don't you think I know how you were worrying about that, Hilary?"

"You do understand everything, Colin," she whispered. "Let us ride home to Syrtis, then, where we can share all these things under your family's roof."

She would still have to face her mother's wrath; but now, she could face even that. Ahead of her was a life as Colin's wife. She smiled at Colin, and thought she would never be afraid of anything again.

ROHANA

Lady Rohana Ardais is one of only two characters in any of my books that I did not consciously create. (The other was Damon Ridenow.) She walked full-blown, like Athena from the head of Zeus, into my first full-length Free Amazon novel, later called THE SHATTERED CHAIN (a title which Don Wollheim, not I, created; I called it FREE AMAZONS OF DARKOVER), which was supposed to be about Kindra. But Rohana Ardais walked into the book, absolutely uninvited, took it over, and turned out to be one of the most popular characters of all.

Here is "Everything But Freedom," which was one of the few longer stories I wrote which were not quite novel length; though when I first wrote SWORD OF ALDONES, it might almost have been a "Cover Novel" for STARTLING STORIES, which just goes to show you what novels were like in those days.

Everything But Freedom

by Marion Zimmer Bradley

"I did not say that I had no regrets, Jaelle," Rohana said, very low, "only that everything in this world has its price. . . ."

"So you truly believe that you have paid a price? I thought you told me but now that you had had everything a woman could desire."

Rohana did not face Jaelle; she did not want to cry.

"Everything but freedom, Jaelle."

—The Shattered Chain, 1976.

I

"Look," Jaelle cried, leaning over the balcony, "I think they are coming."

Lady Rohana Ardais followed her from inside the room, her steps slowed somewhat by pregnancy. She moved slowly to the edge of the balcony to join her foster-daughter Jaelle and leaned to peer down from the balcony, trying to see past the bend in the tree-lined mountain road that led upward to Castle Ardais.

"I cannot see so far," she confessed, and Jaelle, troubled by the angle of the older woman's leaning forward, seized her round the waist and pulled her back from the edge.

Rohana moved restlessly to free herself, and Jaelle confessed, "I am still afraid of these heights. It makes my blood curdle, to see you standing so close to the edge like that. If you should fall—" She broke off and shuddered.

"But the railing is so high," said the third woman who had followed them from the inner room, "she could not possibly fall, not even if she wished! Look, even if I climbed up here—'' Lady Alida made a move as if to climb up on the railing, but Jaelle's face was whiter than her shift, and Rohana shook her head. "Don't tease her, Alida. She's really afraid."

"I'm sorry—did that really bother you, *chiya*?"

"It does. Not as badly as when I first came here, but— Perhaps it is foolish—"

"No," Rohana said, "not really; you were desert-bred and never accustomed to the mountain heights." Jaelle had been born and reared in the Dry Towns; her mother a kidnapped woman of the Comyn, her father a desert chieftain who was, by Comyn standards, little better than a bandit. Four years before, a daring raid by Free Amazon mercenaries had freed Melora and the twelve-year-old Jaelle; but Melora had died in the desert, bearing the Dry Town chief's child. Rohana had wished to foster Melora's children; but Jaelle had chosen to go to the Amazon Guild House as fosterling to the Free Amazon Kindra n'ha Mhari.

Jaelle peered cautiously over the railing again. "Now they are past the bend in the road," she said. "You can see—yes, that is Kindra; no other woman rides like that."

"Alida," Rohana said, "Will you go down and make certain that guest-chambers are made ready?"

"Certainly, sister." Alida, many years younger than Lady Rohana, was the younger sister of Rohana's husband, *Dom* Gabriel Ardais. She was a *leronis*, Tower-trained, and skilled in all the psychic arts of the Comyn, called *laran*.

"You will be glad to see your foster-mother again, Jaelle?" Alida asked.

"Of course, and glad to be going home," proclaimed Jaelle, heedless of the pain which flashed across Rohana's face.

Rohana said gently, "I had hoped that in this year, Jaelle, this might have become your home, too."

"Never!" Jaelle said emphatically. Then she softened, coming to hug Rohana impulsively. "Oh, please, kinswoman, don't look like that! You know I love you. Only, after being free, living here has been like being chained again, like living in the Dry Towns!"

"Is it really as bad as all that?" Rohana asked. "I do not feel I have lost my freedom."

"Perhaps you do not really mind being imprisoned; but I do," Jaelle said. "You will not even ride astride, but when you ride you burden the horse with a lady's saddle—an insult to a good horse. And —" she hesitated, "Look at you! I know, even though you do not say it, that you did not really want another child, with Elorie already twelve years old and almost a woman, and Kyril and Rian all but grown men. Kyril is seventeen now, and Rian as old as I am!"

Rohana winced, for she had not realized that her fosterling understood this. But she replied quietly, "Marriage is not a matter for one person to decide everything. It is a matter for mutual decision. I have had many choices of my own; Gabriel wished for another child, and I did not feel that I could deny it to him."

"I know better than that," Jaelle replied curtly; she did not like her kinsman Gabriel, Lord Ardais, and did not care who knew it. "My uncle was angry with you because you had brought my brother Valentine here to foster, and I know that he said that if you could bring up one baby who was not even of your own blood, there was no reason you should not give him another."

"Jaelle, you do not understand these things." Rohana protested.

"No, and I hope I never do."

"What you do not understand is that Gabriel's happiness is very important to me," Rohana said, "and it is worth bearing another child to make him happy." But secretly Rohana felt rebellious: Jaelle was right; she had not wanted another child now that she was also burdened with Melora's son. Little Valentine was now nearly four years old. Her own sons had not been happy about having an infant foster-brother, even though her daughter treated the baby—now a hearty toddler—like a special pet, a kind of living doll to play with. Rohana was grateful that Elorie loved her fosterling; she herself found it a heavy burden, having a little child around again when she had already reared all of her own children past adolescence. And now, at an age where she had hoped childbirth and suckling all behind her, she must undergo all that again; and she was no longer strong and tireless as she had been when she was younger.

She sought to change the subject, although for one equally filled with tension.

"Are you still determined to take the Renunciate Oath as soon as possible?"

"Yes; you know I should have taken it a year ago," Jaelle said sullenly. "You stopped me then, but now I am fully of age and I cannot be prevented in law."

Jaelle knew it had not been only Rohana's disagreement that had prevented her from taking the Oath which would make her a Free Amazon—a member of the Sisterhood of Renunciates. It had been Kindra herself. She remembered, as she watched Kindra riding toward Castle Ardais, how they had ridden up this road together a year ago, Jaelle sullen and furious.

"I am of age, Kindra," she protested. "I am fifteen; I have a legal right to take the Oath; and I have been two years within the Guild House, I know what I want. The law allows it. Why should you stop me?"

"It is not a matter of law," Kindra protested. "It is a matter of honor. I gave the Lady Rohana my word; is my word nothing, is my honor nothing to you, fosterdaughter?"

"You had no right to give such a word when it involved my freedom," Jaelle protested angrily.

"Jaelle, you were born daughter to the Comyn, Melora Aillard's daughter; nearest heir to the Domain of Aillard," Kindra reminded her, "Even so, the Council has not forbidden you to become a Renunciate. But they have insisted that you must live for one year the life of a daughter of the Comyn, if only to be certain we have not kidnapped you nor unlawfully denied you your heritage."

"Who could believe that?" Jaelle demanded.

"Many who know nothing of the Renunciate way, who do not trust in our honor," Kindra said. "It was a pledge I was forced to make as the price of having you for a fosterling in the Guild House; that when you were of age to be married, you should be sent to Ardais, there to live at least a year—they tried to argue for three—as a daughter of the Comyn, to know—not as a child, but as an adult—just what heritage and inheritance it was that you were renouncing. You should not, they felt, cast it away sight unseen and unexperienced."

"What I know of the heritage of Comyn, I do not want, nor respect, nor accept," Jaelle said stormily. "My life is here among the Guild-sisters, and I swear I shall never know any other."

"Oh, hush," Kindra implored. "How can you say so when you know nothing of what it is that you have renounced?"

"What good was it to my mother that she was Comyn?" Jaelle demanded. "They let her fall into my father's hands and dwell there as no better than concubine or slave—"

"What else could they do? Would you have had them plunge all the Domains into a war with the Dry Towns? Over a single woman—"

"Had Jalak of the Dry Towns kidnapped the heir to Hastur, they would not have hesitated a moment to make war on his account; I know that much," Jaelle argued, and Kindra sighed, knowing that what Jaelle said was true. Kindra herself had no great love for the Comyn, although she genuinely admired and respected Lady Rohana. It had taken much persuasion for Jaelle to agree to spend a year at Ardais as Rohana's foster-daughter, to learn what it was to be born daughter to the Comyn.

Now the year was ended; and Kindra was coming, as she had promised, to take her back to the Guild House, to take the Oath and live forever as a free woman of the Guild, independent of clan or heritage.

She brushed hastily past Rohana and ran down the stairs; as she reached the great front door, Kindra was just riding up the long path. Jaelle, cursing the hated skirts which she had to wear at Ardais, bundled them up in her hands and sped down the front pathway, to fling herself at Kindra, even before the woman dismounted, almost jerking her from her saddle.

"Gently! Gently, my child," Kindra admonished, dismounting and taking Jaelle into her arms. Then, seeing that Jaelle was weeping, she held her off at arm's length and surveyed her seriously.

"What is the matter?"

"Oh. I'm just so—so glad to see you!" Jaelle sobbed, hastily drying her eyes.

"Come, come, child! I cannot believe that Rohana has been unkind to you, or that you could have been so miserable as all this!"

"No, it's not Rohana—no one could possibly have been kinder—but I've been counting the days! I can't wait to be home again!"

Kindra hugged her tight. "I have missed you, too, foster-daughter," she said, "and we shall all be glad to have you home to us again. So you have not chosen to remain with the Domains and marry to suit your clan?"

"Never!" Jaelle exclaimed. "Oh, Kindra, you don't know what it's been like here! Rohana's women are so stupid; they think of nothing but pretty clothes and how to arrange their hair, or which of the guardsmen smiled or winked at them in the evenings when we dance in the hall—they are so stupid! Even my cousin, Rohana's daughter—she is just as bad as any of them!"

Kindra said gently, "I find it hard to believe that Rohana could have a daughter who was a fool—"

"Well, perhaps Elorie is not a fool," Jaelle admitted grudgingly. "She is clever enough—but already she has learned not to be caught thinking when her father or her brothers are in the room. She pretends she is as foolish as the rest of them!"

Kindra concealed a smile. "Then perhaps she is cleverer than you realize—for she can think her own thoughts without being reproved for it—something that you have not yet learned, my dearest. Come, let us go up, let me pay my respects to Lady Rohana; I am eager to see her again."

"When can we go home, Kindra? Tomorrow?" Jaelle asked eagerly.

"By no means," Kindra said, scandalized. "I have been invited to make a visit here for a tenday or more; too much haste would be disrespectful to your kinfolk, as if you could not wait to be gone."

"Well, I can't," muttered Jaelle; but before Kindra's

stern glance she could not say it aloud. She called a groom to have Kindra's horse taken and stabled, then led Kindra toward the front steps where Rohana awaited them.

As the women greeted one another with an embrace, Jaelle stood at a little distance, looking at them side by side and studying the contrasts.

Rohana, Lady of Ardais, was a woman in her middle thirties; her hair was the true Comyn red of the hereditary Comyn caste, and was ornately arranged at the back of her neck, clasped with a copper butterfly-clasp ornamented with pearls. She was richly dressed in a long elegant over-gown of blue velvet almost the color of her eyes; her thin light-colored undergown was heavily embroidered and the overgown trimmed at the neck and sleeves with thick dark fur. Now the rich garments looked clumsy, her body swollen with her pregnancy. By contrast to Rohana, Kindra appeared frankly middleaged; a tall lanky woman in the boots and breeches of an Amazon, which made her long legs look even longer than they were; her face was thin, almost gaunt, and her face, as well as her close-cropped gray hair, looked weathered and was beginnning to be wrinkled with small lines round the eyes and mouth. Almost for the first time, Jaelle wondered how old Kindra was. She had always seemed ageless. She was older than Rohana—or was it only that Rohana's relatively sheltered and pampered life had preserved the appearance of youth?

"Well, come in, my dears," Rohana said, slipping one arm through Kindra's and the other through Jaelle's, "I hope you can pay us a good long visit. Surely you did not ride alone all the way from Thendara?"

Jaelle wondered scornfully if Rohana thought Kindra would be afraid to make such a journey alone—as she, Rohana, might have been afraid. To her the question would have been insulting; but Kindra answered uncritically that she had had company past the path for Scaravel; a group of mountain explorers going into the far Hellers, and three Guild-sisters hired to guide them.

"Rafaella was with them, and she sent you her love and greetings, Jaelle. She has missed you, and so has her little girl Doria. They both hoped you would be with them another time."

"Oh, I wish Rafi had come here with you," Jaelle cried. "She is almost my closest friend!"

"Well, perhaps she will be back in Thendara by the time we are able to return there," Kindra said, smiling. She added to Rohana, "Mostly it was a group of Terrans from the new spaceport; they are trying to map the Hellers—the roads, the mountain peaks and so forth."

"Not for military purposes, I hope," Rohana said.

"I believe not; simply for information," Kindra replied. "The Terrans all appear to have a passion, from what I know of them, for all kinds of useless knowledge; the height of mountains, the sources of rivers and so forth—I cannot imagine why, but such things might be useful even to our people who must travel in the mountains."

They were now well inside the great hallway, and Jaelle noted, standing in the corner where a heap of hunting equipment was piled, Lord Gabriel Ardais, Rohana's husband and the Warden and head of the Domain of Ardais. He was a tall man with a smart military bearing that somehow gave his old hunting clothes the look of a uniform.

"You have guests, Rohana? You did not warn me to expect company," he said gruffly.

"Strictly speaking, the lady is Jaelle's guest; Kindra n'ha Mhari, from the Thendara Guild House," Rohana said calmly, "but though she journeyed here to bring Jaelle home, she is my friend and I have invited her to stay and keep me company now I must be confined so close to house and garden."

Dom Gabriel's mobile face darkened with disapproval as his gaze fell on Kindra's trousered and booted legs; but as Rohana spoke on his face softened, and he spoke with perfect courtesy. "Whatever you wish, my love. *Mestra*," he used the term of courtesy from a nobleman to a female of a lower class, "I bid you welcome; any guest of my lady's is a welcome and a cherished guest in my home. May your stay here be joyful."

He went on, leading the way into the upper hall, "Did I hear you speaking of *Terranan* in the Hellers? Those strange creatures who claim to be from other worlds, come here in closed litters of metal across the gulf of the stars? I thought that was a children's tale."

"Whatever they may be, *vai dom,* theirs is no children's tale," Kindra replied. "I have seen the great ships in which they come and go, and one of the professors in the City was allowed to journey with them to the moon Liriel, where they have set up what they call an observatory, to study the stars."

"And the Hastur-lords permitted it?"

"I think perhaps sir, if we are only one of many great worlds among the stars, it may not be of much moment whether the Hastur-lords permit or no," Kindra returned deferentially. "One thing is certain, such a truth will change our world and things can never be as they have been before this time."

"I don't see why that need be," *Dom* Gabriel said in his usual gruff tone. "What have they to do with me or with the Domain? I say let 'em let us alone and we'll let them alone—hey?"

"You may be right, sir; but I would say if these folk have the wisdom to travel from world to world, they may have much to teach us," Kindra said.

"Well, they'd better not come here to Ardais trying to teach it. I'll be the judge of what my folk should learn or not," said *Dom* Gabriel, "and that's that." He marched to a high wooden sideboard where bottles and glasses were set out and began to pour. He said deferentially to Rohana, "I'm sure it would do you good, but I suppose you are still too queasy to drink this early, my love? And you, *mestra*?"

"Thank you, sir, it is still a bit early for me," Kindra said, shaking her head.

"Jaelle?"

"No, thank you, Uncle." Jaelle said, trying to conceal a grimace of disgust. *Dom* Gabriel poured himself a liberal drink and drank it off quickly, then, pouring another, took a relaxed sip. Rohana sighed and went to him, saying in a low tone, "Please, Gabriel, the steward will be here with the stud-books this morning, to plan the seasons of the mares."

Dom Gabriel scowled and his face set in a stubborn

line. He said, "For shame, Rodi, to speak of such things before a young maiden."

Rohana sighed and said, "Jaelle, too, is country-bred and as well acquainted with such things as our own children, Gabriel. Please try to be sober for him, will you?"

"I shall not neglect my duty, my dear," *Dom* Gabriel said. "You attend to your business, Lady, and I shall not neglect mine." He poured himself another drink. "I am sure a little of this would do your sickness good, my love; won't you have some?"

"No, thank you, Gabriel; I have many things to see to this morning," she said, sighing, and gestured to her guests to follow her up the stairs. Jaelle said vehemently as soon as they were out of earshot, "Disgraceful! Already he is half drunk! And no doubt before the steward gets here, he will be dead drunk somewhere on the floor—unless his man remembers to come and get him into a chair—and no more fit to deal with the stud-books than I am to pilot one of the Terran starships!"

Rohana's face was pale, but she spoke steadily.

"It is not for you to criticize your uncle, Jaelle. I am content if he drinks alone and does not get one of the boys to drinking with him; Rian already finds it impossible to carry his drink like a gentleman, and Kyril is worse. I do not mind attending to the stud-books."

"But why do you let him make such a beast of himself, especially now?" Jaelle asked, casting a critical look at Rohana's perceptibly thickened waistline.

"He drinks because he is in pain; it is not my place to tell him what he must do," Rohana said. "Come, Jaelle, let us find a guest chamber near yours for Kindra. Then I must see if Valentine has been properly washed and fed, and if his nurse has taken him outdoors to play in the fresh air this morning."

"I should think," Kindra said, "that Jaelle would have quite taken over the care of her brother; you are a big girl now, Jaelle, almost a woman, and should know something of the care of children."

Jaelle's face drew up in distaste.

"I've no liking for having little bawling brats about me! What are the nurses good for?"

"Nevertheless, you are Valentine's closest living kin;

he has a right to your care and companionship," Kindra urged quietly, "and you might take some of that burden from Lady Rohana who is burdened enough.

Rohana laughed. She said "Let her alone, Kindra; I've no wish that she be burdened too young with children if she has no love for it. After all, he's not neglected; Elorie cares for Valentine as if he were her own little brother—"

"The more fool she," Jaelle interrupted, laughing.

"He must be quite a big boy now; four, is he not?" Kindra asked.

Rohana replied eagerly, "Yes, and he is such a sweet quiet little boy, very good, biddable, and gentle. One would never think—"

She broke off, but Jaelle took it up.

"Never think he was my brother? For I know very well, Aunt, that I am none of those things, and in fact I do not wish to be any of those things."

"What I was about to say, Jaelle, is that one would hardly think him kin to my sons, boisterous as they are; or that one would hardly think him of Dry Town clan or kin."

Kindra could almost hear what Rohana had started to say; *one would hardly think his father a Dry Town bandit.* She was astonished that Jaelle, who was, after all of the telepathic blood of Comyn, could not understand what Rohana meant; but she held her peace. She liked Rohana very much and wished that the lady and her foster-daughter were on better terms, yet it could not be amended by wishing. Rohana conducted her to a guest chamber and left her to unpack; Jaelle stayed, and dropped down on a saddlebag, her lanky knees drawn up, her gray eyes full of angry rebellion.

"You are still trying to turn me into a Comyn lady like Rohana! I should do this or that, I should look after my little brother, and I don't know what all! Why do we have to stay here? Why can't we start back to Thendara tomorrow? I want to go home! I thought that was why you were coming—to take me home! You promised, if I endured for a year, I would be allowed to take the Oath! Now how long will I have to wait?"

Kindra decided it was time to hit this spoiled girl with

the truth of the situation. She drew the girl down, still protesting, beside her.

"Jaelle, it is not certain that Comyn Council will give permission for you to take the Oath at all; the law still regards the Comyn Council as your legal guardians. Rohana was given your custody as a minor; a woman of the Domains is not like a commoner," Kindra began. "I dare not risk angering your guardians. You know that the Guild House Charter exists by favor of Council; if we let you take the Oath without permission, our House could lose its Charter—"

"That is outrageous! They cannot do that to free citizens! Can they?"

"They can, Jaelle, but in general they would have no reason for doing so; for many years we have been careful not to infringe on their privileges. I am afraid it is just as simple as that."

"Are you trying to say that for all the talk in the Oath of freedom—*renounce forever any allegiance to family, clan, household, warden or liege lord, and owe allegiance only to the laws as a free citizen must* ... it is nothing but a sham? You taught me to believe in it ..." the girl raged.

Kindra said steadily, "It is very far from a sham, Jaelle; it is an *ideal,* and it cannot be fully implemented in all times and conditions; our rulers are not yet sufficiently enlightened to allow its full perfection. One day perhaps it may be so: but now the world will go as it will and not as you or I would have it."

"So I have to sit here in Ardais and obey that drunken old sot and that spineless nobody who sits by and smiles and says he must do what he will because she will not stop him—this is nobility indeed!"

"I can only beg of you to be patient, Jaelle. Lady Rohana is well disposed toward us, and her friendship may do much with the council. But it would not be wise to alienate *Dom* Gabriel, either."

"I would feel like such a hypocrite, to swarm about and curry favor with nobles—"

"They are your kin, Jaelle; it is no crime to seek their good will," Kindra said wearily, unequal to the task of explaining diplomacy and compromise to the unbending young girl. "Will you help me unpack my garments, now? We will talk more of this later. And I would like to see your brother; my hands helped bring him into the world, and I promised your mother that I would try always to see to his well-being; and I try always to keep my word."

"You have not kept your promise to me, that I should take Oath in a year," Jaelle argued, but at Kindra's angry look she knew she had exhausted even her foster-mother's patience, so she began helping Kindra take out her meager stock of clothing from the saddlebags and lay it neatly away in chests.

II

One of the few tasks confronting Jaelle at Ardais which she felt fully compatible with her life as a Renunciate was the care of her own horse; *Dom* Gabriel and even Rohana would have felt it more suitable if she had left the beast's welfare to the grooms, but they did not absolutely forbid her the stables; and almost every morning before sunrise she went out to the main stables to look after the fine plains-bred horse Rohana had presented her as a birthday gift; where she gave the beast its fodder and brushed it down. She also exercised her own horse and rode almost every day. Although she still resented not being allowed to ride astride, she was obedient to Rohana's will, suspecting that yielding on this matter might be the price of being allowed to ride at all. No one could have said or suggested that Lady Rohana was not a good rider, although she was to all outward appearances the most conventional of women.

Jaelle suspected that Rohana was hoping to force her to admit that she could find as much pleasure in riding sidesaddle as in riding Amazon style in boots and breeches; but this, she was resolved, she would never do.

Perhaps, she thought, while Kindra was here—and Rohana could not constrain a guest to follow her customs—Rohana could be persuaded to allow her, Jaelle, to ride as Kindra did. She was intending to try, anyhow. Her own Renunciate clothing, which she had worn when she came here, was too small for her now. She had grown almost three inches, though she would never be really tall. Perhaps one of her cousins could be persuaded to lend her some breeches until she would have proper clothing made on returning to the Guild House; she certainly did not intend to ride back to Thendara in the ridiculous outfit which Rohana thought suitable for a young lady's riding; the sort of riding-habit her cousin Elorie wore, a dark full-cut skirt and elegantly fitted jacket with velvet lapels, would be the mock of every Renunciate in the Guild House!

She took her horse out of the stall and began brushing down the glossy coat. She had heard Rohana and Kindra speak of hawking this day perhaps and meant to ask if she would be allowed to ride out with them. Before long, the horse's coat gleamed like burnished copper, and she herself was warm and sweating profusely, despite the chill of the stable—it was so cold that her breath still came in a white cloud. She began to lead the horse back into its stall when a hand touched her and she frowned, knowing the touch. Her first impulse was to pick the hand off her like a crawling bug, perhaps with a fist-sized blow behind it; but if she was to persuade her cousin Kyril to lend her his riding-clothes, she did not want to alienate him too thoroughly.

Rohana's elder son was seventeen years old, a year older than Jaelle herself; like his father, he had dark crisply-curled hair; many of the Ardais men were dark rather than having the true-red hair of the Comyn. She had heard that this had come from alliances with the swarthy little men who lived in caves in the Hellers and worked the mines for metals, worshiping the fire-Goddess; a few of the Ardais kin, it was said, even had dark eyes like animals, but Jaelle had not seen that; certainly Kyril's eyes were not dark, but blue as Rohana's own. He was tall and broad-shouldered, but otherwise lean and narrowly built; his features were heavy, and at least to Jaelle's eyes he had the same sullen mouth and weak chin as his father. Kyril would look better, she thought, when he was old enough to grow a beard and conceal it.

She shifted her weight a little so that Kyril's hand fell

away from her, and said, "What are you doing out so early, cousin?"

"I could ask the same of you," Kyril said, grinning. "Have you stolen out this early to keep an assignation with one of the grooms? Which one has stolen your heart? Rannart? He is all a girl could desire; if he were a maiden I should swoon over those eyes of his, and I know Eloric seeks to touch his hand whenever he helps her into the saddle."

Jaelle grimaced with revulsion. "Your mind is filthy, Kyril. And already you have been drinking, early as it is!"

"You sound like my mother, Jaelle; a little drink makes the bread go down easily at this hour and warms the body. Yours would be the better for a little warming."

He winked at her suggestively, trying to slide an arm around her waist, and she said, concealing her annoyance and moving as far from him as the confines of the stall allowed, "I am as warm as I wish; I have been currying my horse, and I prefer exercise to drinking. I think you would be the better for a good run, and it would warm you better than whisky, believe me. I don't like the smell or taste of the stuff, and certainly not for breakfast."

"Well, if you don't want whisky, I can think of a better way to warm you in this cold place," Kyril said, and she realized that he had moved to block her exit from the stall. "Come, Jaelle, you need not pretend with me; you have lived with those Renunciates, and all the world knows how they behave about men; would any woman ride astride with her legs showing, unless she wished to invite any man who sees it to spread them?"

Jaelle tried to push past him. She had been a fool; she should have managed to keep the horse between them. "You are disgusting, Kyril. If I desired any man, it would not be you."

"Ah. I knew it; those lovers of women and haters of men have corrupted you! But try it with a real man, and I swear you will like it better." He caught her around the waist and tried hard to push her against the edge of the stall.

"Oh, what a fool you are, cousin! Just now you said Renunciates were all mad for men, and now you will have it that we are all lovers of women. You cannot have it both ways."

"Oh, Jaelle, don't haggle with me; you know I've been hungering for you since you were only a skinny little thing, and now you'd drive any man mad," he said, pushing closer and trying to kiss the back of her neck. She forgot about not wanting to alienate him and pushed him away, hard.

"Let me go, and I won't tell your mother how offensive—"

"Offensive? A woman like you is offensive to all men," Kyril said, and she pushed hard again, driving two stiffened fingers into his solar plexus. He staggered back with a grunt of pain.

"You cannot blame a man for asking," he said, almost smugly. "Most women consider it a compliment if a man desires them."

"Oh, Kyril, surely you are not short of women to warm your bed!" she said crossly. "You are only trying to annoy me! I don't want to trouble Rohana; you know she is tired and ill these days! Just leave me alone!"

"It would serve you right if no man ever desired you, and you had to marry a cross-eyed farmer with nine stepchildren," Kyril snarled.

"What does it matter to you, even if I marry a cralmac?"

"You are my cousin; it is a matter of the honor of my family," he said, "that you should become a real woman—"

"Oh, go away! It is time for breakfast," Jaelle said furiously. "If you make me late, I swear I will tell Rohana why and risk making her as sick as I am when I look at you and smell your filthy breath!" She pushed to the door of the stable while Kyril rubbed his bruised rib.

As the two young people headed for the great hall, she saw *Dom* Gabriel riding up to the great gateway. He was not alone, but she was only vaguely surprised to see the Lord of Ardais out so early; she could not credit that he might have been only in search of fresh air and exercise on a morning ride.

I should not wonder that Kyril is already corrupt; with such a father, it would be a miracle if he were anything else. I only hope he did not awaken Rohana going out so early, she thought, and went up into the Great Hall for breakfast.

Rohana, in a long loose gown covered with a white apron not unlike the housekeeper's, greeted her with a smile.

"You are awake early, Jaelle; riding?"

"No, aunt, only grooming my horse," Jaelle said. Kyril slunk into his place at the table and Jaelle with a fragment of her consciousness heard him order one of the serving-women to bring him wine.

Ugh, he will be a drunken sot like his father within a year! Jaelle thought, and turned her attention to greeting her younger cousins. Elorie and Rian, with their governess, took their seats and attacked their porridge and honey with childish greed. Rohana had a little stewed fruit on her plate, but Jaelle noticed her kinswoman looked pale and was only pretending to eat.

Dom Gabriel made an entrance—any other way of describing it, Jaelle thought, would be an understatement—followed by a slightly built, pretty girl of seventeen or so. She cast a look at Gabriel that was almost pleading, but he ignored her and she assumed a look of hard defiance.

Jaelle understood at once; this was not the first young woman that Lord Ardais had brought to the house under these circumstances; *at least,* she thought, *this one is not younger than his own sons.*

"Gabriel, will you name our guest?" Rohana asked with perfect courtesy.

He stepped to the girl's side and said, "This is Tessa Haldar." The double name proclaimed her at least minor nobility.

Rohana said gently, "She will be staying?"

"Certainly," Gabriel said, not looking at the girl, and Rohana immediately comprehended. Jaelle was not much of a telepath, but she caught the edge of Rohana's emotion.

I suppose he thinks I care who he sleeps with?

Gabriel glared at her, and Jaelle also heard what he would not say aloud before the entire household; *well, you are no good to me now, are you?*

Rohana's face paled with anger.

Whose fault is that? It was you who wanted another child!

Jaelle fought to close her perceptions, flooded with a sick embarrassment; by the time she looked up, Rohana was helping the girl off with her cloak. *Poor child, none of this is her fault.* Rohana said aloud, "Here, my dear, you must be chilled by your long ride. Sit here beside *Dom* Gabriel." She beckoned to the hall-steward. "Hallard, set another place here, and take her cloak. Bring some hot tea; the kettle is cold."

"Forget that swill," *Dom* Gabriel said contemptuously; "After a ride like that, a man wants something warming." Rohana did not alter her cool gracious manner for a moment.

"Hot spiced cider for *Dom* Gabriel and his guest."

"Hot spiced wine, you imbecile," *Dom* Gabriel corrected her rudely. Rohana's carefully held smile flickered, but she gave the order. Her lips were pressed tightly together and there were two spots of color on her cheeks.

Kindra came into the hall and Rohana said good morning. She came to greet Jaelle and took a place among the children.

Dom Gabriel scowled and said quietly to Rohana, over the bent head of the girl Tessa between them, "What's this, Lady? Am I to have a woman in breeches at my own table?"

Rohana said between her teeth, "Gabriel, I have been gracious to *your* guest." He scowled fiercely, but he lowered his gaze and said nothing further. Jaelle gazed into her plate, feeling she would choke on her bread and butter. How could Rohana sit there calmly and allow *Dom* Gabriel to make her confront his new *barragana* at her own breakfast table. And when she was pregnant, too! Yet she sat there politely watching *Dom* Gabriel feed the girl sops of bread soaked in the spiced wine from his own goblet.

Rian asked, "Mother, may I have wine instead of more tea?"

"No, Rian, you cannot deal with lessons if you have been drinking; I will send for spiced cider for you; it will warm you better than wine."

"Rohana, don't make a mollycoddle of the boy! If he wants to drink, let him," Gabriel grumbled, but Rohana shook her head at the hall-steward.

"Gabriel, you gave your word that the children should be wholly in my hands till they are grown."

"Oh, very well, do as you please. Listen to your mother, Rian; I always do," *Dom* Gabriel said with a sickly smile.

"If I were Rohana, I would ... I would kick that girl, I would scratch that smug smile off her face," Jaelle said to Kindra as they were leaving the Hall. Kyril heard and said jeeringly, "What do you know of a man's privileges?"

"Enough to know I want no part of them," Jaelle said. "I thought I had proved that to your satisfaction earlier this morning, cousin."

Rian, Rohana's younger son, a slenderly built boy of sixteen with a perpetually worried look on his face and red hair like Rohana's, said, "Mother is not pleased, I can see that. But it is not the first time. My father will do what he will, and whatever he does, my mother will say before the household that whatever he chooses to do is well done—whatever she may think in private. I agree with you, Jaelle, it is a disgrace; but if she will not protest, there is nothing you or I or anyone else can do."

Jaelle had seen Rian finish the goblet of his father's spiced wine after *Dom* Gabriel left the table, when Rohana was not looking; she looked contemptuously at the boy and said nothing.

Kindra said quietly, "Come to my room, Jaelle; I think we must talk about this."

And when they were alone in Kindra's room, she said, "By what right do you criticize your kinswoman Lady Rohana? Is that what I taught you, who want freedom for yourself, to refuse Lady Rohana her choices?"

"You cannot convince me it is by her own choice that

she allows him to bring his mistress right under her roof and to her own table!"

Kindra said, "Perhaps she would rather know where he does his wenching instead of wondering where he is when he is abroad? I know she is troubled about his health and fears something might happen to him if he goes forth from home. At least here she knows definitely what he is doing—and with whom."

"I think that's disgusting," said Jaelle.

"It is no matter what you think; you were not consulted," Kindra said sharply, "and it is not for you to complain if she does not. When she complains to me or consults me about his behavior, I shall not lie about how I feel; nor need you. But until she makes you the keeper of her conscience, Jaelle, do not presume to be so."

"Oh, you are as bad as Rian!" Jaelle said in frustration. "Rohana can do no wrong."

"Oh, I would hardly say that," said Rohana gaily, coming into the room in time to hear Jaelle's last words, "But I am glad to hear you think so, Jaelle."

"But I *don't* think so," said Jaelle crossly, turning her eyes away from Rohana, and slammed out of the room.

Rohana raised her eyes. "Well, what was that all about, Kindra?"

"Only a bad case of being sixteen years old, and knowing how to settle all the problems of the world, except her own," Kindra said wryly. "She loves you, Rohana; she cannot be expected to be happy at seeing you humiliated at your own table."

"No, I suppose not," Rohana said, "but does she expect me to take it out on an innocent young girl who thinks she is loved by a nobleman? She will learn otherwise, soon enough, and my sympathy is all for her. Why, she cannot be much older than Jaelle."

"I think that may be what is troubling Jaelle, though she may not entirely realize it," Kindra said.

"Well, there is time enough for her to choose among men," said Rohana. "But it would trouble me greatly if she were to decide that all men are like her Dry Town father—or like Gabriel—and turn away from them forever."

"Do you really think she will learn otherwise here?" asked Kindra. Rohana sighed.

"No, I suppose not. Kyril is not much better than his father; I have tried to do my best by example, but it is only natural for a boy to pattern himself after his father. Perhaps I should send Jaelle to my kinswoman, who is happy with her husband. But she has so many little children—there are six not yet eight years old—and they really have no room for another grown girl under her roof. But one way or another, I should make sure she knows that men can be good and decent. Perhaps she should go for a time to Melora's cousins in the lowlands."

"I had trouble enough getting her to come here," Kindra reminded her. "And that was because she loved and respected you. I doubt she wants to learn more about men."

Rohana sighed again. "It is trouble enough having trouble with my own daughter," she said, "but I wanted Jaelle here because she is all I have left of poor Melora. Perhaps I should have let her go to Jerana who was willing to make sure she would have the proper training of a Comyn daughter. Nevertheless, I do not want to think of her as turning entirely against men as they say Amazons do."

Kindra frowned and said seriously, "Rohana, would it really matter to you so much if she should become a lover of women? Are you so prejudiced on that subject?"

"Prejudiced? Oh, I see," Rohana said. "No, it would not trouble me so much; but I want her to be happy, and I am not yet convinced that there is any happiness for women outside marriage."

"I would find it hard to believe that there is happiness for women *in* marriage," Kindra said. "Certainly I found none; I told you the story outside Jalak's house in the Dry Towns."

Years slid away as Rohana remembered Kindra's words. Kindra's husband had felt her inadequate because she had borne him only two daughters; she had risked her life to have a third child and had borne the desired boy, after which he had showered her with jewels. *"I was of no value,* Kindra had said; *the daughters I had borne at risk of my life were no value; I was only an instrument to give him sons. And so, when I could walk again, I cut my hair, and kissed my children sleeping, and made my way to the Guild House where my life began."* Yet Rohana knew this decision had not been made lightly, but with great anguish.

Now she was strengthened to ask what she had never dared before despite their closeness.

"But what of your children, Kindra? How could you leave them in his hands, then, if you thought him so evil?"

Kindra's face was colorless, even her tight lips white.

"You may well ask; before I came to that decision, I had wept through many nights. I thought even of carrying them thither with me or stealing them back when they were big enough. Avarra pity me, one night I even stood over them with a dagger in my hand, ready to save them from the life I could not bear; but I knew I would turn it first on myself." Her voice was flat, but her words came in a resistless rush which compelled Rohana's silent attention. "But he—my husband—was not an evil man; it was only that he could not even *see* me; for him I did not exist, a wife was but an instrument to do his will. And I spoke to many wives, and not one could understand why I was angry or dismayed; they all seemed well-contented with their lot. So what could I do but believe that other women *were* so content—Many of them could not see what I had to complain of. They asked, "He does not beat you, does he?" as if I should be happy just because he did not. So it seemed to me that the fault lay with me, that I could never be content under those terms, that I should die if I was no more than a mother of his children; but even that it was to his advantage to be rid of me and have a truly contented wife happy with her designated place in life, who could bring up my daughters to be happy as those other women seemed to be . . . in finding a husband and being his brood stock. And so I left him as much for his own good and theirs, as my own. And I have heard in the city that he married again and that my daughters married well, and they, too, seem happy. I have three grandsons I have never held in my arms; I am sure my daughters would draw away their skirts as if I bore plague, should I make myself known to them." She swallowed, Rohana could see tears in her eyes. "But I have never looked back. And if I were there again, I would do the same."

Rohana embraced her silently, and did not speak for a long time. She felt touched by the other woman's confidence, knowing it was not lightly given, even to her sisters of the Guild House; she had enough *laran* to know Kindra had never told her tale at this length to even the Guild-mothers.

"I would not swear that I would not have done so in your place," Rohana said, "but the choice never came to me; I bore my two sons *before* my daughter was born, and by the time she was born Gabriel was glad to have her. Gabriel already had a daughter by his first marriage and loved her well. She is in Dalereuth Tower; they say she has the Ardais Gift. She dwelt under our roof till she was fifteen; she had but lately left us when I learned of Melora's plight."

And you were rich enough and had enough servants and ladies at your command that you could leave your own children in the hands of others and go on such a quest, Kindra thought, but Rohana picked up the thought.

"It was not as easy as that, Kindra. Gabriel has not yet forgiven me."

"And this child you did not want is the price of his forgiveness? You pay highly for your husband's good will, my lady," Kindra said, and Rohana spontaneously embraced her.

"Oh, my friend, do not say *my lady* to me. Call me by my name! I may call *you* my friend, may I not? My house is full of women, but I have no real friend anywhere among them! Not even Jaelle—she disapproves of me so much!"

"Not even *Domna* Alida? Not even *Dom* Gabriel's sister?"

"She least of all," Rohana said, still clinging to Kindra and looking up at her. "It troubles her that all things in the Domain have been given into my hands; she knows well that Gabriel is not competent to rule his own affairs, but she feels that since she is an Ardais and a *leronis*, if affairs must be in any hands but Gabriel's own, they should be in hers. I think she would kill me if she could think of a way to escape punishment for my murder. She watches me forever—" Rohana deliberately stopped herself, aware that she sounded as if she were on the edge of hysteria.

"So you can see I am in need of a friend. Stay with me, Kindra—stay at least until the baby is born!"

Impulsively, Kindra embraced her.

"I will stay as long as you want me, Rohana, I promise. Even if I must send Jaelle southward with a caravan before winter."

"She will not like that," said Rohana, smiling wanly. "And to say that is like prophesying snow in the pass of Scaravel at Midwinter—it takes not much *laran*." And having said this, she found herself wondering; did Kindra have *laran* after all? It was unheard of for her to be so much at ease with anyone outside her own caste.

Kindra grinned at her. She said "I told you once in the desert, I think you would make a notable Amazon, Rohana. You have the true spirit. When I go southward with Jaelle, why not come with us? Or if it troubles you to travel when you are pregnant, bide here beneath his roof until your child is born. If it is a daughter, we will take her south with us and foster her in Thendara Guild House; if it is a son, leave it with *Dom* Gabriel since he has other women and all he now desires of you is another son. I think you would be happy as one of the Oath-bound of the *Com'hi Letzii*."

She smiled, and Rohana knew that the offer had been made at least partly in jest; but suddenly Rohana was seized by a great wild desire to ride south with Kindra as once she had done, on their quest to the Dry Towns; to leave all this behind her, and follow Kindra anywhere, even to the end of the world.

"What a mad thought!" she said breathlessly, "but you make it sound very tempting, Kindra. I—" to her own shock and surprise her voice wavered, "I almost wish I could. Almost."

III

A little after Kindra had left her, after she had seen to the welfare of the younger children, and sought out Valentine in his nursery to make certain all was well with her fosterling, Gabriel came to her in the conservatory. He looked ill and tired, and Rohana's heart went out to him as always.

"Are you well, Rohana? You have been more sick with this pregnancy than any of the others. I did not know that, or I would have let you be."

She said irritably, "It is something late to think of that now." At his crestfallen look she repented her cross tone and said, "All the same, I thank you for saying it now."

He said shyly, "I thank you for your graciousness to poor little Tessa this morning. Believe me, I would not have affronted you; I did not mean you to take it like that. But she is in trouble at home and I did not think it right to leave her there to suffer when her trouble was all of my making."

Rohana shrugged. "You know perfectly well it matters nothing to me with whom—or what—you share your bed. As you made clear to me this morning, I am no good to you at present." She did not hear the bitterness in her own voice until she had finished; and then it was too late.

He reached impulsively for her hands and kissed them. "Rohana," he said breathlessly, "you know very well you are the only woman I have ever loved!"

She smiled a little and closed her hands over his. "Yes, my dear, I suppose so."

"Rohana," he demanded impulsively, still breathless, "What has happened to us? We used to love one another so much!"

She held his hands in hers.

"I don't know, Gabriel," she said, "perhaps it is only that we are both growing old." She touched his cheek in a rare caress. "You don't look well, my dear. Perhaps riding so early is not good for you. Are you still taking the medicine sent you from Nevarsin?"

He shook his head, frowning. "It does me no good,"

he protested, "and then when I drink wine, it makes me sick."

She shrugged. "You must do what you think best," she said. "If you choose to have falling seizures rather than giving up drink, I cannot choose for you."

The impatient look she dreaded came over his face again; as always, if she spoke about his drinking he was angry. He said stiffly, "I came only to thank you for your kindness to Tessa," and stormed away again. Rohana sighed and went to the little room where she went over the business of the farm each day with the steward. She let the nurse bring Valentine to play on the floor with his blocks; her own unborn child had recently begun to move in her body, and she thought about what it would be like to bring up another child. Perhaps this son she could shield a little from Gabriel's influence, so that some day he could be some use to her on the estate; she did not feel she could trust either of the boys now. And Elorie was not old enough to know or care much about such things.

She spent the morning discussing with the steward the wisdom of replanting resin-trees at this season against the added dangers of forest-fire if there were too many resin-trees; and the necessity of dealing with the forge-folk for metal to shoe the best of the riding-horses. Of necessity she had learned a good deal about the business of processing resins for paints and wood-sealers to keep wooden fences and buildings from rotting away; the high quality resins could only be processed from the trees whose presence brought the greatest dangers of forest fire.

Not till late afternoon, when Valentine had been sent to the nursery for a nap and his supper of boiled eggs and rusks, was Rohana free to ride; she sent a message inviting Kindra to join her if she wished. She went quickly to her room and changed into a shabby old riding-skirt; when Kindra joined her, she found that she envied the other woman's freedom of breeches and boots, remembering how she herself had worn them on her adventure with Kindra's band.

They were preparing to ride through the gates when Jaelle came into the stable in riding things.

"Oh, please—may I ride with you?"

The question had been addressed to Kindra; she turned to Rohana. "It is for your guardian to say."

Jaelle said sullenly, "You are my guardian," but she turned politely to Rohana.

"Please, kinswoman?"

"Well, since you already have your riding things on—but we shall have no time for hawking; we will only be riding to the Ridge to inspect the resin-plantings," Rohana told her. "Come, if you can keep up."

Jaelle ran to lead out her horse.

"Keep up with you? I will guarantee I can ride harder, faster, further than either of you—or both!" she exclaimed, jumping up swiftly into the saddle.

"Oh, certainly you can ride harder and further than I can now, Jaelle—or any pregnant woman," Rohana said, and pretended she did not see her ward's grimace of distaste.

"Doesn't it make you angry to be tied down that way?"

"Not a bit of it," Rohana returned equably. "Remember this is my fourth child and I know what to expect. Come, let's ride up toward the ridge; I need to see for myself what the winter has done to the resin-trees."

"Why doesn't *Dom* Gabriel see to that?" Jaelle asked.

"Because he has never had any kind of sense for business matters, Jaelle; do you think there is something wrong with the notion that a woman should administer the affairs of the Domain?"

"No, certainly not; but he leaves it all to you, along with all the other things that everyone else agrees are your affair—caring for the house, the meals, the children—so that you do a woman's work and a man's, too—"

"Because I have always been stronger than Gabriel; if I left it to him, all these things would be in a muddle and the estate in great financial difficulties. Or is it that you think I should make Gabriel diaper the babies and count linens, and perhaps bake bread and cake?"

The picture that created in Rohana's mind was so ludicrous that even Jaelle laughed.

"I feel he should do his share," Jaelle said. "If he does not, what good is a man, anyway?"

Rohana smiled and said, "Well, my dear, it's just the way the world is arranged."

"Not for me," Jaelle said.

"Would it surprise you, Jaelle, to know that when Gabriel was younger, before his health was so broken, he did indeed rock the children, sing to them, and get up with them at night so I could sleep? When we were first wed he was the kindest and tenderest of fathers. He did not drink much then. . . ."

Jaelle found that so disturbing that she changed the subject. "When do we go southward, Kindra, so I can take the Oath?"

Kindra opened her mouth to speak, but Rohana said first, "Surely there's no hurry. I had hoped you would give me as much time as you gave the Guild House; three years, to know what you want from life."

Jaelle's eyes flamed.

"No! You promised me, Kindra, that if I spent a year with my Comyn kinfolk, there would be no further delay. And I have given you a year, as you asked." She added scowling, "You spoke to me, at that time, some fine words about honor and the value of your word."

Kindra sighed. "I am not trying to delay you, Jaelle. But I have pledged your kinswoman—who is my friend—that I will remain here until her child is born. You cannot take the Oath here."

Jaelle looked like a stormcloud. She said, "Kindra—"

"I know, I had, perhaps, no right to make such a pledge in view of my word to you," Kindra said, and Rohana interrupted.

"It is my fault, Jaelle; I begged her. Will you deprive me of her company while I am so far from my usual health?"

Jaelle stared at the ground moving past under the horse's feet. At last she said sullenly, "If it is your will, Rohana, then your claim on Kindra is the best." She did not believe this; she frowned even more darkly, thinking; grown-ups always made their own decisions, without the slightest concern for what younger people wanted.

Rohana understood all this as well as if Jaelle had said

it all aloud, but she could not say so. As they rode up the ridge, she drew her horse neck and neck with Jaelle's and said, "I promise to you I will make no further obstacle to your taking the Oath if it is still your desire."

"Can you possibly have any reason to doubt it?" Jaelle asked, "Do you think your life is so fair I would wish to lead it?"

"Still, I would not have you take oath too young," Kindra said. "It would not hurt to delay a little; you might later wish to marry."

Jaelle looked her full in the eyes. "Why? So that I might have children first—and then abandon them, as you did?"

"Jaelle!" cried out Rohana, feeling Kindra's recoil of pain before the words were entirely spoken. "How can you—"

Kindra slapped Jaelle, hard, across her cheek. She said calmly, "You are insolent. Certainly it is better to prevent such a necessity; but I did not do it willingly, and it is better to take thought first. Would it be better to abandon the Oath should you later wish to change your mind and marry?"

"That will take place, kinswomen, when the Pass of Scaravel runs with fire instead of ice," Jaelle said angrily, and stared at the resin-tree stubs broken by the winds of the past winter.

"Well, are they salvageable, or must they be replanted?" Kindra asked. "I do not know of such things."

"Now that I have seen, I can decide at leisure at home," said Rohana, turning her horse about on the trail. "No decision should ever be taken in haste, certainly not one like this."

They rode back silently toward the castle below.

IV

A few days later, Kindra woke early and wondered what had awakened her. Jaelle, in the next room, was sleeping; Kindra could hear her quiet breathing through the opened door. Outside in the corridors was a bellowing, a pounding, an unholy clamor; was it a fire, an attack by bandits? Outside the shutters she could see the dim grayish-pink light of the coming dawn.

Kindra slid her feet into fuzzy indoor boots and pulling a robe round her shoulders, went out into the corridor. Now she could recognize the bellowing voice as *Dom* Gabriel's; hoarse, almost frenzied, shouting, and quite incoherent. Kindra could not help wondering if he was already drunk at this unseemly hour and wondered for a moment if she should tactfully disappear so as not to embarrass Rohana, or whether the presence of a stranger might restrain some dangerous act.

Dom Gabriel came into view at the end of the corridor. Young Kyril, seemed to be trying to restrain his father, who was brandishing something and yelling at the top of his lungs about a horsewhipping.

Kyril said clearly, "I shouldn't advise you to try it, Father; you might find out it is not I who gets whipped. It is not my fault if your women find me more of a man than you."

Now Kindra could see the girl Tessa, scantily clad in a garment revealing even for a bedgown, clinging to Kyril's shoulders and trying to pull the two men apart. Rian came and skillfully in mid-yell wrenched his father off Kyril—evidently he knew some sleight or special skill at wrestling—and pushed his father, abruptly quiet as if he had been stricken dumb, down into one of the chairs placed at intervals along the hall. Lady Rohana, half-dressed, came along the corridor and her face turned sick at the number of people witnessing the scene. She said softly, "Thank you, Rian. Please go and call his body-servant at once, or he may be ill. Gabriel, will you come back to bed now?" she asked, bending over the trembling man. "No, of course not; Tessa will go with you—won't you, my dear."

"Damned little slut," Gabriel mumbled. "Din' you hear? Should be horsewhipped an' I'm the one to do—" He made a half-hearted attempt to rise, but his legs would not carry him and he sank back.

Kyril stepped forward and put his arm round Tessa. "Lay a hand on her, Father, and I swear you'll be the one to suffer!"

Gabriel struggled upward.

"Bastard! Le'me at him! Want to fight? Put yer fists up like a man, I say!" He lurched at Kyril, who launched a blow at him; but Rohana, flinging herself between them, received the heavy blow on the side of the head.

Kyril cried out in shock, "Mother!" and reached out to keep her from falling. Gabriel's reaction was almost the same, but on seeing Rohana dizzy and half-conscious in her elder son's arms, he staggered back and let himself fall into the chair, mumbling, "Rohana? Rohana, you all right?"

"Small thanks to you if she is," Kyril said angrily and lowered his mother gently to the arm of an old settee. Rian had returned with *Dom* Gabriel's body-servant, who was fussing around Lady Rohana with restoratives. She raised her head and said, "Kyril—"

"Oh, yes, blame everything on me, as usual!" the young man said, his arm round Tessa. "If I had had somewhere to take her, this would never have happened."

Dom Gabriel muttered, "Should throw—little slut—right out o' here—"

Kyril looked almost heroic with his arm round the shrinking girl.

"If she goes, Father, I go with her; mark my words! And after this, keep your hands off *my* women—understand?"

Dom Gabriel raised his swollen blustering face, scowled and shook his fist, struggling to speak; then his body twisted into a frightful spasm and he fell, striking his head, twisted and lay with his body twitching, unconscious. Rohana sprang toward him, appalled, but his body-servant knew what to do; the man forced a twisted kerchief into *Dom* Gabriel's mouth so he would not bite his tongue, straightened his limbs a little as the convulsion died down, and knelt beside him, muttering words of reassurance as his eyes opened. Kyril flinched as his father stared sightlessly at him.

"It's all right, Kyril," said Lady Rohana wearily. "When he comes round, he won't remember anything about it."

"Look here, Mother, you can't blame me for this—"

"Not entirely; but you should know that when he has

been drinking for days, this would be likely to happen and anything might set him off." She added to the body-servant, "Call one or two of the stewards and get him to his room and his bed; he will not leave it today nor probably tomorrow. And make sure that when he comes round there is soup or broth for him, but not a drop of wine, no matter how abusive he is nor how he raves. If you cannot refuse him, tell me and I will come and talk to him."

When *Dom* Gabriel had been carried to his room, she looked at the assembled family in the hallway.

"I suppose there is no use in telling people to go back to bed and sleep after all this," she said, and went to her daughter. "Don't cry, Elorie, Father has been ill like this before; he won't die of it, no matter how bad it looks. We must simply try harder to keep him from so much drinking or too much excitement." She turned to Kyril, who still stood with his arms round Tessa. She said to the girl in a clear icy voice, "You are not very loyal to your lord, my child."

"No, Mother," protested Kyril. "It's the other way round. Father knew perfectly well Tessa was my girl. He brought her here to make trouble, that's all, maybe because he was hoping people would think it was *his* child! But how could anyone think an old goat like him—" he broke off abruptly, his voice strangling back in his throat as he looked at his mother. In her light gown, it was perfectly clear that Rohana's pregnancy was well advanced. He stared at the floor and mumbled. Jaelle snickered, her hand held tight over her mouth so only a suffocated sound like a fart escaped. Kindra scowled angrily at her, and Jaelle stared at the floor.

Rohana said wearily, "Well, the girl should be monitored; if the child is an Ardais, no matter which of you fathered the poor thing, Tessa is certainly entitled to shelter here, and protection, and it is my business to see to it. Alida, will you have her monitored today?"

She beckoned to the *leronis,* who said, "Certainly; Gabriel had spoken to me about her child already—"

"Then he did not know—then he thought—" Rohana said half under her breath. She swayed on her feet suddenly, and Kindra supported her with a strong arm.

"Lady, this is too much for you," she said urgently.

"If everyone will—go and dress—I will see to break-fast in the hall—" Rohana said shakily.

Jaelle said in a firm voice, "No, Aunt, you are ill; *Dom* Gabriel is being looked after by his servants; you go back to bed, and Elorie and I will see to breakfast. Kindra, get her back to her room—call one of the women and carry her, don't let her walk! Aunt, for the baby's sake—"

"Why, thank you, Jaelle," said Rohana in surprise, letting herself fall back into Kindra's arms as the wave of sickness threatened to overcome her. She never knew who carried her to her room or her bed.

The light had strengthened considerably when she woke again, and Kindra was sitting by her bed.

Jaelle was just opening the door. She asked in a whisper, "How is she, Kindra?"

"You needn't whisper, Jaelle, I'm awake," Rohana said and was surprised at how shaky her own voice sounded. "Is everything all right downstairs?"

"Oh, yes; everyone had breakfast; Elorie told the cooks to make spicebread, and she had hot cider served to the workmen. Rian told everyone the Master was ill, and the replanting of resin-trees would begin at noon— he would come himself to oversee—"

"Rian is a good boy," said Rohana softly.

"Yes; he knows the estate well, and if Kyril would let him, he could save his father much trouble," Jaelle said, "but Kyril is so jealous that Rian might have some influence with his father—" she shrugged. "It was Kyril who took up some broth and was feeding *Dom* Gabriel; it was, I am sure, a touching sight, but I heard *Dom* Gabriel shouting, as loud as he can shout which is not very loud now, to take away that swill and bring him some wine."

"Oh, dear," Rohana struggled to sit upright, "I must go to him and explain—"

"No indeed," Kindra said urgently, "You must keep your bed, my lady—Rohana," she corrected herself, "or you are likely to miscarry. And *Dom* Gabriel, at least if he were in his right mind, would like that even less than having the stewards refuse his orders."

Rohana sighed and lay flat again, knowing that what Kindra said was perfectly true. Gabriel would simply have to resign himself; though always irritable for days after one of these seizures, he dreaded them enough that he might indeed heed a warning. "But tell him why I do not come to keep him company and sit by his bed," she said.

Jaelle said, "I sent the healer-woman with a message already, Aunt. And I have sent for the midwife; she will know if there is danger."

Thus reassured, Rohana settled herself beneath the covers and lay somnolent, neither waking or sleeping all the morning. She hardly noticed the visit of the estate midwife, who examined her briefly and said she was in no immediate danger of miscarrying but a day or two of rest could do her nothing but good; that the lady was inclined to work too hard for her own good. When she woke in the late afternoon she found Kindra seated by her bed, her needle flashing in and out of a piece of fabric.

"What are you making? Jaelle does so little of this kind of work, I never connect it with a Free Amazon—a Renunciate."

"I find it restful; it is a collar," Kindra said. "I seldom have leisure to sit and do fancywork of this sort. If you like, I will make a piece of embroidery for a baby dress; then if your child is a girl—"

"Oh, no," Rohana said, "I would like a girl well; but it is a son, and Gabriel at least will be pleased."

"I suppose it is your *laran* that tells you that," Kindra said, and Rohana looked startled.

"Why, I suppose so; I never thought of it—I cannot imagine what it would be like to be pregnant and not know whether I bore a son or daughter. Are there women who truly do not know?"

"Oh, yes," Kindra said, "though I always was sure— but I thought perhaps it was my own fancy—at least I always had an even chance of being right."

There was a muffled knock on the door, and Lady Alida came in.

"Are you feeling better, Rohana? My dear, you must not trouble yourself about anything, anything at all; I can see to everything, absolutely everything," she said, smiling, and Kindra thought that the smile was not unlike a plump kitten who had fallen into the cream jar.

"I am sure of it," Rohana murmured.

"But there are a few things which must be settled at once," Alida said, "Kyril must be sent away immediately; this hostility against his father is very bad for both of them. He should go to Nevarsin; he needs discipline and some learning. It is not good for him to be here when you and Gabriel are at odds; he is almost a grown man."

"I suggested this a year ago, but Gabriel would not agree," Rohana said, and Alida smiled her cat-smile.

"Then perhaps there was some good in this morning's altercation; Gabriel will be glad to have him out of the house, I think. And there is something else; I monitored the girl Tessa; and it is indeed Kyril's child she is carrying." Her face took on an edge of fastidious distaste. "Will you really keep her under this roof?"

"What choice have I? If the child is an Ardais—even a *nedestro* has the right to shelter beneath his father's roof," Rohana said.

Alida grimaced. "I have seldom so resented the monitor's Oath," she said. "I was tempted to tell the girl she was lying—she wasn't, of course—and throw her out. I admit I don't have your charity, Rohana."

"I am not displeased at the thought of even a *nedestro* grandson," Rohana said, but Alida shook her head.

"Only a girl. I am sorry if that is not what you wanted."

"A granddaughter I will welcome, if she is healthy and strong," Rohana said. "At home she might be ill-treated, starved, or abused. Make arrangements, Alida: find her a room of her own and someone to look after her, and mind you, don't stint her of anything because Kyril will not be here to see. Anything else?"

"Yes." Alida had been moving about the room, now she came and sat down in a small upright chair. "Rohana, did you know that Rian is a full wide-open telepath, two-way, and probably a full empath as well? Gods alone know where he got it—it's not an Ardais trait."

"Oh, I am not sure of that," Rohana said. "Before he

became so ill, Gabriel had a good touch of empathy; it was what I loved best in him." She paused to consider. "So Rian has it? No wonder he is torn so—"

"Between sympathy for you and for his father," Alida said bluntly, "the strife is tearing him to pieces. He should be in a Tower."

"I had hoped for a year or two of education for him in Nevarsin first—" Rohana protested.

"By no means," said Alida firmly. "He is too sensitive and scrupulous; he would heed every word they tell him. Surely you know that most boys hear only a little of what their elders say—Kyril has never heeded anything he is told—but Rian would take every word to his heart and dwell all his life a prisoner of *cristoforo* scruples. No, Rohana; the only safe place for him is a Tower, and I have already been in the relays; Arilinn will take him. Don't worry; they will educate him as well there as at Nevarsin, be sure of that."

I suppose I should be grateful, Rohana thought, *for Alida has spared no trouble for my sons, but her officiousness infuriates me; she really wants all things in her own hands. She is positively gloating that while I lie here ill, she has arranged everything as well or better than I could have done.*

But she attempted to barricade her thoughts from Alida and to thank her graciously.

"You have arranged everything so well, sister-in-law, that now I will have all my children gone from me— except for Elorie, and she is betrothed—I shall be an idle old woman."

"Idle? You?" Kindra protested. "And you have still Valentine and Jaelle."

"Jaelle makes no secret of it that she is eager to be gone," Rohana said.

Alida said, "That cannot be allowed, Kindra. She must take her mother's place in a Tower; I am sure we could find one that would be glad to have her."

Rohana said, "Have you ever seen any sign that she has enough *laran* for that? I think she would be miserable in a Tower."

Alida said crossly, "You know as well as I that she is blocking her *laran;* and you know why. You told me the story of her mother's death, when Valentine was born. She is not the first young girl whose *laran* was shocked open by a rapport she could not avoid and was not mature enough to endure—a traumatic birth, too close at hand to be shielded, or a death of someone she loved." Certainly, Rohana thought, that described Melora's desert death in childbirth. Alida continued, "But she cannot avoid it forever; some day it will return in full force; and she should be trained within a Tower against that day. Of course her parentage—that Dry Town father of hers—is against her—but they might be persuaded to overlook it. Certainly not at Arilinn. They are so particular about Comyn parentage, but Rian is to go there. I am sure one of the lesser Towers would have Jaelle. Margwenn at Thendara perhaps, or Leominda at Neskaya. Should I try to make such arrangements? I would be happy to try—"

"I am sure you would, Alida," said Rohana, wearily, "but this time your skills at arranging things are not needed; I promised Jaelle that if she spent a year here, I would make no further objection if she wanted to take Oath as a Renunciate."

Alida's mouth fell open; her eyes, very large and blue, stared at Rohana with an unbelieving gaze. "I know you said so when she was a child," she said, "but are you really going to hold to that? Even if she has *laran*?"

"I promised," Rohana said, "and my word is good. I do not lie even to children."

"But—" Alida looked more innocent and confused than ever, "the Council—they will not be pleased, Rohana. There are so few living Aillard women."

"I think I can persuade the Council," Rohana said.

Alida sighed. She said, "You will soon have opportunity. They have sent word to summon Gabriel for the season, and since you still call yourself Aillard and not Ardais, and sit in Council as Aillard, it concerns you, too. But now that Jaelle is of age—and since you are pregnant—I was so sure—"

"You were so sure that you told them that Melora's daughter would be ready to take her Council seat this season, did you not, Alida," Rohana said softly. "Well, you will just have to tell them you were lying or fantasizing, will you not?"

Alida's blue eyes flamed with indignation.

"Lying? How dare you? How could I imagine that you would allow Melora's daughter to elude her duty by such an unlawful commitment?"

"Not unlawful," Rohana said. "The Charter of the Renunciates allows that any freeborn woman may seek Oath among them. It is true there have been times when I thought Comyn daughters were born less free than any small-holder's child; I had never thought you would agree with me, sister-in-law."

"You are making a fool of me, Rohana!"

"No, my dear, you are doing that admirably for yourself. When you informed Council that Melora's daughter was ready for Council, you made a commitment you had no right to make and meddled in something which was really none of your business. I did not bid you speak of this to the Council, and you will simply have to get out of your own lies for yourself." Rohana lay back against her pillow and closed her eyes; but Kindra felt that behind the carefully impassive face Rohana was smiling.

"Rohana," implored Alida, "you cannot do this, the Council will not allow it."

Rohana sat up sharply. "Do you really think they can stop me?"

"Surely there is some other way—"

"Oh, yes, certainly," Rohana said wearily, "I could petition to take the Oath myself."

Alida cried out. "You would not! You are joking!"

"Not a bit of it," Rohana said, "but it is true, I probably would not. But to get freedom for Jaelle, I might well tell the Council how unfit a guardian Gabriel is for any young girl; I might well testify to how he has humiliated and insulted me before my whole household, and petition to dissolve my marriage, to have him confined as a lunatic, and to forfeit his Council position and his place as Head and Warden of Ardais. If Kyril were not worse than his father, I would certainly do so."

"Oh, Rohana!" Alida was sobbing now, "For the honor of the Comyn—this would be a scandal to the

Seven Domains—you would not drag the honor of Ardais in the mud so, would you?"

"I am tired of hearing you babble about the honor of Ardais," Rohana said, "What have you done to preserve it? It suits you well to have Gabriel incompetent to manage his own affairs while it means that *you* can manage them with no chance he will be able to forbid you. Did it occur to you that if Gabriel goes on much longer like this, he will drink himself to death or cause a scandal we cannot keep safe inside these walls? He is my husband, and I loved him once; for his own good he should be subject to someone who can restrain him from killing himself once and for all. I cannot."

"Do you think I want him to die?" Alida asked.

"You are certainly doing nothing to prevent it, and it seems to me that you are fighting all I can do to prevent it," Rohana said. "Can't you admit, Alida, that I am doing the best for the Domain and even for Gabriel? As much as you dislike me—"

"Please don't say that," Alida interrupted. "I don't dislike you; I admire and respect you—"

Rohana sighed and closed her eyes. She said without trying to answer Alida, "The representatives from Council, are they here?"

"They are awaiting audience with Gabriel—or with you if he cannot meet with them."

Rohana said wearily, "Perhaps they had better see him, so they will not think I am merely trying to avoid—"

Alida protested, "But such a disgrace for them actually to *see* him like this!"

"I did not bid him drink himself into a stupor or excite himself into a seizure," Rohana said. "They must see him, Alida, or they will believe—as I think Kyril believes—that I am trying to take over the rule of the Domain for my own purposes. Send for the hall-steward."

Still protesting, Alida went, and Kindra, who had stood silently in the shadow of the bed-curtains, advanced to her side and said, "Are you able to deal with all this, Rohana?"

"It must be dealt with one way or another," said Rohana, "and there is none to do it if I do not. But you should not be—no one should be subjected to my family."

Kindra said, "You should not be subjected to your family," and felt a wave of tenderness for Rohana. *If I could only safeguard her against all this aggravation.*

Rohana lay silent with her eyes closed, hoarding her strength. After a considerable time, there was a soft rap on the door, and Rohana sat up, saying "Let them in; I must speak with them."

Three young men came into the room and bowed low to Rohana. All three bore proudly the flaming red heads of Comyn; the leader bowed to Lady Rohana and said "My lady of Ardais, I am sorry for the illness of your lord; it is all too obvious that he will not be fit to attend Council this season. Will you, as usual, take his Council seat?"

"As you can see, this year I cannot," said Lady Rohana, "My health will forbid it for this season. If my child is born healthy and strong, I might come toward the end of the season."

"What, then, of your ward—the daughter of Melora Aillard?" asked the young man. "May we speak with her and ask if she is ready to be sworn to Council as Heir to Aillard?"

"That you must arrange with Jaelle herself," said Rohana, and when they had gone away, she sent again for Jaelle, who came sullenly to her.

"Jaelle, the representatives of Council are here; you must go South with them to Comyn Council and tell them for yourself that you renounce your rights, through Melora, to Comyn Council."

Jaelle protested "You promised me that I could take Oath—"

"And so you shall, if that is what you wish," Rohana said, "but I cannot renounce your rights for you; you must do that for yourself."

"But how—"

"They will ask you to present yourself before the Council, and they will ask you if you are ready to take your place in Council," Kindra said. "And then you must answer 'No.' That is all there is to it." She added,

"If you are old enough to swear Oath as a Renunciate, you are old enough to renounce Council privilege."

"But what do I do then?"

"Whatever you wish," said Kindra. "If you choose, you can go at once to the Guild House and await my coming to take Oath if you will."

Jaelle said sulkily, "I had thought we would go south together."

"Well, we cannot," Kindra said curtly. "For the moment at least, my duty lies here, and yours in Thendara, at Council."

"Oh, very well," Jaelle said angrily. "If it means more to you than coming to witness me take the Oath." She slammed out of the room angrily, and Rohana heard her talking in the hall to the young men sent from Council.

"Will she ever forgive me, Kindra?"

"Oh, certainly; there is nothing wrong with her but that she is sixteen years old," Kindra said. "She is angrier now with me than with you. Give her a year or two. It would be even less than a year if she were involved in the running of a Domain, but even so, she will forgive you. She will even forgive me my loyalty to you. Some day."

Only one more confrontation remained for the day; at sunset, Kyril asked admission to the room and came in quietly, kissing his mother's hand in a respectful manner.

"I am sorry to see you sick, Mother. When he heard, Father was eager to get up and attend you, but his steward would not let him out of bed."

"I am glad there is a sensible man to look after him," Rohana said. "What do you want, Kyril? Surely you did not come to wish me health."

"Why should you think not, Mother? You have worn yourself out caring for my father's responsibilities; why do you not let him look after his own—"

"This again, Kyril?"

"You are making my father a nonentity and a laughingstock before all of the Domains."

"No, my dear, the Gods did that. I save him the pressure of decisions he is unfit to carry, and I try to keep his honor intact before others." After a moment she said, "Would it be better if the crops went unplanted, the stud-books unkept, the resin-tree harvest ungathered? Are you able to take over that work? I would gladly yield all this to you if you could handle it."

"You mock my ignorance, Mother? That was not my doing either. Now perhaps, if I am to go to Nevarsin, I may learn to manage such things."

"The Gods grant it, Kyril," she said. He knelt for her blessing. She gave it fervently, laying her hands on his curly head.

Then he rose and stared down at her, frowning. "Is it true what Jaelle says—that she is to become a Free Amazon?"

"The laws allow it for any freeborn woman, Kyril. It is her choice."

"Then that is a vicious law and should not be allowed," Kyril said. "She should marry if anyone can be found who would overlook her parentage."

"This saves us the trouble of finding some such husband for her," Rohana said. "Leave it, Kyril; there is nothing you can do about it."

Kyril said angrily "I tried—" and broke off; but it was obvious to Rohana what he meant. A deep blush spread over his face.

She said scathingly, "And you tried to make her see what she might be missing if she refused marriage? You cannot forgive her that she did not fall directly into your arms? For shame, Kyril; this was a breach of hospitality—she is my fosterling. You should have respected her, under this roof, as your own sister! But she goes south to Thendara tonight, so no harm is done." After a moment she said, "Kyril, we part tonight; you go to Nevarsin; let us at least part without hostility. Wish me well, and go to say farewell to your father in peace."

Kyril flung himself to his knees and kissed his mother's hand again. He said, subdued, "I owe you gratitude for caring for Tessa; I was worried about her. Are you sending me away because of that scene this morning—because I made my father look a fool?"

"No, my dear," Rohana assured him gently. "It is high time you were sent away to be prepared for your place in life and in the Domain. You should have gone years ago. Now go and say farewell to your father and refrain from quarreling with him if you can; you set out at daybreak."

"And Rian is to go to a Tower?" Kyril said. "I am glad; he will make a good *laranzu,* and he at least will not contend with me for Heirship to the Domain."

"Surely you never thought he would, Kyril," Rohana said, as she put her arms around his neck and hugged him in farewell. "Good-bye, my dear son; learn well, and make the most of every opportunity. When you come back—"

"When I come back, the Domain will not be in need of woman's rule," said Kyril, "and you, Mother, can rest and confine yourself to a woman's work."

"I shall be glad of that," Rohana said softly, and when Kyril had gone, she sighed and said to Kindra, "and yet he was the dearest and sweetest of little boys. How could I have gone so wrong in his upbringing, that he turned out like this?"

"You were not the only force in his upbringing," Kindra said. "The world will go as it will, Rohana, not as you or I will have it. And I fear that is true of our children, too. Yours and mine, my lady."

V

It was very quiet at Ardais when the young people had departed. Kindra welcomed the quiet for Rohana's sake; *Dom* Gabriel was on his feet again, more or less, looking shaky and weak, but with the aid of his stewards even managing to make some show of supervising the replanting of the resin-trees.

Although no longer confined to bed, Rohana felt unable to be much out of doors or to ride; she allowed the steward to assist Gabriel with the replanting and took such minor exercise as she required, walking in the courtyards. Kindra felt this confining but did not wish to leave Rohana, nor to affront *Dom* Gabriel by coming into his presence unasked. As for Jaelle, Kindra missed her but felt that the absence of her sharp and critical presence made life easier for everyone, especially Rohana.

The only remaining young person besides Elorie, the

girl Tessa, kept a very low profile in Kyril's absence, appearing but rarely in the hall; Rohana was just as well pleased that the girl was content to take her meals in her own room and did not grudge the extra service. There was no reason Gabriel should be reminded of his humiliation at his elder son's hands. Sometimes, at Rohana's invitation, the girl joined the women at their sewing in the conservatory; as far as Kindra could judge she was a harmless, shallow little thing, with nothing much to say for—or of—herself. She did not seem to miss Kyril and made no effort to regain *Dom* Gabriel's interest.

For the most part of a tenday, life at Ardais went on in this quiet way. One morning Kindra wakened to the sound of a great windstorm which roared and wailed around the corners of the building so as to drown out most human conversation. Looking from a window she saw nothing but acres of tossing leaves, trees bending like live things almost to the ground, snapping off short into broken stakes. In her near-forty years, Kindra had seen no weather even remotely like this; no one ventured out except to tend the animals, for any except the strongest farm workers would be blown off their feet. Kindra stepped out on a balcony and had to hold fast to the railing lest she be slammed back against the stone wall. The very air seemed to crackle with weird energy, although there was no thunder. Rohana looked troubled and refused to approach the balcony.

"Is it the wind that frightens you?" Kindra asked. "I have never known anything like it; I am a strong woman but I was very nearly blown off my feet. You could have a bad fall—which could be dangerous for you just now."

"Do you think I would care?" Rohana asked. "I am so sick of being inactive, of doing nothing! I don't care what happens—" Then she broke off and looked guilty. "But this far along in pregnancy, my child is strong enough that I can feel his struggle to live; I cannot endanger that life." Kindra was appalled; she had no idea that any such thoughts had been crossing Rohana's mind. She felt deeply troubled for her.

"Not the wind," Rohana went on, "but the energy in the air; it can ignite fires when the resin-trees are so dry.

We had too little snow last winter. Unless it begins to
rain before the wind dies, we must send out a fire-watch
at first light."

Kindra had never heard of such a thing; though she
knew lightning was the major cause of forest-fire, this
strange storm without visible lightning or thunder was
new to her.

The sun was not visible; in the swirling wind, clouds
of leaves, snow from the crags, and loose gravel occluded
and hid the sun; a mysterious yellow twilight gradually
took over the sky, which toward nightfall turned an eerie
greenish color. There was no visible sunset; the light simply faded toward darkness until it was gone. In the darkness the wind went on howling like some chorus of
demented demons. Whatever lights, torches, or candles
were lighted were blown out almost at once by the drafts
in the corridors; it was difficult to light fires in the main
fireplaces, for the suction of the high winds in the chim-
neys blew back and tried to extinguish them. Elorie
wrapped Valentine in blankets and brought him down
from his nursery to join the others in the great hall before the fitful and smoking fire which seemed perpetually
on the very edge of going out. He was fretful until *Dom*
Gabriel, to Kindra's astonishment, took the child on his
lap before the smoky hearth and croaked old military
ballads in a quavering voice to distract the child.

Elorie said, "It must be terrible to be out in this, Papa,
do you think Rian and Kyril are safe by now in Nevarsin
or wherever they have gone?"

"Oh, yes, for sure they will be in Nevarsin by now,"
Gabriel said, counting on his fingers. "What the devil
ails the fire, Rohana?"

"The wind in the chimney keeps putting it out," Rohana said. "I will do my best to spell it to burn." She
reached into the bosom of her dress and drew out her
matrix, unwrapping the stone and gazing into it. Slowly
the fire on the hearth flared up with a stronger blue
light, and for a little time it burned with an almost steady
light. Rohana had enclosed a candle in a windproof glass
so that it, too, burned strong and clean; against the unholy clamor of the wind the burning hearth fire gave a
curious illusion that all was normal. But after a time the

'suction of the wind pulled the fire raggedly back toward the chimney, and it began to beat uneasily in long ragged flames; behind them the tapestries on the walls bellied out like great sails with flapping sounds. It was, Rohana thought, as if every one of the hundreds of people who had lived and died here were flowing outside in the great screaming winds, howling and shrieking like a chorus of banshees. Yet it was only wind. The servants began to bring in the dinner; Rohana directed that it should be brought to the fire and set up on small tables and benches there.

"You have done well," she said to the cook. "Are the fires in the kitchen burning properly?"

"We have an enclosed stove," said the main cook. "And so we managed to roast a little meat for you and the master, my lady; but there is no bread, for the oven will not draw. Your fire here is the only good fire in the house; we can boil a kettle here for tea, perhaps."

Dom Gabriel said in his rusty voice, "Shall we have some hot mulled wine?"

"Yes, tonight I think so," said Rohana. In this weather, whatever would content him was good. He drank, and fed a few sips to the child in his lap. Valentine coughed and spluttered but enjoyed the attention, and when Elorie protested, Rohana shook her head. "It will make him sleepy, and he will sleep the better," she said. "Let him be for this once." She carved up the fowl and they ate before the fire, balancing the plates on their laps.

But in spite of Rohana's best efforts, the fire was beginning to sink and burn with a bewitched light, pale and fitfully. When the scant meal had been eaten, such as it was, Rohana let the fire sink and die; it was simply too much effort to maintain anything like a natural flame.

"Take *Dom* Gabriel to his chamber, Hallar," she ordered the steward. Her voice could hardly be heard over the wind clanging outside and in; the roar of wind, the banging of branches and shutters against the house.

As the man eased *Dom* Gabriel to his feet, Valentine clung to Rohana and said, "It sounds like the whole castle will blow down. Do I have to sleep alone in the nursery with the wind howling like this? Can I have a light?"

"A light will not burn tonight, *chiyu*," Elorie said, picking him up. "You shall sleep in my room in the trundle bed."

Dom Gabriel said grumpily, "Why not put him in the cradle and be done with it? He's a big boy now, aren't you, Val? Not a mollycoddle, are you, boy? You don't need a light and a nurse, do you, big fellow?"

"Yes, I do," Val said shakily, clinging to Elorie's skirt, and Elorie held him close.

"It's better than letting him be frightened to death alone, Papa."

"Ah, well—at least he is not my son," *Dom* Gabriel growled. "It's nothing to me if he turns out to be no kind of man."

Rohana thought, *Better no kind of man at all than a man like you,* but she was no longer sure that Gabriel could read the thought; there had been a time when it would have been instantly clear to him. In any case it did not matter. She wished Gabriel a good night aloud, and with her arm through Kindra's started through the dark and wailing hallways toward her own room.

Her women were clustered in the corner of her room, moaning in terror, their wails almost drowned out by the shrieking gale; as she came into the chamber, a shutter tore loose and slammed around the room, smashed into sticks of kindling and flailing everywhere. One of the slats struck Kindra and she could not keep back a cry of pain; the women took up the cries. Kindra said sharply, "It's only a stick of wood!"

"But it's cut your forehead, Kindra," Rohana said, and dipped a towel into a jar of water that stood on her dresser, sponging away the blood that trickled down her forehead. The women struggled to haul the shutter closed again. The banging sounded like some clawed thing trying to fight its way in, but something on the shutter itself had broken, so that the shutter would not fasten, and the wind was raging in the room.

"You cannot sleep in here like this," Kindra said, for the room was filled with the choking burden of dust, snow, and dead leaves borne on the howling gale, and the door into the corridor had come loose and was battering to and fro. "I am glad I will not be the one to sweep all these rooms tomorrow."

"Jaelle's room is sheltered," Rohana said, and led Kindra down the hall toward it, turning into the small room enclosed in a sheltered corner of the building, with relief. It was quieter here, and the women could hear their own voices more easily. As Kindra helped Rohana into her night things, she knew Rohana was still tense, straining to hear the wind, to know the worst.

"I am as foolish as Valentine," Rohana said, "afraid to be alone where a candle will not burn and I cannot be sure the walls will not fall around me."

"I'll stay with you," Kindra said, and slid into bed beside her. The women clung together in the dark, listening to the banging of shutters, fighting of branches against the walls and shattering of the few glass windows in the building.

After one such outburst of noise, Rohana, tense in the darkness, muttered, "Gabriel will be beside himself with despair; we have so few windows and glass is so expensive and hard to have fitted. For years now he has been trying to make the place weathertight, but a storm like this . . ." and she fell silent. "Even a few months ago, I would have gone to him and tried to calm him, but now he would mock me—or there might be someone with him who would mock me—I would even be grateful if that girl Tessa would go to him and comfort him—" her voice drifted into silence.

"Hush," Kindra said, "You must sleep."

"Yes, I must—after all this there will be work for everyone tomorrow," Rohana said, closing her eyes and snuggling against Kindra. A faraway battering sound made her wonder what other structure had come loose, fighting wildly against the storm. Then there was a sudden swashing sound, a rushing against the shutters.

"Rain," Rohana said. "With this wind it is being thrown against the walls like waves. But at least now we need not fear fire before daylight."

The sound was like a river in full flood, but Rohana had relaxed. Kindra held her close, troubled for her, knowing that it was as if the weight of the whole Domain rested on this single body, which seemed so frail and was so surprisingly strong. *And all the weight is on her; now, when it sounds as if the whole world is breaking down into wind and chaos, she bears it all on her shoulders—or in her body like the weight of her child.* Kindra held Rohana close, wishing that she could ease the burden for her friend; *It is too much for one woman to carry. I have always thought that the wives of rich men were idle, letting their men determine what they might do; but she is as powerful and self-determined as any Renunciate. The Domain could not be better managed by five strong men!* she thought, holding Rohana tenderly in her arms, *yet she is not strong, she is a frail woman and not even in good health.*

Gradually the distant sound of the roaring wind seemed merged into a song, a lullaby on which she cradled and rocked the woman in her arms. And at last, knowing Rohana slept, she slept, too, in spite of the great howl of the wind.

VI

Rohana woke to silence; sometime before sunrise the wind had died. She was still nestled in Kindra's arms and for a moment she felt a little self-conscious; *I went to sleep clinging to her like a child.*

It reminded her a little of the days when she had still believed that Gabriel was strong and had all things under his control. She had felt so secure then; and she had been sure that whatever was beyond her strength, she could turn to Gabriel for his help. Now, for these many years, not only could Gabriel not help her, he was not even strong enough to carry his own burdens and she must look after his welfare as if he were one of the children. She thanked the Gods that she had always been strong enough to look after herself and Gabriel, too, but it had been sweet to feel Gabriel's strength and enjoy his protection—and his love. It had been so long since there had been any strength on which she could lean.

Love. She had all but forgotten that there had truly been a time when she did love Gabriel— and when, in truth, he had loved her. She had clung to that long after his love for her was gone, even after her own love had died out, starved into death by lack of response; that illusion that if only she could cling to her own love, his might one day return.

Was love always an illusion, then? She supposed that Gabriel did love her in his own way—a fondness, born of habit, provided she demanded nothing, asked nothing of him. She still cared for him, remembering what once he had been. *I love my own memory of the illusion that once was Gabriel's love,* she thought, and began to turn over in bed, knowing she should rouse the servants; there would be much to set to rights after the great storm.

Then she froze as far above her in the great tower, a bell began to toll with insistent regularity, in groups of three; clang/CLANG/clang, clang/CLANG/clang. She sat upright, her breath coming swiftly. Beside her, Kindra murmured "What is it?"

"It is the fire-watch bell," Rohana said, "Somewhere on the estate, a fire has been sighted; probably during the great wind, a fire was ignited and smoldered unseen, too sheltered to be put out by the rain. It is not the danger signal yet." She put her feet to the floor and sat up, steadying herself with her hands as the room seemed to swing in slow circles round her.

She managed to get up, thrusting around with her feet for her slippers, her bare toes avoiding the cold stone floor. Kindra got up and found her robe, then followed Rohana toward the hall. The floor lay thick with dust, dead leaves, little knots of foliage, gravel in little piles. *What a cleaning project for someone!* The fire-watch bell continued its slow pattern of tolling.

The great hall was filled with people gathered for the sound of the bell; obligatory gathering, for the purpose of dealing with the single greatest danger in the mountains, or, for that matter, anywhere in the Domains; fire. Little Valentine, like all children made wild by the break in routine, was running about, shouting; Rohana made a step or two to capture him but could not; she sat down and said firmly "Come here, Val."

He came to a halt an apprehensive few steps from her;

she reached out, grabbed his shirt-tail, and beckoned to Elorie.

"Find Nurse Morna, and tell her that her only responsibility for this day is to keep Val safely above stairs, out of danger and out from under people's feet."

"I could look after him, Mother." Elorie offered.

"I am sure you can; but I have other things for you to do today. You must be my deputy, Lori. First —" Rohana found a seat on a bench and established herself; one of the women brought her a cup of tea while the old nurse was found and Val, yelling with rage at missing all the excitement, was carried away.

"Now," she directed Elorie, trying to recall everything that must be done, "go to the head cook and tell her that if the ovens can be lighted, we must have at least a dozen loaves and as many nut-cakes. Then if anyone has been butchering, we must have at least three chervine hams roasted for the workmen, and she must kill three fowl and put them over to make soup. And you must go to the west cellar and bring up the barrels there—get two of the stewards to carry them, you cannot even lift one barrel—and a couple of women to help unpack the barrels; they will have a hundred each of clay bowls and mugs. And at least four dozen pairs of blankets and so forth—and three or four sacks of beans and dried mushrooms, and barley and so forth, for the camp—and have Hallert harness up the big cart to take the men up to the ridge."

Elorie hurried away to the kitchens, and Rohana beckoned to one of the stewards.

"One of you must stay close to the master today," she said, addressing herself to Hallert. "You or Darren; try to see that he does not become too excited." There was no way she could prevent him from drinking, when law and custom demanded for every man on the fire-lines his fill of wine or beer; but if Gabriel collapsed on the fire-lines as he had done before, or had a seizure, she could only arrange that it did not disrupt the serious business of fire-fighting.

"I will look after the master," promised Hallert; he had been with the family since *Dom* Gabriel's father died.

"Thank you," Rohana said fervently. Outside they heard the old cart rumbling up to the door, and the men and the younger, more able-bodied women went to climb in. Rohana was about to join them when Lady Alida stepped in front of her.

"You know a ride in that jolting cart would be really dangerous now," she scolded in a low voice.

Rohana sighed. She knew this already; she felt heavy and sick, constantly and painfully aware of the weight of pregnancy, frantic with fear for her child, but conscious of divided duty and loyalty.

"What other choice is there, Alida? Can we let the Ridge burn?"

Kindra said, "If you will trust me, Rohana—this would not be the first fire-camp I have managed."

Rohana felt an overpowering sense of warmth and gratitude. Kindra was there, yes, able and trustworthy and fully capable of doing what she, Rohana, was not strong enough to do.

"Oh, could you, Kindra? I would be so grateful," she said with overpowering warmth, "I will leave it all in your hands, then."

"Indeed I will," Kindra said, taking Rohana's hands in hers and putting her firmly back into a chair, "Everything will be all right, you'll see; we have got at it quickly and it will not get out of hand."

Alida scowled; "They will not obey an Amazon," she pointed out to Rohana. "She is not an Ardais."

"Then they must obey her as they would obey me—" Rohana said, "*Or you*. You must see to it, Alida; it is that, or I must go no matter what."

Alida, she knew, might otherwise sabotage Kindra's efforts out of pure spite; she did not know Kindra well enough to trust her simply for the good of the Domain. "Promise me, Alida; for the good of the Domain. Gabriel really is not strong enough to do this, and—just now—neither am I. Do not try to tell me that you could boss a gang of fire-fighters."

"No; certainly not. How would I have learned such a skill?" Alida said haughtily.

"The same way I did," Rohana said, "but fortunately

for Ardais' safety this day, Kindra n'ha Mhari is willing to take over. *If* you will back her up."

Alida stared angrily into Rohana's eyes, and Rohana knew it was alien to her—to submit to the authority of the strange Amazon. But at last Alida said, "For the good of the Domain. I promise." Rohana heard what she did not quite dare to say aloud:

Some day, Rohana, you will pay for all this.

"No doubt I will," she said aloud. "When that day comes, Alida, call me to account; for now, I do what I must, no more. Promise me, on the honor of Ardais."

"I promise," Alida said, and added to Kindra; "*Mestra,* anyone who does not obey you as myself, shall be dealt with as a traitor."

Kindra said solemnly, "Thank you, Lady." She clambered up into the cart over the tongue, stepping up agilely between the animals, and took her place at the front of the workers; the driver clucked to his beasts and the cart lumbered out of the yard. Alida, standing beside Rohana, said with a reproachful look, "How is it that you could not see reason when I bade you, but for that Amazon you immediately saw sense in what I was saying—"

Rohana said, more gently than she intended, "because I have known Kindra a long time, and I know how efficient she is; whatever she does will be as well done as I could do myself."

She went into the house, and set herself to conferring with the cooks; in another hour or two, the smaller cart, laden with food and with field-ovens, went up toward a flat spot short of the actual fire-camp, from which the men would be fed and cared for during the emergency.

And then there was really nothing to do, except somehow to occupy her time, sewing on baby-clothes, a neglected pastime—in all of her previous pregnancies she would have had a full layette for the prospective newcomer at least a month before this. Her women, the few who had not gone to the fire-lines because of age or inexperience, were all pleased to see her finally making provision for the coming child and more than glad to help her at it; by noon there was a basketful of stuff assembled, small blankets, diapers, even quite a number of pretty little embroidered dresses and petticoats salvaged from the other children. Rohana's mind, no matter how she dissimulated, had not been entirely on what she was doing, and she broke off to say, "Oh—I was afraid of this." She hurried clumsily to the courtyard; it was not the small cart, as she had thought from the sound, but a wheelbarrow, into which his steward had loaded the unconscious *Dom* Gabriel, as the only available vehicle, and trundled him down from the ridge; Rohana thanked the man, and with Alida's help she set herself to applying restoratives and getting the sick man to his bed; she showed him, with soothing words, the baby-clothes and blankets she had gotten together for the baby, knowing it would please him to think of the child; after all, he was the one who had wanted it.

At last Gabriel dropped off to sleep and Rohana went to her own room and to bed. She slept but ill, tossing and turning; twice she dreamed that she had gone into labor on the very fire-lines and woke crying out in fear. It would be more than a few days, she knew, perhaps a full moon; babies tended to be born more readily at the full of the largest moon, Liriel, and Liriel was just beginning to show her narrowest new crescent in the evening sky.

She was in no hurry; she dreaded the thought, with the household in such disorder ... the boys away, and not yet recovered from the great storm. Also, though she had not counted her time very accurately, it seemed too soon; she felt her child was not yet ready to be born strong and healthy. But the constant dreams—she knew this from experience—meant that the unborn child's *laran* was intruding on her own. If she must have a child, she wanted one who was vigorous and strong, not a feeble premature one who would need a lot of care. Which reminded her that unless she wanted to breast-feed it herself—she didn't—she must consult the steward or estate midwife about another pregnant woman who would be having a child about the same time and could breast-feed her child with her own. If I am to go to Council, I cannot be troubled with feeding a babe; it must be sent out to a nurse. So she determined to make inquiries about a healthy wet-nurse so that she could do her duty

to Comyn Council without harm or neglect even to this
unwanted son coming so late in her life.

*Forgive me, child, for not wanting you. It is not you I
do not want; it is the trouble of any child at my age.* She
wondered if anyone would understand this. Other
women she talked to seemed only to feel that she was
exceptionally blessed, having a child after the regular
age to hope for such things was past. But did they really
feel that way, or was it only that this was what women
were supposed to feel? Kindra had spoken of other
women seeming always content with their lot. Am I simply, like Jaelle, constantly rebellious and questioning? I
had thought myself wholly resigned—are then the Renunciates really as dangerous to the institutions of contented, happily married women as Gabriel—and
Alida—think they are?

Certainly Kindra was the only person who had even
seemed to understand how she felt. *And truly that could
be dangerous,* she thought, without bothering to ask herself why.

Toward afternoon of the next day they could still
smell the smoke; Gabriel was up and around, but looking exhausted and weary. Most of the day Gabriel was
content to lie on a balcony overlooking the Ridge where
they could smell and see the smoke and the distant fire;
but he was too languid and weary to worry. Rohana did
enough of that for both, and found that much of her
worry was about Kindra; would the woman expose herself to peril, or have enough sense to safeguard herself
from the worst dangers?

VII

The sun was still invisible but the sky was darkening
and night was evidently falling. Rohana jerked erect as
if pricked painfully with a needle; somewhere within her
mind, a signal had flared into brilliance, a warning. But
with whose *laran* had she unknowingly made contact? A
pattern of fire, fear....

There was no one on the fire-line with sufficient *laran*
to reach her this closely except Alida; Alida, who was
herself a *leronis* and who had spent, like Rohana, several

years in a Tower in training. But the general lack of sympathy between herself and Alida would prevent casual or accidental communication of this sort; this time it was obvious that Alida for some reason had deliberately reached out for her.

Warned by that silent signal, Rohana withdrew her mind from what was happening around her and concentrated on the matrix jewel inside her dress.

What is it? Alida, is it you?

You must come, Rohana. The wind is rising again; we must have rain or at least keep the wind from raising a firestorm which it will be likely to do.

Sudden dread clutched at Rohana, a warning of clear danger; at this stage in her pregnancy it was not safe to use *laran* except in the simplest and most minimal way. Yet if the alternative should be a firestorm which could ravage the entire Domain of Ardais and threaten every life in the countryside, what alternative did she have?

I cannot come out to the fire-lines; I cannot ride now, and I should not leave Gabriel. You will have to return here and we will do the best we can.

A silent sense of acquiescence; and the contact was withdrawn. Rohana sat silently with her eyes closed. Gabriel, with too little *laran* to know precisely what was happening, but too sensitive to let everything pass unaware, turned to her and asked gently, "Is something amiss, Rohana?"

"*Laran* signal from the fire-lines," she murmured, glad of an opportunity to speak of what she felt. "We desperately need rain, and there has been no opportunity to gather a *laran* circle together. Alida is returning, and she and I will try to do what we can—at least to keep the wind from rising again."

He lay without moving, except for his eyes, too exhausted and languid to have much to say. At last he murmured, "It is at times like this, Rohana, that I regret I have done so little to learn use of my *laran*. I am not wholly without it."

"I know that," she said soothingly, "but your health was never really strong enough to let you make full use of the talent."

"Still, I wish I had been able to do more," he insisted.

"I would not now be so completely useless to the Domain. With fire approaching, I feel so helpless—more helpless than any woman—since it is you women who must do what you can to save the Domain and I am here useless, or worse than useless, just another body to be protected. Perhaps we were too quick to send the boys away, Rohana; both of them have some *laran*."

"It would have done no good to keep them here, Gabriel. I could not work in a laran circle with my own sons."

"No? Why not, pray?"

"There are many reasons; for one reason and another it is not done." Rohana did not want to go into the many reasons why parents and their grown children were barred from working together in matrix circles. "There is no reason to trouble yourself about it now, my dear," she said peacefully. "Alida and I will do what we can; no one alive can do more. And try not to be concerned or your fears and worries will jam the circle." Vaguely she wondered if she ought to make sure that he was drunk or drugged before they began whatever it was that they would have to do. Now she was conscious at the edge of her mind of a horse being ridden breakneck— Alida was usually a careful if not an overcautious rider; now she was afraid and racing for Castle Ardais at an almost dangerous speed. Rohana felt a burst of fear; if it could so override Alida's caution, the danger must be great indeed. She resisted the temptation to look back at the advancing fire through Alida's eyes; that could only exaggerate her own fears, and now she must be calm and confident.

Now she could hear the rider's hoofbeats in the courtyard below the balcony where she sat. She laid her work aside, scornfully looking at the embroidery and being grateful that she had something more to give her Domain and people. How must Gabriel feel at a time like this? Well, she knew how he felt; helpless, he had said, *helpless as a woman.* But I am a woman and I am not helpless; I suppose that is just Gabriel; he associates helplessness with women in spite of the fact that I, a woman, am the strongest person in his life.

Alida was dismounting in the court, and to Rohana's relief, Kindra was with her.

"Let us make ready quickly," she said, and the women went up to the conservatory. Rohana and Alida seated themselves in two chairs facing one another, knee to knee.

"Can I do nothing to help?" Kindra asked, concerned.

"Not much, I fear, but your good will can do us no harm," Rohana said.

Alida added, with instinctive tact, for once knowing how Rohana felt, "Sit here with us and make sure we are not disturbed; that no one should break in on us."

Alida had her matrix in her hand. "Do not look at the stone," she warned Kindra with a quick gesture. "You are untrained; it could make you seriously disoriented or ill."

Helpless, like the rest of us, but, unlike us, not knowing it.

Rohana, knowing that she was delaying, swiftly thrust the field of her concentrated attention within the stone, moved upward and outward to survey, as if from a great height, the fire raging on the ridge above the Castle. With her enormously expanded senses she could see the air currents that fed the fire . . . she seemed to ride upon them, hungry to feed the swirling updraft of the fires. For an instant the exhilaration of it swept over her, all but carrying her to become part of it, but conscious of the link with Alida keeping her earthbound, she controlled herself, searching for remedies to the inexorable strength of the fire.

If there were enough moisture in these clouds to bring heavy rains—

But there was not; the clouds were there, heavy laden with enough moisture for rain—but *not* enough to drown the threatening firestorm. She felt Alida reaching out, making swift strides through the overworld. It was as if hands clasped theirs, wings beat beneath them as they flew.

How can we help you, sisters?

Rain; it is fire we face; give us clouds for rain.

The faceless voices—Rohana sensed they were from Tramontana Tower—swiftly grasped them, displaying the mountains below as if on a giant picture; only a few scant clouds, and when pushed toward Ardais, not sufficient at this season for anything but raising more wind from the imposed motion, so that the best they could do was worse than no help at all.

The voices from Tramontana were gone, and Rohana, with a sense of helplessness knew there was nothing to do with the fire but let it burn as it wished, down the ridge toward the Castle, where it would be arrested by the stretch of deeply plowed fields and by the stone of the Castle itself.

She opened her eyes and lay back exhaustedly against the cushions of her chair.

"I have never felt so helpless," Alida said.

"It is not your fault, Alida, it is only that sometimes there is nothing that can be done." She was suddenly seized by a wave of weakness, a gnawing pain reminding her that matrix work this late in pregnancy could bring on premature labor. With great bitterness she thought that she had risked her last child—and without even the justification of accomplishing what she had tried to do, the saving of Ardais. Bent over, gasping with pain, she said, "Alida, warn them, the fire will come this way, they may have to fight at the very house doors ..." and felt a wave of blackness sweep over her. When she woke, she was lying on her own bed in her own room, and Kindra was beside her.

"The fire—"

"Lady Alida is gathering them together with soaked blankets and rugs; I knew not how strong she was in a crisis," Kindra said.

Rohana said flippantly, "I have not wanted to give her time to develop her strength; but now I am glad she has it." She started to rise, but was checked by pain, and Kindra held her back.

"Your women will be with you in a few minutes; *Dom* Gabriel became troubled and had to be taken to his rooms and put to bed, too," Kindra said.

Rohana lay quietly, feeling the powerful forces working within her body. It was out of her hands now, inevitable, and she felt the usual resistless terror. Now she could not escape. She clung to Kindra's hands almost feverishly, but the Renunciate made no sign of leaving her though her clothes were smoke-stained and still reeked of the fire-lines.

The women came and examined her; none of them could say whether or not she was actually in labor; they would simply have to wait and see. Rohana, knowing that nothing she could do or say could do anything one way or the other, tried to rest quietly, ate and drank the food they brought her, tried to sleep. Far away she heard voices and cries; but there was no way even the worst of fires could cross the wide band of plowed lands around the castle—thanks to all the gods that it was not late in harvest when these lands would be covered with dry plants which would burn—and at last the very stone of the castle would resist fire. She was grateful that Gabriel had been carried to his bed; close-quarters fighting at the kitchen doors would agitate him beyond bearing. She hoped Alida had given orders for a sleeping-draught for him, at least.

That abortive attempt to link with Alida and use *laran* against the fire—had been her only failure ever in use of *laran*. She hated to fail, though she knew that even a fully trained Tower circle could have done no better. The very cooks fighting with soaked rugs had done better; one of them had stepped on a live coal and burned through his shoe sole, but had not been seriously hurt. All was well, the castle had suffered no harm; only she felt this intangible sense of utter failure. *Everyone sooner or later finds something he or she cannot do,* she told herself, but she did not believe it; she was not allowed ever to fail at anything.

She lay fitfully slipping in and out of sleep; when she woke again, she knew it was late morning of the next day; the sun was shining through a smoky sky, and she knew she had escaped the consequences of her rashness; she was not in labor, not yet: this child would not be born today, at least.

Kindra came when Rohana's women came to look after her, and Rohana stretched out her hands in welcome.

"How can I ever thank you? You have done so much for me—for all of us."

"No," Kindra chided, "I did only what was necessary; I could hardly have denied that kind of help no matter where I guested." But she smiled and bent to embrace Rohana. "I am glad nothing worse was to be faced. And this morning you look well!"

"I am very fortunate," Rohana said and meant it with all her heart. "And not the least of my fortune is to have such a friend as you, Kindra."

Kindra lowered her eyes, but she smiled.

"Sit here beside me; I have been told by these women that I must stay in bed and do no more than a flowering cabbage, lest I excite my naughty baby to trying again to be born before his time; I am so bored!" Rohana exclaimed. "I was not born to be a vegetable! And these women think I should take for my model a nice contented cow!"

Kindra could not help laughing a little at the image. "You, a vegetable, never! But perhaps you could pretend to be placid, perhaps like a floating cloud—"

"When I was a young girl, I had a cousin who traveled southward to the sea; he told me of sea animals who are graceful in the water, but when they try to go on land they are so heavy that their bodies cannot support their weight, and they can only crawl and flop about." Rohana, trying heavily to tug herself upright and turn over in bed, showed Kindra what she meant. "See, I am like one of these beached fish-creatures. I think this must be a very big baby; I was not as heavy as this even a tenday before Rian was born, and he was the largest of my children."

Kindra sat on her bed and patted her hand comfortingly. She said, "I seem to remember that older women with later children always feel heavier and more fretful; you forget how hard the last one was. Probably just as well, or who would ever venture to have a second child, let alone a third."

"I am certainly less patient than I was at nineteen when Kyril was born; I had been out on a nutting party, gathering nuts till it was too dark to see," Rohana said, "and when I woke in the night, I thought only that I had eaten too many nuts, or the stew I had eaten for supper had upset my stomach. It went on an hour before

even Gabriel thought to call the midwife . . . and he was
not inexperienced; his first wife had borne him a child.
The midwife laughed at me, saying it would be noon at
least before anything happened—but Kyril was born an
hour before dawn. Even my mother did not believe how
quickly it was over!"

"Then you are one of the lucky ones who gives birth
easily?" Kindra asked.

Rohana grimaced. "Only that one time; Rian took two
days to get himself born after he started signaling he
was ready—and he has always been late for everything
since, from dinner to birthday-parties. As for Elorie—I
will never tell anyone much about her birth lest young
girls hearing should be frightened. But I hope this one
is not so bad as that." She shivered, and Kindra
squeezed her hand.

"Perhaps you'll be luckier this time, then."

A serving woman appeared with Rohana's breakfast
on a carved wooden tray.

"Lady Alida said you would not be getting up today,
Mistress."

"For once," Rohana said, "I am grateful for Lady Alida's wish to show that she can manage everything as
well as I do. Let us see her opinion of what a pregnant
mother should eat; a little toast with honey, perhaps?
Or did she have sense enough to consult the midwife?"
She uncovered the tray; porridge and honey, with a lav-
ish jug of cream, a dish of boiled eggs and one of cut-
up fresh fruit. Evidently Alida *had* consulted the midwife—or Gabriel, who knew that pregnancy never affected her appetite. Thinking of Gabriel made her ask,
"What of the Master? I heard he was sick again last
night—"

The woman said, "Aye; Lady Alida ordered him a
sleeping-draught; he was abed late this morning, and he's
roaming about downstairs with his eyes swollen, growl-
ing as if he were spoiling for a fight."

Oh, dear. Well, at present she could not get up and
deal with it. Perhaps Alida would have the sense to offer
Gabriel some remedy for the after-effects of her sleep-
ing-draughts. Rohana applied herself to her breakfast
with an appetite only slightly diminished by the thought

of Gabriel roaming around looking for something to grumble, complain, or storm about. She was safe and insulated here.

"You said I was like an Amazon, but not nearly enough," she said to Kindra, spooning up the last of the eggs in her dish. "You are braver than that, I suppose. You would not hide away to avoid an unpleasantness. Yet I wish I could stay here in this bed till the baby is safely born—Gabriel could not complain at me then."

"We have a saying; take care what you wish for, you might get it," Kindra said, accepting a slice of fruit. "But if you do wish to stay abed, would anyone stop you?"

"Only my own sense of what needs to be done," Rohana said. "I could not justify more than two days, say, abed, considering how well I feel. Then it is all to be faced again. Gabriel grows no better, and his drinking, I fear, is the last step in his disintegration."

Kindra asked, as the women took away the tray, "How came you to marry Lord Ardais, Rohana? Was it a family match? For he seems not entirely such a man as I would have expected you to wed."

"I could defend myself and say so," said Rohana, "for surely my parents were more eager for the match than I. Yet it is not entirely true. Once I liked Gabriel well—no; I loved him." She added quickly, "It is only fair to say he was much different then; his sickness was something which passed across him now and then like a shadow—a look now and again of absentmindedness; forgetfulness—he would not remember a promise or a conversation. And then he had not begun drinking so heavily; I thought at that time that the drinking was only an attempt to keep his pace among some roistering companions, not a fault within himself."

"I still feel you were designed by nature for something other than domestic cares," said Kindra.

Rohana smiled; Kindra thought the mischievous smile was at odds with the heavy body and swollen features.

"Kindra, is that a polite way of saying that I am not sufficiently dignified for a pregnant, middle-aged mother of three children who are already men and women?"

After a moment Kindra realized that a very real insecurity lay behind the flippant words. She hastened to reassure her.

"No indeed. I meant only—you seem too large of mind to be confined to domestic trivialities. You should have been a *leronis,* a wise-woman, a—I have a friend in the Guild House who is a magistrate, and you could fill that position at least as well as she."

"In short," Rohana said, "an Amazon."

"I cannot help feeling so," said Kindra defensively. "I still wish it were possible."

Rohana took her hand. She said, "Ever since I journeyed with you, I have wished it might have been so. Had I been given a real choice, I might have remained in the Tower as a *leronis;* Melora and I both wished for it. You know what befell Melora—and in a sense, when I wedded as my family desired, I felt that I was comforting them for what Melora could not. . . ." Her voice trailed off into silence. She sought Kindra's hand and said softly, "I think sometimes that Melora meant more to me than anyone in my life; this is why Jaelle is so dear to me."

There are times when I feel you understand me almost as she did. . . . The women were silent, then Kindra leaned forward and put her arm round Rohana. They embraced in silence; then, abruptly, the door swung open and *Dom* Gabriel stood in the doorway.

"Rohana!" he bawled. "What the devil is this? First I catch your slut of a daughter in the hay with a groom, and now I find you—" he broke off, staring in consternation.

"Now do I begin to understand why you have avoided my bed these many months," he said deliberately, "but if you had to console yourself, could you not find a man—instead of a woman in breeches?"

Rohana felt as if she had been kicked, hard, under the solar plexus; she could not catch her breath. Kindra would have moved away from her, but Rohana clung to her wrists.

She said, "Gabriel, I have suspected for many years that you are not only sick, but demented; now I am sure of it." She added, hearing her voice bite like acid,

"Leave my room until you can conduct yourself decently to our guest, or I will have the stewards drag you out!"

His eyes, red-rimmed, narrowed and Rohana, wide open, could read in his mind speculations of such obscenity that she thought her heart would stop. She felt sick and slimed over with his thoughts; she wanted to scream, to hurl her porridge bowl at him, to shriek foul language that she herself only half understood.

Kindra broke the deadlock; she rose from the edge of the bed, leaving Rohana against the pillows, and said swiftly to the chamber-woman, "Your mistress is ill; attend her. Send for the midwife!" Rohana let her eyes fall shut; her hand released Kindra's and she collapsed, half fainting, as the woman scurried away.

Dom Gabriel snarled, "One word from me, and three dozen women on this estate do just exactly as they please! Does no one hear me?"

The midwife, coming in in time to hear this—in fact Kindra suspected she had been in the next room waiting for such a summons—lifted her head where she bent over Rohana attentively, to say, "Lord Ardais, in this chamber alone you may not give orders; I beg you, go and give orders where you may be obeyed. May I summon your gentlemen?"

"Rohana's not as sick as all that; time I made a few things really clear to her, what I will an' won't put up with," *Dom* Gabriel grumbled. "Going to throw me out of my own wife's bedroom? Then throw that damned she-male in britches out, too!"

"My lord, I beg you, if you *will* stay here, be silent," demanded the midwife. Rohana heard all this as if from very far away, through wind and water, very distant. She struggled to sit up, hearing another sound; the distant sound—or did she hear it only through her *laran*—wild, hysterical sobbing; then Elorie, weeping, burst into the room. She ran and flung herself down at the edge of Rohana's bed. The midwife said "You must not disturb your mother, Mistress Lori—" but Rohana struggled upright.

"Elorie, darling, what is it?"

"Papa—" she sobbed, stumbling over the word, "He called me—he—" Her face was red with sobbing, her cheek bleeding with a long cut, one eye already blackened and swollen.

"Gabriel," Rohana said firmly, "what is this? I thought we agreed you would never strike the children when you were not sober."

Gabriel hung his head and looked wretched.

"Am I to sit by and watch her play the slut with any stable-boy—"

"No!" wailed Elorie, "I didn't, and Papa is *crazy* if he *really* thought so!"

"So then what were you up to with that young—"

"Mother," Elorie sobbed, "it was Shann. You know Shann; we played together when we were four years old! I scolded him because he had not properly curried my pony, and I took the currycomb in my own hand to show him what I wanted! Then when we finished, we were looking in one of the loose-boxes—"

"Watching the stallion, an' makin' all kinds of lewd filthy jokes about it," *Dom* Gabriel snarled, "I *heard*!"

"Oh, Gabriel; the children are farm-bred; you cannot expect that they will never speak of such things," Rohana said. "What a tempest over nothing! Elorie—?" She looked at her daughter, and Elorie wiped her eyes and said, "Well, we were talking of Greyfoot's foal, true— but Shann meant no harm, and when Papa began to strike him with the crop, I tried to grab it—Mama, is he really *crazy*?"

"Of course he is, darling, I thought you knew that," said Rohana wearily. "You should know better than to provoke him this way. I wish you could learn to be sensible and discreet enough not to set him off."

"I didn't do anything wrong," Elorie protested.

"I know that," Rohana said wearily, "but you know your father; you know what will upset him."

Kindra interrupted, "Elorie, your mother is not well either; can't you see that? If you must have a tantrum like an eight-year-old, can't you find your old nurse or someone like that to have it in front of, and not trouble your mother? If there is more of this, she could go into premature labor, and that would be dangerous for her and for your little sister or brother."

Elorie mopped at her eyes and snuffled. "I don't see

why she wants to have a baby anyhow at her age; other ladies don't," she grumbled.

Gabriel's steward had entered the room. He said in a soft, self-deprecating voice, "By your leave, sir," and gave Gabriel his arm. Gabriel shook him off and walked to the bedside.

"You going to let them throw me out of here, Lady?"

"Gabriel, I beg you," Rohana said in a stifled voice, "Truly, I am too ill to deal with all this now. Tomorrow when I am better, we will talk—that I promise you. But please go away now."

"Whatever you say, my love," he mumbled and went, turning back to say, "You too, Elorie; don't you pester your mother," and the door closed.

Rohana had the sense that she wanted to cry and cry until she melted into one vast lake of tears. She held painfully to composure though her heart was pounding. She held out her arms to Elorie, who was crying harder than ever.

"Mother, don't be sick, don't die," the girl begged, and Rohana could feel the frail shoulders trembling in her arms.

"Don't be foolish, love; but I must have rest," she said, "That is all I need; your father has upset me terribly. Please run along now."

The midwife rose from the foot of the bed and said "I want it quiet in here," and Elorie, still sobbing and wiping her face, hurried out.

Rohana still clung to Kindra's hand; when all the other women had gone away, she whispered to Kindra, "Don't leave me. I could not blame you if you refused to remain here another minute; but I beg you not to leave me alone with—" she broke off, choking. "But why should you stay? I should never have exposed you to such—such unspeakable accusations—it is my fault. . . ."

Kindra squeezed her hand. She said, "There is no honor in contending with a madman or a drunkard. I have heard worse. And—I asked you this once before in a somewhat different form—does it really offend you so much? Is it such an unspeakable accusation as all that?"

Shocked and startled—of all things this was the last she had expected to hear—Rohana said, "Oh. That. Oh, I see. No; I loved Melora and I swore an oath to her, but it was the way Gabriel said it; as if it was the filthiest thing he could think of to say—about you *or* about me—"

"To the lewd of mind, all things are filthy," Kindra said. "He did not spare his own daughter, I noticed, and on flimsier evidence yet. The truth is that I really love you, Rohana, and I feel no shame about it, according to custom or not. I would not have spoken of this while you are sick and busy with other things; but he has brought it out; I feel no evil in loving a woman, and if he were an example of loving a man, I would feel disgust for any woman who chose men instead."

Rohana said in a low voice, "I can certainly understand that. I said to you once—in the Dry Towns—that in the Domains, when two young men swear the oath of *bredin,* that they will be friends all their lives, and that not even a wife or children shall ever part them, there is nothing but honor for them; but if two maidens swear such an oath, no one takes it seriously, or at best, take it to mean only—*I shall love you until some man comes between us.* Why should it be so different?"

"I would say—and I do not know if you would agree—" Kindra said, "that it is because men never take seriously anything women choose to do unless it concerns a man. But that is why I am a Renunciate and you are not. But I would willingly swear an oath with you, Rohana."

And if you were a Renunciate I could love you without caring what people said; my primary vows and commitments are to my sisters.

It was not the first time Rohana had suspected Kindra had more than a little *laran.* She was touched and overwhelmed by the thought that Kindra loved her; she had thought before this that the Renunciate was the only person who understood her; but it seemed that Gabriel's accusation had fouled a thing she thought wholly innocent. *No, she does not understand this about me, I love her, but not like this,* and almost without realizing it, she withdrew her hand from Kindra's.

The Amazon looked sad; but as she had said, this was why she was a Renunciate and Rohana was not. She had not expected Rohana—certainly not in her present state of turmoil—to understand. She said gently, "Hush, you mustn't worry about anything now; there will be time enough to talk about all this when you are stronger."

Rohana was almost relieved at the sense of exhaustion and weariness that swept over her. She reached up her arms and hugged Kindra childishly, grateful for her kindliness and strength.

"You're so good to me," she whispered. "The best of friends."

Kindra thought, *I would have spared her that scene with Dom Gabriel. Yet it is what he is and it is what she must face sooner or later.*

She kissed Rohana again on the forehead and silently went out of the room.

If we are fortunate, it will not send her into premature labor.

VIII

Rohana woke from a nightmare of going into labor alone, unprepared and in the desert outside the Dry Towns. Waking, she realized with enormous relief that she was not in labor, and the child in her body was quiescent, with only the routine dreaming movements. All the same she knew from experience—after all she had already been through this three times—that such dreams were a warning. Labor was near, though not imminent. She rose sluggishly and dressed in an old unlaced house gown. She was not able to face the thought of breakfasting in the Great Hall, but Alida would be only too pleased to deputize for her. She sent for some fruit and tea; when she had finished, one of her women appeared at the door.

"My lady, the Master asks to see you."

At least he had not pushed his way in unannounced. Rohana sighed.

"Drunk, I suppose."

"No, *Domna;* he looks ill, but sober."

"Very well, let him come in." She could not, after all, avoid his presence indefinitely here at Ardais.

But when this child is born, I shall go to Thendara for Council, or to my sister Sabrina, or home to Valeron. . . .

Gabriel looked small, almost shrunken inside his untidy old farmerish clothes. His face held the crimson discoloration of the habitual drunkard, but he seemed wholly sober. His hands were shaking; he tried to conceal them within his sleeves, but although he had carefully shaved himself, his face bore many small telltale cuts.

"My dear," she said impulsively, "you should have your man shave you when you are not well."

"Oh, well, you know, my dear, a fellow don't like to ask—"

"Nonsense; it's the man's duty," she said sharply, and heard the harsh note in her voice. "You shouldn't need to ask; I'll have a word with him."

"No, no, my dear, let it go. I didn't come for that. I am glad to see you lookin' so well, now. The little feller in there—he's quiet still?"

"I don't think it will be today, and perhaps not tomorrow," she said, "but it will be soon. We are fortunate—with the fire—"

And that terrible scene yesterday—she forebore to say that aloud, but he heard it anyhow and awkwardly put an arm round her waist. He did not for once smell of wine and she managed not to pull away when he kissed her cheek. All the same she could sense, at the touch, the confusion and fuddlement in him, and it repelled her.

"I knew I'd need to be sober if you were in labor," he said and reached in the old way for *rapport;* instinctively she flinched and he did not press for it but said aloud, "I know yer angry with me. You should be; I was filthy drunk. I shouldn't a been so rude; no matter what *she* is, I know *you*, Rohana. Forgive me?"

Have I not always forgiven you? she asked, not in words, but she shrank from the thought of the long hours of labor when by custom they must share the birth in full rapport, telepathically entwined. *Trapped together in their minds. . . .* She *could not* endure it. He had been so different when Kyril was born, and during Rian's birth, which had been prolonged and very difficult, she had clung to his strength as to a great rock in a flood that was drowning her; his hands, his voice and touch holding her above the flood, pulling her back from the very borders of death. This would be the fourth time that they had gone down together into the inexorable tides of birth.

Yet how could she endure it after these intervening years of struggle and humiliation, after his foul accusations? He meant well; she was touched at the dreadful effort it must have taken to present himself here, sober and shaven after a profound drinking bout; *his poor shaking hands, his poor cut face,* she thought with a wave of habitual tenderness; but she clung fiercely to her pride and anger; if he wished to revive his view of himself as strong supportive father, let him go to Tessa when *her* child showed signs of being born! Then she remembered: he had not fathered Tessa's child, but he must have had reason to think so: disgraceful! He should not think that with one day's sobriety and attentiveness he could wipe out a decade of neglect, abuse, and humiliation.

Yet there was no alternative; by iron-bound custom, the father endured childbirth with the mother, and she would be given no choice. Somehow she must steel herself to endure the hours of birth in his presence, and thank the gods if he did not present himself drunk.

Rohana asked deliberately and was shocked at the cruelty in her own voice, "Have you visited Tessa this morning? She would, I am sure, be relieved to see you well and sober."

His face twisted, half in anger and half in humiliation.

"Oh, Kyril's girl—if you like, me dear, I'll send her away. We could have her married off to somebody decent—"

"No," she said deliberately, "Alida told me there is no doubt it is an Ardais child and she, too, has a right to her father's roof. She is not offensive to me."

"You're better than I deserve," he muttered, "I ought never to ha' brought her here."

"It doesn't matter," she said. "Gabriel, I am very weary; I want to rest; and so should you. Thank you for coming—" *And thank you for being sober and gentle; I couldn't bear another scene. . . .*

He kissed her clumsily on the cheek and murmured a formal prayer for her health, then went quietly away; and Rohana stood staring at the closed door behind him, in something very like horror. At least when he was a drunken beast she could protect herself by despising him; but how could she protect herself against this well-meaning mood and humility?

Not today and not tomorrow, she had told Gabriel; and as the day and the next day wore on toward sunset, Rohana, dragging around from hall to conservatory, from conservatory to kitchen, telling herself she was making certain all would go well while she was laid up abed, felt weary to the point of sickness. In vain she reminded herself of what she had told other women in her state; the last tenday is longer than all the other months together. She could settle to nothing; not to a book, not to a piece of fancy-work nor to plain sewing, not to her harp or her *rryl;* she took up one thing after another restlessly, and felt as if she had been pregnant forever and would be so for the rest of her life, if not for all eternity.

As the afternoon of the third day dragged wearily toward sunset Rohana watched the sun sink toward night with distaste; another day over and another night to come, during which once again she would not sleep, but lie restless in the dark, tossing and turning and hearing the clock strike the dark hours . . . she could not remember when she had truly slept.

She had set all in order with kitchens and estate—she had even brought the stud-book records up to date and made notes of some of the sales agreed upon at the last horse-fair; two of their good breeding mares to be sold into the lowlands, one more to the Kilghard Hills—the Master of MacAran would travel here to fetch them, but the payment had already been received. They needed another saddle horse—Elorie was outgrowing her pony, but there was no saddle horse on the estate which was right for her. She had thought of Rian's horse—but it was a big, ugly raw-boned gelding, no ride for a girl . . .

at least not if the girl was Elorie who was very concerned about beauty and elegance in riding-clothes and mount. Why Elorie should be so concerned with outward appearances Rohana did not know; somehow she had failed to educate her about what was important; but it could not be remedied in the next few days.

"It is a pity," she grumbled to Kindra, "that the Guild Houses do not educate girls as the *cristoforos* at Nevarsin do boys; I am sure that a year in a House of Renunciates would do Elorie all the good in the world."

"It might," said Kindra. "We must consider it. But alas, most of their fathers would fear we were teaching them what they should not know; and I fear much of what we teach would not please their fathers nor even many of their mothers."

"Well, there should be some place where girls should be taught—if only in charity, to keep down madness among their mothers—but you would not know," Rohana said. "You left your daughters, you said, when they were still little children."

"And ever since," said Kindra, "I have been raising other women's half-grown daughters—which in one way is simpler, since they are not my own and if they make preposterous she-donkeys out of themselves, it is no blow to *my* pride or self-respect. And sooner or later they do grow up to be a credit to us. Lori will, too, you will see."

"That's not much comfort to me now," Rohana said. "I look at her and feel I have raised a simpering idiot who cares about nothing but the color of the ribbons on her ball-dress—or whether she should arrange her hair in curls or braids for any particular occasion."

Kindra asked gently, "Did you never so?"

"Never; I was a *leronis* at her age, and too busy for such things," Rohana said crossly. She went out into the courtyard, her long gown trailing, and toward the stables.

"Where are you going?" Kindra asked.

"Nowhere. I don't know. I'm tired of being in the house. I'll think of something." Her voice was absentminded and irritable. Inside the stable, she went and offered a lump of sugar to her favorite mare. "Sorry, little one, I cannot ride today," she muttered, fondling the horse's nose. She passed down through the line of horses, caressing here, offering a tidbit there, drawing back and closely examining others.

When Kindra came up inquiringly, she said, "I should make ready for the horse fair, it is only a handful of tendays away ... this year we should put up a pavilion for anyone for whom the sun is too hot, so that we can talk business out of the sun's rays."

It seemed fantastic to Kindra that at this point Rohana should be thinking about the horse fair, but no doubt it was habit—many years of thinking first and always about the management of the Domain.

Rohana wandered out to where two men were repairing saddle tack and said, "Hitch the small cart."

Kindra demanded, "What now? Surely you cannot go from home—"

"Only to the top of the Ridge," Rohana said. "I must know whether the fire damaged too much, and how the replanting is coming along."

"You mustn't really. No, Rohana, it's impossible. Suppose you went into labor on the way—"

"Don't worry so," Rohana said, "I'm sure I will not. And if I did, at least it would be over!"

There was really no more Kindra could say. In spite of her extreme courtesy, Kindra was abruptly reminded that her friend was a lady of the Comyn, and the Head of a great Domain; further she was Kindra's hostess. It was really not for Kindra to say what Rohana could and could not do. She watched, feeling helpless. This really was not wise; in the Guild House they would have forbidden a woman—at this stage of pregnancy and after more than one false alarm of labor—to stir beyond the garden!

The cart was hitched, and Rohana climbed into it. "Come with me, Kindra; this is our gentlest horse. She could probably take the cart to the Ridge herself. Elorie drove her when she was only seven; she used to carry the children and their nurses everywhere before that." Kindra, unwilling to let Rohana drive off alone, climbed in and took the reins. Rohana did not protest.

And it was true that the old mare plodded along very gently. Along the Ridge, the earth was still scorched with the impact of fire; but already, along the rim of the hill where a long line of evergreens sheltered the field a little, a group of men were setting out a wavering line of resin-tree seedlings.

Along the Ridge, stark against the sky, there was a small stone hut, evidently a shelter for workmen caught by bad weather or for travelers. Rohana alighted from the cart and turned her steps toward the shelter; Kindra followed helplessly.

"What are you doing, Rohana?"

"The shelter must be checked, the law requires that it be kept stocked and in good order, and Gabriel would come up here a hundred times and never think to stick his nose inside." She disappeared into the darkness and Kindra followed.

"Disgraceful," Rohana exploded, "the mattresses are rat-eaten, the blankets have been stolen, the pots broken. I will send someone up here tonight to restock the place; if I could lay my hands on the criminal who tore this place up—I would rip him asunder! To do a thing like that—it is not only inconsiderate, but a traveler who destroys a place like that should be hanged! For he condemns anyone who comes here in bad weather to possible death from cold and exposure!" She staggered slightly and sat down unexpectedly on the bench. Kindra had not expected to see her so angry; she had not betrayed anger like this even when Gabriel brought Tessa home. But Rohana was still agitated as she shook her fist at the damaged supplies in the travel-shelter; Kindra came and held her upright, and she could feel Rohana actually trembling, see the beating of the blue pulse in her temples.

"I beg you, don't excite yourself; I am sure there is someone, do let me go and call one of the men to go down and give the orders for you," Kindra said, trying to speak in a soothing tone of voice.

"And look, someone has dumped a load of fresh hay in here; how annoying! For warmth, I suppose, but the danger of fire at this season seems to me too strong: They should not have done that." Rohana was walking around agitatedly, scowling; she stopped and sat down unexpectedly on the bench again, with a surprised look on her face.

"What is it, Rohana?" asked Kindra, but before Rohana could reply, she knew the answer.

"Is the baby coming?"

Rohana blinked and looked startled.

"Why—yes, I think so; I didn't really notice, but—yes," she said, and Kindra groaned.

"Oh, no! You cannot possibly be jolted all the way back in that cart!"

"No," said Rohana, almost smiling. "Here I am and here I must stay, I suppose, till it is over. Don't look like that, Kindra, I am certainly neither the first nor the last woman to give birth in a barn; you can send the men down for the midwife and one or two of my women—the ones I had chosen to help me."

"Shall I ride down myself?"

"No, please—" Rohana's voice suddenly wavered "Don't leave me, Kindra, stay with me."

Annoyed as Kindra was at this sudden development, she was touched and could not draw away from Rohana. "Of course I'll stay with you," she said in a soothing tone. "But now let me go out and send the cart down for your women and the midwife."

Reluctantly Rohana let go of her hand, and Kindra went out to where the cart waited. She said to the man on the seat, "You must go down quickly; the Lady is in labor and cannot be moved. Go down and fetch the estate midwife, and her women, and clean blankets, and everything she will need here; and *Dom* Gabriel and Lady Alida, of course," she added as an afterthought. She was not sure Rohana wanted either of them, but she could not take the responsibility of keeping them away.

"I'll go at once," said the man. "Truth to tell, *mestra*, I wondered about that when I saw her come up here. Something about the look on her face—when my own wife is near her time, she gets restless like this."

"I wish you'd warned *me*," Kindra muttered, but not aloud.

IX

Rohana rested on the load of fresh hay, vaguely musing on the lucky coincidence that had brought it here fresh when everything else in the shelter had been damaged or destroyed. With the automatic confidence of a trained *leronis* who had been a monitor, she ran her trained senses through her body, keeping pace with what was happening. Labor, for having started so recently, was progressing very rapidly; the contractions were already coming at intervals of a couple of minutes apart. All seemed well with the baby, who was already in the deep pre-birth trance of some babies; the alternative was a state of agitation mingling terror and rage at the process, and Rohana was just as grateful she need not—as was often the case and had been the case with Rian at least— spend all her own strength in calming the baby's terror. She had heard a lot of debate among the *laranzu'in* in Arilinn and elsewhere about which state was better for the child's ultimate welfare; but Rohana was not sure that any of them knew any more than she did about it, and at the moment she found it easier for her own sake that this baby was one of the tranced ones. She would not have imposed a trance on a wide-awake and angry one, as some of the women who debated the two view-points considered to be best, just for her own convenience; but she found herself whispering to the child: *Just sleep, rest, little one; let me get on with this and you can wake up when it's over.*

The intensity of the contractions was by now very painful, but Rohana was so relieved that the waiting was over that she did not care how quickly it went; although she hoped she could hold out until the midwife got here; she did not really want to give birth alone. The unwit-nessed birth of a child, no matter how regular the cir-cumstances or how certain the parentage, invariably left, for the child's whole lifetime, his ancestry open to ques-tion except from the most charitable. Rohana lay back and tried to relax, knowing that, even though it was going well and quickly, there was a long way to go.

It seemed a long time—she lay alone. There was con-siderably less light in the shelter when she heard the heavy crunching of cart wheels, and Annina, the estate midwife of Ardais, rushed into the shelter, bearing a lantern, an armful of blankets, and what seemed like a cartful of other impedimenta. She immediately took charge.

"Marga and Yllana, lift her there—careful—spread out those blankets and the sheet on the hay—now ease her down. There ye are, my lady, all comfy, aren't we?"

It was a considerable improvement over lying on the prickly hay, and when they slipped her into a warm nightgown, it felt good. The midwife managed to get a small fire lighted at the far end in a small enclosed stove, and Rohana smelled the comforting smell of herbs for tea. She hoped the water would boil soon; she wanted a cup.

Alida knelt beside her.

"Rohana! Oh, we were all so worried about you, dearest! You should never have gone up to the Ridge, it was unforgivable of that Amazon to take you up there, but you should have had better sense than to listen to her. But now at least you're safe and warm—it looks like snow tonight—"

Rohana had reached a stage where she could not focus on Alida's chatter.

"Go away, Alida," she said, trying to get the words out between the careful breaths that were all that allowed her to stay at least mentally on top of the pain. "I have work to do. Don't blame Kindra. It was my doing entirely. She didn't want to come—without her I'd have come alone, and she knew it, so she came along." She stopped and concentrated on her breathing again, reached for Kindra's hand and held it, squeezing it in a bone-crushing grip. It felt good to focus on Kindra's strength, which in her heightened, wide-open state was as palpable as the heat from the stove or the swish of the rain outside the shutters.

Thrusting into the comfort of Kindra's touch was a familiar, unwanted touch, a sullen glow of suspicion in it as Gabriel's eyes rested on her hand in Kindra's.

"You gave us all a scare, me dear," Gabriel said, and to Rohana the tenderness in his voice was smooth and false. "But ye're safe now. Shall we send away all these people so you and I can get on wi' our work? Annina, o'course, can stay, that's her business but none o' these others—right, love?"

With a painful shock, Rohana surfaced from the carefully held focus on the contractions. One of them got a head start on her, and galloped across her consciousness so that it took all her effort to keep from screaming aloud.

She took a great breath, bracing herself against the next.

"No!" she cried out. "No! Go away, Gabriel! I won't have you here!" And with her last strength, a great blast of voiceless rejection, "Go *away!*"

"Oh, you mustn't talk like that," Alida crooned at her. "Gabriel, she doesn't know what she's *saying!* Never mind, Rohana, he's not angry at you, are you, Gabriel? Of course not, at a time like this—"

"O' course not," said Gabriel, and held a cup of wine, from which he had already taken a sip, to her lips. "Here, love, drink some o' this, now, it'll make you feel better—"

With dull amazement she remembered that this ritual had actually been welcomed at Kyril's birth and Rian's. Now it filled her with such disgust she thought she would vomit. *Serve him right if I did, all over his best shirt,* she thought and did not know whether to cry or giggle or weep. She thrust the wine back at him, spilling it all over his hand.

"No; I want some tea, Annina. Tea, do you hear? Gabriel, get out of here; out, out, OUT!" She was screaming now and knew she sounded hysterical; the blast of revulsion, purely automatic and without thought, reached Gabriel and Alida and Alida looked pale and rushed outside; Rohana heard her vomiting just outside the shelter.

Well, she got the message, Rohana thought; *I wish Gabriel were half that sensitive; it would save me a lot of trouble.* For Gabriel was still kneeling beside her smiling stupidly.

"Never mind, me dear. I know she don' know what she's sayin'," he confided in the midwife, "I wouldn't leave her for a thing like that—"

"If you don't—" she said, trying to aim her fury and revulsion at him alone, "I will—"

I will faint, I will die, I will vomit all over him, I will get up and run screaming out of here and have my child in the deep woods alone and after dark where we will be eaten by banshees. . . .

She saw with definite satisfaction that Gabriel turned a dirty-white color and rushed outside. This would be a tale creating scandal through the Domain and the Kilghard Hills; but she felt she absolutely *could* not bear his presence. Her fingers tightened on Kindra's, and the other woman gently patted her hand.

Well, that's over, she thought, without any sense of triumph, simply that now she could breathe freely without the oppression of Gabriel's presence, *now let's get this over with. . . .*

X

The night wore on, endlessly; the lantern burned low and was refilled; Rohana seemed to float outside her body, conscious only of Kindra's presence like a lifeline.

Why do I want to survive this anyhow? Gabriel will never forgive me. I have lived long enough; my older children no longer need me; better to die than to make the decision to walk away from Ardais and Gabriel forever, yet if I live I cannot return to the kind of life I have been living these last few years. Nor will I ever again agree to bear a child for Gabriel's pride of fatherhood or for the Domain. . . .

That reminded her of the phrase in the Renunciate Oath; *never to bear a child for any man's pride, position, clan or heritage . . .*

I should never have returned to Gabriel; when I returned from the Dry Towns, I should have stayed with the Free Amazons; Kindra at least would have welcomed me . . . and I should not be here fighting for the life of a child who should have never been conceived, a child I do not want. . . .

Then she realized sharply; *it is not only the child's life for which I am fighting; it is mine. My own life.* But what good is my life to me now? That was the question she could not answer. *Why should I live to nurse a drunkard? My own son is a worse monster than his father, so it is no good saying I am keeping the Domain for Kyril. And whoever comes after Kyril, for all I know, may be worse yet. Why not let the Domain collapse now, as it would do if I died, as it would have done a dozen years ago if I had not married Gabriel. The Domains will survive, as they survived without the Aldarans. Or it will go to the Terrans who are so eager to claim it ... to map it, to know all about it.*

My life is over anyhow....

Then, opening her eyes for a moment between pains, she looked directly into Kindra's encouraging gaze; and thought;

Even now, if I live, this need not be the end of my life; but for certain if I die, there will be nothing more; and I will never know what might have happened.

She began to listen again to the insistent suggestions of the midwife, to her murmured instructions. No, she would not die; she would fight to live, fight for the life of this child. Outside the shutters the light was growing and the wind had dropped so that she could hear the hissing of the snow.

Later, she knew that Gabriel had stood outside the shelter all night in the snow, lest he should be summoned, believing that she would die, praying that he could speak to her before she died, that she might speak a word of forgiveness. That was much later; for now she did not want to know.

She was conscious only of endless pain and struggle, effort which seemed to demand more fight than it would have been to die.

More and more seemed to be demanded of her.

"I can't—" she whispered, and without words the challenge came; *You must....*

And then at the very end of endurance there was a moment of surcease, of rest; and she knew (*from experience*) that she should now feel relieved and triumphant; and she heard the midwife cry out in triumph:

"A boy! A son for Ardais!"

Not for me? Rohana found herself wondering and wished she could fall asleep; but there was Gabriel, his face flushed (and, all the Gods at once be thanked, still sober) his shaking hands gently holding the boy—bending to kiss her carefully and clumsily, holding the small wrinkled infant wrapped in an old baby blanket she had knitted for Elorie twelve years ago. She thought Elorie had taken it long since for swaddling her dolls.

"Won't you look at our son, Rohana? A third son. Aren't you glad now that I wanted this, now that it's all over?"

"Over for you," she said. "For me it is only beginning, Gabriel, fifteen years or more of trouble. Must I bring this one up, too, to fear and despise his father?"

He said shakily, "No. I swear it, Rohana, by whatever Gods you wish. This night—this night I knew if I had lost you, I would have lost the only good thing ever to come into my life."

Yes, but you have sworn before this, too . . . so many oaths, she thought, but did not bother to speak aloud. She took the blanketed baby into her arms, holding him close, and snuggled him against her bare breasts; almost at once, with the singleminded obsession she remembered from her other confinements, struggling to undo the blanket, to count every precious finger and toe, memorizing them, then to count them again in case she had missed one, to run her hands lovingly over the softness of the little round head. She remembered the old story she had been told in Arilinn—that for the first hour after their birth, babies remembered their past lives, before the veil of forgetfulness was lowered again. He was awake, looking at her with watery blue eyes.

Gabriel said "He's a pretty child, Rohana. But, boy, if you ever give your mother this much trouble again, I'll box your little ears—"

"Oh, fie, Gabriel, what a way to greet the poor babe—threatening to beat him," she murmured, not really listening, focused on the child. She murmured to him, carefully edging the words with the strongest touch she dared of telepathic rapport;

"Hello, my darling; I'm your mother. You will meet your father later . . . he was holding you, but I'm afraid you didn't notice him."

Just as well, she thought, but tried to shield the thought: he was not old enough to face hostility.

"You have two brothers—I'm afraid they won't be much good to you ... and a sister; she at least will love you; she loves all babies. I have decided to name you Keith ... I hope you like the name. It is a very old name in my family, but as far as I know, not used in Gabriel's. ..."

She could not think of anything else to tell him, so she returned to smoothing his little body with her hands memorizing him, feeling such a flood of helpless love she felt she could not endure it. *To think I didn't want you!* It was like the monitor's touch she had learned so long ago. ...

Over and over his tiny body went her loving hands, as if she could enfold him forever in her tenderest love, and keep him forever safe. But already she knew the truth, and knew the very instant when her youngest and last child slipped away from the touch and left her holding a lifeless bundle of chilling flesh. She flung herself into Kindra's arms and wept, hardly knowing it when they lifted her into the cart and carried her through the falling snow down to Ardais and into her own room and her own bed, still holding the little blanketed bundle, trying to soothe him and search out where her lonely baby had gone, alone into the snowstorm ... when they took him from her, she let him go without protest and heard Gabriel weeping, too. But why should he cry? He had not really known the child as she had even in that single hour of his life.

"No, my lord," said the midwife firmly. "It would have happened even had the child been born here in her own bed, on her own cushions. It was nothing she did, certainly nothing *Mestra* Kindra did, nothing anyone could have known or prevented. His heart was not formed to beat properly."

Rohana was still crying; she knew she would never stop crying again until she died. ...

She cried for two days; toward the end of the second day Eloric came in, crying, too, and Rohana hugged her fiercely, thinking, *This, then, is my baby, the youngest child I shall ever have.*

"Do you mind if he is buried in your doll blanket, Elorie? I had no time to make him one of his own; it was what he wore while he lived, the only thing I could give him. . . ."

Elorie said, subdued (*her eyes were red; had she been crying, too? What had she to cry about?*) "No, I don't mind; let him have it. I'm so sorry, Mother, I'm really so sorry."

Yes, she is: she wanted another baby to play with. I'm sorry she didn't get it. When she had gone, Rohana lay in her somnolent daze, not wanting to move—it hurt too much—or to do anything except lie there and remember the few minutes she had held the living child in her arms, vainly needing time to stop so that she could hold on to them and to him. But already the fleeting moments were fading from her mind and Keith was only a fading dream. He had gone where the dead go, and she could not follow.

Life goes on, she thought drearily. *I don't know why it has to, but it does.* Now she was remembering the nebulous half-plans she had made before the birth; *when this is over, I shall go South, away from here.* Painfully she realized that, sincerely as she mourned, deeply as her body and soul hungered for the child who had gone from her, now she was free to make plans which did not involve being tied to a frail newborn for at least a year. This realization was slow and guilty; as if by realizing that freedom was welcome, she had somehow created the situation and was guilty of desiring it.

I did not want this child; now when I do not have him, I ought to rejoice, she thought; but her grief was too new, too raw, too real to accept that yet. Nevertheless, she was beginning to accept that when the shock of birth and loss faded, she would indeed be grateful; that her state at the moment was a purely physical state of shock.

Accepting this, the next time one of her women came tiptoeing in to ask if she wanted anything, she made the fierce effort of dragging herself upright in bed and said, "Yes; I want to be washed and I want some soup."

The women brought the things, and with Kindra's help

she managed to wash herself and to eat some soup. She realized that Kindra had not left her for more than a few seconds since the birth and that she had taken this for granted; now she was aware of it and grateful again, now that she could look a little outside the circle of anguished pain and preoccupation of the last couple of days. It was like surfacing from a very deep dive, clearing her lungs and mind of water at last. . . .

She said, "As soon as I am better, I must travel South. Perhaps for the Council; but in any case I cannot stay here. Shall I travel with you, then, Kindra? You will not be sorry, I think, to get away from here."

"I will not," Kindra confessed. "Not of course that you have failed in any way in hospitality. . . ."

Rohana laughed dryly. "The hospitality of this place I think is cursed," she said. "I swear I shall never impose it on any other."

Kindra smiled at her.

"I have said before this that you have the spirit that would make you a notable Free Amazon, Rohana. I wish you might return with me to the Guild House and there take Oath as one of us. . . ."

Rohana said through a dry mouth, "I am trying to decide if there is any way in which I can in honor do exactly that, Kindra. It is clear to me that I am not needed nor wanted here."

Kindra's eyes glowed. She said softly, "I have prayed for days that you would see how right that would be. If you are not wanted by anyone here, you would be so welcome there." She added, almost in a whisper "More than this . . . I would swear an oath to you."

"And I to you," Rohana whispered, almost inaudibly; but Kindra heard and impulsively kissed her. Rohana remembered that moment—now it seemed a lifetime ago—when Gabriel had burst into her room with unspeakable accusations; now she did not care what he said or what he thought.

Who would *not* prefer Kindra's affection and her company, to his? And if he chose to make of that choice something evil or perverted, that was only evidence of his own foul mind.

But I must not detain Kindra selfishly here; she has

work and duties of her own, which she has generously sacrificed to stay with me while I needed her so much. She tried to say what she felt for Kindra; but the woman said only, "There is nothing that cannot wait until you are able to travel, and then we will go together."

"Together." Rohana repeated it like a pledge. Oh, to be free of the burden and weight of the Domain; of knowing that the welfare of every soul from Scaravel to Nevarsin was in her keeping; of managing everything from the planting to the stud-books—well, now Alida would manage all that, and be glad of the chance.

She began to think for the first time in many years of what things she would take with her, if she were going south not only for the handful of tendays of Council season, but for an indefinite stay—perhaps forever, whether to her family's Domain in Valeron—surely there would be some place to go—or to a Guild House where she would no longer be Lady Rohana of Aillard and Ardais, but simply Rohana, daughter of Liane. She would have no regrets about laying down the larger identity; she had borne it too long. There were not many possessions; her clothing, (and little enough of that, for most of what she had would not be suitable for a Renunciate; a few riding suits and some changes of under-linen) her matrix stone, locks of the children's hair . . . no; not that, no keepsakes; she must put the Rohana who had been Lady of Ardais wholly behind her. The Lady of Ardais will disappear forever; will anyone ever know or care what has become of me? Surely it would never occur to anyone to seek within a Guild House. . . .

And I who for years have sat in Council, dealing the laws of this land, who will sit in my place, who will speak for Ardais? Will there be anyone to speak for my people? Will they be left to Gabriel's whim or Kyril's selfishness? Or Alida's cold, self-interested pride?

That is nothing to me; for eighteen years I have borne that burden which is not even mine, simply because Gabriel would not or could not—it matters not which. Now he must do his destined work or it will go undone; he can no longer shift this burden, unwanted, to my shoulders, *I have served long enough, I will serve no more.*

That afternoon she felt stronger, and when Gabriel

came to see her, she told the women to let him in. He was still, to her mild surprise, sober; this had been his longest sober stretch in years. Well, she no longer cared whether he were drunk or sober; what he did was now nothing to her. But she wondered numbly why he had never attempted this when it had mattered so much to her, when she had wrung herself inside out trying to keep him sober enough and strong enough to deal even with the smallest matters of the estate, when this sobriety would have meant so much to her; when she had loved him.

His hands were shaking, but he was beginning to look a little more like the handsome young *Dom* Gabriel she had married eighteen years ago. His eyes were clearing; she had not remembered how blue they were.

"You look better, Rohana."

"Thank you, my dear; I am better. Physically at least."

"Too bad," he said bluntly, "I was kind of looking forward to havin' a little feller around again. Somebody else to think about." He added with great bitterness, "Somebody to try an' stay sober for. You don' care any more, do you?"

The directness of that made her flinch; but this new, sober Gabriel deserved honesty.

"No, Gabriel, I'm afraid I don't. I'm sorry; I wish I did." She added after a moment, "Elorie cares, my dear. Her father means a great deal to her."

He said broodingly "I suppose it makes no sense to try. Sooner or later . . ."

Sooner or later he would begin having seizures again, and only drink would ease the pain and formless fears. And there was no reason to care. It was too late to begin again. If the child had lived . . . perhaps there might have been some reason to try again to rebuild a life together. They might have done so with a child to begin again. Even so, it was probably too late for Gabriel. He could not endure the pangs of returning to sobriety, to a decency he would only see as deprivation. With the child they would have had a reason to try. Now there was no reason and she was free; the pain she felt was only the pain of a closing door.

She could not help thinking of Gabriel looking at her

and Kindra, accusing her of the unthinkable. Now when he knew she had gone away with Kindra, nothing would ever convince him he had been mistaken; perhaps, she thought with a pain, he had not been mistaken. Maybe she had failed with Gabriel because at the heart of her innermost self what she wanted was not anything Gabriel could provide. Perhaps what she had really wanted all along was the womanly tenderness and strength which Kindra could give her. So Gabriel, in his drunken accusations, had spoken more truly than he realized.

Was it that? And if it is so, is it my fault? Or if it is my fault, is it a crime? Was I ever consulted about whether I wanted a husband at all, much less whether it was Gabriel I wanted? I certainly never considered marrying anyone else, nor in eighteen years of the gatherings of the Comyn, of men of my own station and caste, have I ever looked on any single one of them with desire or a longing that fate had cast me into his arm and not Gabriel's. Unhappily married women look elsewhere—I am not so naive that I do not know that. But if it is simply that I married the wrong man, then why, in Evanda's name—who is Goddess of Love both lawful and profane—why do I not dream of some handsome young man of Comyn kindred? Why then do all my dreams of freedom center upon a woman—upon a Free Amazon—upon Kindra, in fact? Why?

I was given to Gabriel, and I have done my duty—and his—without looking back, for eighteen years. After all this time, am I not entitled to some freedom and happiness for myself? Why must I give what remains of my life as well as what I have already given?

Gabriel had turned away and was moving aimlessly around her room in the way which always made her fidget; she always wondered what he wanted of her. Whatever it was, she had never had it to give. She wondered if he knew the decision she was making. There had been a time when he always knew what she was thinking. Well, if he did, she need not explain herself. And if he did not, he deserved no explanation. She would do what she must; she would take her freedom. No one could expect more of her than she had already given. The women of her own Domain, the Aillard, would understand; and if they did not—well, at least she would have her freedom.

The words of the Renunciate Oath, which Kindra had explained so many years ago, were ringing in her mind;

From this day forth I renounce allegiance to any family, clan, household, warden, or liege lord, and take oath that I owe allegiance only to the laws of the land as a free citizen must: to the kingdom, the crown, and the Gods.

No longer a symbol of a great Domain; but simply and solely herself. I have lived all these years by what I owed to others; never by what I owed myself.

She watched Gabriel leave her room and go down toward the Great Hall. As she surmised, he was heading straight for a drink. It would be madness to try again.

And what would they say in Council, when it was known that Lady Rohana, head of the Domain of Aillard, and by default, holding the Domain of Ardais, in Gabriel's place, had been lost to the Guild House?

The Renunciates held their charter by suffrage. Kindra had explained to her once that the Renunciates were not allowed to seek recruits, but only to accept such women as sought them out.

It does not matter if a few craftsmen's wives or farmer's daughters, battered wives or exploited children, run away to the Guild House. But if the Guild House should reach out to take the Head of two Domains, will they still be tolerated? Or will the Council seek redress from the Guild House? Could their charter survive if they seduced from her sworn duty, say, the Keeper of Arilinn? Ludicrous as the picture was of Leonie Hastur fleeing the Tower in her crimson veils and taking the vows of a Renunciate, still it must be faced as a possibility. If she, Rohana, could be tempted from her clear duty, was any woman in the Domains above suspicion? Would this, then, mean the destruction of the Comyn? And was it worth preserving at such a price—that women should all be enslaved and without choice?

No, there was no question of that. She was free to do as she would; but then she must decide to live for herself without taking thought for the duty she owed to everyone else. Should she sacrifice Domain, family, the well being of every man and woman in the Domain in order that she might do whatever she wished and live for herself alone? To Kindra, the price was too much to pay; she had chosen the duty to herself; but then, Kindra had never owed a duty to anyone, nor chosen that duty; Kindra had been given in marriage, no doubt without inner consent; while she, Rohana, had long enjoyed the privileges of a Comyn lady; and should she enjoy them while they exacted of her nothing, and refuse the burden when it grew heavy? And if she chose to take her own way and live her own life, would the Council not revenge themselves upon the Guild House—even withdraw once and for all the tolerance extended to the Guild Houses and withdraw the Charter given to the Renunciates? *That could destroy Kindra, too....*

No; with all my prestige I will fight for that right— none shall touch the rights of the Guild House while I live. And I am Comyn; who could deny me even should I demand for myself what any small-holder's daughter can have ... my freedom?

Gabriel was in the Great Hall. Rohana, still shaky on her feet, followed him down and saw him fill a glass from a decanter on a sideboard. She sighed; she need only remain silent, and there would be no need for confrontation or choice. Would he even know she was gone—or care? Would he not be relieved, even, to know himself alone with his bottle, to find in it the death he was certainly seeking? Had she any responsibility, then, to him? He drained it quickly, raised his hand to the steward demanding the decanter be refilled.

Rohana said, "No. No more."

She stood before the steward, bracing herself weakly with both hands.

"Listen to me, Hallert," she said. "From this moment forth, when you give the Master more drink than enough for his thirst, it is not his anger you will face; it is mine. Do you understand? *Mine.* The Master needs to be well and strong for the days that are coming soon at Ardais." She saw Gabriel scowl and said urgently, "I will help you, but you must work with me. Kyril is not ready for the Domain, Gabriel. You must somehow stay strong so that he cannot take it from—from us—which he would be all too ready to do."

For a moment an old determination flickered in his eyes. It would be enough for now; there would be struggle ahead, and he would fight her about this again, but somehow she would preserve the domain for Gabriel; and perhaps by the time Kyril reached maturity, he would have improved and matured enough to be trusted with the Domain. And if not—well, they would face that when the time came. At least it would not—now—come this year or next.

"You're right," Gabriel said. "That young upstart—not ready for the Domain. We'll keep it for a while yet."

Rohana suddenly realized that without any conscious act she had made her decision; she had acted almost without thinking. And therefore there could be for her no other choice; this was her allotted destiny, the road she would walk whether she would, or no. The world would go as it would, not as she would have it.

She was filled with a great and terrible sense of loss; she had lost everything else long ago, and now she knew that without any deliberate choice or renunciation she had lost Kindra, too, and all the hopes she had had for another life.

She said to the steward, "Bring the Master some cider or apple juice; he is thirsty." The man scurried away and Rohana sighed, looking in her mind into Kindra's stricken face when she knew of the decision which had been already made, flinching from the long and lonesome road she must tread alone. Kindra was freedom and—yes—love, but this love and freedom could not be hers. She was not even free enough to seek freedom.

DYAN ARDAIS

Few things in the history of Darkover have ever surprised me as much—no; that's not true; everything about the Darkover books has surprised me; but few things have surprised me as much as the popularity of Dyan Ardais. He was invented for the commercial rewrite of the original SWORD OF ALDONES, in which, running the whole thing hurriedly through my typewriter, I invented him by combining three of the spineless villains I invented for Sword, and I have now totally forgotten what the other two were like—even their names. I can only imagine my readers thought Dyan was enough villain for three.

His ghost persisted in walking; first in "The Hawkmaster's Son," which I still think better than the original book in which Dyan appeared. This story was written after Dyan made a small but memorable appearance in the rewritten BLOODY SUN.

"Oathbreaker" was written to study an always unanswered question about why Dyan Ardais had been dismissed from a Tower. "A Man of Impulse" arose out of a phrase in SHARRA'S EXILE; in which Dyan, informing Danilo of the existence of his son, justifies himself by saying Danilo had always known he was a man of impulse.

And finally, I think "The Shadow" is the finest of my own short stories; I generally am not infatuated with myself as a short story writer. I wrote this story to tell myself how it was that Danilo and Regis had gone from the affectionate but ambiguous relationship depicted in HERITAGE to that in SHARRA'S EXILE. So I could not resist the temptation to present it here.

Dyan has been by far the most popular character I ever invented. Like Spock in STAR TREK, fans have been unable to resist the impulse to write stories bedding him down with everybody except the Terran Legate—and I'm not too sure I didn't read one or two of those in the slush sometime. The popularity of the "Relationship" story in STAR TREK fandom was once compellingly explained to me by Diana L. Paxson as the temptation "to be the perfect man and make love to the perfect man." But then, what is the explanation for all these Dyan Ardais stories? To be the worst man making love to the worst man? Not that Dyan—or even *Dom* Gabriel Ardais is the worst.

Oathbreaker

by Marion Zimmer Bradley

In the cool of the evening, Fiora of Arilinn moved silently through the Keeper's Garden, the Garden of Fragrance. Here she had come to be alone, to enjoy the drifting scents of the herbs and flowers planted by some long-ago Keeper. She wondered who that Keeper had been, the Keeper who before recorded time had created this peaceful place, her very own retreat. Had she, too, been blind? Or, perhaps he—for Fiora knew that in ancient times some men, too, had been Keeper—even in Arilinn. Some day, perhaps, when work was not so pressing, she might undertake Timesearch and try to discover something of that long-ago Keeper.

Fiora smiled, almost wistfully. When work was not so pressing—that was like saying, when oranges and apples grew on the ice walls of Nevarsin! The life of a Keeper, certainly of a Keeper of Arilinn, was too crowded to allow for the indulgence of purely intellectual curiosity. There were novices to be trained, young people to be tested for *laran,* and, if possible, claimed for a period of service in Arilinn or one of the few remaining Towers. And there was much other Tower work, complicated by the unending service in the Relays. From this last, however, Fiora was exempt; a Keeper had more important work to do.

For this moment Fiora was at liberty to enjoy the privacy of this special garden, her own particular domain. But not for long; she heard the sound of the garden gate, and even before her mind reached out to touch him, she knew who it was from the fumbling step and the faint scent of kirian which hung always about him; Rian Ardais, the aging technician she had known since childhood.

He was drunk again with kirian. Fiora sighed; she hated seeing him this way, but how could she forbid it, even though she knew he would sooner or later destroy himself? She remembered that Janine, the old Keeper who had trained her when she was new-come to Arilinn, had mentioned Rian's continual intoxication:

"It is the lesser of two evils. It is not for me to refuse him whatever it is that he needs to keep his balance. He never allows it to affect his work; in relay and circle he is always perfectly sober." Janine had said no more, yet Fiora had heard the unspoken words clearly, how can I stop him or deny him that surcease, when the alternative would be that he could no longer tolerate his work here at all?

"*Domna* Fiora," the old man said unsteadily, "I would not intrude upon you in this condition without necessity. You have earned leisure, and—"

"Never mind," she said. She had seen the old man once, before the illness which had deprived her of her sight. She still saw him as handsome and erect, though she knew he had grown skeletal and his old hands trembled. Except, of course, working in the lattices, when they were always perfectly steady. How strange that was, that he should retain the ability to remain steady within a matrix lattice, when he could not so much as shave without cutting himself.

"What is the matter, Rian?"

"There is a messenger in the outer courtyard," he said, "from Ardais. Young Dyan is needed at home, and if it is possible, I must go, too."

"Impossible," Fiora said, "You may go, of course; you have certainly earned a holiday. But you know very well why Dyan cannot." She was shocked that he should even ask; the strictest of laws stated that for the four months after a novice had been accepted at Arilinn, nothing might intrude on his training. Drunk or not, Rian should have been able to handle that without appealing to a Keeper. "Send the messenger away and tell them Dyan is in isolation."

Then she realized that the old man was shaking. Fiora reached out with the awareness which served her better than sight. She should have known. He would not have interrupted her here without need, after all, and it was really far more urgent than she had believed. She sighed, realizing how hard he had tried to keep any hint of his distress from reaching her, and came all the way back from the peace of the garden.

"Tell me," she said aloud.

He spoke, carefully disciplining his thoughts so that Fiora need not pick up anything but the spoken word if she chose.

"A death."

"Lord Kyril?" But that was small loss to any, thought Fiora. Even in the isolation of Arilinn, the young Keeper had heard about the Lord of Ardais, about his dissolute life, his fits of madness. So many of the Ardais clan were dangerously unstable. Kyril mad; Rian himself, though he tried his best, addicted to the intoxication of kirian. It was too soon to know about young Dyan, though she had hopes for him.

"Yet even for a death in the family Dyan may not be released so soon." Although, if it were Kyril, Dyan would be Heir to Ardais and there would be no question of allowing him to take oath at Arilinn in service to the Towers.

"It is not Kyril," Rian's voice was shaking, and though he tried to keep rein on his thoughts she heard it clearly, would that it had been no more than that! "It is worse than that. The Gods witness I love my brother and never once envied him heirship to our house; I was content to make my life here."

Yes, Fiora thought, so content that you cannot get through a tenday without making yourself drunk with kirian or some other drug. But who was she to mock the man's defenses? She had her own. She only said, again, "Tell me."

Yet he hesitated. She could feel him thinking; Fiora was Keeper, sworn virgin, such things should not be spoken before her.

At last he said, and she could feel the desperation in his voice, "It is *Dom* Kyril's wife, the Lady Valentina. She has been an invalid for years and his youngest daughter—Dyan of course is the eldest, his son by his first wife—his daughter Elorie has been acting as his hostess. Some of Kyril's parties are—dissolute," he said, carefully choosing the most neutral word he could.

So Fiora had heard. She nodded for him to go on.

"The Lady Valentina was reluctant for Elorie to appear at these parties," Rian said, "but Kyril would not have it otherwise. So *Domna* Valentina appeared, despite her illness, to protect the girl's character. And Kyril, in a drunken rage—or worse—struck her."

He paused, but Fiora already knew the worst.

"He killed her."

It was indeed worse than Fiora had believed. Kyril had always been a dissolute man—the roster of his bastards was said, and not altogether in jest, to equal the legendary conquests of *Dom* Hilario, a notorious lecher of folk-tale and fable—and there were tales that he had more than once paid heavily to hush up a brutal beating. Fiora was too innocent to be aware of the sexual implications of this, and would have believed it meant no more than ordinary drunken brutality. But murder, and of a lawful wife *di catenas*—that was something else, and probably could not be hushed up at all.

Still Fiora hesitated. "You are Regent of Ardais till Dyan is of age," she said after a moment's thought, "and I am hesitant to interrupt his training. We know he has not the Ardais Gift, but he is potentially a powerful telepath. An untrained telepath is a menace to himself and everyone around him," she added, quoting one of the oldest Arilinn maxims of training. "I know this is a serious crisis in Ardais and perhaps in all the Comyn, *Dom* Rian; it may well demand Council action. But must it involve Dyan? You are *Dom* Kyril's brother and Regent. And you may go as soon as you wish; I will give you leave at once. But why must Dyan accompany you? It is not even as if the Lady Valentina were his mother; she was no more than his stepmother. I think you should go at once and that Dyan should remain here."

Rian twisted his hands. Fiora could sense the man's desperation; she did not need sight for that. Once again she was aware peripherally of the strong smell of the drug that clung to him, blocking out the scents from the garden, and felt with irritation that he had profaned her favorite retreat; she wondered if she would ever walk in it again without the overpowering scent of drug and misery which she could feel on the evening breeze. Silence; the blind woman was tense with the pain of the man who faced her.

Rian was not, Fiora thought, really an old man; it was sorrow and perhaps the side effects of the drugs which made him seem so. He should have been in the heartiest stage of his middle years; he was more than a year *Dom* Kyril's junior. Yet he seemed decrepit, and she had seen him so in the eyes of everyone at Arilinn. He still stood silent before her, and after a moment she heard the small sound of the stifled sob.

"Rian, what is it? Is there something else?"

He did not speak, but the Keeper, open in empathy to the misery of the man before her, was overwhelmed with his despair. In that moment she knew why Rian drugged himself, why he seemed an old man when he was younger than Kyril, as she heard his first stammering, shamed word.

"I am—I have always been afraid of Kyril. I dare not, I have never been able to face his—his anger, his brutality. Ever since I was a young man, I have tried never to face him at all. Dyan is not afraid of his father. I dare not go home, especially not now, unless Dyan is with me."

Fiora tried hard to conceal her shock and pity, realizing it was not untouched with a contempt of which she knew she should be ashamed. Rian's weaknesses were not of his own choosing. Yet she knew nothing would ever be the same again between them. She was Keeper; she had won through to that high office by achievement, hard work, and an austerity which would have broken nine women out of ten. She was Rian's superior, but the man was her elder, and she had always liked and even admired him. The liking remained unchanged, but she was shocked and distressed by the change in her own feelings. Nevertheless, the young Keeper made her voice gentle, without judgment.

"Well, then, Rian, it seems there is no help for it. I will speak with Dyan. If it can be done without totally wrecking all his training so far, I will give him leave to go with you to Ardais. Send him to me—" she hesitated,

"—but not here." She would not have her garden further spoiled for her. "I will await him, an hour from now, in the fireside room."

Dyan Ardais at this time of his life—he was about nineteen, she thought—was still as slight as a boy. Fiora, who of course could not see him, had seen him often enough in the eyes of the others in the circle at Arilinn. He was a darkly handsome young man, dark hair coarsely curling about his face, which was narrow and finely made. He had also eyes of the colorless steely gray which, Fiora knew, often marked the strongest telepaths. If Dyan was a telepath, though, he had learned to barrier his thoughts perfectly, even from her.

In the training which had made her Keeper, she had learned to be impervious to all men; and Dyan was no exception. But though Fiora was innocent, she was a Keeper and a telepath and in the course of the early training, when Dyan had first come here, she had learned many things about him, and one was this; he would forever be impervious to her or to any woman. That did not matter to Fiora; he was neither the first nor the last lover of men to make a place and a reputation for himself in the Towers. What troubled her was that a boy so young—Fiora herself was not past twenty, but a Keeper's training made one age rapidly in both body and mind—should be so braced, so impassive and invulnerable. At his age, a novice in a Tower should be open to his Keeper. Was it some early warning sign of the Ardais instability, which might later show itself in becoming, like Rian, addicted to some drug? Or—in fairness, she remembered what she knew of *Dom* Kyril—was it only the effect of growing up in the presence of a madman? As far as she knew, and she would have known, Dyan used kirian only for the necessary work in the Towers and for training. And though some Ardais drank far too much, she had noticed that he drank only moderately and at dinner. He had, as far as she knew, no glaring character flaws; some Keepers might have considered his homosexuality a flaw, but it did not trouble Fiora as long as it created no trouble within the circle, and so far she had not heard of any dissension that it had caused; the others in the circle were tolerant and seemed to like him. He seemed a quiet, inoffensive youngster, yet something about him, something subliminal which she could not yet quite identify, still troubled her; why should a youth of Dyan's age be opaque when to his Keeper he should have been transparent?

Dyan bowed and said, in the musical voice which was, to Fiora, one of his most attractive qualities, "My uncle said you wanted to speak to me, *Domna*."

"Has he told you anything about what it is?"

"He said to me that there was trouble at home, and that I was needed there. No more than that ... no; he said, too, that it was important enough that I should have to go home even though I have not yet passed my first period of probation here." He paused, expectantly.

Fiora asked, "Do you want to go home, Dyan?" And for the first time she sensed a trace of emotion in his voice.

"Why? Has my work here been unsatisfactory? I have—have tried very hard—"

She said quickly, "It is nothing like that, Dyan. Nothing would please me more than that you should complete your training with us here, and perhaps work with us for a time, perhaps many years; although, as you are Heir to Ardais, you cannot spend a lifetime here. But, as Rian has told you, there is trouble at home which he feels he is not competent to meet alone. He has asked us as a favor that you be allowed to go with him. This is very unusual at this stage in your training, and I need to assess whether it will do any damage to interrupt your training at this point." She added forthrightly, "If you are here only because you are unhappy at home, as you can see, your dedication to Arilinn is certainly in question."

She could feel that he smiled. He said, "It is true that I have no great love for living at Ardais. I do not know how much you know about my father, Lady, but I assure you, a desire to escape the chaos of life at Ardais is a healthy sign of a sane mind. That I find pleasure in my work here—is that a bad thing?"

"Of course not," she said, "and I have no particular

fault to find with you at this point. Who has been training you?"

"Rian, for the most part. He has told me that he thinks I will make a technician. And *Domna* Angelica has said she believes I have mastered the work of a monitor. She said she thought I was ready for the monitor's Oath."

"That I will certainly authorize," Fiora said, "and it is even your right to take it at my hands if you desire. Even so, you must have realized while we were talking that you have not answered my question, Dyan. Do you want to go home?"

He sighed, and that heavy sigh answered her question. Fiora was not a maternal woman, but for a moment she felt she would have liked to shelter the youth in her arms; a fleeting sensation, and one, she knew, which would have distressed Dyan as much as herself. Recalling herself to the duty of questioning, not only in words, she reached out to him; she could feel the tension in his shoulders, the weight of the lines in his face, telling her better than sight what the answer would have been to her question.

"I do not. But if I am needed, how can I refuse? Rian means well, but he is not—" he paused, and she felt him searching for truthful words which would not reflect on his kinsman, "not worldly."

She did not challenge the polite evasion of what she had really asked him; though she felt, with some distress, that he should have been willing to be more honest with his Keeper.

"Dyan, you are a responsible young man; what do you think? Will it harm your training? I shall leave it to you."

The sigh he gave seemed drawn up from his very depths. He said "I thank you, *Domna,* for asking that question. The only answer that I can give is that if the Domain demands my presence, I must not think of anything else."

Again, without really knowing why, Fiora felt an enormous pity for the young man before her. "Spoken like an honorable man, Dyan."

She could sense the very stoop of Dyan's shoulders,

as if he bore the weight of a world on them. No, not a world. Only a Domain. She said gently, "Then it remains only to give you the monitor's Oath, Dyan; you must not leave here without that. Then you are free to do as your conscience bids you."

She took leave of them a few hours later at the front gates of Arilinn. Rian already in his saddle, stooped and looking older than his years; Dyan standing beside his horse, his handsome face drawn with tension which Fiora could sense, without sight, from her distance of several feet. He bent over her hand respectfully and she could feel the lines drawn in his face.

"Farewell, Lady. I hope to return to you soon."

"I wish you a pleasant journey."

"That is impossible," Dyan said with a faint tinge of amusement. "The journey to Ardais lies through some of the worst mountains in the Domains, including the Pass of Scaravel."

"Then I wish you a *safe* journey: and I shall hope that you may be able to return soon and that when you arrive at your home you find the problems less serious than you have foreseen," she said, and they mounted and rode away. As he went, Fiora felt enormous anger. *No, she thought, I should never have let him go!*

The kinsmen rode in silence for some time. At last Dyan said, "You knew that Fiora had insisted that I take the monitor's Oath before I left the Tower. Is such haste usual, uncle?"

Rian sighed and said, "Indeed, it is customary to give the Oath even to children at the first moment they are old enough to understand its meaning."

"Then it was not a personal statement that Fiora did not trust me—that she was in such haste to bind my Oath?" Dyan asked.

Rian frowned and said "Of course not. It is customary."

"Indeed."

"You can hardly have any qualms of conscience about taking the Oath of a monitor," exclaimed Rian, recalling the words of the Oath ... *to enter no mind save to help or heal, and never to force the conscience of any.*

"Perhaps not," Dyan said after a moment, "yet I cannot help but feel as if I had ceded some right over my own conscience. I thought not that I needed any to keep my conscience, nor an Oath to bind me to ethical use of *laran.*"

"The Oath is needed most by those most reluctant to take it," said Rian, "those who feel they need it not should surely have no qualms about it."

He felt that Dyan wanted to say more. But he didn't.

The journey took four days, at the best speed they could make over the mountains. When they came in sight of Castle Ardais, Dyan noticed that the crimson and gray pennant was flying which announced that the Head of the Domain was in residence.

"He is here," Dyan said. "Perhaps I wished that he had fled us. The Domain is in mourning; this is arrogance."

"More likely," Rian said, "he feels himself so justified that it would not occur to him to flee justice."

Dyan said sighing "I remember him as he was *before*—when I was a little child. I loved him; now I can hardly remember when he was not a brute. I remember hiding in a cupboard from him when he was drunk and roaring all over the castle, threatening us all ... I think it the saddest of all that Elorie will remember nothing but this and has no memory of a father to love; because despite everything, Rian, never doubt this; I love my father well, whatever he has done."

"I never thought to doubt that, lad," Rian said gently. "Once I loved him, too."

Almost on the threshold, Elorie appeared, pale as death; it looked to the men as if she had neither slept nor eaten since her mother's death. She flung herself, weeping, into Dyan's arms.

"Oh, my brother! You have heard—my mother—"

"Hush, little sister," Dyan said, stroking her hair. "I came as soon as I heard. I loved her, too. Where is our father?"

"He has barricaded himself in the Tower room and will let no one near him, not even his body-servants. For a full day afterward, he was drunk and shouting and roaring all over the castle, offering to fight anyone—" Elorie shivered, and Dyan, remembering similar episodes when he himself was very young, patted her as if she were a little girl. "Then he hid himself in the Tower room and would not come out. I had to arrange everything for—for Mother—"

"I am sorry, little sister; I am here now, and you need not be frightened of anything. You must go and rest now, and sleep. Tell your nurse to put you to bed, and give you a sleeping draught; I will take care of everything, as befits Warden of the Domain," said Dyan. "And as soon as your mother is buried, you cannot stay here alone with Father, not now."

"But where can I go?" she asked.

"I will find a place to send you; perhaps you could be fostered at Armida or even in one of the Towers; you are Comyn and nobly born," Dyan said, "but now you must sleep and eat and rest; you must look seemly and lady-like when your mother is laid to rest. You do not want to look as if you dwelt under siege here—even," he added shrewdly, "if that is what you feel like."

"But what of Father? Will you let him hide there in the Tower saying evil things of how Mother drove him to kill her?"

Dyan said quietly "You must just leave Father to me, Lori, child."

And at her look of relief he stroked her hair again and said to Rian, "Ring for her nurse now, will you, and tell her to take Lori away to her rooms and look after her properly."

"Oh," Elorie sighed, and he could see that she was near to collapse, "I am so weary, so glad you are home, brother. Now you are here, everything will be all right."

When Elorie had been taken to her own rooms, Dyan went into the Great Hall, and called the *coridom*.

"Lord Dyan, how good to see you," the man said, and curiously repeated what Elorie had said; "Now you are here, everything will be all right." It was like a weight on him; Dyan thought, with smothered rage, they should be seeking to make things easy for him, instead of all waiting until the burden could be put on his shoulders.

He was not ready for the weight of the Domain; could he not even complete his education? He should have known when he was summoned, a year earlier than he had been promised from Nevarsin, that he might assume the place of Warden of the Domain, when his father was ill with the autumn fever; they had feared he might die and had lost no time in naming Dyan as Warden. *It was the fever that did it,* Dyan thought; *some injury to his brain. Before that he had been drunken and dissolute, but sane, and only rarely cruel.*

There had never been any question, he thought dispassionately, of naming Rian as Kyril's successor. Not even the most optimistic of Ardais kindred had believed Rian fit for that office; they were all ready to dump it on the shoulders of a boy of nineteen.

The *coridom* began telling how the ill-fated feast had begun; but Dyan waved him to silence.

"None of that matters; how came he to strike down my stepmother?"

"I am not sure he knew he struck down any; he was drunk."

"Then, in the name of all the Gods," Dyan shouted in frustration, "when all of you know he has these rages when he is drunk, why do you not keep him away from drink?"

"Lord Dyan, if you who are his son, or the Lady who was his wife, cannot forbid it, how are we who are but servants to do so?"

Dyan supposed there was some justice to the question. But now it was too late to leave such things to servants or chance.

"There's no help for it; the man's mad, he must be watched over, perhaps locked up so he'll do no harm to himself or others," Dyan said.

"And what of the Domain, with my Lady dead and you all away in the Tower?" asked the *coridom*.

Dyan sighed heavily and said "Leave that to me. Now I will go and see my father."

Dom Kyril had barricaded himself inside the topmost room of the north tower, and Dyan struggled in vain with the heavy door. Finally he shouted and kicked at the door, and at last a quavering voice came from inside.

"Who is there?"

"It is Dyan, father. Your son."

"Oh, no," the voice said. "You can't get me that way. My son Dyan is in Arilinn. If he were here, none of this would be happening; he'd make sure my rebellious servants did my will."

"Father, I journeyed last night from Arilinn," Dyan said, feeling his heart sink at the crafty madness—real or feigned?—in his father's voice. *If I had been here, it is true, this would not have happened; I'd have had him chained first.*

"Damn you, Father, open this door or I'll kick it in!" Dyan backed up the threat with a mighty kick that rattled the hinges.

"I'll open, I'll open," said the voice petulantly. "No need to go breaking things."

There was a creak in the mighty lock, and after a moment a small crack widened and Dyan saw his father's face.

Once *Dom* Kyril had been handsome, with the good looks of all the Ardais men. Now his eyes were bloodshot, his face puffy and swollen, the features blurred with drink and indecision, his clothes filthy and disheveled. He looked with hostile grimaces at Dyan and muttered "What are you doing here, then? You were so anxious to go off to the Tower and get away, now what are you doing back?"

So that would be his defense? Pretending to ignore what had happened and putting Dyan on the defensive?

"I went with your leave, Father. Was I to think the Domain could not be trusted with its ruler? Come, Father, don't pretend to be madder or drunker than you are."

Dom Kyril's bloodshot eyes grimaced closed; he said "Dyan, is it you? Really you? Why is everybody angry with me? What did I do this time? I need a drink, boy, and they won't bring me wine—"

Dyan was not surprised; but now he understood his father's ravings. A long-term drunkard, abruptly deprived of all drink—by this stage no doubt he was seeing things crawling out of the walls at him.

He could understand the servants; but at this point if they were to have any rational discourse, his father must have at least enough of the poison to give him the simulacrum of sanity. His brain had grown unused to functioning without drink; Dyan could see the shaking hands, the uneven gait.

He should never have been allowed to come to this point. No doubt they found it simpler to abandon the man to drink himself to death, rather than contend with him for his own good. *If I had been here*, Dyan thought painfully, looking at the wreck of the father he once had loved. *But as he says, I was eager to get away from the problem, and so it is as much my fault as his. I am no better than Rian.*

"I'll get you a drink, Father," he said.

He went down to the foot of the stairs and found wine and told the *coridom* to bring food. His father drank with haste and eagerness, slopping the wine on his shirt-front, and after, when the shakes had subsided, Dyan managed to persuade him to drink some soup.

The shivering and trembling slowly stopped. Now, when he had had a drink, Dyan thought, his father seemed more sober than when his system was free of the drink. It was true that he could no longer function normally without it.

"Now let us talk sensibly," said Dyan, when the man who faced him had been restored at least to a semblance of the man he had once known. "Do you know what you have done?"

"They were angry with me," *Dom* Kyril said, "Elorie and her mother—damn all puling womenfolk—I shut her up, that's all," he said craftily, "Never was a woman didn't deserve a lick or two. Won't hurt them. Does them good, and they like it really. Has she been bawling to you because I hit her?"

But Dyan heard the craftiness in his father's voice; he was still pretending to be drunker than he was, and madder.

"You wretch, you killed her," he exploded. "Your own wife!"

"Well," murmured the drunken man, staring at his knuckles. "I didn't go for to do it, I di'n mean any harm."

"All the same—no, Father, look at me, listen to me—" Dyan insisted. "All the same, you are no longer fit to rule the Domain, and after this—"

"Dyan—" His father tugged at his arm, "I was drunk; I di'n know what I was doing. Don't let them hang me!"

Dyan brushed off his grip with distaste. "There's no question of that," he said. "The question is what's to be done with you so you won't kill the next person who crosses your path. I think the best thing for you to do is to turn the Domain over, formally, to me or to Rian, and confine yourself to these rooms except when you're in your senses."

"So that's what this is all about," his father said furiously. "Trying again to get the Domain away from me? I thought as much. Never, hear me? It's my Domain and my rule and I should give it over to an upstart boy?"

"Father, I beg you; no one shall harm you, but when you are incapacitated, I can care for the Domain safely in your place."

"Never!"

"Or if you do not trust me, give it over to Rian and I will stand by him faithfully—"

"Rian!" His father made an inexpressible sound of contempt. "Oh, no, I know what you're up to. Look at me, Gods—" he spread his hands and began, drunkenly, to weep. "My brother, my children—all my enemies, trying to get the Domain out of my hands—lock me up—"

Dyan never knew when he had made the decision he made now, but perhaps at first it was only a desire to silence the drunken whining. He reached out with the new strength of his *laran*—it was the first time he had used it since training began at Arilinn—and gripped his father with the force of it. The words trailed off into incoherence; Dyan gripped harder and harder, knowing what he must do if this was ever to be settled and the Domain of Ardais free of a madman's rule.

When he stopped he was white and shaking, stopping himself with force before he killed the man. He knew, shamed, that this was what he had wanted. His father

was slumped on the floor, having slid, during that mon-
strous battle, from his chair.

Dom Kyril mumbled, "Of course ... only rational
thing to do. Call the wardens an' we'll have it done."

Silently, without a word, Dyan went and summoned
the *coridom*. All he said was, "Summon the Wardens of
the Domain; he is rational now and ready to do what
must be done."

Within the hour they came; the council of old men of
the Domain, who had been notified of the emergency
days ago; by whose counsel and agreement the Ruler of
Ardais held his power.

"Kinsmen," Dyan said, facing them; he had gone to
his room and changed into a sober suit of the formal
colors of the Domain. He had also summoned his father's body-servant and had him washed and shaved and
made presentable. "You know what sorry urgency brings
us all here. Even before the Lady of Ardais is laid to
rest, the Domain must be made secure."

"Has he agreed to turn the Domain over to you? We
tried to persuade him, but—has he agreed to this of his
own free will?"

"Of his free will," said Dyan. *Even if he had not, what
other choice have we?* he wondered, but did not speak
the question aloud.

"Then," said the oldest of them, "we are ready to
witness it."

And so they all stood by as Kyril Ardais, calm now
and evidently in his right mind, went through the brief
ceremony where he formally and irrevocably laid down
the wardenship of the Domain in favor of his eldest son
Dyan-Valentine.

When it was over and the Council of Ardais had given
Dyan their allegiance, Dyan relaxed the stern grip he
had kept on his father's mind through the ceremony.
The man slid to the floor, whining incoherently and
retching. Dyan told himself; this had had to be done,
there was no other way; but it left a bad taste in his
mouth. This he knew to be a misuse of his *laran*. They
should have kept him at Arilinn. . . .

What was the alternative? he asked himself grimly. Put
his father into the hands of healers—for a year per-

haps—until he came entirely to himself? No time for that. No, he had done what he must: No man can keep another's conscience. No, nor any woman either, he thought, scalded by the memory of Fiora and the monitor's Oath. This was, no doubt, why he had been reluctant to take it. Well, he could not cede the right to do what his own conscience bade him, not for many oaths. But it should never have happened. He would not even see Elorie; she was among those who had forced him to this.

Fiora of Arilinn had been informed of the arrival of the men from Ardais; she sensed some tension in each of them not consonant with only settling family affairs. Rian seemed calm; yet, reading in his mind what had befallen, she was angry. No, Rian was not on the surface the kind of man to rule a Domain; yet it was not right, either, that he should have been passed over. Given the responsibility, he might have grown into it; now he would always accept his own weakness and unfitness. It was wrong that he should be allowed to hide here, forever unable to grow to his own strength, forever immature. Her hands went out to him, impulsively. "Welcome back, my old friend," she said, clasping his hands. "I had feared you were lost to us." Feared? She had *hoped* he would achieve the strength to take his brother's place; but in the test he had not done it.

And turning her attention to Dyan, she realized that he seemed weary, but calm, and the barrier had dropped; he was not opaque to her; he had arrived at some inner strength, achieved some unknown potential.

"Dyan, I am glad to see you again," she said, truthfully if inaccurately, and she touched his hand lightly; and at the touch he was transparent to her, he no longer even wished to hide what he had done, or why; and in that moment she was shocked. She said, "Dyan, I am sorry to see what has happened to you."

"I have done what I must, and if you know what I have done, you know why. Hypocrites, all; none of them had the courage to do what must be done. I did; and now you, too, will censure me?"

"Censure you? No. I am the Keeper of Arilinn, but

not the keeper of any man's conscience," she said, knowing it was not true; she had sought to bind his conscience, and had failed. "I say only that now you may not return to us, and you know why. Recall the words of the monitor's Oath; *to enter no mind save to help or heal and never to force the conscience of any. . . ."*

"Lady, if you know how I forced my father's assent, you know well why I did so, and what alternatives I had." Dyan said, his face carefully impassive, denying her touch. Fiora bent her head.

This was wrong, what she must do. Now they could have no control over him, no link to right whatever wrong had been done; he was forever beyond even a Keeper's help or touch.

"I do not judge you. I only say that having violated that Oath you have no place here." But where, then, she thought wildly, could he go, having stepped beyond her judgment, gone further than he had ever wanted to go. Already his life was to be led outside the laws laid down for them all. Must he be an outlaw before he was out of his teens? Desperately, she realized that he had put himself outside even her help. She said slowly, "Will you take my blessing, Dyan?"

"Willingly, Lady." His voice shook, and she thought, with deep pity, *he is only a boy, he needs our help more now than ever. Damn our laws and rules! He had the courage to break them; he did what he must. I wish I dared as much.*

She said, slowly, holding out her fingertips to him, "You have courage. If you always act in accordance with your own conscience, even when it violates the standards of others, I do not censure you. Yet if you will let me counsel you, I would say you have embarked on a dangerous path. Perhaps it is right for you; I cannot say."

"I have come to a place in my life, Lady, where I cannot think of right or otherwise, but only of necessity."

"Then may all the Gods walk with you, Dyan, for you will need their aid more than any of us." Her voice broke, and he looked down at her—she felt it—with pain and pity. *For the first time and maybe the last in his life he is reaching out for help and I am bound by my own oaths and laws not to help him.* She said quietly, "You may send Elorie here when you will."

Dyan bent over Fiora's hand and touched his lips to the corpse-pale fingers; he said "If there are any Gods, Lady, I ask their help and understanding; but why came they not to my aid when I needed it most?" He straightened, with a bleak smile, and Fiora knew he had barricaded himself again; he was forever beyond their reach. Then he rode away from Arilinn without looking back.

The Hawkmaster's Son

by Marion Zimmer Bradley

Dyan Ardais laid down his pack on the narrow cot, covered with a single rough blanket, which would be his in the cadet barracks, and started to transfer his gear into the wooden chest standing at the foot of the bed.

Third year; the final year as a cadet. He was just enough older than the others to put him out of step as a cadet; he had spent his first two cadet years here before his father's inexplicable decision—and all of his father's decisions were inexplicable to Dyan—that he should spend several years in Nevarsin Monastery. Now, an equally inexplicable whim had brought him back here.

He thought, with resignation so deep that he did not fully realize how bitter it was, that his family did not seem to care where he was—Nevarsin, the cadet corps, in one of Zandru's nine hells—so long as he was not at Ardais.

He had been glad to leave Nevarsin, however. He had learned much there, including the mastery of *laran* denied him when the Keeper of Dalereuth Tower had refused to admit him to a Tower circle; he had seriously wished to study the healing arts and medicine, and he had been given ample opportunity, at Nevarsin, to study these things normally denied to a son of the Comyn. More than this; he had been able to forget himself there, giving himself up to his first love, music and singing in the great Nevarsin choir. The Father Cantor had admired his clear treble voice and gone to some trouble to have it trained; the saddest day of Dyan's life had been the day his voice broke, and his mature singing voice turned out to be a clear, tuneful but undistinguished baritone.

But it was not really suitable, that a Comyn heir should live among *cristoforos*. He had accepted their discipline with calm, cynical obedience, as a means to an end, without the slightest intent of taking their rules of life into his personal world-view; and when the time came, he had left them without much regret. Tempting as it might be, to give his life to music and healing, he had always known that his real vocation, the path laid out for every Comyn son, was here; to serve, and later to rule, among the Comyn. There was a Council seat awaiting him, as soon as he was old enough to take it.

And as soon as he completed this mandatory third year in the cadet corps there would be an officer's post in the Guard. The Commander of the Thendara City Guard, Valdir Alton, had only one son of an age to command; Lewis-Valentine Lanart was nineteen. Valdir's younger son, Kennard, had been sent to Terra, a few years ago, as an exchange student for the young Terran, Lerrys Montray. Dyan had known Lerrys, a little, during his own second cadet year; Lerrys had been allowed to serve a single year in the cadets, in token that he was taking up the obligation of a Comyn son. Dyan had heard his superiors say that the young Terran had been a credit to his people, but Dyan felt cynical about that. They could hardly expel or harry a political guest, so they would find tactful praise for whatever he did right and ignore his blunders, and it would make for excellent diplomatic relations.

Dyan wondered why the Comyn bothered. It would be better to send all of those damned Terrans yelping back to whatever godforgotten world had spawned them!

Dyan remembered Lerrys Montray as a pleasant-looking, amiable young nonentity, but he could have been a dozen times as capable and competent and Dyan would still have loathed him. For Larry had taken Kennard Alton's place—and for Dyan, no man alive, not the legendary Son of Aldones, could have done that. Dyan had fiercely resolved that this Terran intruder get no joy of his usurped place; he flattered himself that he had made things damned difficult for the presumptuous Terran who thought he could stand in Kennard Alton's boots!

As if some trace of precognition had sent the thought of Kennard to his mind moments before the reality, a voice behind Dyan said softly, "You're here before me, cousin? I had hoped to find you here, *Janu....*"

Only one person living, since Dyan's mother had died ten years before, had ever dared to use that childish pet-name. Dyan's breath caught in his throat, then he was swept into a familiar kinsman's embrace.

"Kennard!"

Kennard hugged him tight, then held him off at arm's length. "Now I really know I am home again, *bredu* ... so you interrupted your time in the Cadets, too? Third year?"

"Yes. And you?"

"I finished my third year before I left, remember? But Lewis has gone to Arilinn Tower, so Father wants me as his *seconde* this year. I'll be your officer, Dyan. How old are you now?"

"Seventeen. Just one year younger than you, Kennard—or had you forgotten, we have the same birthday?"

Kennard chuckled. "Why, so I had. But you remembered?"

"There isn't much I don't remember about you, Ken," Dyan said, with an intensity that made the older lad frown. Dyan saw the frown and quickly went back to lightness. "When did you come back?"

"Only a few days ago, just time enough to pay my respects to my foster sister and my mother. Cleindori is at Arilinn now, and of course, there is talk of marriage, or at least handfasting, for all of us. And what about you, Dyan? You're at the age when they start talking about such things."

Dyan shrugged. "There was some talk of marrying me to Maellen Castamir," he said, "but there is time enough for that; she is still playing with dolls; there might be a handfasting, but certainly not a wedding, not for ten years and more. Which suits me well enough. And you?"

"Talk," Kennard said, "There's always talk. Time enough to listen when it's something more than talk. Meanwhile I can renew my old friendships—and speaking of old friendships," he said, and broke off as two young men came into the barracks.

"Rafael!" he said, then laughed, looking at the second youth. "I mean, of course, both of you!"

Rafael Hastur, Heir to Hastur, a slight, handsome youngster, with eyes nearer to blue than the true Comyn gray, smiled merrily and held out both hands to Kennard. "It is good to see you again, cousin! And you, Dyan—do you know Rafael-Felix Syrtis, my paxman and sworn man?"

Kennard smiled at him, "We probably met as boys; before I was sent to Terra. But I know your family, of course; the Syrtis hawks are famous."

"As famous as the Armida horses," young Syrtis said, smiling. "I heard you were to be one of our officers, Captain Alton."

"Kennard will do," Kennard said genially, "There's no need for formality here, kinsman. You know my cousin Dyan, don't you?"

Dyan frowned and gave Rafael Syrtis the most distant of nods, his frown reproving Kennard's effusive friendliness. A Syrtis, the son of the hawkmaster, and a *cristoforo*, too, as the Syrtis folk had been for generations, was no suitable paxman or companion for a Hastur heir, and, to look at the two of them, Dyan sensed they were not paxman and master alone, but *bredin* as well! Young Syrtis addressed his master in the familiar inflection, and he saw that the young Syrtis, though he was only a minor noble, wore in his sheath a dagger with the fine Hastur crest. Well, Rafael Hastur might have a taste for low company, but he could not force his commoner friend on other Comyn! He began talking to Rafael Hastur, pointedly ignoring young Syrtis' sycophantic efforts to be friendly. Young Hastur tried to include his friend in the conversation, but Dyan gave him only brief, frigidly courteous replies.

After a time Kennard went to attend on his father, and one of the armsmasters sent for Dyan; Rafael Hastur and Rafael Syrtis remained in the barracks, helping each other put away their possessions.

Rafael Hastur said, in apology, "You must not mind Dyan, my friend. The Ardais are proud . . . he was disgustingly rude to you, Rafe; I regard that as an insult to myself, and I shall tell him so!"

Rafael Syrtis laughed and shrugged. "He is very young for his age," he said. "He has always been a bit like that, acting as if he thought himself far above everyone else, probably because he is self-conscious ... his father, you know. I should not say so about a Comyn Lord, but old Lord Kyril is a disgusting old sot, the most unpleasant drunk I have ever met."

"You won't hear any arguments from me about that," Rafael said, "I have no love for my Uncle of Ardais. But Dyan used to be a nice lad."

Rafe Syrtis shrugged. "Well, I can live without his liking. But I'm sorry for the lad; he has not many friends. He would have more, no one would blame Dyan for the old man's faults, but he is prickly and over-swift to take offense and slight others before they can snub him. *Dom* Rafael, shall I go and look at the duty lists and see where and when we are assigned?"

"Go by all means," Rafael Hastur said. "Bring me word of where I am assigned, and forget not to take note of when we are off duty, so that we pay our respectful compliments to my sister Alisa and to her companion ... ha, Rafael, you see, I can feel the wind when it blows from the right quarter, and need no weather vane for that!"

Rafe Syrtis made a gesture of laughing surrender. "You know me, *vai dom caryu* ... indeed, I am eager to pay my respects to the *damisela* Caitlin. . . ."

"But not too respectfully, I hope," Rafael Hastur teased, then sobered. "No, I won't make fun of you, *bredu*. I am truly glad you have found someone you can love, and she is worthy of you in all ways, my foster sister Caitlin."

"But I am not worthy of her ..." Rafe's voice trembled. "How could I look so high. . . ."

Rafael Hastur laid his hand on his friend's shoulder. He said vehemently, "No, Rafe, don't speak like that. My father knows, we all know, your worth and quality. My father, too, values your father as one of his most loyal men. To me, Caitlin is only one of my cousins, all eyes and teeth, and what you want with that scrawny buck-toothed little thing—"

"Scrawny! Caitlin scrawny!" Rafe Syrtis cried in indignation, "She is divinely slender, and her eyes . . . those eyes. . . ."

"When she was a little girl, Alisa and I used to call her Pop-eyes," Rafael teased, "and I cannot see that she has grown a whit prettier. But, Rafe, don't trouble yourself. She is my father's ward, and Alisa loves her well, but she is not wealthy, so in that respect she is not too far above you; and although her family is very good, so is yours. Father will be well content to give her to you. I do not think any other has offered for her, but even if someone had done so, I will speak to Father for you, and if you will, I shall stand for you at your handfasting. Thus Caitlin will remain in our family and close to my sister as she has always been."

Rafe Syrtis' voice trembled. "I don't know how to thank you. . . ."

"Thank me?" Rafael said, "Merely by being what you have always been, my most loyal paxman and my sworn brother. I wish I thought, when the time comes for my father to find me a bride, he could find me one I was half so eager to marry. As yet I have seen no maiden in Thendara who seems better to me than any others; Father has spoken of the daughter of Lord Elhalyn; but she is still a child." He laid his hand, shyly, on his friend's arm. "Perhaps some of your good fortune will come to me, too, and I too shall be lucky in love. But promise me, Rafe, that you will never let this new tie part our company."

"Never," Rafe Syrtis pledged, "I swear it."

For the first tenday or so of the cadet season, the business of honor guards, of escort for Comyn lords and ladies, of assessing the training of new cadets and assigning suitable duties to older ones, kept them all too busy for the renewing of old friendships. On the morning of Festival Night, Kennard and Dyan met in a small office near the Guard Hall, where Kennard was making up duty lists before leaving for the ceremonial duties of the night's ball.

"Will you be there, Dyan? But of course you will, there is no other representative of the Ardais Domain here." He looked at the younger lad with sympathy. Dyan's father, *Dom* Kyril, was well known to be subject to recurring periods of derangement when he had little sense of what was fitting and proper; during one of his lucid intervals, he had arranged for Dyan to perform the ceremonial duties of the Domain, so that he might not, in a moment of vagueness or madness, bring disgrace upon them.

Kennard said, "I am fortunate in that my father and my brother Lewis are both fit to perform the public duties of the Domain; I have no liking for ceremony. I could take pride in the important business of Council, but to stand up in public and be admired like a racehorse because of my pedigree ... no, I should find that tiresome."

Dyan said stiffly, "I hope I shall never fail any duty to Comyn, no matter how tiresome it may be."

Kennard put his arm briefly around his friend's shoulder. He said, "That's what I love about you, *bredu.* But truthfully, Dyan, it is a boring business, isn't it?"

Dyan chuckled. "I wouldn't say so in public, but it's as you say. I wonder if the prize horse gets tired of being dressed in his finest harness and paraded in the streets?"

"It's a good thing we don't know, isn't it, or we'd never have the heart to hold parades," Kennard said. "No, actually, I do know, a little. One of the things I like to do, when I have leisure, is to train our saddle horses, and I can sense, just a little, with *laran,* how they feel about the bit and the saddle. But they come to accept it, just as you and I accepted learning to stand long watches, and to write, and to do all the other things we have to do. And, speaking of tiresome duties, Lewis said that Father had chosen a wife for me, some tiresome daughter of one of the minor Hastur clans ... have you heard any gossip?"

Dyan shook his head. "I am not particularly interested in women and I hear very little about marriages."

Kennard said with a shrug, "Women, that is one thing. I discovered that, at least. But as for marriage ... oh, I suppose it would have its merits, an established home, children for the clan ... I bear the Alton Gift; Lewis does not. So it is more urgent for me to marry and to have sons."

"As to that," Dyan said, "I suppose, as always, I will do whatever my duty is to the Domain, but when I was so young I was so sickened at my father's women—" He did not look at Kennard, and his calm, musical voice did not change its inflection, but Kennard, who had a sizable portion of the Ridenow empath gift, sensed that Dyan was forcing the words through layers of pain and shame.

"You probably do not know ... there were times when he brought them to Ardais, flaunting them in my mother's face, jesting about the old days when wives knew their duty, and if they did not delight in their husband's bed, choosing some woman to please their husbands ... he forced her to foster all of Rayna Di Asturien's bastard sons and even daughters ... even though the woman was cruelly arrogant to my mother. And he did not stop at—at making advances even to her own serving maids, and worse, before her eyes, and forcing her to witness ... the idea that I could ever behave so dishonorably, it makes me physically ill! And yet he could not ... could not help himself; the idea that I could ever be so enslaved to a ... a concept of manhood, of virility ... so that I would hurt and humiliate a good woman who had done me no harm, to whom I owed honor ... someday, I suppose, I shall marry properly and do my duty to the Domain, but the idea that I could ever be so—so enslaved to my own lusts ... before I could behave like that I hope I would be honorable enough to make myself *emmasca* as the whining *cristoforos* do!"

Kennard was appalled at his vehemence; he squeezed Dyan's arm with silent affection, but there was nothing he could say before the younger boy's revelation. He had had no idea ...! At last, after a long time and diffidently, he said, "Your father ... he is not in his right senses, *bredhyu,* you must not let his wickedness deform your life."

"I will not," Dyan said, guarded again and defiant, "but I am in no hurry to have a woman's happiness and honor placed in my hands. It would be a—a terrifying responsibility. And suppose I should find myself so enslaved to the desire for women. . . ."

Kennard said, half lightly and half seriously, "Oh, I shouldn't think there is much danger of that. Women are pleasant enough, but I have no wish to limit my attentions to only one. I would rather make them all happy, not give any one of them the right to jealousy and reproaches."

"How can you be so cynical!" Dyan said in horror.

"Dyan, I was joking! But truly, my brother, I am not particularly interested yet in marriage, I have not been home long enough even to renew all my old ties and friendships, and I would rather wait a while before forming new ones. And speaking of old ties and friendships, you and I have hardly seen anything of one another! Shall we plan a hunt? Or—Rafael Hastur spoke of spending a tenday at Syrtis—*Dom* Felix knows more of hawks than anyone from Dalereuth to the Kadarin, and he has promised me one trained to my own hand. Both of them, I know, would be delighted if you joined us."

"I do not care for hawking," Dyan said stiffly. So Rafael Hastur thought he could force his friend, the hawkmaster's son, on Kennard Alton by laying him under obligations with this kind of courtesy—this kind of bribe!

"Well, as you like," Kennard said. "We'll ride in the hills, then, just the two of us, if you'd prefer that. I can take three days' leave, and so can you, a few days after Festival Night."

A day or two later the invitation was actually forthcoming from Rafael Hastur to join them at Syrtis—his sister and foster sister were also to make up the party—but Dyan refused, saying that he and Kennard had made other plans. Riding at Kennard's side along the lower ridges of the Venza Hills, Dyan felt perfectly happy, as if, after all these years, they had returned to a happy boyhood. Kennard, too, seemed happy. He told Dyan something . . . not much . . . of his years on Terra, his struggle against the heavy air and the dragging gravity, the long trip from star to star, the curious offworld customs. And the loneliness, among those mostly ungifted with *laran*.

"Only once did I find real friends," he said. "On

Terra, of all places, some kindred of the Montrays, who had lived on Darkover, and knew how that light hurt my eyes ... that was the worst, the pain of the light, and even when the sun was not in the sky, I sometimes felt I should go mad under the frightful cold light of that terrible white moon ... do you know that their word for madness is akin to their word for moonworshiper? There was a girl—her name was *Elaine,* that is Yllana in our tongue ... but she was kin to Aldaran, too. I do not suppose I will ever see her again. But she understood, a little ... how I feared that terrifying moon."

Dyan said, "Moon madness is easy enough to understand; we have that proverb, *What is done under four moons need never be recalled nor regretted....*"

"True," Kennard laughed, "and I see there are three in the sky, and later tonight, Idriel will rise too, and then we, too, will perhaps have some adventure of madness!"

All the moons were indeed high in the sky when they made camp and cooked their meal, roasting a bird Dyan had brought down with his *courvee,* the curved throwing-stick used for hunting in the Hellers. "I have lost my skill," Kennard lamented, "it has been so long!"

They sat long beside the coals of their fire, lighted by the four moons, talking of their own childhoods, the early days in the Cadets.

"I was so wretched on Terra," Kennard said, "I wonder, often, if Larry was equally so in my place. His kindred were so kind to me, and tried so hard to be understanding. I know my father would have been kind, but what about the others, Dyan? Was he happy in the Cadets? Did any befriend him? I would have commended him to your kindness as my sworn friend."

Dyan said stiffly "Do you think anyone alive could take your place? I think we all made him realize what an interloper he was, to try that!"

Kennard shook his head in dismay. "But we were friends, Dyan, I would have had you treat him as you would have treated me, as friend and brother ... well, it is past, I won't censure you," he said, "but I wish you could have come to know him as well as I do; believe me, he is worthy of it, *Janu.*"

But he used the old pet-name of their childhood, and

Dyan knew that Kennard was not angry with him, of course not, Kennard would not quarrel with him over any *Terranan*!

The fire had burned low. Kennard yawned, and said, "We should sleep. Look, we have the four moons after all ... what madness shall we do?"

Dyan said, with a shyness that surprised him, "Hardly madness ... but shall we, then, renew our old pledge, *bredhyu,* after so many years?"

For a moment Kennard was motionless, startled. Then he said, very gently, "If you will, *bredhyu.*" He repeated the word with the special inflection Dyan had used, only for sworn brothers between whom there were no barriers. "It would need no renewal to be as strong as ever; I do not forget what I have sworn. And you are old enough, I would not have thought to treat you as a boy too young for women ... but if you wish for it, my dearest brother, then, as you will."

He drew Dyan to him, their lips meeting, barriers going down in the most intimate of touches, until their minds were as exposed to one another as their young bodies ... and in that moment, something deep within Dyan Ardais cracked asunder, never to be whole again.

Kennard had not ceased to love him. He would never cease to love him. He welcomed their reunion, and now he had given himself up completely to the warmth and tenderness of this physical reconfirmation too, he was withholding nothing. And yet ... yet there was a profound difference, a difference heartbreaking to Dyan. What was, to Dyan, the needed, desperately longed-for wellspring of his existence, the core and renewal of his being, was nothing like that to Kennard. Kennard loved him, yes, cherished him as brother, friend, kinsman, with a thousand kindly memories. But the very center of their love, this mutual affirmation which was the whole reason for Dyan's existence, was to Kennard only a pleasant kindness, he would have been equally content if they had clasped hands and slept apart ... and before the agony of that knowledge, Dyan Ardais felt that the whole core of his being was cracked, torn, broken into fragments.

Even while he was held tenderly in Kennard's arms,

wholly absorbed in the mutual sharing, he felt the ice of death surrounding him, like the icy halls of Nevarsin, cold, alone ... even dissolving in the mutual delight was agony, he knew he was sobbing uncontrollably, and through his own despair he sensed Kennard's bewildered grief and regret. He could not even be angry with Kennard; Kennard's thoughts were his own, *What can I do? He cannot be other than he is, nor can I. I love him, I love him dearly, but love is not enough....*

"Dyan, Dyan ... *Janu, bredhyu,* my beloved brother, don't grieve like this, you are breaking my heart," Kennard pleaded. "What can I say to you, my brother? You will always be more dear to me than any man living, that I swear to you. I beg of you, don't grieve so ... the world will go as it will, and not as you or I would have it ... there is no one, no one I love more than you, Dyan, it is only that I am no longer a boy ... Dyan, I swear to you, a time will come when this will not matter to you so terribly ... all things change...."

Inwardly Dyan raged, *I will not change, not ever,* all of him was crying out in anguished rebellion, but slowly he managed to bring his weeping under control, withdrawing behind an impenetrable barricade of calm, good manners, almost lightheartedness. He reached for Kennard again, with skillful, seductive touch, just letting Kennard sense his thoughts, *at least there is this, and Kennard cannot pretend he does not find pleasure in it....*

Kennard, still troubled, but grateful for Dyan's calm, reached for him with gentle urgency, saying aloud ... he could not bear the deeper touch of minds, not now, "I will never try to pretend that, my brother."

Summer moved on. One day, as Kennard was changing in the small room off the Guard Hall, after giving some younger cadets lessons in swordplay, he said to Dyan, "Well, it's happened. Father has found me a wife."

Dyan lifted an ironical eyebrow. "My congratulations. Am I acquainted with the fortunate young woman?"

"I don't know! I don't know the girl at all. Father says she is suitable, of a minor Hastur sept; he said that she is not particularly beautiful, but she is not ugly either, and she is amiable, and accomplished, and gifted with *laran*—and that is enormously important to me. He has no doubt whatever that we will like one another and live well together. Beauty may be important in a man's mistresses, but good temper and friendly disposition are more important for sharing a home and a life, and I have no doubt we will be happy enough. She is foster sister to Rafael and Alisa Hastur; have you met her? Her name is Catriona, Catrine, something like that."

"Caitlin?" Dyan asked, and Kennard nodded. "I think so. You know her?"

"No," Dyan said, "but I know who she is."

Inside he was laughing triumphantly. That would teach Rafael Syrtis to lift his eyes to a girl of Hastur kindred! Now that they had a proper husband for the girl, Rafe Syrtis would learn that there were limits to a commoner's ambition!

He said formally, "I wish you every happiness, kinsman," but his own happiness overflowed when Kennard smiled and said, "The girl is nothing to me, dear brother. I have never yet met the woman who can be more to me than a sworn brother, and I heartily pray that I never shall."

He was curious to know how the two Rafaels would react to this knowledge; and he was not long in finding out. Actually he was out of earshot, doing some small chore in the barracks while Rafael Hastur and Rafe Syrtis were ostensibly playing cards at the other end of the room; but he heard them mention Kennard's name and felt not the slightest ethical hesitation in extending his senses to listen in, telepathically, to what they were saying.

I could hardly believe it, Rafael Syrtis said, *I knew of course, that she was gratified and glad to see me when I sought her out, but I had never believed that she would actually send for me, would beg me ... Rafael, I could not bear it, she had been crying so, her poor little face was swollen with tears, I think the very stones of Nevarsin Peak would have melted with pity! And of course that father of hers thinks only of what it will mean to her, to marry a Comyn heir . . . what shall I do, Rafael? I cannot lose her, not now, not when I know she cares about me as much as I. . . ."*

Dyan felt savage gratification. So this damned commoner was learning he could not force his way into Comyn circles by marrying a foster sister to Rafael Hastur, after all! Well, let him suffer, it would teach him a lesson! Then, in outrage, he heard what Rafael Hastur was saying to his friend. A Hastur, to speak like this? Disgraceful!

If you and Caitlin both have the courage . . . I will stand by you. Freemate marriage cannot be gainsaid, if it has been consummated; if you spoke to my father, he would say it was only a boyish fancy, but if you have shared a bed, a meal, a fireside . . . I do not know if the girl has the strength of mind to defy the old people's wishes, but if she does, and you, you will want witnesses, and Alisa has promised that she, too, will stand by you. . . .

And then they were discussing horses, and directions, and Dyan turned off his listening-in, as Rafe Syrtis turned and looked uneasily at him . . . had that damned commoner some scrap of *laran* after all? But he did pick up the rendezvous, *the traveler's hut on the road to Callista's Well. . . .*

You have nothing to fear from Dyan, Rafael Hastur said calmly. *He, too, has suffered from the whims of an overstrict father, he would not betray us.*

Would I not! Dyan thought, enraged. Even if he had not been infuriated by Rafe Syrtis' presumption, daring to raise eyes ambitiously to the ward of a Hastur, he was angered for Kennard's sake. Who was this girl Caitlin, to prefer some impudent nobody to Kennard Alton? What a slap in the face for Kennard it would be, if it became gossip in Council that his promised bride had run away to marry someone else! And for whom? For a prince, for a nobler marriage? Not even that; for the son of her guardian's hawkmaster! What an insult to Kennard! Dyan thought, in a fury, that if he had had the offending Caitlin before him, that he would have spit on her!

Kennard must know at once—that Rafael Hastur and

that insolent and presumptuous favorite of his were conspiring to cheat him of his bride!

As he went in search of Kennard, he was rehearsing in his mind what to say, to make Kennard aware of how he was being insulted by the Hastur heir! Those false friends and traitors were conspiring to cheat Kennard, to make him lose face before the Guards and the Council.

Yet his mind persisted in presenting Kennard to him, not grateful to Dyan for warning him of this humiliation they were planning, but as angry with Dyan for his meddling; it seemed he could almost hear Kennard's voice, saying, *Zandru's hells, Dyan, do you think I care about the girl? At this time of my life, one girl is very much like another to me, provided she is suitable, I've never even seen her.* And the more Dyan argued in his mind, trying to convince Kennard that he could not consent to lose his pledged bride to a commoner, the more his mind rehearsed Kennard's logical reply:

What pleasure could I possibly have in marrying a girl who is helplessly in love with another man? There are plenty of women who would as soon have me; why not let the Syrtis boy have this one, and welcome, if they want each other; who knows, perhaps some day I might be fortunate enough to find some woman who could care as much for me as this one does for Rafe!"

Confused by the voices in his mind, Dyan felt grave misgivings. Should he simply hold his peace? If Caitlin Lindir-Hastur and Rafe Syrtis cared so much, why should he rend them asunder to give Caitlin into the hands of a man who did not care whether he had her or another? Then, in a last moment of anguished self-knowledge, still stinging with that unintended rejection from Kennard, he knew he did not want Kennard to marry a woman who would mean to him what Caitlin meant to Rafe ... *what no woman, I know it now, will ever mean to me. . . .*

Firmly he dismissed his compunctions. Loyalty to Comyn demanded that he prevent young Hastur from defying the will of the Council, that Kennard Alton should have Caitlin as a wife. Kennard should not be humiliated by being shown that his pledged bride preferred to be the wife of a commoner, a hanger-on, the hawk-master's son!

Kennard will know that I hold his honor as a Comyn Lord dear to me as my own; he will be grateful to me, I will still mean more to him than any woman. . . .

His hands were shaking. He realized that he was outside the Hastur apartments, and as he told the grave-faced servant to say that Dyan Gabriel, Regent of Ardais, wished to speak to the Lord Danvan Hastur, or, failing that, to the ancient Lord Lorill, he rehearsed, mentally, his opening words.

Do you know, my lord, what they are planning, your son and his shameless paxman, the son of your hawk-master? They are planning that Kennard, Heir to Alton, shall be cheated of the marriage designed in Council. . . .

They were a small party; all of Comyn blood, or long-trusted Guardsmen who could be certain not to spread scandal. Danvan Hastur himself rode with them, and Dyan himself was the youngest of the party riding northward to Callista's Well. Old Hastur had inquired discreetly; when he heard that the lord Rafael and Alisa, with Rafael's paxman, young Syrtis, and Alisa's foster sister, had ridden out before midday, taking hawks as if it were an innocent holiday, he had gathered the party and ridden swiftly forth. Now they sighted the small traveler's shelter, and outside, they saw four horses, one of them the white stallion which Rafael Hastur rode.

Danvan Hastur's voice was low and bitter.

"Spread out; circle the house. Who knows what they will do, these rash young ones? Disobedience, certainly; perhaps dishonor and disgrace." With his paxman at his side, he struck a heavy blow with his sword hilt on the door; Dyan could see that the elderly Lord of Council was prepared for anything, even brute defiance.

But no blow was struck. Dyan could not see, and from his post, never heard what words were exchanged inside, but after a long time, Danvan Hastur came forth. His face was cold and set; he held the weeping Caitlin by the hand. Lord Hastur signaled to two Guardsmen to ride at either side of Rafe Syrtis, who looked as white as his shirt.

"Guard him lest he do himself some hurt," Hastur said, not unkindly. "He is distraught. He has been ill-advised by those who should have known better." His eyes rested on his son Rafael, and his face was like stone.

"As for you," he said, "I know where to lay the blame for this disgraceful affair; you are fortunate that your cousin Alton does not challenge you to a duel, since Comyn immunity covers you both. No, not a word—" He raised his hand imperiously. "You have said and done quite enough, but through good fortune and fast horses it came to nothing. I shall deal with you later. Get to your horse and ride, and don't presume to speak to me tonight."

Rafael's lips moved inaudibly in protest, but his father had already turned away. He himself set Caitlin on her horse, saying, "Come, my child, no harm is done, though your folly was great. I'll pawn my honor Kennard shall never hear of this, and fortunately he has nothing to forgive you. Alisa!" His voice suddenly cut like a whip. "Get to your saddle, my girl, or I shall have you lifted there! No, not a word!"

Alisa drew her green cloak around her face; it seemed to Dyan that she was weeping, too. But his eyes were on the slumped back of Rafael Syrtis. Now, indeed, that detestable commoner had learned his lesson!

In the end nothing came of it; Alisa was sent away in disgrace—to Neskaya, they said; but there was surprisingly little gossip. The Guard Hall was full of it, but Dyan answered no questions; his honor had been engaged to keep silent. A few days later the handfasting was duly held, and Caitlin Hastur-Lindir was pledged to marry Kennard Alton *di catenas.* Dyan, watching the bride and groom dance together, with courteous indifference, at the ceremony, felt a curious hollow emptiness. Kennard, when he came to speak congratulations, greeted him affectionately.

"Let me present you to my promised wife, Dyan.... *Damisela,* this is my kinsman and sworn brother, Dyan."

For a moment the girl's dead face came alive with a

flicker of wrath and resentment, and Dyan realized she must have seen him in that circle of politely averted faces, at the hut on the road to Callista's Well ... then it was gone, and Dyan knew she no longer even cared about that.

"I wish you every happiness," he said formally, and Kennard replied something equally formal and meaningless; only Dyan caught his imperceptible shrug.

"Here is your foster brother to dance with you, Caitlin," Kennard said, and delivered her up to Rafael Hastur. "Come back to me soon, my lady." But he watched them move away together with an almost audible sigh of relief.

"I do not think Caitlin likes me overmuch," he said. "I suppose, soon or late, she will resign herself to the idea; I'll try to be as kind and friendly as I can, and I suppose we will agree together as well as any other married couple. She is certainly no beauty," he added candidly, looking after the girl, "but she seems to have a sweet disposition, even if she is sulking now; and she is well-spoken and gentle, and she seems to be intelligent enough! I would hate to be married to a fool. I suppose I am not really ill-content," Kennard finished, without much conviction. "My father could have done worse for me, I suppose. Well, if she gives me a son with *laran*, I won't ask much else of her." Almost visibly, he shrugged. "Oh, well, it is an excuse for a festival and a merry-making, shall we have a drink? Dyan—listen to me. Of all my acquaintances in the Guardsmen, only Rafael Syrtis has not come to congratulate me or wish me well. My brother, what can I possibly have done to injure him that he should dislike me so much?"

Dyan felt a tight constriction in his throat. It was not too late, even now ... instead he heard himself saying, "What the devil does it matter to you what he thinks, Kennard? Who is this Rafael Syrtis anyway, that he should snub you? Nobody—the hawkmaster's son!"

"We married your father to someone we thought suitable," old Hastur said, "and they dwelt together in perfect harmony, and total indifference, for many years."
                                        —The Heritage of Hastur

Man of Impulse

by Marion Zimmer Bradley

"You keep good company, *chiyu*," Marilla Lindir blazed
at her brother. "By all accounts you are just what he
likes, the Lord Ardais—a boy not yet a man, old enough
to be almost a companion, young enough that you will
never contest his will, and pretty as a girl—has he yet
made you his—"

Merryl heard the word in her mind, and colored before she spoke it, but he said stubbornly, "You do not
know Lord Dyan as I do, Marilla."

"No, and I thank all the Gods for it! Is it not enough
that all our Aillard kin think you sandal-wearer because
you shirked your term in the Cadets—"

"That is not fair, either," said Merryl quietly. "What
ails you, 'Rilla? Are you angry because for once there
is something we do not share? You have woman friends
and I do not grudge them to you. You know why I could
not go into the Cadets; after our brother Samael died,
Mother thought always that I would melt in the winter
rains or catch the fever in a summer heat, and truly I
did not ask it—to be coddled and made a housepet, tied
to her sash even when I was grown to be a man. Now
for once there is a man of our kinfolk who accepts me
for what I am; a man, a telepath . . . and does not mock
me for what I cannot amend, that I grew to manhood
without the company of my own kind. He *accepts* me,"
Merryl repeated, and Marilla, through her anger, felt the
pain in her brother's voice, steadied though it was. She
swallowed hard. Perhaps it was true, perhaps her anger
was only jealousy . . . she and Merryl, twin-born, had not
been separated as most brothers and sisters were when
one moved into manhood and the other was confined to
the narrow limits of a Comyn lady. Was she jealous, that

now Merryl moved on where she could not follow, into the larger world? She reached for Merryl, and he hugged her close. She was still almost as tall as he; and though her hair was braided in a flaming rope down her back, while his clung in tendrils around his freckled face, her shoulders were nearly as broad as his own.

For years, our father said I was more the man of us two; I can ride as fast and as far as Merryl, my hawks are better trained than his, I even practiced with him at such weapons-training as he had . . . because Mother always felt that the rough lads around stable and barracks would contaminate her precious baby boy. But Mother is gone now and there is none to keep Merryl from becoming a man. And I . . . Marilla shrank from the relentless implications of that, *must I become no more than a woman? Because I was allowed to share what little Merryl had of manhood, have I been spoilt for the only life that must be mine?*

She drew a long breath and said, "True it is that I do not know Lord Dyan as you do. Yet I feel he is using your—" she sought for a word that would not offend him, considered and rejected *hero worship*, and finally said hesitantly, "using your—your admiration for him. I am not a fool, Merryl, I know that—that young men, boys, care for one another this way, and I would never have grudged you that—"

"Would you not?" he broke in angrily, but she shook her head and gestured him to silence.

"Truly, had you had such a friend . . . companionship I have given you and such friendship as you have had—"

"Marilla, Marilla—" he held her tight again, "Do you think I am censuring you because—"

"No, no—wait—that is not what I mean; I am your sister, there are some things a friend, man or woman, could give you that I, your sister and twin, could not, and I—I would have tried not to grudge you that," she said honestly. "The world will go as it will, not as you or I would have it . . . a man is free to explore in this way and a woman is not. . . ."

"That is not quite true, 'Rilla—"

She smiled at him a little and said, "Maybe not; I

should have said, a boy is something more free than a woman, since they need not fear disgrace—"

"And I have no wish to disgrace any woman or bring shame on her," Merryl said quietly, "but I have had no *bredini* either."

"Till now?"

A flare of anger; the barriers were down between them, but she felt them slam shut. Merryl had never before shut her out of his mind. She said urgently, "Merryl, listen to me! For you, perhaps, this is right, this is the time for such things—but in the name of all the hells, in the name of Avarra the merciful—I can see why you love Dyan, perhaps, but what does he want with you? He is old enough to have outgrown such things before either of us were born, he could be our father's father—"

"He is not so old as that," Merryl interrupted. "If he had been grandsire, then would he have been wed full young—and what of that, anyhow? Would you judge a man by the years he was numbered, rather than by what he *is*?"

"Of what he is, I know only that he is a man past his first youth, at least, who seeks lovers among boys not yet grown to manhood," Marilla blazed. "What kind of a man is that? And I heard, if you did not, of the scandal in the Cadets six years ago, when he seduced a boy so young that he had to be sent home to his family because—"

"I might have known you would throw Octavien in my face," Merryl said, with an odd, smug smile. "Dyan told me before any other could rake it up against him. He took Octavien into his own quarters just *because* he was young and childish and the other lads who were more mature, bullied him—Dyan had been small and frail too, and knew what it was to be bullied, and he thought perhaps he could make a man of the lad by treating him as one ... he taught him, supervised him, stood friend to him. But the truth of the matter was only this; Octavien was a whimpering child who should never have been sent into the Guards at all, and under the double strain he broke and his mind snapped ... he got it into his head that the other lads were talking about him night and day because of Dyan's friendship and attention, that they had nothing better to do with their time than to taunt him and call him weakling, sandalwearer, catamite—and then he began to weep night and day and could not stop himself, and, like all such sicknesses of the mind, he turned on the very one who had most befriended and helped him, and accused Dyan of such unspeakable things ... and so they hurried him away, poor brain-sick child, before he could grow worse."

"That, I suppose, is Dyan's version," said Marilla.

Merryl said, "I am enough of a telepath to know when I am being lied to. Dyan spoke truth—nor would he have stooped to lie about it. Had he known how frail was Octavien's hold on reality, he would have sent him home before—but he had grown to love the boy, and Octavien did not want to be parted from him then, he said Dyan was the only one who cared for him and understood him, and Dyan felt that sending him away would have been to hurt him worse." Merryl was silent, but Marilla could read even what he did not want to say aloud to her, *Dyan wept like a child himself when he knew what had befallen Octavien; he did not tell me this, but I saw it in his mind. . . .*

Marilla thought: *Dyan could have stood friend to the boy without seducing him first to his bed; and it served him right that he did not observe the proprieties.* One of the strongest taboos in the Hellers was that which prohibited such affairs between generations; it came from the days when any kin of the mother's or father's generation might have been the true mother or father, since marriages were group affairs and true parentage often unknown. "Could Dyan find no men of his own age for his favorites and friends?"

"You are prejudiced, Marilla. Like all women, you think a lover of men has insulted all your sex—"

"Not so," she said, "but he, too, is prejudiced, then, like to a man who deserts his wife of thirty years who has borne him many children, because of her wrinkles and gray hairs, and takes a younger and prettier maiden. Does he think, if all his lovers are young, that no one will see the lines in his face?"

Merryl flushed, but said stubbornly, "Nevertheless, he is my friend, and as long as you keep my house, you will be civil to him and receive him with courtesy."

"Oh, is it so?" she flared. "While I do your will at all times, we are as equals, but when our wills clash, you say only, *I am master of this house and you are no more than a woman*?"

He lowered his head. "I say not so, Marilla, Evanda forbid—but sister, will you not be kind to my friend for love of me?"

She said crossly, "It is for love of you that I would show him the door," but when her brother spoke in that tone, she could only grant him what he wished. She said, "I neither like nor approve of the man. But you must do as you will," and turned away from him.

Lord Dyan, she thought, was rather like a hawk: proudly poised head, lean to emaciation, high-bridged nose, and now and again, when he laughed, the far hint of wildness in the harsh sound. His manner to her was delicately punctilious; he called her, not *damisela*, but *Domna Marilla*, in recognition that she was chatelaine of Lindirsholme. In the evenings when they sat in the hall or danced to the sound of the house-minstrel, he was always first to ask her to dance, and even courteous to her lady-companion and the elderly chaperone who had been her governess and Merryl's. During the days he was out with Merryl, hunting or hawking, or simply riding across the broad lands; in the evenings, sometimes, he borrowed a harp from one of the singing-women and sang to them himself, strange sorrowful ballads older than the hills themselves, in a voice well-trained and musical, though without much tone. Once he said, with a faint, rueful shrug, "A boy's tragedy is always this—that no matter how beautiful his voice before it breaks, there is no way to tell whether his mature voice will be anything but another well-trained croaker."

"Yet the songs are beautiful," Marilla said, truthfully, and he nodded.

"I had them from my mother ... she spent years studying under one of the great minstrels of the mountains; of course my father could not abide music, so she sang only to me. And I learned more in Nevarsin."

"Were you destined then for a monk, Lord Dyan?" she asked him. He laughed, that harsh bird-sound.

"Not I! I have no call to fasting and prayer, and less, perhaps, to the way of the ascetic ... I like good food and warm beds and the company of those who can dance and sing ... only the music kept me there; I would have endured more than that for such learning. No, I was apprenticed to be a healer, and now—"he shrugged, "I have scarce enough skill in these to set a broken bone for a dog." He stared at the long delicate fingers which moved so skillfully on the harp. They were still fine, but the joints showed lumps and knots and calluses from sword and reins. "For one of our kind, there is no task worthy of a man, they say, but the sword. Duty called me there, and I did what I was bound in honor to do. How lucky you are—" his eyes sought Merryl's, "that you escaped this destiny."

"At the cost of manhood," Merryl said bitterly.

"Faugh!" Dyan made a harsh, guttural exclamation, "If that is manhood, perhaps 'twould be a saner world if we all put skirts about our knees, lad!"

Marilla asked him, "Do you truly think women are better off than men?"

He shook his head. "Perhaps not, Lady Marilla—I am no judge; my grandmother Rohana ruled the Ardais lands better than any man could do, and my father—" he shrugged. "I never saw him sober, or sane, after my thirteenth year. My sister was Keeper, *leronis* at Arilinn, and no man could be her master, yet she gave that up to die in trying thrice to bear a child to her Terran-reared lover. My mother endured my father's madness and folly till she died of it. My grandmother lived all her life subject to a man who was scarce her equal, yet she treated him always as her better. Can you blame me for saying I understand not women? Nor, for that matter, men ... even you, lad—" his smile at Merryl was so frank, so warm and tender, that Marilla winced, "you have escaped the worst of what your clan demanded of you, yet you pine as if you had been forbidden something splendid! I would have given much for just such incapacity as yours, so that I might have had my own choice . . ." and he sighed. "No matter. The world goes as it will. . . ." And he bent his head to the harp and began to play a merry and not too decorous drinking-song about a most inept crew of raiders from the mountains.

> "We have to tell them again and again,
> Rape the *women*, and kill the *men*,
> I think sometimes they'll never learn,
> *First* you plunder and *then* you burn."

Not long afterward, Marilla rose, with chaperone and lady-companion, and withdrew; Merryl embraced his sister, and Dyan bent over her hand; for an instant she was shocked, wondering at herself, *Did I want an embrace from him, too?*

And late in the night she woke, shocked, from a dream such as had seldom come to her, she was held in someone's arms, caressed tenderly, mind and body touched in such depths that her whole body seemed to melt into a jelly of delight. . . . She woke in startled amazement, feeling arms still about her, the pleasuring touch still lingering in her body . . . but she was alone, and then, catching her breath in dismay, she slammed down a barrier; but it was Dyan's hands, Dyan's arms in the dream . . . or was it a dream? And slowly, shamingly, she knew what she had shared . . . she had guessed, of course, that Dyan shared her brother's bed, and the bond of the twin-born was stronger than any other telepathic bond. . . .

But I knew not that it was like this . . . Merryl has this and I, ah, merciful Evanda, I am virgin and I lie alone . . . till my family gives some man rights over my body without my will . . . and Dyan, Dyan wants no woman, he would turn from me in scorn, turn to my brother. . . .

The barrier was in place again. In her cold and lonely bed, Marilla wept herself to sleep. And in the morning she sent down word by her chaperone that she was ill in bed; she could not face Merryl, she could not face Dyan . . . certainly he had known that they had touched her. . . .

I never want to see him again. I will stay here in this

bed until he has gone away, and damn him, he can take Merryl away with him, I never want to see either of them again! But she knew that she was lying. The next day, self-possession armoring her again, and chill irony, she managed to come down and be civil, to endure Merryl's and Dyan's kind inquiries about her illness. But she held herself tightly with dread, and watched, with something she now knew was envy, as Dyan and Merryl walked arm in arm. And once, when she sat among her women, sewing, she heard one of them giggling and speculating.

"What in hell's name can two men do with one another? It seems silly, doesn't it? And what a waste! I've heard that the *Comhi'Letzii* take one another to bed like lovers, but I've never been able to figure that out either . . . maybe they don't know what they're missing—"

"Maybe," Marilla said coldly, "they have more imagination than you do, Margalys," and left the room, hearing their curious chattering voices rise behind her.

It was that night, as they sat at music, that Merryl took the harp and began to sing, but broke off in a fit of coughing; and Marilla reached for his hand; it was hot as fire.

"You have fever," she said accusingly.

"Well, there is fever in the village, and I went to see how many of the farm-people would be away from the harvest," Merryl said, sighing. "True 'tis, that old saying, lie down with dogs and you will rise up with fleas. . . . I will be well enough, sister." He struck her hand away. "You are not our mother, to coddle me now!"

Dyan reached for Merryl's forehead, touching it expertly. "No, now, lad," he said. "Away to your bed; you have fever-bark? And if you are not well in the morning, we will ride another time, but you must not endanger yourself."

Merryl colored, but he rose and signaled to his body-servant, taking leave of Dyan with an embrace. He looked sick and flushed.

"I will see you, then, in the morning—it will be well enough," he said crossly. "Marilla is like all women, she likes having men sick and under her control."

"Only because men are too much fools to admit when they need care," said Marilla, just as crossly, and frowned. But as she climbed the stairs, to search out fever-bark from the stillroom and pour a dose into the protesting Merryl, she had already formed the plan in her mind.

She had still the riding-breeches of Merryl's which their mother, four years ago, had forbidden her to wear; and Merryl's tunics were only a little too broad for her shoulders. She slipped into Merryl's room where he lay restlessly tossing about with fever, and slid his sword from the rack, belted it about her waist. She had had enough training to walk without bumping it on things; and she took his cloak and slid her feet into his boots. They were too big for her; she pulled on another pair of thick socks so she could walk in them without blistering her heels. In the stable, Dyan was already saddled and waiting.

"Well! You look well recovered," he said gaily. "Did not that sister of yours jump at the chance to keep you abed like a child?"

"Do you think I would let her?" Marilla blessed the deep contralto of her voice; she could never have carried this off if her voice had been high and light like her companion's. She was glad to realize that she could, in breeches and boots, jump into the saddle as lightly as Merryl himself; only once had Dyan seen her ride and then she had been cumbered with riding-skirts and a lady's saddle which was, Marilla had always felt, an insult to a self-respecting horse.

"You said I might fly Skyclimber," Dyan said. "Have you a hawk chosen?"

Marilla nodded. She said, wondering at her own calm, "My sister told me that Wind Demon is not being flown enough, and she is too busy to ride; she asked me to handle her today."

Bold as she was, she would not venture to handle Merryl's hawk, Racer; Racer was a nervous haggard who let no one but Merryl himself touch her.

But with Wind Demon on her saddle, she felt competent to match Dyan himself at hawking. She rode in the crimson sunrise, feeling the dawn wind in her face with excitement, the delight of freedom; how long it had been since she rode like this, forgetting the household duties which lay behind her! Surely she would be missed, but what did that matter? There were plenty to care for Merryl and for the household, and if she could not have one day of absolute freedom, what good was it that she was Lady of Lindirsholme?

The sun had begun to angle downward from the zenith, and noon was far past; Dyan began to loosen the hawk again from the saddle, then shrugged.

"We do not need any more birds," he said, "and the hawks, too, are full-fed; do we need to take more? You promised we should ride one day to the waterfall; is there time before sundown?"

"I think so," Marilla said, and beckoned to the hawk-master who rode far enough behind them not to interfere, but close enough to take charge of the birds if he was needed. "Take them back to the castle, and the game too, Rannan."

"Certainly, *vai dom*," Rannan said, "but ye're not going to ride farther this day, are ye? Lord Ardais, ye wouldn't be takin' the boy all that way with fever just past and a storm comin' on?"

"Storm? I see no sign of storm," Dyan said, "but if Merryl wishes to return—"

Marilla sniffed the wind; it did not seem to her to smell like storm. Rannan had always pampered Merryl. She said coldly, "You are not now in my mother's pay, to keep me housebound. Take the birds and go."

The man ducked his head and rode away, and Dyan chuckled.

"When I was a lad, they used to have a saying for a boy growing up—*Well, lad, ye'll be a man before yer mother will*," he said, imitating, with a droll twist of his mouth, the country accent of the man. "You may have been kept from manhood much of your life, but you make up for lost time now. But are you sure you are not wearied with riding? It is true we have come a long way, and no doubt the waterfall will wait on our pleasure."

Marilla was not accustomed to this much riding; she ached and was saddlesore. But she would not yield before this man! She hardly knew why she had come; *perhaps*, she thought, *I wished to know what Merryl sees in him....*

And she knew; a charming companion, ready with jest and game, now and again tactfully suggesting a better way to handle the hawk ... though, indeed, earlier he had said: "You grow better at this than you were; last time we went hawking, you did not handle Racer so well as this—"

Marilla had said lightly, "I have learned from your company and example, my lord."

Dyan smiled and leaned close and said, "I thought we agreed you were to call me only Dyan—or, if you will—*bredhyu*—" and she felt the questing touch of his mind, but she kept her barrier in place; she could not pretend to be her brother, not now ... but still she could read Dyan, a little.

I like it that he is still shy, that he does not presume nor grow bold....

"The waterfall lies beyond this ridge," she said, and set her teeth, racing ahead. How dared Merryl share this with Dyan? That had been their own private place, their rendezvous, the place where they went to share confidences from early childhood; and now Merryl would bring this man here? She felt simmering resentment; and yet ...

I can see it now, she thought, *why Merryl loves him so well.*

The sky was darkening with cloud when they came in sight of the waterfall, and a few drops of rain had begun to fall. Yet the rushing cataract drowned out all thought, all sound, all speech; and Dyan, staring with delight at the great jagged cliffs with rushing water, was silent, too. He stood there without words, looking downward at the torrent, and after a time she could read his thoughts again.

Now do I know why you brought me here. There are not many who will own to their love of such beauty. Nor do I—much—when there are others near. It is the second—nay, the third most beautiful thing I have seen at Lindirsholme.

So close they were, so deeply sharing the silence, that

for a moment Marilla was tempted to open her mind to him; she did not want to deceive him, let him show the tenderness he meant only for Merryl. But the thought of his rage and fury at being deceived, kept her barriered tightly, and after a little Dyan sighed and turned away, and again she could read his thoughts. *Still he defends himself against me, but perhaps tonight when we are together he will not barricade his thoughts from me. . . .*

In a wild confusion of feeling, dread and shame and some unidentifiable thing, she turned quickly away and hurried to her horse. Dyan turned in surprise and looked up, troubled, but she said swiftly, "Look, we cannot stay here ... look at the sky, Rannan was right about the storm."

Within minutes, she knew, it would break and they would be drenched. Dyan threw himself into his saddle and was off after her, racing ... he drew angrily abreast and said, "You are a child indeed. If you knew this storm would break, and if your clothes are soaked to the skin again, you will have fever worse than ever—are you always going to act like a child or a silly girl? This is such a trick as your sister might have played! Is there any place we can shelter from this, out of the rain for a little?"

"You are like my mother," Marilla snarled in Merryl's voice. "Think you I will melt in the rain?"

"Nay, but I hunted in these hills before you were more than a gleam in your father's eye," said Dyan, and again Marilla caught a picture in his mind, two lads racing over the hills breakneck on their horses ... who was the other boy, younger than Merryl was now? She neither knew nor cared. Dyan said, "I know how quickly this rain can turn to sleet or ice at these latitudes ... even now, feel that," and Marilla was aware of the sting of sleet against her cheeks. "We cannot reach Lindirsholme without freezing; must I seek a cave or ditch as we were taught to do at Nevarsin against bad weather?"

She said, shivering against her will, "There is a—a shepherd's hut." It had stood unused for years, since their father had sold his sheep and turned to breeding the black horses of the Leyniers. She and Merryl had kept childish treasures there, when they rode to the wa-

terfall, and brought food and drink for out-of-door meals
away from governess and tutors.

*No doubt Merryl would have shared this, too. He cares
nothing for our old secrets now, only for Dyan. Well, let
it be so.*

Even Dyan was blue with cold by the time they forced
the hut's stiff door open, and knelt at once to make a
fire. When it was blazing up, he unsaddled the horses,
brushing away Marilla's attempt to help.

"Stay by the fire, lad, you are chilled through, and
I have not just risen from a fever-bed!" He laid the
saddleblankets down beneath his outer cloak, pushed
Marilla down on it. "Nor need we go supperless to bed,
I kept the last bird, thinking we might cook our dinner
out of doors."

She knelt upright on the blankets and said, "Let me then
spit the bird for roasting while you deal with the horses."

Her hands were too cold and stiff still to do much at
plucking it; she finally held it to the fire to singe the
feathers away. He came when she had half finished, and
took it away from her.

"Here could you use some of your sister's housewifely
skills," he said, laughing, "Plaster it in mud and ashes,
lad, and the feathers will break away when 'tis baked.
Did she learn your skills of riding and hawking without
teaching you such things as this?"

Marilla flared at him, "Would you have me learn to
cook and sew? Already I was womanly enough, was I
not?" And as she spoke she knew she was speaking the
very words Merryl would have spoken, the rage and resentment at never sharing a man's life ... well enough
it was to bring Marilla into a man's world, but if he had
tried to enter hers, then would he have been ridiculed
or worse....

Dyan said, still laughing, "In the Cadets I learned to
cook or go hungry, even if it was no more than grain-
porridge and such field cookery as this; there are no cook-
maids on the battlefield, lad. And my paxman darns my
socks and mends my cloak—it is the price I pay for having
no woman about me." As he talked, he was plastering
mud and ashes on the bird; now he thrust it into the coals.
"Leave it there to cook, and get out of your wet cloak,

lad." He pulled it from her shoulders. His hand lingered at the nape of her neck. "Such fine hair—'tis pity you cannot let it grow long like your sister's. . . ."

Marilla bent her head. She would have to face that some day, too; and she thought with a sting of regret of the long braid of hair left on her floor. She forced herself not to shrink from Dyan's intimate touch. . . . *Yes, they have shared more than this, he has a right to expect it. . . .*

"I suppose you wonder why I would have no woman about me," said Dyan quietly. "I thought it not fair to marry as many of the Comyn do, to women with whom they have no more in common than horse or dog, to use a woman as a breeding-animal, no more. Once I dwelt with a woman for a year, and she bore my son; I had him legitimated, but he died, years ago. I have an heir by adoption—I think you may have seen him in Thendara; Hastur's paxman, young Syrtis. I do not dislike women as much as all that." He raised his eyes and looked at her directly.

"What do you want with me, Marilla?" he asked.

She bent her head. How long had he known?

"Since we stood together by the waterfall," Dyan said quietly. "I am no *laranzu;* yet telepath enough to know something of what you felt. Do you understand how much I love your brother, Marilla? I know you have hated me; yet I mean him no harm. He will leave me; a younger lad always does; I will have no choice but to find another. My—my friends seem somehow to grow to manhood, and I—well, perhaps it is something within me—" he shrugged. "Why am I explaining myself to you?"

She turned away and bent her head. Her voice was stifled. "You owe me nothing, my lord."

She wished he would not look at her; and as if yielding to her wish he got up and busied himself at the far end of the shelter where the horses were; he gave them grain from a bag, hauled some of the fodder stacked at the far end and spread it for them. She came and stood close, tearing apart the baled fodder so the horses could get at it to eat, and he smiled.

"What? Now I know you are a woman, you do not leave me to do the men's business here?"

"When I ride with Merryl, I am a boy with him; should I be less with you, *vai dom*?"

"You are his equal, aye," Dyan said softly, "I would you were his twin brother, not his sister . . ." and she lowered her eyes before the sudden heat in his. He reached out and took her between his hard hands, holding her so that she faced him. "You have come here with me, Marilla—what do you want, truly?"

She turned aside, swearing that she would not cry. How could she say, *I want what it is that you have shared with Merryl and never with me, what you can give to no woman—ah, fool that I am, caught in my own trap—*

He pulled her against him, stroking her hair, stroking the nape of her neck. After a time he lowered his lips against hers, and a little later he carried her to the bed of saddleblankets.

"But you are a child—" he said, after a time, hesitantly, "and, if I make no mistake, virgin—do I repay hospitality by violating the sister of my host?"

She half sat up, her arms still round his neck. She said fiercely, "You did not ask my leave to take my brother to your bed! What sort of ninny do you think me, that you must have permission from him to take me, when I myself have given you that leave? I am my own—my own woman, I belong not to my brother but to myself—nor to you, Lord Dyan! I give and withhold myself at my own will, not that of some man!"

He laughed softly, and for a moment she thought he was laughing at her, but it was a laugh of pure delight.

"One thing more you have learned of your brother's world, Marilla—if all women were like you, I doubt I should be such a man as I am today—" His lips sought hers again and he whispered softly, against them, *"Bredhya."* Then he pulled her down again on the bed of saddleblankets.

"I must take care, then, if you are a maiden; I would not reward you for this with pain," he said, touching her more gently than she had believed was possible, and she sighed, letting her mind open before him as her lips opened under his, feeling his delight and surprise and wonder.

I thought you cared nothing for woman, Dyan. . . ."

*I am a man of impulse ... you know that of me, if
nothing more. ...*

And then even thought was lost.

They rode home early in the daylight, holding hands.
As they came within sight of Lindirsholme, Marilla
halted, looking at Dyan with a certain dismay.

"Merryl will know ... again I have stolen from him
what he wanted; when we were little children, my father
said always, I should have been the man, I was the
stronger of the two ... and always I bested him at riding
and hawking ... and now even at this I have stolen what
he wanted most. ..."

Dyan clasped her hand and held it hard.

"You have taken from Merryl nothing that is his," he
said gently. "And I shall tell him, believe me, that it was
for love of him. ... I cherish you, *bredhya,* but without
my love for Merryl, you would have been no more to
me than any of the hundreds of women who would lure
a Comyn lord into their bed ... do you think women
have not tried? Had you been older, more guileful, I
would have thought it of you, and turned away from
you, but my friend's sister was something else ..." he
lowered his eyes again and was silent. "Now he has
shared with me what was the dearest of his possessions,"
he said at last, "his sister's love. Is it not so, Marilla?"

She clung to his hand. "It is so, Dyan."

Merryl met them at the gate, holding out his hands to
each of them as they dismounted. "I was frightened,
when I knew what you had done," he said. "The storm
was so fierce—but you took him to our own old place,
Marilla. ... I am glad!" And, meeting his eyes, she knew
that he was aware of what had befallen them, as she
had wakened to share his delight in Dyan's arms. Dyan
reached out and hugged them both together, turning his
head from side to side to kiss them, Marilla's soft cheek,
Merryl's downy one, and for a moment it seemed to
Marilla, in an insight she never lost, that somehow Dyan
was not a bearded, scarred, aging man, but somehow,
inside, a laughing boy her own age or Merryl's. ...

She took his hand and her brother's, and, walking between them, walked through the gates of Lindirsholme.

*　　*　　*

Dyan rode away ten days later, Merryl at his side.

"I wish I might come with you to Thendara," she said rebelliously, as she said farewell.

"So do I," Dyan said softly, "but you know why it cannot be." Already, with her *laran*, she knew that the night they had spent together had been fruitful; she bore Dyan's child, and already guessed that it was the son he needed and desired so much. He held her face between his hands again and said, "You have given me the one thing Merryl could not, Marilla. No one else, ever, can take your place in that. I will marry you if you will—" he added, hesitating, but she quickly shook her head.

"If I held you in those bonds, I should desire of you what you cannot give . . . what the bonds of marriage demand," she said. "You would come to hate me . . ." and at his look of pain, she added quickly, "not to hate, perhaps; but you would resent me, that some one had put reins to your freedom . . . I have this." With a curious new gesture she held her hands, sheltering, across her body where the child lay cradled. "I am content with that . . ." and she raised her lips for his farewell kiss. And as he turned away, riding at Merryl's side, she whispered to herself:

Once you called me, bredhya. But I know, if you did not, that what you truly said was . . . bredhyu.

She turned before they were out of sight, and went inside the gates. There were those who would think that Dyan had taken from her what she had to give, and left her nothing; but she knew now that it was not true.

She was mother to the son of Lord Ardais; mother to a Comyn Heir. Now no kinsman could force her, unwillingly, to marry some man for house and name; she had status enough of her own, wed or no. She was her own woman, now and forever; and Dyan had given her this, which was better than marriage.

Some day—perhaps—there might be another man; and perhaps not. Perhaps she was never meant for marriage. But some day, certainly, she would find someone to share her life who could accept her in freedom; and when she found that person, man or woman, she would know. Dyan had given her that.

The Shadow

by Marion Zimmer Bradley

Danilo Syrtis signed the estate books and handed them back to the steward.

"Tell the people in the Hall to give you some dinner before you start back," he said, "and my thanks for coming out in this godforgotten weather!"

"It was no more than my duty, *vai dom*," the man said. Danilo watched him leave and wondered if he should go to his own dinner now, or send for some bread and cheese here in the little study he used for estate business. He did not feel like making polite conversation with the steward about business or the weather, and he supposed the man, too, was eager to get back on the road and be home with his wife and children before dark set in. There was more snow coming tonight; he could see the shadow of it in the great clouds that hovered over Ardais.

Snow coming, and it was cold in the room. And by nightfall I shall be on the road ... and Danilo started, wondering if he had fallen asleep for a moment. There was no such luck coming his way, that he should be on the road, away from here, by nightfall. Danilo rubbed his hands together. His feet were warmed by a little brazier of charcoal under the desk, but his fingers ached and he could see the breath between his mouth and the books which lay on the desk before him. He had never grown used to the cold in the Hellers.

I wish I were in the lowlands, he thought. *Regis, Regis, my brother and* bredu, *I do my duty here at Ardais as you in Thendara; but though I am Regent here at Ardais, I would rather be in Thendara at your side, no more than your sworn man and paxman. I shall not see my home*

*again, perhaps not for years, and there is no help for it.
I am sworn.*

He put out his hand to the bell, but before he could ring it, the door opened and one of the upper servants came into the study.

"Your pardon, *vai dom*. The Master would like to see you, at once if convenient; if you are still occupied with the steward, he asks you to name a time when you can attend him."

"I'll go at once," said Danilo, puzzled. "Where will I find him?"

"In the music room, Lord Danilo."

Where else? That was where Dyan spent much of his time; *like a great spider in the center of his web, and we are all in his shadow.*

Dyan, Lord Ardais, was Danilo's uncle; Danilo's mother had been the illegitimate daughter of Dyan's father, who had had many bastards. Dyan's only son had been killed in a rockslide at Nevarsin monastery; when Danilo proved to have the *laran* of the Ardais Domain, the catalyst-telepath Gift believed extinct, the childless Dyan had adopted Danilo as his Heir.

He had been at Ardais now more than a year, and Dyan Ardais had proved both generous and exacting. He had had Danilo given everything he needed for his station as the Ardais Heir from suitable clothing to suitable horses and hawks; had sent him to a Tower for preliminary training in the use of his *laran*—more training than Dyan himself had had—and had had him properly educated in all the arts suitable for a nobleman; calligraphy, arithmetic, music and drawing, fencing, dancing and swordplay. He had himself taught Danilo music, and something of mapmaking and of the healing arts and medicine.

He had also been generous to Danilo's father, sending breeding stock, farmhands and other servants, and a capable steward to manage Syrtis and to make life comfortable for the elderly *Dom* Felix in his declining years. "Your place is at Ardais," Dyan had said, "preparing yourself for the Wardenship of Ardais. For even if I should some day have another son—and that is not altogether impossible, though unlikely—it is even more unlikely that I should live to see that son a man grown. You might need to be Regent for him for many years. But your own patrimony must not be neglected," he stated, and had made certain that the estate of Syrtis lacked for nothing which could be provided.

As he approached the door of the music room, a slender young man, fair-haired and with a sort of feline grace, brushed past Danilo without a word. But he gave Danilo a sharp look of malice.

Now what, I wonder, has happened now to displease him? Is the Master harsh with his minion?

Danilo disliked Julian, who was Dyan's house *laranzu;* but Dyan's favorites were no business of his. Nor was Dyan's love life any affair of his. If nothing else, Danilo realized, he should be grateful to Julian; the presence of the young *laranzu* had emphasized, to all the housefolk, that there was an enormous distance between the way Dyan treated his foster-son and ward, and the way he treated his minion. He himself had nothing to complain of. Before Dyan had known who Danilo was, or that he had the Ardais Gift, when Danilo was simply one of the poorest and most powerless cadets in the Cadet Corps, Dyan had tried to seduce him, and when Danilo had refused, in distaste, Dyan had gone on pursuing and persecuting him. Danilo was a *cristoforo* and in their faith it was shameful to be a lover of men. But never once, in the year since Dyan had adopted him as Heir, had Dyan addressed a word or gesture to him not completely suitable between foster-son and guardian. Yet the shadow of what had once been between them lay heavy over Danilo; he had, he believed, forgiven Dyan, yet the shadow was dark between them, and he never came into Dyan's presence without a certain sense of constraint.

As far as he knew, he had done nothing to displease his guardian. But it was unprecedented that Dyan should send for him at this hour. Normally they met only for the evening meal and spent a formal hour afterward in the music room; sometimes Dyan played for him on one of the several instruments he had mastered; or had his minstrels and entertainers in; sometimes, to Danilo's distress, he insisted that Danilo play for him; he had required that his foster-son learn something of music, saying no man's education could be complete without it.

Dyan was standing near the fireplace, tall and lean in the somber black clothing he affected. Despite the fire, it was cold enough to see his breath. He heard Danilo come in and turned to face him.

"Good day, foster-son. Have you had your noon meal?"

"No, sir; I was about to have it when I received your message and came at once."

"Shall I send for something for you? Or, there is fruit and wine on the table; please help yourself."

"Thank you, sir. I am not really hungry." Danilo noticed that Dyan's mouth was set; he looked grim. He felt a little inward clamping, tight inside him; he was still a little afraid of Dyan. He could not imagine what he could have done to bring that look of displeasure to his guardian's face. Mentally, he ran over the events of the last tenday. The estate accounts, with which he had been trusted for the last four moons, were all in order, unless the men had all conspired to lie to him. As far as he knew, his tutors would all give good reports of him; he was not really a brilliant scholar, but they could not fault him for industry and obedience. Then he saw Dyan's eyes shift a little in his direction and was suddenly angry.

He is trying to make me afraid again. I should have remembered; my fear gives him pleasure, he likes to see me squirm. He drew himself up and said, "May I ask why you have sent for me at this hour without warning, sir? Have I done something to make you angry?"

Dyan seemed to shake himself and come out of a daydream. "No, no," he said quickly, "but I have had ill news, and it has distressed me for your sake. I will not keep you in suspense, and I will not play at words with you. I have had a messenger from Syrtis. Your father is dead."

Danilo gasped with the shock, though he knew the bluntness was merciful; Dyan had not left him to worry and wonder while he broke the news in easy stages.

"But he was perfectly well and strong when I left Syrtis after my birthday visit. . . ."

"No man of his age is ever 'perfectly well and

strong,' " Dyan said. "I do not know the medical details;
but it sounded to me as if he had a sudden stroke. The
messenger said that he had finished his breakfast and
thanked the cook, saying he planned to go riding, and
suddenly fell on the floor. He was dead when they
picked him up. It was to be expected at his time of life;
you were born, I understand, at an age when most men
have grandchildren on their knees. He had ill-luck, I
know, with his elder son."

Danilo nodded, numbly. His older brother had been
killed in battle before Danilo was born; he had been
paxman to Regis Hastur's father. "I am glad he did not
suffer," he said, and felt tears rising in his throat. *My
poor father; he wanted me to have a nobleman's education, he never stood in my way. I hoped a day would
come when I would know him better, when I could come
back to him as a man, free of all the troubles of youth,
and know him also as the man he was, not only as my
father. And now I never will.* His throat closed; he could
not hold back his sobs. After a moment he felt Dyan's
hand on his shoulder; very gently, but through the touch
he felt something like tenderness; inwardly he cringed
with revulsion.

*He thinks, because I am grieving, he can touch me and
I will not draw away from the touch . . . he never stops
trying, does he?*

Abruptly the touch was withdrawn. Dyan's voice was
distant, controlled.

"I wish I could comfort you; but it is not my comfort
you wish for. Before I sent for you, I made inquiries
through my household *laranzu.*" Now Danilo understood the look of malice Julian had given him.

"I learned through the Towers that Regis Hastur was
in Thendara, and is riding today for Syrtis; he has said
to his grandfather that as your sworn friend he owes a
kinsman's duty to your father, and he would await you
there. You may go as soon as the necessities are packed,
unless you would rather wait until the weather clears . . .
only the mad and the desperate travel in the Hellers in
winter, but I did not think you would want to wait."

"I am not afraid of weather," Danilo said. He still felt

numb. He had wanted to see his home, and Regis; but not like this.

"I took the liberty of asking my own valet to pack your clothing for the ride and for the funeral. But have some food before you ride, my son."

Startled at his tone—Dyan was indeed showing extraordinary gentleness—Danilo raised his eyes to his guardian's face. Dyan said gently, "Your friend will be waiting for you when you reach Syrtis, foster-son; you need not face the funeral alone, I made sure of that. I would myself come to do him honor but . . ." Dyan took Danilo's two hands formally in his own; he was perfectly barriered, but Danilo sensed a threat of some emotion he could not quite identify; regret? sorrow? Dyan said quietly, "Your father was one of the few men living who dared to incur my displeasure in honor's name; I have great respect for his memory. Stay as long as you wish, my boy, to set his affairs in order. And convey my compliments to Regis Hastur." He released Danilo's hands and stepped back, formally dismissing him. Danilo bowed, his emotions too mixed to say anything. Regis Hastur, already awaiting him at Syrtis? He went slowly to his room, where he found Dyan's body-servant packing his saddle-bags; Dyan had sent a purse of money, too, for the expenses of the journey and to make gifts to his father's servants. He had told off three men to escort him, and as Danilo went down to the hall, he found a hot meal, which could be eaten quickly, already on the table and smoking. Danilo was too weary and troubled to swallow anything, but he noticed distantly that the *coridom*, or hall-steward, brought a basket of food and packed it with the saddlebags on the pack-animal; inns were almost nonexistent and travel-stops few and far between.

II

The snowflakes were falling into the open grave, mingling with the lumps of dirt there as the men and women of *Dom* Felix's household, one after another, stepped to the side of the pit and let a handful of dirt fall on the coffin.

". . . and the Master said to me, 'your daughter, she's a good clever girl, it's too bad for her to stay here milking dairy-animals and scrubbing pots all her life.' And even though we were short of kitchen help, he sent her with a letter to the Lady Caitlin at Castle Hastur, and the Lady took her into her own household as a sewing-woman and later she became the lady's housekeeper and married the steward, and he always asks . . . asked me about her," the old cook finished, her voice shaking, and crumbled the lump of dirt between her hands, letting it fall with the snowflakes into the grave. "Let that memory lighten grief."

Each of the housefolk had told some small anecdote, some kindness done, some pleasant memory of the dead man. Now the steward Dyan had sent last year was standing at the graveside, but Danilo hardly heard what he said. Regis was behind him; but they had had no more than the briefest chance to greet one another. And now Regis stepped to the graveside; and as he looked up, his eyes met Danilo's for the first time since they had greeted one another that morning. Between Dyan's efficient steward and *Dom* Felix's own men, there had after all been very little to do. Danilo had been beginning to think that he might as well have stayed at Ardais for all there was left for him to do here.

"When first I saw *Dom* Felix," Regis said, the snowflakes falling on the elegant blue Hastur cloak and on his coppery hair—he had, Danilo thought dully, gone to considerable trouble to present himself as prince and Heir to Hastur before these men—"he snarled at me as if I had been a naughty small boy come to rob his orchards. He thought I had come to trouble his son's peace, and he was willing to send me away angry and incur the ill-will of Comyn, to protect his son. Let that memory lighten grief."

But that, Danilo thought numbly, was almost exactly what Dyan had said; would no doubt, have said if he had come here; that his father would face angering powerful men for his son's sake. He thought, *I should have been a better son to him.* He took the crumbling ball of earth Regis had put into his hand. He was remembering how Regis had sought him out here at Syrtis. *We sat over there,* he thought, *in the orchard, on that crumbling log.* At the time he had been no more than a small-holder's son, without even a decent shirt to his name; no one knew he had the Ardais Gift. Yet Regis had said, *I like your father, Dani.* Regis had come here when Dyan had contrived to have him expelled in disgrace from the Cadet Corps. And *Dom* Felix had been rude to him. Danilo said, blind with pain and unable to pick and choose at his words, "My father cared nothing for the court, or for riches and power for himself. His older son had been taken from him—" *Taken from him twice; once when my brother Rafael chose to follow a Hastur as his sworn man, and then when he followed that Hastur to death. And I struck him a blow on that old bruise. Yet . . .* "Yet he willingly let me go from him when most fathers would have kept me at his own side, to serve him in the obscurity he preferred. He let me go first into the Cadets, and then to Ardais. Never once did he seek to keep me at home for his own comfort. Let that memory . . ." his voice broke and he could hardly finish, "lighten . . . grief . . ."

His fingers tightened convulsively, crumbling the lump of dirt. He felt Regis' hand over his own, and suddenly he felt numb. It would soon be over, and all these people would go away, and he could go inside and drink hot soup . . . or hot wine which might be more to the point . . . and get warm, and sleep. The funeral feast was over, the burying was over, and now he could rest.

Brother Estefan, a *cristoforo* monk who had come from the village, was saying a few kindly words at the graveside. ". . . and as the Bearer of Burdens bore the Worldchild across the swollen river of Life, so our departed brother here strove all his life to help his fellow-men bear their burdens as best he could; *Dom* Felix was not a rich man, and much of his life he lived in great poverty, yet many in the country round here can speak of having been fed in his kitchens when the winter was hard, or that he sent his men to bring firewood to cold houses when that was all he had to give. Once I came late after visiting some sick folk on his estate; his cook and steward had gone to bed, so he welcomed me in with his own hands and brought me to warm at his fire;

and since he said his cook had left him too much supper, he simply poured half of his soup into my bowl and cut a chunk from his own loaf, and because there was no one to make up a room for me, he set down some saddleblankets by the fire to make up a bed for me. Let that memory lighten grief; and may the Lord of all the Worlds welcome him to the Blessed Realms, having held there in store for him all the kindnesses which when he dwelt among us he shared with his fellow men." He made the Holy Sign over the grave and signaled the workmen to start filling it in. "So we on earth may cease to grieve and allow our brother to journey to the Blessed Realms untroubled by the thought of our mourning. Farewell."

"He has laid down his burdens; farewell," chorused the watchers beside the grave, and turned away. *So, Danilo thought, there he will lie, in an unmarked grave here on his own lands, resting beside my great-great grandfathers before him, and my sons and grandsons after him. Or does he truly feast this night in the Blessed Realm, in the presence of his God, with my mother on one hand and my elder brother on the other? I do not know.*

Only Brother Estefan returned to the house with them. Danilo went to fetch some of the money Dyan had sent with him to make gifts to *Dom* Felix's men, and came back into the hallway; the priest had refused to enter the main Hall, saying he knew Danilo needed to rest after the long journey and the funeral feast and burying. Danilo knew he was eager to get back to the Longhouse in the village.

"The snow will be heavy tonight; what a good thing it did not begin to come down so hard until the burying was over," Brother Estefan said.

"Yes, yes, a good thing," Danilo said, thinking, *Surely he is not going to stand here and make small-talk with me about the weather!*

"You will remain here at Syrtis now, my lord, in your rightful place, and not return to Ardais? All through the Domains and beyond, it is known that Lord Ardais is a wicked man, fearing no gods, licentious and wicked . . ."

"He has behaved honorably to me," Danilo said, "and

he is the brother of my own mother; I am sworn as his Heir. It is my duty to my mother's blood, and to Comyn."

The priest's mouth tightened and he made a small expressive sound as Danilo said, *Comyn.* "Your father was never really at ease about you in that place. And it is rumored that Lord Regis is one of the same debauched stamp; he is neither married nor handfasted, and he is eighteen already. Why has he come here?"

"I am his sworn man and paxman," Danilo began, but behind him in the shadowed hallway Regis Hastur said, "Good Brother." Danilo had not noticed before that Regis' voice had deepened and strengthened to an almost organlike bass.

"Good Brother, if anyone you know has complained to you of my conduct toward him, I am prepared to make an accounting of my behavior, to him or to you. If not, I have not appointed you as keeper of my conscience, nor is that office vacant. May I send a servant to guide your donkey through the storm? No? Are you sure? Well, good night, then, and the Gods ride with you." And as the door closed behind the priest, he muttered, ". . . or anyone else who is willing to endure your company!"

Danilo felt almost hysterical laughter rising in his throat, but he turned away into the main Hall. Regis caught at his sleeve; at the touch memory blazed between them, but then Danilo drew away, and Regis, shocked less by the withdrawal than by the refused rapport, said vehemently, "Naotalba twist my feet . . . I am a fool, Dani! I know you do not want it gossiped, especially among those who are all too ready to seek scandal of Comyn!" He laughed, embarrassed. "I am to blame, that I thought myself above suspicion, perhaps; I had only feared to expose you to rude jesting, not to Brother Estefan's long-faced concern about the state of your soul and your sins!"

"I don't care what they say," Danilo blurted, "but I can't bear that they should say such things about you . . ."

"My own honor is my best safeguard," Regis said quietly, "but then I am not exposed to their talk; there are

not many who will dare speak slander of a Hastur. I, at
least, am not ashamed of the truth. Of all evils I hate
lying the most ..." They were still standing in the doorway, and the old cook, who was still setting out a simple
supper in the Hall—porridge sliced cold and fried with
bacon, a baked pudding which smelled of dried fruits,
bowls of steaming soup—raised eyes still blotched and
red to summon them. She said with the freedom of an
old servant—when Danilo was very small she had fried
him dough-cakes and mended the torn knees of his first
riding breeks—"You should ha' asked the Brother to
dine with us, *Dom* Dani ... Master Danilo," she corrected herself quickly.

"True," Regis said in a lazy voice. "We could have
done with his company, I suppose, for an hour more, if
we must, and it is a pity to send the poor man out into
the snow with nothing in his belly. What would they say
to you at Nevarsin, Dani?"

"He will dine better in the Longhouse, nanny," said
Danilo to the old woman, "and he would probably not
wish to dine in the house of a sinner; I made it clear I
was none of his flock."

"And I am just as glad to be spared his company,"
said Regis. "I had all I could stomach of pieties when
we dwelt together in Nevarsin, Danilo; I had enough for
a lifetime and more, of their solemn nonsense. Oh, I
suppose some of them are good men and holy; but I
cannot believe what they believe, and there is an end to
it. I do not wish to be rude about your father's religion,
but it is not mine, and I feel no particular obligation to
your priest. Well ..." his face sobered, "we have had
no time to talk. I was eager to see you again, *bredu,* but
not like this." There was a stone jug of wine on the
table, too; he poured a cup and handed it to Danilo.
"Drink first, my brother, then eat. You are exhausted,
and no wonder, and I saw that you could eat but little
at the funeral feast."

Danilo drank off the wine, feeling it warming him all
the way down. Then he put a spoon in his soup; but he
felt Regis' eyes on him, puzzled.

Damn that priest, he thought; *now it is all between us
again. I had not wanted to think of that. It is enough that*

I dwell in Dyan's house and am forced to turn my eyes away from that accursed Julian, flaunting Dyan's favor, and the knowledge that Dyan's household thought, for a time, that I was there in that position, Dyan's favorite, his minion or catamite ... I am sworn to Regis. But what lies between us is more honorable than that.

His mind returned for a moment to a small travel-hut in the Hellers, where he and Regis had acknowledged the bond between them, had been, through their *laran,* more open to one another than lovers. Surely no more was wanted nor expected of him. *I cherish Regis, and I love him with all my heart. But he would never ask more than that of me. Perhaps, if we had come to one another as young boys ... but that was spoilt forever when Dyan sought from me what it could never have been in my nature to give.* And tonight in the hallway Regis had been apologetic about exposing him even to the accusation.

He reached up for the bowl of fruit-spread for his fresh porridge, and met Regis' eyes. Regis smiled at him and said, "What are you thinking, my brother?"

Danilo said impulsively, "Of that night in the travel-shelter ..."

"I have not forgotten," Regis said, reached across the table and squeezed Danilo's hand in his own. And at the touch, for a moment, they were there together, wholly open to one another, and a moment when Regis had drawn back, saying softly, "No. You don't want to stir *that* up, do you. Dani?"

And they had both withdrawn ... it is acknowledged between them, but they had both drawn back. The shadow of Dyan lies heavy on us both ... neither of us wished, then, to admit what we wished for. It was enough that we knew. ...

But the elderly cook was standing before them again.

"I made up the first guest-room for Lord Regis last night, sir," she said to Danilo, "and I had the Master's own room made up for you; was that right?"

Not right, thought Danilo, but customary and to be endured. He nodded acquiescence at the old woman and stood up, taking a candle in his hand.

"I am tired, nanny, and I will go up now. Go to your own rest now, and thank you for everything."

She came and kissed his hand, and he saw her blinking hard as if she were about to start crying again. "There, there, nanny, go and sleep now," he said, and patted the old woman's cheek. She went out, clutching her apron to her face, and Regis took an apple from the bowl on the table and came after him. "I like your apples here," he said. "Could your steward send me a barrel of them in Thendara?"

"Nothing is easier. Remind me to tell him tomorrow," Danilo said, and together they went toward the stairs.

III

In the upper hallway, Danilo hesitated before the heavy carven doors of what had been his father's room. He had not been inside it a dozen times in his life. He said at last, "I ... I can't go in alone ..." and Regis' hand was firm on his shoulder.

"Of course you can't. She should not have expected it of you. If you were coming back here to live it would be different." He pushed the door and they went in together. Danilo touched his candle to a branch of candles that was setting on the old carven desk, and light sprang up, gentle to the faded tapestries, the shabby carpet; but the old furniture was well-kept and shining with wax. The big bed listed heavily to one side where the old man had slept in it alone all these years; on the other side was a still high, firm, untouched bolster, in pathetic contrast to the flattened, lumpy old one which had, all these years, known the weight of his father's graying head.

Seventeen years now, since I was born in this bed and my mother died there on that same day. That sagging, one-sided old bed struck him as unutterably pathetic. *He lived alone here, all those years, and I left him even more alone.*

"But you are not alone here," Regis said quietly. "I'll stay with you, Dani."

"But I ... you ..." Danilo looked helplessly at Regis, and his friend smiled a little. He said, "No, Dani ... we must talk about this now. Neither of us could face it *then,* I know. But ... we are sworn. And you know as well as I what that means. ..."

Danilo looked at the threadbare carpet. He said, striking out in protest, "I thought ... you were as ... as shocked, as *sickened* as I was ... by what Dyan wanted of me. ..."

Regis' mobile face twisted in the candlelight, his brows coming almost together.

"I still am ... by force or unwillingness," he said, "but what made me sick was Dyan's ... insistence, not his tastes, if you understand me. Those are ... no mystery to me. On the contrary. But ... freely given and in bond of friends. Not otherwise. I thought ..." as if from a very great distance, Danilo knew that his friend's voice shook and barriered himself against the naked outrush of that emotion, "I thought you truly shared that—that we were as one, but that we had simply set it aside for another time. A time when we were not ill, nor terrified, nor in danger of death, nor under the shadow ... the shadow of your fear of Dyan. And I believed no time would be better than now ... to confirm what once we swore to one another, that we would be together. ..."

Moving through intense embarrassment, Danilo managed to reach out to Regis, to take him into a kinsman's embrace. He kissed him shyly on the cheek. He remembered when he had done this before, that day in the orchard. He said, groping for words, "You are ... you are my beloved brother and my lord. All that I am, all that I can give in honor ... I cherish you. I would give my life for you. As for the rest ... *that,* I think, it is not in me to give ..." and he could not go on.

Regis held him hard, his hands sliding up to grip Danilo by the elbows. He stared into his eyes. He said softly, "You know I want nothing of you that you are not willing to give. Not ever. What I do not understand is why you are not willing. Dani, do you still believe that what I want of you is ... is shameful, or that I want you ..." No less thān Danilo, the younger boy knew, Regis was groping blindly through a forest of uprushing words, avoiding the deeper touch of *laran.* "Do you think I want you for pride, or to show my power over you, or ... or any of those things? You said, once, that you knew I was not like Dyan, and that you were not afraid of me . . ." But he sighed and let Danilo go.

"Truly, his shadow lies heavy on us both. I cannot bear that he should still come between us this way." He turned a little, and Danilo felt cold, aching at the distance between them. But it was better this way.

"Well, you should rest, Danilo," Regis said quietly, "but if you do not want to stay here alone, I will stay with you, or you can come and share the guest-room with me. Look, your father kept your picture here beside . . . I suppose that is your mother?"

Danilo picked up the two small paintings; he had seen them here beside this bed ever since he could remember. "This is my mother," he said, "but this cannot be my picture; it has been here since I was old enough to remember."

"But surely it is you," said Regis, studying the painted face. Two young men stared at one another, their hands clasped, and Danilo realized, bewildered, who it must be.

"It is my brother Rafael," he said, "Rakhal, they called him."

Regis said in a whisper, "Then this must be *my* father. His name was Rafael too, and if they had their pictures painted together, this way, they, too, must have sworn the oath of *bredin* . . ."

They were both named Rafael; they were sworn to one another and they died trying to shield one another, and they are buried in one grave on the field of Kilghairlie. The old story had brought them together as children; for a moment they stood together beneath the old shifting lights of the Guard-hall barracks, children in their first Cadet year, caught up for a moment in the old tragedy. Time seemed to fold in upon itself and return, and Regis remembered the father whose face he had never seen, the moment when Danilo had somehow *touched* him, awakening the *laran* he had never believed he had. . . .

"I never saw my father's face," he said at last, "Grandfather had a picture . . . I never thought; it must have been the other copy of this; but he could never bring himself to show it to me, but my sister had seen it. She, of course, can remember our father and our mother, and she said, once, that *Dom* Rakhal Syrtis had been kind to her. . . ."

"Strange," Danilo said in a whisper, turning the little portrait in his hand, "that my father, who so much resented the Hasturs, since they had taken from him first my brother, then myself, should keep this here at his side for all these years, so that both their faces were before him always. . . ."

"Not so surprising," Regis said gently. "No doubt all he remembered at the end was that they had loved each other. It might even be, at the last, that he was glad you, too, had found a friend . . ." he looked again, with an abstracted smile, at his father's face. "No, I am not really much like him, but there is a resemblance, after all; I wonder if that was why my grandfather could hardly bear to look on my face for so many years." He laid the picture gently back on the table. "Perhaps, Danilo, when it has been for years beside you, you will understand . . . come, my brother, you must rest; it is late and you are weary. You waited upon me like a body-servant at Aldaran; let me do as much for you."

He pushed Danilo into a chair and bent to tug off his boots. Danilo, embarrassed, made a gesture to prevent him.

"My lord, it is not fitting!"

"A paxman's oath goes both ways, my brother," Regis said, kneeling and looking into his face. He moved his head slightly to indicate the picture, and Danilo could see the face of the first Regis-Rafael smiling into the eyes of Rafael-Felix Syrtis. "I doubt it not . . . if he had lived, your brother would have been a second father to me as well . . . and I should have had a different life altogether, even if my father had died."

"If he had lived," Danilo said, with a bitterness he had never known was in him, "I should never have been born. My father took a second wife when most men are content to rock their grandchildren on their knees, because he would not leave his House without an Heir."

"I am not so sure." Regis' hands closed over his again, "The Gods might have sent you to your brother as a son, to grow up beside my father's son . . . and we should have been *bredin* as it was foreordained. Do you not see the hand of destiny in this, Dani, that we should be *bredin* as *they* were?"

"I know not whether I can believe that," Danilo said, but he let his hand remain in his friend's.

"It seems to me that they are smiling at us," Regis said, and then he reached forward, holding out his arms to Danilo. He burst out, "Oh, Dani, all the Gods forbid I should try to persuade you to anything you felt was wrong, but are we to live in the shadow of Dyan forever? I know he wronged you, but that is past, and will you always make me suffer for what he tried to do? Why, then, your fear of him is stronger than your oath to me...."

Danilo wanted to cry. He said, shaking, "I am a *cristoforo*. You know what they believe. My father believed, and that is enough for me, and before he is cold in his grave you would have me here, even in that very bed where he slept alone all these years...."

"I do not think it would matter to him," Regis said very softly. "Because for all these years he kept beside him the faces of his son and the one to whom his son had given his heart. Would he do so if he hated the very face of a Hastur? There are portrait painters enough who could have copied his own son's picture so that he could have consigned the face of the Hastur prince who had taken his son from him, to the fires of this chamber, or to those of Hell! As for what he believed ... I would not care for a God who spent his powers in trying to take away joy and love from a world where there is such a lack of either. Of my Divine forefather I know nothing, save that he lived and loved as other men, and it is written that when he lost the one he loved, then he grieved as do other men. But nowhere in my sacred books is it written that he feared to love...."

I said myself that I could never fear Regis. What, then, has cast this long shadow between us? Is it truly Dyan, after all? Our hearts are given to one another; I hated Dyan then because he sought to impose his will on me. Yet am I not also hurting Regis this way? Am I free, then, of Dyan's taint?

Or is it only that I wish to think that what I feel for Regis is pure and without taint, that I am somehow better than Dyan and that what I feel for Regis has no shadow of what he flaunts with Julian?

I have hurt Regis. And worse ... the knowledge flooded suddenly into him. *I have hurt Dyan because I do not trust him; he has accepted me as a son and found another lover, and I have been unwilling to trust him enough to accept a father's kindness from him. I have kept feeling myself superior, accepting what Dyan gives grudgingly, as if I were a better man and conferred a favor upon him by accepting it, as if I wished him to court my favors. . . .*

And as I cannot accept Dyan when he wishes to show me a father's love, so I have refused to accept Regis for what he is, to accept the need in him for love . . . he is not the kind of man who could ever seek for that love casually. It would require trust, and affection . . . something that leapt from my heart to his when I touched him, and wakened his laran. *But giving with one hand I took back with the other; I accepted his devotion and his love, but for fear of idle tongues I would give no more of myself.*

Regis was still holding his hand; Danilo leaned forward and embraced him again, not formally this time. He felt overwhelmingly humble. *I have been given so much and I am willing to give so little.*

"If my father kept their pictures all these years beside him, then," he said, "and if he let me go from his own hands into yours, my brother . . . why, then, the Law of Life is that we should share one another's burdens. All that I am and all that is mine is forever yours, my brother. Stay here with me tonight . . ." he smiled deliberately at Regis and spoke the word for the first time with the inflection used only between lovers, *"bredu."*

Regis reached out to him, whispering, "Who knows? Perhaps they have truly returned in us, that one day we may renew their oath . . ." and as he pulled Danilo close, the picture overturned and fell rattling to the floor. Regis reached for it; so did Danilo, and their hands met on the frame. It seemed to Danilo that Regis' smile tore at his heart, there was so much in it of acceptance and love and joy. There was, for an instant, something like a struggle as each tried to take the picture and set it aside; then Regis laughed and let Danilo set it on the little table next to the bed.

"Tomorrow," Danilo said, "I must go through my father's personal things; who knows what else we shall find?"

"If we find nothing else," Regis said, holding Danilo's hands tightly, his words coming breathless, "we have found already the greatest treasure, *bredhyu*."

IV

"The Master had your message," said Dyan's steward, "and he asks, if the journey was not too fatiguing, you would join him for a little in the Music room."

Why, he, too, is glad to see me home. I have made a place for myself here. Danilo thanked the man and let him take his traveling cloak, and went toward the Music room. Inside he could hear the small sound of a *rryl*, and then Dyan's deep and musical voice.

"No, my dear, try fingering it like this . . ." and as he stepped inside he saw Lord Ardais, his hands laid over Julian's, arranging his fingers on the strings. "See, you can strike the chord and go on at once to pick out the melody . . ." he broke off, and they both looked up; the light was on Dyan's face, but Julian's face was still in shadow, and Danilo thought, *He is content to be in Dyan's shadow. I never understood that. I thought that he sought favors from Dyan as a* barragana *gives her body for rich presents . . . but now I know it is more than this.* Dyan nodded at Danilo, but his attention was still on Julian. He said, "Let me hear you play it again properly this time," and as the boy repeated the phrase, he smiled, his rare smile, and said, "You see, that is better; one can hear both melody and harmony so. We need both." He stood up and came to Danilo in the entrance of the library.

Danilo thought, with a curious intuition, *he knows.* But it was no secret, nor did he shrink from it now in shame or fear. What he and Regis had shared, what they would, he knew now, continue to share for most of their lives to come; it was not after all so different from what

Dyan and Julian shared, but now he was not ashamed of the similarity.

If I am no better than he, I am no worse. And that is not . . . he thought, remembering Dyan's hand gently guiding Julian's on the strings of the harp, *entirely a bad thing. I thought because I would never acknowledge that likeness, that somehow I was a better man than Dyan. Or Julian. It is a strange brotherhood we share. But nevertheless it is brotherhood.*

He took Dyan into a kinsman's embrace. "Greetings, foster-father," he said, and even managed to smile hesitantly at Julian. "Good evening, kinsman."

"I trust you have set everything in order at your home?"

"Yes," said Danilo, "I have indeed set everything in order. There was . . . a great deal of unfinished business. And the Lord Hastur sent you his respects and greetings."

Dyan bowed, formally acknowledging the words. "I am grateful. And I am glad to see you returned safely, foster-son."

"I am glad to be here, foster-father," he said. And for the first time the words were spoken unguarded. *I have lost my father; but losing him, I found I had another father, and he means me well. I never believed that before, nor trusted him.*

"Julian," Dyan said, "pour our kinsman a drink. There is hot wine; it will be good after long riding in the cold."

Danilo took the mug between his fingers, warming his hands on it, and sipped. "Thank you."

"Chiyu," Dyan said to Julian, in that tone which was half deprecating, half affectionate, "play for us on the *rryl* while I talk to Danilo. . . ."

Julian's face was sullen. "Dani plays better than I do."

"But my hands are cold with riding," said Danilo, "and I cannot play at all. So please go on." He smiled at Julian. They were both young. Each had his own place in Dyan's home and affections. *And there is another brotherhood, too. My heart is given wholly to my lord. And so is his.* "I would be grateful to you, kinsman, if you would play for us."

As the notes of the *rryl* rose in the room, he took a seat beside his foster-father, preparing to catch up with his neglected duties. Tomorrow, perhaps, he would show Dyan the painting he had brought from Syrtis; Dyan had known Regis' father, when they were boys together. Perhaps he had known Danilo's elder brother, too, and perhaps Dyan could talk of him without pain, as his own father had never been able to do.

He relaxed in the heat of the fire, knowing that he was home again, that he had stepped out of Dyan's shadow and taken his rightful place at his side.

DAW

MARION ZIMMER BRADLEY, Editor
THE DARKOVER ANTHOLOGIES